Freedom's Forge,
Striking the sparks of Liberty

by Nelson Abbac

This book is dedicated to

The members of the Appleseed Project,

who rise early every weekend and come home after sunset,

trying to remind their friends and neighbors of the pains

taken by our forefathers to gain us our freedom.

And most specifically

To my beautiful, long suffering wife, Jennifer

Who is bored to death by history,

yet has endured countless trips to historic events and all my "what if"

discussions.

I love you, this one is for you.

No author works in a vacuum, the process of weaving events and imagination into a coherent, interesting story requires the input of patient teachers and guiding friends.

Special thanks to my proof readers. Bob V, Tom T, Tom H, Bradley "Slim" S, Joanne N, Donalynn M, and Richard S.

Prologue

Gulls swirled in a graceful arc, white dots against a steel grey
December sky, cruising through tight turns as they spun, lower and lower to the
Atlantic shores of Boston Harbor. It could mean only one thing; food, something
dead. A grey-winged carrion bird of many years perched upon the prostrate form
of a man among rocks, ship's debris and dead fish, braying loudly to summon
his brethren to the feast. Then, in mid-call, the bird took flight as his meal
groaned and turned onto his side. Flapping its wings against the biting Atlantic
winds, the bird departed for easier pickings.

The man pried open salt crusted eyes, the rocky ground beneath him
did not move as the ship's deck had, he mused, and looked up at the spires of
Boston, Massachusetts. Muscles screaming, the exhausted Scot wrenched
himself over onto his back. "Jesus wept," he whispered piously, or tried to
around a curiously thick tongue. Daniel Ferguson drew a simple brown leather
bag tied with a piece of ship's cord from his mouth and remembered all.

* * * * *

The *Beaver* was some fifty days at sea, and tempers aboard were thin.
Disputes among the crew came often to blades, with the captain turning a blind
eye to them. "Sailors are a temperamental lot," he said dismissively, "best to
allow them their distractions. Exercise wards off the doldrums."

"Doldrums my bleeding arse," the Irish carpenter muttered at the Captain's dismissals, "we near port, and the more of us stuck, bleeding and dying upon the decks, the greater the gold he pockets."

The sunburned Scot's mind was heavy on these things as his cool blue eyes marked the mass of ships at anchor outside Boston Harbor. A fisher they had parlayed with yesterday told tales of bully boys blockading the colonies ports, stopping off-loadings.

"Call themselves parrots, no, patriots, something of the sort. They are blockading imported goods bearing a tax. Tea and paper, I hear," said the sail-maker, twisting a length of cordage into some useful thing as he smoked a pipe. Tea was their primary cargo, every member of the crew had spent enough time below on the bilge pumps to know. "The Captain worries his private stock of goods might be unsold, and a small fortune lost." Then the sail-maker reached down to pick up a pottery tankard at his feet.

"That be mine." A drink-scarred voice rasped, and ended the Scot's conversation.

"I bought it in Espanola last year," lashed back the sail-maker as a sun bronzed sailor snatched at the garishly painted grog cup in his hands, "or do you dispute it?" Scarred hands snatched belted knives and Daniel Ferguson hastened away from the flashing blades on the rolling deck, stumbling full into someone.

"Ferguson!" Captain Harlan snarled, turning upon the Scot like a man-a-war as the officer's daily rum ration dribbled down the front of his wool coat.

"You incompetent Scots brigand, you'll taste 'me lash for this!" The Captain's hated, ever present leather strap quested for his face.

Daniel rolled out of his way, gaining his feet at the ship's rail, and his hand chanced upon one of the hickory belaying pins racked there. The captain, bellowing like a charging bull, thundered toward the Scot with the long leather strap cocked back over his shoulder.

Reaction, hard learned and long drilled took over Daniel's body and the hickory pin lashed out. The Captain's right arm broke with a sharp, wet "Crack", and the officer let out a pained squeal, cut short as the 14-inch long wooden pin burrowed deep into his guts and took his wind.

Momentary silence descended upon the deck like a wet blanket and the Scot's eyes swept his fellow Jack Tars, on the deck and in the sheets. Then, much like the voice of the Lord, Captain Harlan's voice thundered. "Seize that mutineer!" He bellowed.

Striking a ship's officer was a flogging offense, and the crew reacted with immediate obedience to the Captain's voice; such things were the difference between life and death upon a ship at sea. Daniel raised the belaying pin to defend himself, but surveyed the faces of his shipmates, men he had shared food and drink, laughed with and Daniel realized he could not strike these men. The pin slipped from his hand.

Arms seized him, grasping at his limbs and Daniel had a moment of dread. A small leather pouch was thrust into his hand, and a familiar voice declared, with an Irish lilt. "Over the side with him, boys! Let the deep have the treasonous bastard!"

Before he could catch a breath, he was over the side, jettisoned like so much ship's garbage. As he hurtled through the space, the Scot twisted his head, and caught sight of Paddy's face at the *Beaver*'s starboard rail, and the Irishman winked broadly before the briny, frigid Atlantic waves washed over him.

Chapter 1

The clanking leather bag contained a handful of gold and silver coins of a dozen different lands. Not enough to buy a man a castle or an earldom, but enough to keep him fed and warm for a while. And the first matter of keeping a man warm was to find something to fill his belly.

The *Green Dragon* was a small, dimly lit tavern within scant walking distance of the waterfront with a surprising clientele for early evening. The bartender was a smiling gentleman with the corded arms of a seaman and inquisitive, intelligent eyes. "Drink?" Daniel inquired.

"Drink we have," The man agreed amicably, "what'll it be?"

"Something hot," Daniel requested, noncommittally. He knew he was a sight, without a bath to speak of for long months, raw boned and wasted from the hard life and indifferent foods of the sea. A young man of some twenty years, with blue eyes and dark hair gone sandy from the unforgiving sun, something over medium height as Scots tended to be. Shoeless, baggy ships trousers and shirt stained and patched, his leather belt was cracked and stained from hard use, but the long dirk thrust in his belt was free of rust and sharp.

Those suspicious eyes narrowed. "You don't mean tea, do you?" Silence fell over the shadowy denizens of the bar. Daniel remembered the fisher's warning. "No," the Scot said hurriedly, "give me an ale flip."

The barkeep's eyes did not unknit. "That'll be two penny."

Daniel momentarily pawed at his sporran, the belt pouch of his homeland that now held all his worldly possessions. He had several coins in it, besides the windfall from the decks of the *Beaver*, but he was reluctant to show such fortune in a strange tavern. Instead, he drew a hand along the belt he wore, decorated with studs of silver, copper and gold, found one by touch and wrenched it free, laying it upon the bar.

The barkeep registered the offering and swept it up before it had stopped rocking. With a nod, he turned to the preparation of the drink and Daniel absently watched the man at his labors as, inwardly he brooded upon his case. But for the clothes upon his back, the sum total of his life was left aboard the *Beaver*, lashed to the beams over his hammock, and he lamented the loss. He considered and discarded plans faster than the beat of a seagulls wings. Sneak aboard? Bluff his way back onto the ship? None seemed plausible, or even within the desperate realm of fantasy.

The Bar-keep slid the drink in front of him. Ale, the flavor stained to a warm, smoky nuttiness by thrusting a hot poker into it, and he let himself forget his difficulties for a brief moment. The first mug he drained in a rush, the warmth and potent spirit filled him with an ardor that left his head swimming. The bar keep watched this distractedly as he tended other duties, concocted a second flip and pocketed another starburst copper rivet from Daniel's belt without comment for his troubles.

"God save King George!" Someone shouted from the door, and was greeted by a desultory grunt. A dandy clad in the finery of the Royal Courts sauntered into the tavern without removing his gaudy hat, his long walking stick tapping at the ground as he moved. Men muttered at his passing, and the dandy seemed to revel in their disdain. "Why do I come here?" He simpered in answer to some overheard question. "I find great comfort in the familiar, my good man. And when I need to seek the commonplace or the constant, I ride the ferry 'cross the Charles from Cambridge, come here and find dear Doctor Warren and his Sons of Liberty plotting treason and regicide."

One of the men at a table rose and bowed elegantly. "My good lord Trenton is too kind to come out among the lowly this evening to offer us comforts." Doctor Warren answered with evident sarcasm. He was a thin man with a handsome round face, a singularly strait, almost aquiline nose and the sensitive mouth of an aristocrat. His sandy hair decorated by a fashionable earlock pin.

Trenton waved the words off as if they had been offered as praise, tossing his head grandly to allow his longish hair to dance about. "Perhaps this evening you will join me for a mug, and a toast to our gracious, good King."

Warren shook his head sadly. "I fear that to be a toast I cannot offer."

"But surely, you cannot but extol the leniency of our Majesty in his late conduct.", goaded Trenton with exaggerated flair.

"My dictionary lists no lenient tyrant." The good doctor stated curtly.

"You paint our Regent with the tyrant's brush, yet we find ourselves ten years free of the Seven Years War, our French antagonists and their painted savages safely quelled. The Crown is in debt for our defense…"

"Too bloody right and what does Georgie do, but tax us!" A voice called from the rear, to a clattering of sympathetic sounds. "Sugar and molasses, painter's lead, the Stamp tax, the bloody Townshead acts...."

"All of which are repealed, my man." The Tory soothed. "Repealed but for a pittance upon tea, the mildest of requisition, to assist the war debts."

This last caught Daniel's ear. Tea?, he thought, these Sons of Liberty must be the patriots blocking offloading of ships.

"There is no mild theft." The Patriot physician countered again, "no matter how gently taken."

"And how," the Tory fop hissed, "am I to take that."

"Take it as you like, my good man!" Warren rebuffed. "By our gracious sovereign's Declaratory Acts he grants himself the right to tax us, and by his Navigations Acts, he harnesses us to the East India Trade Company like oxen and denies us the right to seek fair trade for our products. We are powerless to advocate against these things, as we are denied representation in parliament. All that is left us is to blockade the cargoes from our harbors."

"Perhaps you hope these traders will run aground this night, so you can burn them to the waterline, as was done to the *Gaspee*." Daniel almost choked on his ale, word of that had reached England. The British Navy's sloop *Gaspee* had ran aground upon colonial reefs, and that very evening, the Navy ship was boarded, and set ablaze, her captain shot.

Doctor Warren was the equal of his opponent. "These sad events are no worse than Good King George's troops firing on his own, upon King Street."

"Remember Christopher Seider!" An emotional voice commanded from the anonymity of the shadows, sadly adding. "Dear little martyr."

"Indeed, remember the little delinquent, but do not forget the beaten soldiers of the King, at the Pearl Street Rope works!"

A rue chuckle went through the tavern, one that turned to a raucous laugh. "Aye, beaten bloody they were." Some wag agreed. "Again and again!", and dark laughter filled the bar.

"We forget them not." Still another voice in the shadows added. "Tis' what gives us hope."

"But," the simpering Trenton opined, attempting to forge a more successful path. "Were the good King such a despot, as you claim, then answer me this. Why does the *Dartmouth* and the *Eleanor* sit, her holds stuffed with Chinese tea, as you Sons of Liberty demand, when Redcoats aplenty lounge at their leisure, awaiting but a word from King George to offload it at bayonet point. Answer me that!"

'That, I can answer." Heady with drink, Daniel abandoned his half conquered flip, turning on the velvet wrapped fop. "You of the colonies complain of the King's boot upon your neck, we of Scotland have felt his lash. Walk my streets, I invite you! There you will find Kirks, churches, that lack a roof because the Crown had want of copper. Men feed their bairns stews of sheep shanks and leeks, or watch them starve, so that the higher cuts of meat may go for taxes." He paused, reaching for the ale flip as stunned, attentive voices in the darkness bellowed "Hear hear!" and stamped their feet. "I am

Daniel Ferguson, of the clan Ferguson, but we lack the gold and food for my found, so I make my own way here in the new world. That is the benevolence of your good King George; starve your child, but be late not with your taxes."

"Ferguson, you say.' The foppish Trenton drawled thoughtfully. "I recall meeting some of your kinsman, in New York, or was it York. They seemed much more....tractable."

"If my Laird sees fit to lick royal ass to keep his own in his castle, do not judge me by his weakness." Ferguson snapped. "It is for that I bring myself to this new land, for I detest the man who would submit to it as much as the royal German usurper who might compel it."

"You speak treason." Trenton snarled, drew back his expensive walking stick as a bludgeon.

Like a coiled spring, his long dirk flashed from the scabbard thrust into his belt and bit deep into the bar top. "I speak truth!" The Scot roared, his scarred hand left the quivering blade, pointing like the finger of doom at the pretentious fop before him. "Be that treason, then what does that say of your good King George?" With that, the Scot tuned his back upon the perfumed dandy and took up his tankard once again.

The dirk was over-long for a Ship's knife, sixteen inches from lethal tip to the black carved handle. The blade quivered in the bar top like the rattle of a rattlesnake's tail, and every man in the bar saw it for what it was, a warning carved from steel.

The Tory dandy made a few starts at rejoinders, but his eyes seemed transfixed by the vibrating blade. "I would expect no less from a Border reaver." The Lord Trenton spit, finally. "What color was your cockade in the '45?"

The '45, Daniel thought for a wistful second, Culloden, the last charge of the Highlanders and their decimation in the face of Redcoat guns. He might almost will himself to be among the fallen on that swampy field than to see his clan so diminished and destitute. He raised the half-full glass of flip high in the air. "Bonnie Charlie!" He bellowed. "God bless the Royal Prince, last of the Stuart line, true King of Scotland and England!" He said it to shock, and it did not fail to do so as a hush fell over the room, broken when someone whistled a few bars of "The white cockade", a jaunty Jacobite fife tune. With that, Daniel drained his flip in one long draught and when he set it down, he found two interesting things.

The foppish Trenton had taken his leave of the *Green Dragon* in a very feminine huff, and Daniel found yet another Ale flip set before him. Daniel again reached for his belt and sporran, but the barkeep waived him off. "T'was already paid for by your new friends."

"You are mistaken, sir, I am new to the colonies and have no friends."

"New you may be." The bartender allowed. "But you have made fine inroads to making friends, and enemies. Now, if you would be so kind, please remove your cutlery from my bar top."

Daniel slid his dirk back the scabbard with practiced grace. The ale flip, still warm from the hot iron, was welcome in his belly. When he regretfully set the mug down, a new face had assumed the space beside him at the bar.

"Who was that popinjay?" The salt-encrusted, sodden Scot asked, but corrected himself. "Your pardon, you called him a Lord, who was that royal peacock?"

"Old money from the old country," the newcomer stated with some venom, "landowners of some sort. His family makes their bread by trading, but 'tis said he needs not tip his hat to John Hancock if he does not wish. Might not be royalty back in merry ol' London, but 'tis close enough for the colonies."

Daniel nodded, though he had no idea who John Hancock was. "So he is a nabob with heavy pockets." He growled with even more hatred in his voice.

"There is no call to damn a man for sleeping warm."

True enough, Daniel cursed himself and whispered a silent prayer for a more civil tongue before asking. "And who are you, my newfound friend, and state your business."

"My name is Bodkin," He announced, conspiratorially, "if you meant the things you said, I know a place for you this night."

He had a mousy, quick manner like a thief expecting to be collared. But Daniel had no other prospects. "Go on." He said, noncommittally.

"A quorum of like minded gentleman gathers not far from here to discuss the current dilemma."

"And what dilemma would that be?" He asked, pointedly not looking at the man as he drew on the tankard again.

"A dilemma of taxes and deprivation of rights, of despotism and liberty."

Of being hanged for treason, the Scot added, his head swimming with drink. But, hanged today or starved tomorrow, the result was the same. He drained the tankard with another pull. 'How do we get there?"

* * * *

A pungent odor emanated from the *Green Dragon*, mutton too long from the butcher's stewing in onions to hide the tang. It assailed his nose all the more as his vision was dimmed by a scrap of cloth bound across his eyes.

Bodkin said, in a kindly voice as he took Daniel's hand. "Come with me, now," then he set out. With the certainty of a man used to navigating ships in the darkness, the canny Scot knew they traveled back toward the wharf. Just as certainly, he knew they would not reach it, Boston was not so lost to anarchy it would endure without comment a blindfolded man lead about their streets.

More so, the loquacious Bodkin was too nervous a sort to remain silent. "You find yourself joining our society at a most momentous time. Much hangs in the balance." As Daniel had supposed, Bodkin turned off the street to a dirt floor alley

Much hangs in the balance? Such as what? Daniel wondered silently, but kept that council. "What society might that be, good Bodkin?" He asked instead, "and what events?"

"We are the Sons of Liberty." Bodkin answered, but let the other question drift away in the wind as he nonsensically lead Daniel three times about a particular house like a maypole dance before returning the way they had come. A dog with a high-pitched bark chased them behind a short distance of fence and the rat-like little man commented, nervously. "That is quite a blade you wear, Mister Ferguson. I had always heard you Scotsman went about with knives in your socks. You must have quite the socks, eh?"

The blindfolded Daniel laughed so hard he almost lost his count of their paces. Had I a Skien Duhb, he thought, I would have it in my sock, had I socks, or shoes for that matter. Had I another dagger than my dirk, I would carry that, but I do not. That train of thought drew him back to his ejection from the *Beaver*, and the loss of his dunnage. Daniel began to despair again when the scent of old mutton and onions returned to his nose. Bodkin hurried him to the rear of the tavern.

The door was closed behind him and barred before the blindfold was removed. Daniel looked about, blinking owlishly. Heavy blankets were draped over the few windows, a man stood upon a chair, his face blackened with soot, then painted with blotches of blue and red in a recurrent pattern. His hair was blackened and spiked up, like a wild Celt. He wore a much repaired scrap of blanket from one shoulder and had a hatchet stuck in his belt. Stunned, Daniel stood and stared, it was the first sight he had ever had of a real Red Indian.

Then the painted man spoke and Daniel's image was shattered. "Let there be no thievery!" The Indian commanded, in a voice used to obedience. "If but one leaf is stolen, it all becomes a robbery, and we are undone." His eyes were chestnut brown, and burned with passion and purpose. "I will request of the duty officer the keys, and let us all pray God that he complies. But if not, we will do as we must. What is broken, we will fix, or pay for...."

Daniel looked at the men bustling about the dark, cramped space. All were done up like the speaking man, as Indians in war paint, buckskin and blanket, knives and hatchets abounded. "What goes on here, Bodkin?" He asked over his shoulder, only to see his guide also donning soot and war paint.

"What goes on here?", quoted the speaking man in clear, clipped tones, "protest, sir, perhaps the most dire petition of redress ever conceived. We have weathered the Townsend acts, we have protested and petitioned, but the crown remains deaf. They are bled white from a long war, they and their agents in the East Indian Tea Company, and see our colonies as a cash cow to be milked dry."

"You look like a chessboard," Daniel declared to the man dressed as an Indian on the warpath.

"It's supposed to be a rain of fire and ice," rejoined one of the painted men, apparently one of an artistic bent.

"Still looks like a chessboard," Daniel observed defiantly. "Now, what of me? What is your purpose and why am I summoned here."

"To answer a riddle, those of our Committee of Observation keep a careful note of the happenings of Boston; The movements of troops, the comings and goings of ships from the sea, and at harbor. Some ships more than others. Today, it was noted that a ruckus was a'acting upon one of those ships as it journeyed toward our harbor, and one man leapt overboard, or was thrown."

There seemed little point in denying it. "Thrown," Daniel intoned.

The chessboard painted man nodded grandly, a nod that was almost a bow. Then he continued as if he had not been interrupted. "Our greatest dread is our duty. Your newly arrived *Beaver* sits at anchor, her captain says she is infected with smallpox and he smokes her out before he will dock her."

"He lies," Daniel snapped, bitterly, "the canny fox. I was aboard the *Beaver* this very day, with no disease aboard."

"As we thought, but thank you for your council," the painted man reached beneath the blanket draped from his shoulder and produced a pistol, checked the priming pan and held it thoughtfully in his hand for a moment. "But a cagey captain I fear more than a diseased ship. We must board this ship, and a suspicious mind can only know that. We must board the *Beaver*, and I fear it will lead to blood."

Daniel thought a bare moment, dread washing over him was like the freezing, endless Atlantic. There were arms aboard the Beaver, muskets, swords and cannon besides. In his mind' eye, he saw friends shot, men bleeding and broken upon the *Beaver*'s decks, and he saw in these men the opportunity to once again walk the deck of the *Beaver*, and collect his things. "I can get you aboard that ship without blood." He said. "Give me that grease paint."

All eyes turned to the checkerboard painted leader, "and we shall," he promised, holding out a Bible for the Scot to swear his silence upon, "but with one small service we should ask of you."

Daniel looked at the Holy Book, and at the painted man who held it as he solemnly intoned. "Ours is a dire errand, this we all know, perfect secrecy is our only armor. Do you swear upon this most holy of Holies that you shall keep these events secret, now and forever, upon not pain of death, but of your immortal soul and eternal torment?"

Daniel took the book from the painted hand and flipped it open randomly, his finger searching out a verse without looking, indeed with his eyes shut. He opened his eyes and read. "Gird your sword upon your hip, mighty warrior, in splendor and majesty ride on triumphant."

"Aye, I do so swear." Daniel nodded.

* * * * *

"I entreat you, sir, one last time to return your cargoes to England, undelivered." The man speaking at the Old South Meeting House dais was blessed with a huge nose and forehead, beneath a mop of lush, even bushy white hair, Daniel was told his name was Samuel Savage.

The entreated man, of middle age and paucity shook his balding head sadly. "Should I return these cargoes," he said, in the sing-song of repetition, "my ships and the cargo would be seized and I ruined." His name was Francis Rotch, a Quaker, though apparently not one afraid of a profit. He said the words like a man tired of saying them, which he likely was, as in the hour Daniel had been in attendance in Old South, this was at least the eighth repetition.

The church was large, the impressive elevated dais as its focal point, and a multi-level balcony above. Even with all that seating, the crowd was greater than Daniel had ever seen before, standing room only, and damned little room then, crowding about the windows and at its doors to hear what went on.

At his left elbow, his checkerboard painted leader whispered. "There yet remains a slim hope." His outlandish costume seemed less strange to Daniel, as he, too was now clad as a Mohawk, in a green hunting shirt of a stiff cloth, a blanket roll slung from his left shoulder. His sandy brown hair was blackened and spiked up like an ancient Celt, his face smeared with soot and a garish red handprint across the whole of his face.

A slim hope? Daniel prayed not. The long wait and dread had sobered him, but the greater agony was fear. Fear of the sketchy plan his painted leader had laid out for him, but Daniel knew this was his last, best shot to be back aboard the *Beaver* to get his dunnage.

A commotion at the door broke his silent reverie. A young man, the image of Rotch, bareheaded and a mud splattered riding cloak, looking all the world like a man who had ridden his horse to death to be there, rushed in. Sparing no time for the questioning crowd, he hustled to the podium and spoke hurriedly to his father.

The simpering Quaker leaned toward his son in a regal way, spoke in hushed tone for several minutes, then turned to the men sharing the podium with him and shrugged dramatically. "My latest entreaty to Governor Hutchisson has been rebuffed. I have done what I can."

"You have done what you can," Savage repeated, and then demanded, "now what are your intentions?"

The Quaker paused momentarily. "For my own protection, if ordered by the Royal authorities, I will offload the tea."

The silent audience suddenly roared with their discontent, like a waking beast. One of the assembly leapt upon the pew rail and declared. "Who knows how tea will mingle with salt water?" and the crowd approved, their response electric, and vengeful. A dark muttering began to rumble through the crowd. In the balcony, the Mohawks began to pointedly shuffle toward the exits.

"Wait!" Their painted leader commanded, loud enough to make Daniel's ears ring. He flinched at his own volume, smiled apologetically to Daniel and added, in a more hushed tone. "Wait for the signal!"

The crowd was taking a decidedly dark tone, even high above in the balcony, Daniel could feel it. One of Mohawks whispered that a full third of Boston was there, they thought it a fine showing. Daniel thought of bloody riots in the streets and it worried him. He was apparently not the only one, as Rotch began backing away from the podium rail. Then, Samuel Adams, until now sullenly thoughtful in a chair like a wooden statue rose to his feet, and ascended to the speaking platform. He was a solidly built man, with a prominent forehead over bushy eyebrows. His very presence bespoke of intellect, a man of circumstance, his appearance at the dais was like a tonic upon the crowd, and they settled into silence to hear his words. "This meeting can do no more to

protect our country."

His leader's checkerboard face twisted strangely in confusion. He had

been busy hushing down his Mohawks when Adams spoke and had not heard

the simple phrase. "Did he say country, or colony?" He queried.

"Country," Daniel supplied.

The simple word send his fearless leader into action, he leapt to the

high second story railing, cupping stained fingers to his mouth. "Boston Harbor

a teapot tonight! Hurrah for Griffin's wharf! The Mohawks come!" A shiver

went through the crowd, Indians abandon the balcony with whoops and shrieks

to wake the dead, men in the crowd shifted from their seats, casting off the

finery of civilization for war paint, hunting shirts, buckskin and blankets.

The Scot stood for a long moment at the railing, watching the room

shimmer into life, men casting off the trappings of civilization and marching

toward the door in a warlike state of mind. Others, women and men who had not

thought to bring war paint to the meeting followed with defiant utterances and

shaking fists. Then, as the first few pews were already vacant, a well dressed

nabob his war painted compatriots had identified as John Hancock rose from his

bench and fairly leapt to the dais. In the manner of a man trying to appear to be

leading a parade by having the last word, he stood before the emptying hall and

pronounced to the fading assembly. "Let each man do as he feels is right."

Their indefatigable leader was at Daniel's side, blue and red dots upon

his face like a puzzle. Daniel's own puzzle was if the painted man was his tour guide or his jailer, but his eyes glowed with an intense, infectious excitement, white teeth showing through a blackened mouth as they stalked through the town. The dirt path turned to the cobblestones of Hutchisen Street, then wood as they gained the pier.

There were about sixty of them, certainly not more than eighty. Others were joining the war party as it marched, scaling chimneys to rub their faces with soot in imitation of the Indian costumes. Painted Mohawks had already boarded the *Eleanor*, ordering the night watch from her decks, more gained the *Dartmouth*. Daniel and his compatriots kept walking to three whalers moored in the shadows of Boston's docks.

His heart pulsing in his ear, the Scot took up an oar, reflected that of all his new found friends, he might be the only one who knew how to row, but his checkerboard painted leader proved to be the better man, taking up oars beside him with a wink and an appraising look.

* * * *

Thirty days of night watch, Paddy reflected upon the pilot's deck, thirty days with little or no sleep. But it was right to do, even cutting that sadist Captain's purse and slipping young Ferguson the loot, he would be repaid in Heaven, the Irishman piously reassured himself, and chuckled at his pranks. When Harlan demanded "who gave the order to heave him overboard! Who gave it!", daft Irishman he was, Paddy said. "Bless me, sir, I thought you did!"

A clatter from starboard caused Paddy to scurry to the *Beaver*'s rail, afraid the ship had run into a shoal, or some floating bilge that could damage her. There, he was greeted by a vision from Hades scaling up the side of the ship. Head like a porcupine, all spikes and quills, and a bloody handprint upon its face. Paddy stumbled back. "God save Ireland!" He squealed, looked in all directions for the ship's musket he had forgotten.

"Paddy," said the vision from the depth staring up at him. He opened his mouth again and the Irishman was surprised not to see fangs. "It's me."

The voice tickled his memory. "Ferguson?" The superstitious Irishman croaked. "Ferguson, is it you? Alive?"

"Alive and well," Ferguson confirmed, hurtled the rail to land on bare feet. He wore a green shirt and a tattered blanket over one shoulder, a hatchet was thrust into his belt beside that great Scottish knife of his, "and, with friends." He turned and whistled shrilly over the side.

With that, a mass of men with blackened faces, clad in feathers, blankets and buckskins swarmed aboard. Paddy whistled through his teeth at the sight of them. One of the group, a stocky one with a checkerboard pattern on his face stood strait and militarily erect, walking toward him. "Watch officer," He said, officially, "take me to your captain, please. I'll need your keys."

* * * *

Daniel breathed the heady scent of Bohea tea, all the way from China. Sealed in red chests highlighted with blue and crowned with the golden East Indian Tea Company insignia, the *Beaver* freighted one hundred fourteen of these chests, and painted Mohawks brought each of the heavy wooden crates in turn to the deck using the ship's tackle and lines. There, the dirty work of the evening began, already the rhythmic sounds of hatchets set the evening's tempo.

Daniel studied the Rampant lion holding the world in an outstretched paw, called the "Cat and the cheese" by salty Jack Tars. He reflected on the sweat and blood he had expended this month past bringing it safe to this new world, only to bring a hatchet crashing down upon the lid, dead in the middle of that golden lion's chest.

The painted wood gave way with surprisingly few blows, releasing a pleasant scent to the salty air as a riot of Mohawks leapt upon white muslin bags of fragrant tea with grasping hands. Daniel surveyed the destruction of the cargo he had succored, and found it strangely satisfying. Quick as thought, sharp knives laid bare the dried black leaves and Mohawks hefted bags to their shoulders, trudging to the Beaver's rail. Daniel ran the sharp blade of his hatchet over one of the sacks, jammed the weapon into his belt and hauled the heavy sack to his shoulder, joining his fellows in the walk to the rail. The sack was heavier than it looked, hefted like a fattened pig and shifted unpredictably as the tea flopped about, some dropping down the back of his shirt like mud, but his experienced sea legs gave him the edge in the race to the ship's rail.

He felt tea in his spiky hair, more trickling down his collar. With a grunt the Scot hefted the bag onto the wooden rail he had polished for hours in the hot sun and cutting Atlantic winds. Tea boiled from the rent in the fabric bag, dried tea leaves fluttering in the nighttime wind with the rolling Atlantic.

It was a moment of liberation in an act of sedition to Daniel as he dumped the bag of hated tea into the white capped surf to join others that had preceded it. Daniel shook the sack like a terrier snapping a rat's neck, then wadded the cloth into a ball, and consigned it also to darkened waves churning with tea. The waves claimed it, driving the bag underwater forever and Daniel felt his anger swept away too. There was something about this land, something strange that bewitched him like no other land, even Scotland which he would always call his home. He stared down into the waters, black but for the reflection of the odd star, and felt strangely satisfied. Then he turned to the Mohawk standing beside him at his labors, abashed at his own wool gathering. "Three pence a pound-weight, eh?" Three hundred sixty pounds a chest, one hundred fourteen chests aboard the *Beaver*, alone, Daniel thought, the *Eleanore* and the *Dartmoth* doubtless carried about the same. "That'll give King George indigestion, I reckon."

"Brother, 'tis not the sum, but the principle." The words he said sounded so strange coming out of the mouth of a man with half his face painted a bloody red, the other half dark blue. "England refuses us a seat in Parliament, nor are we allowed say in our own governance." He paused to slap Daniel on the back, and was gone back to his labors before the words sank in.

The ship rocked as the Mohawks dashed about the *Beaver*'s decks, tea laden waters lapped at the Beaver's sides, to Daniel's mind, it sounded like applause. His ears perked, it was applause, through the haze and distance, Daniel could make out the docks of Griffin's Wharf, chocked with people. Men and women, children even, cheering the Mohawks in their evening's employment.

The next painted and soot stained man beside him at the rail dumped his bag bodily overboard. "A nice night's work, eh, brother?"

"Indeed." Daniel agreed, and paused long enough to smile at the man before returning to his work.

Sacks of tea fell from the ship like fat snowflakes. Mohawks hurried at their duties, divesting the ship of tea, bags and even the garishly painted boxes of red, blue and gold. Time lost its meaning in the strange duties, Daniel hefted another uncounted sack to his shoulder, time and repetition had found cutting the bags open a forgotten inconvenience in their hurry when two of His Majesty's warships had drifted silently to the Harbor's mouth. They were content to simply sit there at anchor, but their gun ports were open in an obvious threat. Hurried council supposed them to be awaiting orders, and the Mohawks wanted to be long gone when those orders arrived. Daniel heaves the sack as hard as he could over the Beaver's side, watched it clear the rail with a certain dark satisfaction that had not yet left him, and heard a muffled "thud".

"Thud?", he muttered, exchanged a glance with the painted compatriot who happened to be beside him, and the two hesitantly stepped to the ships rail and peered over. White muslin bags were piled in an irregular mound up to the *Beaver*'s scuppers, small vents in her rail to allow the water free passage from her decks during storms or hard seas. Daniel looked at them again with dawning understanding, glanced in confusion at the painted Mohawk beside him. "The tides out, they'll float on the morning tide, but…"

"What is it, brother?", called the red and blue painted leader from the pilot's deck. Beside the Mohawk commander, the dejected Captain Harlan looked on in interest also, his arm still wrapped up in a sling.

Daniel cupped his hands to his face. "The bags are floating! Piled to the scuppers, cap… er…brother!" Beneath ash and paint, Daniel flushed. Long months of repetition making him address the mast as Captain, almost giving himself away.

"Starboard side too!" Another voice called from that side, and a moment of indecision crept over the war party.

"It's the tide!" Another of the Mohawks opined. "The damned tide's buggered us, boys."

Then the Mohawk beside Daniel, a tall powerfully built man with the arms of a blacksmith requested. "Hold these for me, brother." He stuffed two heavy bags, which he had been carrying on each shoulder, into Daniel's arms, and with the gingerly footing of a land lubber at sea, straddled the rail and gained his footing upon the unsure, shifting bags. His hands spread for balance, he tested his footing upon this new perch, and a cheer that was almost a war cry let up from his compatriots as he commanded. "Hand 'em out to me, boys!"

More bags of tea flew to the burly armed man, who dispersed them just as quickly into the deep. Daniel's chest and arms ached from the exertion, but at the same time, he could feel the energy of the world pulsing around him. The feeling that he was part of something incredible, something momentous grew as he watched the murky, star-lit Atlantic receive the tea like some pagan gift to the gods. The Mohawk beside him trod upon Daniel's foot and begged forgiveness, and the Scot almost wept, wanted to embrace the man.

It had been an exhausting three and a half hours, throwing the bags into Griffin's Harbor. Daniel looked with sinister satisfaction on the work of the evening, on the Pilot's deck, beside his checker board faced leader, Captain Harlan looked on sullenly and slack jawed as white bags of Bohea splashed into the Atlantic, slowly absorbing sea water and slipping beneath the waves. Now, the tackle and rigging were stowed and his Mohawk companions had taken mop and brush in hand and were cleaning the decks. They appeared to be determined to leave the ship in better condition than they found it, less the offending tea. None could dilute their message or claim them vandals or brigands when they worked so diligently to return the ship to perfect order. Daniel was about to join their efforts, when the glowering face of Captain Harlan jogged his memory, and the time seemed proper for a journey below.

With a month or more of experience finding the stair in the ocean's dark, Daniel ascended into the ship's bowels. Two of his Mohawk brethren were below, cleaning up the lower deck of any mess. "Uh…me know you." Daniel offered them the evening's agreed upon recognition signal.

The two were of a more liberal mood. "Evening, brother," one offered, "where you headed."

"Come with me." Daniel ordered, finding the trap door to the belly of the ship. One of the Mohawks handed him a sputtering ship's lantern and Daniel slid through the trap door. The hold, always impossibly cramped before, seemed strangely open and bracing now, even with the constant scent of mildew in the air. Where before he would have been climbing over and around crates of tea to find what he sought, now it was comparatively easy to find the cask sized chest marked with the sadistic Captain's name. "This is it." He said, mostly to himself, then commanded his two comrades. "Take this up to the deck."

Feet moving familiarly on decks that had been his world for the last month, he followed his two Mohawk brothers and their heavy chest. Then, at the spot between two ship's beams where his hammock hung each night he tarried. Four hammocks hung between each pairing of beams, the last so low your ass drug upon the deck with each ship's roll. Daniel had been one up from the bottom, a bare eighteen inches between he and those above and below him. Thus he would hang each night, smelling another's farts above him, and getting kicked in the back from below.

Hanging from cast off netting was the thing that had pulled him back onto this mildewed, floating torture chamber. A bundle not thirty inches long, rolled in his own tartan. The overhead beams were of a height he could easily conquer, below decks most of the crew had to at least squat, and the bundle quietly clanked a metallic greeting as he claimed it. A piece of cast off line was knotted into a convenient strap about the tartan wrapped bundle, and he quickly cast it over his shoulder and beneath his blanket, finding himself rushing back above decks, as the sounds of booted feet above boded trouble.

Captain Harlan, his right arm splinted, had drawn his cutlass backhand and stood defiantly over his trunk. It was a stubby weapon butted with a gleaming dull iron guard that covered his whole hand, a wicked, inelegant, razor sharp cleaver that was lethally efficient in practiced hands. "You said you had no quarrels with commerce or private property," he raged at the Mohawks checkerboard painted leader, feigning clumsily with the stubby blade, "yet you drag my personal dunnage to the decks for destruction!"

With a "thud", Daniel's hatchet spun through the air and chewed itself solidly into the thick wooden hide of the Deck Captain's trunk. "Hold!" Bellowed the young Scot from the deck stair, with newfound courage, he stalked across the deck and retrieved the hatchet.

The captain stared unknowing into the insolent eyes of the Scot he had doomed to flogging. Daniel met those eyes and with a deft chop of the little axe, hacked the chest's padlock aside. He threw open the chest's lid without looking, and the bracing scent of fine tea drifted about the decks. The contents of the oversized trunk were divided meticulously; one side being taken up by shirts and other linens, the other side was stuffed with cotton bags of fine tea. The Mohawks cheered and someone commanded, "Over the side with it, boys!"

"Brigand." The infuriated Captain hissed through clenched teeth as his fortune was slit open like a pig and cast to the sea like a chamber pot. His face reddened like a man too long in the sun, and suddenly he lunged, the heavy boarding cutlass cutting the air at Daniel's exposed back. There was a shout of warning and the blade met his back with the ringing clang of steel upon steel. Before Harlan could redirect the blow, a dozen Mohawks were upon him.

The world swam around Daniel. Dazed, he did not remember dropping to his knees, felt the throb of his arm and saw blood pouring copiously down his left sleeve, dripping from numb fingers. Trailing from his shoulder was a discolored scrap of blanket wool now stained crimson. With his working right hand, he touched it in confusion before recognizing it as the bloody shred of the blanket he had worn draped over his shoulder, now shorn in half by the chop of the Captain's cutlass. His stumbling caused the bundle beneath the blanket to shift and his sword swung out, hanging from the slashed tartan like an accusation and Daniel remembered his carefully concealed bundle beneath the Indian blanket.

"This bundle belongs to one of my crewmen." The captain protested, pointing to the purloined package now all but bared upon Daniel's back, but spoke directly to their painted leader. "You, my Mohawk charlatan, with your fine speeches and morals, all now comes to naught and you are exposed as the base pilferer of a poor seaman's bag." He stood imperiously, staring down his nose at the painted men in judgment.

"A fine voice you have." Daniel said from the deck. "You speak so highly of Seamen's rights and property, you who have sent more men to sleep with Neptune this last week than the rest of the voyage before. Hypocrisy suits you." His bloody hand fell heavily on the wooden chest, and he dragged himself to his feet. The Captain recoiled as if he were under eternal judgment, until

Daniel snatching a loose shirt from the piles inside the chest and began

vigorously scrubbing at his face with it. When he pulled it away, his true visage

glared at his former captain. 'You know me now, don't you sir?"

In a just world, Harlan's sadistic face would have fallen, mouth agape

as he recoiled from the reappearance of this vengeful wraith claimed by the

briny deep. But he did not. Instead, he stared at Daniel in evident confusion and

the Scot bit his lip in impatience as a long, awkward moment passed. The

impatient Scot was about to speak and name himself, when Paddy leapt into the

fray. "Daniel Ferguson! In the flesh, he is!" Still, this was not enough, as no

light of recognition glimmered on the captain's face and the Irishman added.

"God save us from mutineers!"

"Mutineers." Captain Harlan mulled the word over in his mind, and

then his eyes grew wide. "Ferguson! You return like the prodigal son."

"And this is my bundle." Daniel confirmed the Captain's recognition,

belated and assisted though it might be, touching the long blade in his belt. "Or

do you dispute it?"

The *Beaver*'s captain knew all to well what the soot stained, bleeding

man intimated at, and his eyes went wide in sudden fear. "No." The captain said,

too quickly. "No, I do not dispute it. You have retrieved your property, in that

you are just. But it is your errand I find damning. You are a wolf's head now,

young Ferguson. There is no place you may go to escape the King's justice,

nowhere which the law will not follow."

"Did you see me in brigandage?" Daniel demanded with a wicked smile and blade in hand. "Can you testify that you saw me in any act? Me, mind you, my good Captain, not my compatriots here?" The Captain's red face drew a smile to Daniel, his white teeth glowing through sooty blackened skin. "I will pay you for that lock." He said, magnanimously, and withdrew from his sporran a small decorated leather pouch bound with a strand of ship's cord. He dropped it to the *Beaver*'s deck with the joyful jingling of coins.

* * * *

The deck was cleaned and mopped of both Chinese tea and Scottish blood, the Mohawks removed their footgear and shook them over the side, expunging themselves of the last vestiges of the hated tea. Nearby the checkerboard-faced leader stood with the crestfallen Captain and asked. "There you are, sir, all ship shape and Bristol fashion, to your satisfaction, sir?"

The seaman, rubbing at his splinted arm, inwardly admitted the painted Indians had done a fine job of clearing his decks. But from the pilot's deck, he could see bags of tea slowly sinking into the harbor and sickened at the loss, he could only nod.

One by one, the Mohawks returned to their rowboats, onlookers cheered from the docks, watching the Indians take their places. The other Mohawks had long since finished their errand and watched their brethren gain their oars. The last man to board had inexplicably wiped his camouflaging paint from his face, and cradled his arm. A Mohawk with checkerboards painted onto his own face helped that last aboard, and the little ships cast off.

"He is cut badly." A burly Mohawk with jagged lightning bolts crisscrossing his face observed of the injured Daniel.

"True enough," Checkerboard said with thoughtful, worried eyes. "There are Fergusons over on King Street among the sail makers, I think. At times like these, a man needs his kin close. When we make shore, send a man and...."

"No!" The voice came from the longboat's deck. The wounded man lay in a bloody slump, he had seemed barely clinging to life, but he mustered the strength to speak, and there was urgency to his voice. His good hand, coated with new and dried blood reached out and gripped the checkerboard chief's rolled sleeve. "No Fergusons, swear it to me. No...Fergusons."

The leader of the Mohawks felt the grip slack and gently guided the hand back to the wooden floor of the longboat. The Scot's blood coated the bottom of the boat and would need to be well scrubbed before dawn. Blood that might have been from all of them, had the man not risked all to help. He considered that a moment, and made a snap decision. "I will take him to my home, send Doctor Warren as soon as he is found."

Light headed and strangely drowsy, Daniel dimly heard Revere. Even staunching the bleeding wound with the remnant of the Captain's shirt was becoming an effort. He lay his head on the mildewed hull of the longboat and felt nothing for a long time.

Chapter 2

He had dim memories, nightmares almost, of awaking as a feathered,
painted Mohawk stitched at his arm. But the terror subsided as the painted man
introduced himself as Doctor Joseph Warren, and his checkerboard faced leader
stepped from the flickering shadows of candlelight, holding a candelabra. The
checkerboard pattern of blue and red had been indifferently scrubbed away, as
Daniel was sure he looked, too. His leader of the evening introduced himself as
Paul Revere, and vouched wholeheartedly that Doctor Warren was an ardent
Son of Liberty, patriot and lover of freedom. Dour faced Sam Adams stood in
the shadows, speaking soberly to all.

"This is a dark omen for our mission. We endeavored that no blood be
spilt, nor thievery. I have ordered Charles O'Conner's coat nailed to the
whipping post for the theft of a few leaves of tea, and here this Scottish stranger
walks off the *Beaver* with..." his hands played over the piled sum of Daniel's
possessions, inexpertly picking up the brass basket hilt and almost cutting his
left hand upon the sword. "...all this. It will be our undoing."

"It need not be." Revere leapt to the Scot's defense. "Daniel merely
retrieved his own property, nothing more."

"Her Captain need only cry brigandage . . ." Adams said, shaking his
great, craggy head, trying to divine the purpose of a plate like brass disk with a
threaded hole punched in its middle.

"But he will not," Doctor Warren protested as he stitched, 'less the law too closely examine his own actions both this night and before."

"Aside," Revere added, "the only man to identify him was an Irishman, and as we left he drew close and whispered that, if pressed, his memory would be vague as to the identity of the wounded Mohawk."

Then, the fever had taken Daniel and he remembered little else. Almost nothing but for Revere's kind face, speaking to him gently as he rowed him across Boston Harbor, explaining to the delirious fevered Scot, "we must get you out of Boston, you have become.. Popular." He remembered that, and nothing else.

Time passed without his mark or knowledge, until his fever broke in the midst of an unforgiving Massachusetts winter. For his recovery, he had been granted the anonymity of a corner of the kitchen, a blanket and several sacks stuffed with straw for his bed. The scrap of tartan, barely enough to bundle a babe, which had borne his possession to this new world was mended of its tear by Captain Harlan's cutlass and was now pressed into service as a blanket.

His hand drifted to the kitting scar on his arm, the heat there had mostly dissipated. Like his burning fever, the swelling was all but gone. Drowsily, he drew on his shirt, trousers and belt. He found his baldric and drew it on as he sought his way to the tavern. His sword now hanging familiarly at his left hip, Daniel had dim memories of reassembling the pieces of it from his torn bundle after regaining it from the *Beaver*.

The Black Horse Tavern was known far and wide as the jewel of the little town of Menotomy. A tiny scattering of homes and milk cow farms between Cambridge and Lexington, Menotomy had little to speak for it but the Black Horse. It was known by its sign, a carving of a rearing black stallion, and revered for its flowing tap and ebullient good cheer. It was said that the 'Horse, when her doors were open, never lacked for business. It offered a small number of rooms on her upper floor, too small a number for Daniel to be spared one.

Pelenore, the indentured man, spoke with a French accent and feigned high breeding. His airs fit poorly with his duties about the Black Horse, which were mostly of the chop wood and muck out the stalls variety. He walked with a strange gait and affected his dark brown hair in a queue, the masculine ponytail so popular in the civilized world, bound with a well used, but much loved, silk ribbon. Working in the kitchen was Abigail, a half black woman servant of some thirty years who seemed confined to the stove. She was a barely passable cook and an indifferent nursemaid, but kept the fire burning warmly. She woke Daniel with her rattling before the dawn each morning, and never failed to do so again, forgetting to wish him good night in the evening as she left.

Too precious for the kitchen was Meg, who seemed to never leave the bar. A comely lass of some twenty years, in a brown skirt of home-spuns that traced at the rough plank floor and a red bodice over a white blouse, the bright red bodice complemented her hair well, a glowing auburn that flowed down her back like a sunset. She had a laugh and a smile for each customer that you would never guess was perfunctory until you had heard the real one, ringing joyously through the meager backyard of the Black Horse at some antic of one of the house cats, or one of the owner's dogs.

The owner of the Black Horse was a prosperous old-country Scot going by the name of Trotter, but he had the long, mile eating pace of a mountain striding Highlander, not of the bandy, bow-legged horseman of the rocky lowlands. He had the erect manner of a Soldier, and his back bore the marks of the lash. Daniel guessed him a deserter of His Majesty's Army from the "Seven Years war", or the "French and Indian War" as it was known here, there was something in the way the man watched the door and kept a ready eye on strangers entering his Tavern, something that hearkened Daniel back to Scotland, and watching wanted men in their daily life, but Daniel had also known enough men to know that small indiscretions like desertion from the King's army did not mark a man to be one of bad character.

Trotter was a bustling thunderbolt of activity, dashing from table to table on the crowded floor. Daniel watched the tireless man as he spread good cheer and *joi-de-vivre* about his establishment, never too busy to fill a glass or slap a back. Daniel had dim memories of a different sort of Trotter, leaning over him in the grip of his fever with the serious look of a man contemplating burying a kinsman. Then, the Tavern keeper saw Daniel and had him away from prying eyes in a corner table before the young Scot realized. Likewise, he had returned and departed before the wounded man could form a question to his tongue, a bowl of stew and a mug of beer left in the wake of his passing.

The food was good, and most welcome, Daniel ate hungrily and was pleased to see his stomach did not rebel. Trotter returned to him, and sat down across from the younger Scot, to Daniel's very great surprise. They studied each other a long moment, Trotter with a medical eye, Daniel because he had never seen the man so still before. "You seem none the worse for wear." The Tavern keeper announced, smiling with the perfunctory, easy grin those of his profession could summon at will, a smile that somehow never got to his guarded eyes. "Thought you were a goner, but God has other plans for you, it seems."

"How long was I a'fever?" Daniel asked, rubbing his chin. He reckoned his face wore about a week's worth of beard, enough to make him scratchy, though not enough to be called a respectable beard yet.

The tavern keeper shrugged. "A while." He muttered noncommittally. "If it helps, it is later February, 1774."

Daniel gaped at the revelation, chewed slowly for a long moment as he phrased his next question. "A man a'fever may rave of... things."

"True enough." The Tavern keeper nodded, his Scottish brogue creeping thickly to his voice as he spoke. The injured Scot did not elaborate, just stared evenly at his expatriate kinsman. Finally the tavern keeper sighed and spoke. "I know you are no stranger to killing, your speech was plain enough to that. I ken you a soldier to a Laird of the old country."

Daniel cursed himself as a loose lipped fool. "And?"

"Bosh, 'tis not my business." He said, waving his hand dismissively. "A Taverner knows when to be deaf, and when to forget."

Daniel was not assuaged, the Tavern-master was a glad hand, but Daniel had met many men in his years. Some, like Revere, were true as steel and there were others, like this man, who were out for one and one only, themselves. "And?", he repeated, "I can tell there is more by the way you look at me."

"There was a night…" The Tavern-master stammered, as if he hesitated to bring up this knowledge. "You were a'fever and raving, making enough noise to wake the dead. That malingering Abigail of mine had wound a blanket about her head to ward out the noise and…well, cursing a streak in Gaelic, I was, and you sat up and looked at me, first time you had. Then you spoke in Gaelic."

Daniel swallowed, and not because he was finished chewing the tough piece of beef in the stew. "And what did I say?"

"You said you would not take the shilling. You'd die before you wore a red coat. And then you fainted dead away."

"Anything else?"

"In truth, I left your care to Abigail," Trotter held up a hand and lied, "tended you like her own babe, she did. You had many concerned for you, Revere left word for you, should you live."

"Revere was here?" Daniel asked, amazed the man had made the effort to keep abreast of his health. "He asked after me?"

"Keep your voice down, with that!" Trotter snapped, glancing in all directions, "Menotomy is as much Tory as Patriot." Satisfied that none had overheard, the tavern master sighed and continued. "As often as he could, Revere came, and we kept him informed by express message. He left us word for you, for once you are fit to travel."

The Tavern door opened and shut, outside the world was painted white with a very broad brush, an ill wind howled at the building's walls. Daniel shivered at the thought of finding his way with a wounded arm and no real prospects, but his fierce Gallic pride would accept no other thought. "Fit I am, for whatever end."

"Good man you are, then." Trotter enthused, eager to have the man out from under his roof. His was a life of business, not ideology, and while it was good business to have a friend in Revere, the business man did not readily accept the idea of another mouth to feed in his inn, and a wanted mouth at that. This man had the odor of a King's bounty about him, and Trotter wanted him long gone, for a lot of reasons. "Paul left word that you were to set up lodging in the old Cavanaugh place. I will have my man show you where it is. It hasn't been occupied for some time, will likely need some work."

Suspiciously, Daniel considered his host's largess. "How does Mister Cavanaugh feel about this?" He asked.

"Doubt he cares," Trotter spat. "He's dead, dead a long winter ago."

Abandoned at least a year, the residence would undoubtedly need lots of work. Daniel did not relish the thought of the likely repairs in his weakened condition. "How did he die?" He asked the tavern master.

The answer he got was a simple shrug. "People die."

Gallic pride urged him to refuse, but his hasty evacuation from Boston leapt to his mind. Undoubtedly, soldiers of the Crown sought a man wounded upon his left arm, in Scotland that would mean brass muskets butts upon the door in the darkness and men carried away, homes put to the torch and inhabitants bayoneted or worse, Daniel's eye wandered to the comely Meg at the bar, adding her lighthearted laughter to the din within the establishment. In his mind he saw a gleaming seventeen inch bayonet mounted to a Brown Bess musket, and that laughter heard no more.

Impatient with his wool-gathering, Trotter abandoned the table to be swallowed by the crowd. The younger Scot leapt from the bench intent on pursuit, when a mischievous foot appeared from the milling crowd, struck his heel and Daniel went lurching into another table, upsetting it onto the patron seated there.

"Clumsy oaf!" The harsh tones of the new world lash at Daniel's ears. "You Boarder Reivers have the upbringing of Goats! If you cannot go about on two feet, kindly return to all fours. Then the rest of us need not concern ourselves with herding you!"

"Mind your tongue," the Inn's rigid, high backed chairs had bruised his ribs, and the Scot gasped for wind as red rage filmed his mind at being tripped, "doddering old fool!"

The musical ring of steel sent the familiar muttering of the tavern to a sudden stand still. The hushed, frightened silence was worse than a scream. Daniel struggled to get bare feet beneath him and looked at his antagonist. His grey hair hung long about his shoulders. His wardrobe, what was not spattered when Daniel upset his dinner upon him, was of a somber and utilitarian cut. "Do not allow my years to embolden your tongue, boy." He breathed, and Daniel

caught the scent of a heavy red wine upon his breath. His arms were twisted

steel, holding his blade in an unwavering grip. It was a curving saber ending in

an ornate cup hilt that protected his hand and aimed unerringly at Daniel's heart.

"I have buried more men than twice your years!"

"Buried more bottles, you mean." Daniel quipped.

The attempt at humor did not quench the man's anger and he blustered

with a black, killing rage. "You are impudent." He snapped.

Daniel paused a long moment. "What does that mean?"

"It means follow me out onto the common, boy and die there!"

* * * *

The common was a scrap of grassy field in the middle of the town

were, each Sunday after worship, the men of the Militia would gather and

practice their martial arts. They would form their squares and march in lines.

From the kitchen of the Black Horse, Daniel had watched them march and

parade, endlessly practicing forming into tight groups bristling with their

collection of mismatched muskets.

He stood now in the frozen grass, felt the dusting of snow there on his

bare feet. He was numb but not from the cold, rather he was numb with fear of

the events swirling around him like a storm at sea. Daniel drew his blade, a

basket hilted, single edged sword of some thirty inches from tip to butt. It was

an artifact of his clan, none the worse for its travel across the Atlantic lashed

between the beams below deck on the *Beaver*, a Falchion blade wedded to the traditional Highland basket hilt, built to hard use unlike the decorated, aristocratic weapon his opponent carried.

His opponent, whom the townspeople were calling Samuel Whittenmore carried his ornate sword on a military belt. It was fine steel, and the man hefted it like one familiar with its lethal purpose. The blade was of the French style and had such a curve to it, it almost appeared to be stolen off a farmer's sickle. Around them, Daniel could hear the townsfolk talking, this old man had been a soldier in the King's army, an elite Dragoon horseman, and was known to be good with blade or gun. He had stayed in this new land after the French and Indian wars, and fought again in the Seminole wars against Pontiac and his warriors. He had buried a wife, and unknown numbers of men.

The February wind cut through his threadbare shirt and trousers. Daniel fought down a shiver and wondered if it were the cold, or the effects of his injury. A crowd was gathering, Puritan roundheads who ordinarily abhorred a duel came to watch a pair of savages kill each other, one a Highlander from the old country come among them a stranger, the other one of their own, who held himself aloof by his skills and his past.

His opponent unclipped the lacquered scabbard from his plain, serviceable belt and set it aside. In quiet pantomime, Daniel drew off his baldric and dropped it, facing the grey haired man with his Falchion at a pretty, practiced high guard he dimly recalled was referred to as St Michael's Guard.

The Dragoon looked queerly at Daniel as he stood awaiting him, The Scot realized dimly that St. Michael's Guard was usually used when paired to a targe, a small leather faced shield that the rest of the world had left behind but was still in vogue in Scotland. Daniel allowed the blade to drift to a more typical, classical inside guard.

With a flourish, the gaudy, gilt handled sword slashed the air like a dizzying whirlwind, and Daniel felt himself gape, dropping his guard so that the blade almost struck the ground. His foggy mind forced bleary eyes to return to his opponent, now standing in a pretty dueler's stance. "I await you!" Whittenmore declared belligerently.

"What?" Daniel heard himself dumbly ask. His vision momentarily swam, his injured arm ached as he moved it but that had nothing to do with his crawling stomach.

Whittenmore muttered something with the sharp edge of a curse, closing the distance between them with the footwork of a dancer and with that inauspicious opening, the duel began. Daniel warded off the French sword's searching point with a hacking slash that barely saved his flesh. He had no time to celebrate the victory as the former Dragoon's blade seemed to magically return, again and again, the 35 inch long strip of gleaming, curving steel stretched out to prick at his knees, another kiss of steel barely avoided. Daniel lunged in attack, slashing out with his shorter more common falchion's wicked single edge, which the former Dragoon easily deflected.

The Scot pressed his attack again, and Whittenmore dealt his blade a rattling slap with his saber that vibrated up Daniel's arm. "You swing that cutlass like you are reaping hay!" The old man taunted. "Dirt farmer!"

"I reap souls." Daniel snarled back.

"With a pistol, perhaps." The Dragoon goaded as his blade suddenly swept high and Daniel barely avoiding it. The injured Scot hacked a mighty swath with the broad bladed falchion that the older man seemed to take no notice of. Instead the black clad Whittenmore stabbed that metal point unerringly at Daniel's navel. The Scot leapt aside, felt steel nip his loose shirt.

The Scot clapped a hand to his belly, trained in the blade since his birth, he was watching his life melt away before this withered old man. His head swam as he saw the former Dragoon lunging toward him in another assault. Daniel hacked the falchion in a whirling figure-8, forcing his opponent back, trying to buy room to think. The grey haired swordsman danced back further than the Scot expected, dropped the blade of his saber almost to the earth, watching warily. Daniel allowed his own blade to drift toward the earth, and the somberly dressed former Dragoon lunged with his shuffling footwork, and just as quickly danced back when Daniel drew up the blade into a hanging, inside guard, the curved blade suspended from his hand, but drifting down.

He's getting tired, the Scot realized, he's breathing hard, at least as hard as Daniel was, and the Scot pressed his assault with a vengeance. He hacked out with the Arabesque's single edged blade, a killing blow from a blade made for shearing, hacking cuts. It was a slash that would take a man's limb, had it connected. But it did not, the nimble old man danced out of the path of the stubby blade, and the trap was closed. Whistling through the air, the razor sharp saber hurtled down like a guillotine blade. Seeing his neck in the trap, Daniel sucked in a breath, instinctively swung up his left arm into the path of the descending French steel.

The old soldier's eyes went wide, his hand worked with a nimbleness belying his years and the descending blow, which should have taken Daniel's hand clean off his wrist, instead dealt a stinging, bloodless blow to the Scot's forearm with the flat of his blade. Then the man danced back out of range, the curving French blade no longer a ward against Daniel's assault, but forgotten in his hand. His left hand now came up, finger aimed at Daniel in righteous indignation. "That blow would have taken your arm."

There was no arguing that, and Daniel's infection addled brain was too dizzy to do so. "Yes." He agreed.

The old Dragoon spoke the next like an accusation, "And you are used to a target!"

Target, another word for the small shield Daniel called a Targe, which usually graced his left arm, and that he had spent countless hours using in his martial training. "Yes." Daniel answered truthfully to the older man's statement.

The old soldier cocked his head queerly. "Do you have a target now, sir?" He asked in perfect, almost jarring, politeness. "I will tarry here and allow you the time to go fetch it."

"I have yet assembled it." Daniel allowed, shocked by the sudden turn in the man's demeanor. "I lack the pieces,"

"I will stop the duel then, until you have." Whittenmore announced with finality, turning with military crispness and walking with the rolling gate of a horseman back to his abandoned scabbard in the frozen grass.

For the second time in less than an hour Daniel felt insulted, but this time it stung worse. He felt not unlike a poor student before a disapproving teacher. His Gallic pride boiled to the surface. "No!" He declared in a bellowing roar, and lunged at the old soldier's back with his outstretched blade in the back stabber's attack.

The swordsman was a blur of motion, dodging aside from the hacking falchion blade, whirling like a Spanish dancer and Daniel found himself flying through the air, landing in a disreputable lump. "First blood! First blood!" Cried one of Menotomy's citizens, one eager to end the contest of honor or eager for blood none could say, but the man pointing at the fresh crimson spreading upon the prostrate Scotsman's shirt.

The crowd muttered excitedly, pressing in close to observe the bleeding man prostrate upon the snowy earth. Looking numbly from face to face, Daniel tried to control the sudden urge to vomit.

Whittenmore was forcing his way through the milling mass, also. "Hold, I landed no blow!" In an officer's parade ground voice, he bellowed, tossing men bodily aside. "I drew no blood!" Despite the mass of bodies around him, the old Dragoon seemed to suddenly appear at Daniel's side, examining the Scot's injured arm in no time at all. "I see you have dueled before, my young friend." He muttered in a voice tinged with concern. "And what blackguard gave you this? This is no honorable wound." Strong hands jerked him onto his feet. "Come, we will fix it."

A strong arm protectively around Daniel, the man in black stalked through the Menotomy crowd to one of the salt box houses arranged along the roadway. Daniel not so much walking as being swept along in the man's wake.

* * * *

The house was furnished in Spartan style. A table, a chair before the fireplace, simple, utilitarian tools hung at places of greatest convenience, without regard for more genteel decorative fancies. A respectable pile of firewood lined on wall in comfortable reach of the fireplace. "I take you for a bachelor, Mr. Whittenmore."

"Buried my wife, Elizabeth some years ago" The grey haired man said precisely in clipped and emotionless tones, as if simply stating dates and facts, but a look in his eyes spoke a different story. "A beautiful lady, with a fire to her unlike any I had ever experienced before. But such fierce fires cannot burn forever, this is the hardest lesson a man must learn in his time upon this earth." The grey haired man dropped his saber upon the table with a clatter, knocking aside dishes, papers and a dozen half completed projects. He hooked the bench with a foot and shoved Daniel down onto it without niceties. "Sit." He commanded in a voice used to obedience. "I will fetch what I need." With that, he was gone, returning moments later with dried herbs and a corked bottle.

He set the bottle before the injured Scotsman, "Drink," he ordered, and Daniel happily uncorked the bottle with his teeth. It was a heady French red wine, thick with the scent of the grapes, and the old country. "Drink! It will thicken your blood!"

Daniel took a long pull on the bottle, felt the warmth of the wine flow through him, "very good," he smiled, "French?"

"No, I made it." His benefactor answered, took a long pull from the bottle himself. After which, he busied himself stoking the flames in the fireplace for a while. "A man upon these new frontiers needs to have many skills, my newcomer friend."

"Daniel." The Scot named himself. "Daniel Ferguson."

"Samuel Whittenmore," the older man returned, adding, "formerly of His Majesty's Dragoons. I came to this land a horseman for the King, and fought the French. I found this new land to my liking. In truth, I fell in love with a lady. Mister Ferguson." The kettle over the flames was bubbling cheerfully, a full rolling boil, but Whittenmore eyes were focused into a time long ago. Daniel watched his benefactor wetting a folded strip of cheesecloth containing the herbs he had fetched, dipping the poultice in the boiling water over and over. "But I did not bring you here to hold you captive as I babbled about the past."

The two former combatants fell to talking like old friends, sharing the bottle from hand to hand as the older man ministered to his injury. "An interesting wound you have here. A fine cleaving cut delivered with some skill, but then patched with greater skill. Since then, it has been neglected, or rather tended with poorer skills, but it is not beyond repair, I think." The old soldier commented as he drained Daniel's arm of odiferous corruption while he kept up conversation as if they had undertaken each other company after a fine meal and not upon the dueler's field. "What will you do now, Daniel Ferguson, if you survive the winter?"

"I do not know." Daniel shrugged, winced as pain raced through his arm and cursed his lack of thought. "My skills are few, and fewer still that relate to farming."

"And what would those skills be?"

He shrugged and winced at the pain the slight movement gave him. "I was a member of the *Buchannacan* for the house of Ferguson, as my father and his father before."

"*Buchannacan*, eh? I took you for a fellow soldier." Whittenmore smiled, patiently.

The man had a passing knowledge of Gallic, Daniel realized. "The Laird had scant use for warriors, and less to feed them. I am afraid such experience lends little to life behind a plow hereabouts. Doubt there is much call for raiding cattle hereabouts."

"This is milk country." Whittenmore said, investing the words with great importance as he carefully placed the poultice of herbs on the Scot's arm. "Wolves and dogs harry the cows, make off with yearling calves. A deliberate sort of man, with skills of shooting and the hunt could make a living culling their sport."

"Perhaps," Daniel conceded, the warmth of the pad of herbs like a balm to his spirit, "for a man with perseverance, aim and a long gun. I have no musket."

The old Dragoon chuckled at that, but seemed to consider the offhanded comment, then wordlessly placed Daniel's hand on the bandage and walked deliberately to an oblique niche in his wall. It was, or rather had been an incidental cavity left in a partition wall inside the salt box construction, but the Spartan Whittenmore had pressed it into use as his arsenal, decorating it with a half dozen or so firelocks, and no few blades and hatchets. He drew several different muskets from it and made an inspection of each, they seemed to remind him of a story, or perhaps a person. With that brief contemplation, he selected one and returned with it. He set the brass stock of the weapon on the ground by Daniel's bare foot, leaned the long browned barrel against the Scot's good shoulder in token of transfer of ownership. "You do now."

Daniel mouth fell open in shock as the grim, spare man walked past him as if an act of no great importance had just been committed. "I am in no position to return your largess." Daniel protested, and Whittenmore reached high above himself on his tip-toes, drawing from the rafters a burlap bag which contained a handful of powder horns and shooting bags. "I cannot accept a gift of this magnitude."

"You have pride, boy," Whittenmore observed, setting aside a sparsely carved horn and sorting through the leather bags, "but I would expect no less. Do not let it be the end of you. Take the gun."

"I cannot."

"Don't be ridiculous, you have need of it, I do not." He had found a handful of lead musket balls in one of the pouches, dumped them into a spare scrap of cloth and cast the leather bag into the blazing fire.

Daniel looked at the gun. He did have great need of it, if he had a hope of surviving the winter. It stood about five feet tall, of 72 caliber or so, what was called a Militia fowler, designed to pass muster for a Militia call up, but still useful for a man to hunt bird or beast. This one had a brass sunburst set into the stock, with the initials B.R carved expertly into the metal. "This is not your musket." Daniel said, sharply.

"It is now." Whittenmore said blandly, taking no offense as he returned the burlap bag of accoutrements to its hiding place. "And as I said, I have no further need of it."

"Who is B.R?" He asked, dimly remembering that the shooting bags the old man had sorted through all contained carving and other marks of ownership upon them, too

"Do not worry." The old soldier said, cryptically. "They have no further need of it, either." A long moment passed before Whittenmore spoke again. "You said you were for the Cavanaugh place before, as I worked on your arm. How do you like it?

"I don't know."

The old Dragoon raised a suspicious eyebrow. "How do you mean?"

"Well, I was about to go there, with Trotter's man, when this crotchety old Dragoon challenged me to a duel, and…" Daniel allowed his voice to trail off pointedly.

Whittenmore let out a barking laugh at the Scot's rib. "Ah, but you were going to go out there with Pellenore? That dozy Norman could not find his way out of a ship with the holds open." He forced an involuntary curse from Daniel's lips as he cinched the bandage tight. "That will not do, I will take you there. Bring the bottle." He volunteered, turning to gather items from the nearby shelves and the table. "Better yet, I will bring the bottle." He laughed, took the bottle and tipped it back robustly.

Daniel used his new musket as a crutch to gain his footing. Then he paused a long moment. "Samuel, what does "impudent" mean?"

The soldier paused also, watched the Scot a long moment. "In truth, I must admit I do not know myself." Then he let out that harsh bark of a laugh again as he strode toward the door in the easy rolling gate of a horseman.

Chapter 3

Winter came and went, snow turned to puddles, melting puddles growing to flow into the rivers and back out to the bold Atlantic. Thin deer, hungered from a lean winter, journeyed from the greening wood to feast on fresh Spring shoots. Hibernating bears shook off the veil of sleep to begin a new year.

Men knew no such time, laboring regardless of the snow or grass, Paul Revere thought, riding a jaunty stallion with a piebald flash over one eye on the trail from Waltham to Lincoln. It had been a unforgiving winter, the second in so many years, and he feared for what that portended for his new dreams.

Tucked beneath his riding cape, close to his heart were bundles of letters for the Correspondence Committee of Bedford, Patriots who saw a future as Revere did, and had the gall to act upon those dreams.

The sun sank low in the West; time was of the essence.

Others were stirring that night also, for their own reasons and Revere slowed the piebald stallion to cede the road as a familiar wagon appeared out of the setting sunlight.

"Greetings Paul Revere, where go you at so late an hour?", hailed a happy, boisterous voice.

"Greetings Friend Trotter, I go to Bedford on the Express," Revere called familiarly to the man driving the wagon. "Hope to make it before the setting of the sun."

The Tavern-keeper turned in his seat, observed the sun for a long moment. "You will be hard pressed to that, I fear. Pity you do not have a guide like mine." He nodded toward the woman in the wagon beside him as the fresh breezes played at his graying hair. "Eyes like an owl in that pretty face, she has. I swear it!"

The red haired girl respectfully inclined her head in a nod that was almost a bow. "Greetings, Mister Revere." She smiled at him, demurely. She cloaked herself in a colorless cast-off scrap of wool blanket as a shawl against the dreary, threatening mist and self-consciously tucked bare feet beneath a long, modest skirt of worn blue gingham. Beneath the scrap-blanket shawl, she wore a fiery red bodice laced close to show off a trim waist and a loose blouse of pale yellow. A fine image of a woman, her long red hair trailed down the drab shawl like a flaming sunrise overtaking a solemn dawn. The sort of girl with the promise of warm summer about her that made a man resent his wedding vows. Any man but Revere, that is, who instead found his thought upon his new bride patiently awaiting him back in Boston. Rachel Walker had happened by his shop one afternoon, about quitting time as Revere was hurrying from his anvil to one of his many meetings. Newly widowed, his happy meeting with Rachel had been the only one he relished that day. But still, Meg's face drew Revere's stare, hazel eyes that were both world weary beyond their years and childlike in their openness, sharp eyes that observed the world like a hawk. Lips that ached to smile, but could draw up no more than a tired, world weary line. Not a sad face, not even a tired face, just inured from the hard life around her.

Revere bowed to her from the saddle, removing his hat as if he greeted the Queen herself, and Trotter grimaced like a man afflicted with gout. Meg inclined her head shyly, drawing his eyes from her womanly charms to the mass of hide cutting in her lap. She was an industrious lass, braiding rawhide into a rope as she played the passenger in Trotter's wagon.

Industrious, or nervous, Revere pondered, looking at the three passengers in the empty wagon. Only a fool would not know where they went in this late hour. To some sheltered cove, to meet a Dutchman. The Crown's Townshend acts had meant to force the colonists to purchase their goods through a single agency, the East India Tea Company, and by extension, the Crown, grantor of the monopoly. This was part of the royal efforts to extinguish their war debts, but it had a different effect. Dutch traders purchased their goods from the same European merchants, in the same boxes and smugglers aplenty were eager to bring them to the colonies. Men like Trotter were also eager to bring them to the colonists, who showed no compunctions in saving a coin or two buying them.

But first, Trotter and his crew would need to meet that smuggler ship. The former soldier fidgeted in his seat, looking at the sinking sun with calculating eyes divining the distance and time. The dim sun was sinking fast in the grey sky, they would need his girl's eyes and soon. "Come you back through Menotomy, please look me up, Paul."

"I have plans to do so. I believe we have a mutual friend, in old Lexington towne," Revere smiled warmly, "at Cavanaugh's."

That brought him up short, he winced at the name the way a murderer might at the name of his victim. "I had heard it occupied again," Trotter nodded blithely, looked in all directions and shifting in his seat, "I presumed squatters."

He plays me cagey, Revere noted, but why? Trotter could be forgetful, but the silversmith doubted Daniel to be a man who would not leave an impression. Then Revere found himself looking at the two in the fore of the wagon again. The nervous way the red haired girl sat, pressed to one side of the wagon. Revere judged the tavern keeper at fifty or better, though he had never asked the fact. You old satyr! Revere smiled to himself. Imagine a man of his years attempting to bed a girl of not more than 20 summers. "No, he is a good friend." The silversmith defended the man that Trotter evidently feared the girl coming into contact with. "Should he be there still, he would be a good man for you to know, a man of wit and industry."

Trotter nodded hurriedly, nervous of the time, or the conversation. "Then I will call upon him, at your recommendation, Paul." The Tavern-master momentarily gazed up at the sky, critically marking the time. "But I should be on now. Time, and the tide wait for no man."

* * * *

An aromatic mixture of beeswax and beef fat perfumed the air about Cavanaugh's old abode, a long earthenware vessel called a grisnet contained the bubbling mixture, Daniel had salvaged it from the casts-offs scattered about the old shack. It had lost one of its simple ring handles, but functioned to Daniel's purpose still, much to the consternation of a half dozen dogs that milled about and whined in distress at the wondrous odors it emanated.

From a stack of forage, he drew out split rushes, fibrous and well dried, and cut them to the length of the grisnet, then submerged the fibers in the waxy grease with the help of a whittled twig, dipping them over and over before drawing out the makeshift candles to hang off a convenient nail to dry and cool as other rushes were so treated. His hands were stiff and coated with wax but he kept to the task until he could juggle no more. By this time, the mess of beeswax and fat was running low, to the point his home-made candles were not evenly coated, and he gathered them and headed for the door.

He carefully judged the time by the setting sun. The disappearing light would allow just enough time for Daniel to stack the scattered wedges of wood his earlier chopping had produced. The Cavanaugh house was situated on a hill, over-looking the scattered dwellings of Lexington as the town hurried to its evening rest. Like most towns, Lexington was just a collection of houses and buildings at the crossing of the roads to Concord, Bedford and Boston, by way of Cambridge.

The church, or meeting house as they termed it, was three full stories and sat right across the road from the town's Tavern, called Buckman's. The town also boasted a school and a blacksmith's, as well as a fine military green. It was a fine town, the people a friendly enough lot who knew when not to ask questions. They were mostly dairy farmers, raising milk cows for the local markets. The only path from dear departed Cavanaugh's old home ran downhill to the Bedford road, almost upon the fields of the parsonage, and giant of a parson with the flowing hair of a lion and the booming roar to match.

The holy man's name was Jonas Clarke, and he could deliver a fiery oratory from the pulpit when the occasion called for it, but he was also a gentleman who allowed others their sins. Daniel had passed the winter and the flowering of spring absenting himself from the fires of the meeting hall, his Papist ways afraid to mingle with the zealotry of the Puritans, until he had happened into the wedding ceremony of Joshua Simonds and his new bride, Betty. The long winter had been good to them, she showing her belly in at least her third or fourth month of pregnancy, and none of the Papists even casting an eye that way.

He was set apart, his simple one room log cabin in the vestiges of the forest so different from their salt box houses of split timber and shingle, just as he was different from them. They did not speak of it, but even in their kindness he felt it. Even now, as he stood in the warmth of the setting sun, draping rush-light candles from a branch, he did not feel invited among them.

One of the half dozen dogs that had taken up residence at the house growled and the others sprung to their feet, some barking and some racing in all directions. "Good day, friend Daniel," haloo'd a voice from the road, "and how are things for you? Do you live? Did you weather the winter in good spirits?"

Daniel smiled, and turned his eyes from the dimming lights of Lexington, somewhat chagrined that his wool-gathering had left him blind to the approach of horse and rider. "And a good day to you, friend Revere. You find yourself a long way from Boston."

"Not so much as you would think, I thought I might inquire as to your health," he said, sliding from the saddle. What a sight the Scot was, the baggy ship's trousers were gone, replaced by buckskins fastened with buttons of horn. He wore a sleeveless muslin shirt, perhaps the same from that fateful night upon the *Beaver*, but the sleeves gone to some other purpose. His shaggy hair was now gone to a long mane that hung past his shoulders, his beard unkempt and long enough to make Revere wonder if the cabin held a mirror.

Revere's eyes fell upon a stump in front of the modest home, mainly because an axe protruded from it. Well split wedges of wood were scattered about it. "You have been busy," he jested.

Daniel gave a half smile. "Splitting colonial wood is no different than Scottish, but that there was so much more of it."

Revere nodded, looking at the piles of firewood, and the Scot's shoes. His formerly bare feet, so common for sailors, were shod in Scottish brogues, soft deerskin soled with heavy ox hide and the whole dyed to a deep, respectable walnut brown. In truth, the dye was uneven and blotchy, undoubtedly a tannic stew of the husks from black walnuts, but it showed a persistence and adaptability that Revere was glad to see. "All this could not have done well on an injured limb."

Daniel made a show of a few fists. "I reckon it'll suffice."

Revere, wearing a tri-corner hat and blue wool jacket beneath his riding cloak, sauntered lightly across the grass to stand before the Scot he called a friend and seemed to drop the issue, casually drawling. "My business regularly brings me through Lexington, delivering posts for the Committee of Corresponce. I was to ride on to Bedford today, but I tarried and have need of a friendly bed this night." He offered the man his hand, the left, in familiar greeting and when the Scot took it, delivered a sudden, stout blow to his shoulder, watching the man's eyes for reaction, and grinned widely. "You do seem well mended."

One of the dogs growled ominously at the silversmith's blow, but the Scot waved it off with a pass of his hand and the dog gentled. Daniel rubbed at the scar on his left arm, grinned back. "And what brings you to Lexington today, friend Revere?"

"Liberty." Revere intoned pregnantly, allowed the monumental word a moment to set in before speaking again, patting the head of one blonde dog who had journeyed close to sniff at him. Nearby, there was a wooden teepee structure, green deer hides wrapped around it in the process of being smoked into leather. The scent of cooking meat drifted from the area, Daniel was killing two birds with one stone, cooking meat and curing hides at the same time. The thought of meat brought him back to other thoughts. "Have you had supper?"

"No, not yet," the Scot admitted, "I can offer you a fine rabbit stew, and brewed raspberry tea?" The attacks upon the East India tea had not ended on that manic December night in Griffin's Wharf, many Patriot groups had organized private embargos on the stuff, offering recipes for substitutes including Chamomile, rose hips or raspberry leaves.

"Sounds fine," Revere nodded, "but I was thinking steak and a beer, at my expense, and an offer." With that, the two began an amiable stroll toward town. Daniel walked at the silversmith's side, and the man put a kindly arm about his shoulders. "You work late into the evening.' Revere ventured.

"Some of the King's troops happened through on a march this afternoon. I whiled an hour observing them at their tasks." Daniel looked over his shoulder at the rushes and shrugged. "The time must be made up."

"They have been doing more and more of that, General Gage claims he is limbering up their legs after a long winter, toughening them up." Revere nodded at that admission from the Scot. "What tasks were they about?", he asked cagily.

"Merely marching, but they stopped some distance from Lexington to practice forming skirmish lines." Daniel answered guilelessly. "How are things in Boston?"

"Fine, fine," the silversmith said with an assurance he did not feel. "It has actually been a strange homecoming for me today. Not three hours ago, I found myself in the welcome presence of Tavern-master Trotter of Menotomy."

Daniel's only welcome memories of that time were glimpses of the Black Horse's Tavern maid. Rather than speak on this, he scratched at his beard as if he had only just now noticed it and asked. "How is the old beer slinger? And Pelenore, and...everyone?"

Revere smiled coyly. "Everyone is fine."

* * * *

"A bit more back into it, please, Mister Collins."

In response to the goad, the British soldier, and he could only be a British soldier, wrenched harder at the corpse's shoulder, sawing with a use-dulled knife at the arm to disjoint the body like a hanging beef. The civilian clothes he wore could not disguise his trade, if the military cartridge box and musket did not betray him; he had neglected to take his hair out of the queue hanging grease black and stiff at the nape of his neck.

Meg covered her face behind her arm as the shoulder separated and the arm popped loose with a nauseating, wet sound. She stifled a whimper, trying to become invisible in the shadow of the wagon she had been riding in, and was now bound to, her hand drawn through the wagon spoke and bound to the other with a strip of woven rawhide, the same rawhide she had spent the last few days weaving, as if to pour salt in the wound.

A half dozen soldiers in the dress of day laborers swarmed among the scene, some mutilating the two bodies and others hurriedly searching the contents of the heavily laden wagon, scattering them on the ground in their rush. One of them had hacked open a hogs-head of Jamaican rum and appointed himself quartermaster, rationing out goblets and tankards of the potent spirit from a box of silver drinking mugs and plates shattered on the dirt road beside him. Another amused himself with Trotter's tinderbox, kindling a fire of trade goods worth ten year's of his salary in the middle of the muddy, stony road.

Passing by both of them, their officer, muffled in a riding cloak but bearing an expensive sword and gleaming gorget on a silver chain about his neck, refilled his chalice for the fourth time.

He was a handsome rogue, with ash-blonde hair and haughty green eyes in an aristocratic face. His body was slim and muscular and he moved like a cat, at his waist were a gleaming sword and a heavy looking pistol. She knew him for an officer by his airs, seeing himself as a gentleman among peasants as he busied himself walking pensively among his men, issuing orders barely concealed as requests.

The officer paused beside a chest, casually tossed from the wagon by one of his riotous men, deigned to draw his pistol and, with a shot that elicited a scream from her, blasted the padlock free. The trunk was full of papers, and he crouched, rifling through them for a moment before rising again. Whatever he was looking for, it was not in the leather faced chest and in a disappointed huff, he scattered a handful of the papers upon the fire.

Regaining his inebriated composure, he looked about the scene to note any who might have listened, and his eyes fell upon the slumped corpse of Trotter staring lifelessly at him in the roadway. "Sargea...er, Mister Kincade, scalp that corpse. Remember, we endeavor to approximate a renegade Indian attack." The barrel-chested sergeant rushed to the task, reaching for a sheathed knife at his belt. The officer began to turn, but stopped and pivoted in a poised manner, "and, do use your hatchet, Mr. Kincade, please." He glanced at the papers still negligently clutched in his hand, let them fall to the dirty trail, and sauntered with an urgent, forced casualness toward her.

Lieutenant Edward Wainright, of the Newcastle Wainrights, supernumerary to His Royal Majesty's Light Infantry here in the Continents, amused himself poking among the treasures scattered about the bed of the wagon, found a piece of iron strapping and toyed with it as he approached. She could not tear her eyes from him, like a sheep stares at the circling wolf. Her teeth chattered, she was so afraid, and the officer seemed to relish that, looming over her in the shadows of his cloak, the meager moonlight dancing on his belt buckle and scabbard. She felt a finger brush down the line of her cheek, and his rum soaked breath buffeted her face.

Her humdrum, quiet, provincial life was turned on its ear, the glow of slight adventure in an evening meeting a Dutch smuggler was wrecked forever. Armed men thieved, pillaged and mutilated the dead around her. Their officer, a gentleman of breeding and poise, bore the unmistakable marks of a sadistic beast. She looked frantically in all directions, but escape was impossible. But even if she did manage to free herself, the rutted, muddy roadway in both directions was a long strait away as good as a target range, the east was tufts of shrub and grazing land for dairy cattle, no better than another shooting range. Behind her, to the west, were the Sudbury marshes, with their tangling thorny vines and beasts with claw and fang. But, better to die in there, than here. Better by her own hand, even her own folly, than to once more suffer to callous men's cruel intentions and then share in the fate of Trotter and Pelenore.

"A short few months ago," the officer spoke, looking down his nose at her, "the property of the East India Tea Company was vandalized, in the amount of eighteen thousand pounds, were you aware?" She barely had time to draw a breath to answer when he clouted her across the back of the head with his gloves. "Of course you are, you treasonous peasants have been strutting about like cocks since the first leaf hit the water."

She saw stars and was afraid to talk. The disguised soldier clucked his tongue and continued. "I will have the names of your leaders, your superiors, locations of your military supplies, I will have them, I will have them all, and I will have them now."

A long moment of silence slipped between them as Meg looked at him agog. Her mouth worked like a landed fish. "M'lord!", she finally managed," I could no more tell you what you ask than the day of the Resurrection! The best I might do is showing you a few secluded coves where Mister Trotter might meet the odd Dutch trader, or fingering a few folks here about who bought tobacco or yard cloth…"

"Or powder?"

She shook her head vehemently. "Mister Trotter didn't trade in powder."

Her interrogator sighed dramatically, made a show of dropping the iron strap into the fire kindled in the roadway, a fire fed on French yard cloth and wooden boxes from the wagon's bed. Then he seized the wagon wheel with a suddenness that made her shriek, threw his back into rotating the wooden spokes like a ship's wheel. It moved with a sound like stones grinding corn as the wheel rolled through the muddy, gritty rut in the roadway, the girl's hands wrenched painfully through the spokes until she found them buried past the wrists in the rut's thick, cold mud. Melted snow mixed with the roadway's muck to an icy gruel rushed back into the rut, cold enough to make her gasp. "Protest all you like," her tormenter snarled. "The company you keep shows you out."

Doubled over, almost to the point of falling head over heels, Meg leaned heavily against the spokes just to keep hope of balance. She looked under her own arm, at the dizzying, inverted sight of the British officer tending the coals of the flames while his men raced in the shadows like imps about their bloody business. "General Gage has been far too lenient with you colonials, with your machinations and airs," the officer growled. "Patience is finite, my dear, and at an end."

He strutted about the helpless girl, seized her skirts and what petticoats she had, and threw them as far over her head as he could. The fine ladies of England wore pantaloons beneath their petticoats, but this less fortunate girl was bare from muddy feet to the fine mounds of her rump. This sudden assault on her modesty elicited a frightened squeal that melted into a keening sob bordering on hysterics.

Again the kidskin gauntlets flashed, raising a welt on the cheeks of her bottom. "Stop that noise, you treasonous bitch!" The pain brought her up short with a gasp, and he seized that moment to hold the glowing tip of the red hot iron up for her horrified perusal. "This night is young, and we have much to discuss."

"M'lord," she sobbed with terror tinting her voice, "I know nothing."

Unsatisfied, he drew the hot iron between her legs, lifting it slowly and methodically, his eyes glued to the way she moved as she stood on tip-toes to escape the heat. He said nothing, just lifted the hot iron mechanically, unstoppably upward.

Words boiled from her mouth, coming quickly in hope of soothing her tormentor. "I am not a rebel, I am a loyal subject. I swear it, just a girl trying to make her way." Tears running freely now, "I could not name a rebel if I wanted to, but for Paul Revere."

That name made the glowing iron stop. "Go on."

"There was another, after the … the tea was thrown into the harbor. He was brought over from Boston, wounded."

"Wounded?" That little fact had been kept from most.

"Yes sir, a great ugly rent in his arm, I saw it."

"And his name?", the Redcoat officer demanded, "What was his name, girl? Out with it!"

"Name?" She parroted, and the hot iron moved higher. She pondered the stranger's face, remembering those deep blue eyes, the furrowed, fevered brow before the present heat of the smoldering iron snapped her back to reality. "I don't know, sir. I never heard it. Mr. Trotter knew it, but he's …dead."

"But you could find out? Right?" Lieutenant Wainright menaced.

"Yes," she gasped, breathless from fear, the hot iron singed at her delicate parts, but her thighs burned from the strain of standing so long on tiptoes in the frigid, slippery mud. "Yes."

"Too right you could!" The officer spat. "Use your feminine charms to out this rogue, provided I don't burn them off, here tonight?" Her breathless feminine voice was so base, so primal, the Lieutenant wondered what sounds the girl might make flat on her back. That was the rum talking, he knew. At the thought of the liquor, he looked over at the battered hogs-head, yearned for its fortifying warmth and courage, and impetuously staggered back toward it. "I have use for you, girl," he muttered aloud, punctuating the words with the glowing iron, "One who's charms are available for..."

"I am not a whore!" She sobbed, teeth were chattering in fear. Her fingers were numb from immersion in the icy mud, and from the woven leather cord which bound her wrists so tightly. She was cold, achingly cold, the frigid Atlantic winds sliced through the trees, lashing at bared parts of her body which had never seen such treatment before.

"Nonsense, girl, you're all whores, to one style or another. The difference is merely of degrees, and circumstance," he said, plunging a neglected tankard into the rum and thrust it, dripping rivulets like blood, to his mouth. Drink was his weakness, he had known it long ago, but free drink was a particular weakness, and he found he could not turn away from the half-drained wooden cask until he had dipped the chalice once again into it. "I want information, you want to live. The exchange is. . ." He turned back toward her, tossed the iron in a lazy arc so it clattered in the mud before her eyes, the glowing point sizzling and popping in the frigid mud, sputtering to a dull grey again. A stranger, more intriguing sight caught his fancy in the crackling shadows of that lonely trail. One more interesting, more possibly rewarding, that the red haired girl bound to a wagon wheel with her most intimate parts bared to the Atlantic winds. Deftly, he balanced his rum on her bared backside, the cold silver tankard nestled upon her spine and sent a chill through her. "Be still, don't spill that, not one drop." He warned, and reddened her backside with his glove again so she would remember it.

In the half light, one of the King's loyal servants deftly put a boot to the side of Trotter's scalped, cold head and rolled him over, staring at the deceased Scottish tavern keeper's face with a queer look.

"What troubles you this fine night, Mister Trenton? The Lieutenant asked as he sauntered slowly toward him.

John Trenton did not speak immediately, for fear of voiding his dinner upon the stony roadway. With great deliberation, he lowered the flint on his pistol and clipped it to his belt with a shaking hand. His eyes were not able to leave the dead face of the man lying in the cold, muddy roadway. "So strange, Lieutenant," he mused thoughtfully, "to come all this way to kill a fellow Cambridge man."

"A Cambridge man you say, sir?" Lieutenant Wainright smiled condescendingly. "I understood him to be something of a pimp and a taverner in Menotomy."

"I mean," Trenton continued as if the Lieutenant had not spoken, "I could have shot this bloke any day of the week; he toiled just down the road."

"In Menotomy," the British officer added again, afraid he was getting the pronunciation wrong, or some such difficulty.

"Well, yes in Menotomy, but that is only. . .what, not even five miles, two hours by horse." Admitted Trenton, he spoke to the soldier of the King, but also to himself. "I mean, speaking freely of course, Lieutenant, I am chiefly a buyer of commodities and have no experience for this sort of thing."

True, thought Wainright, to the King's forces in the America's, this man's chief recommendations were his knowledge of the roadways and his unquestioned loyalty to the crown. His family owned properties both in Cambridge and in several of the surrounding towns, Concord, Waterton and Sudbury being only a few of them.

"Until I was approached, as a loyal servant of the crown, about serving as a guide I had no idea that this sort of thing happened."

"Yes, you are not supposed to know. When these sort of policing actions are required, they need to be carried out with the utmost discretion and …. secrecy." The lieutenant invested the last word with great importance, then added an observation. "I take it this is the first time you have killed for your King and Country?"

"Well, yes," he admitted without rancor, and paused. "And I take it this is not new to you, killing your fellow countrymen?"

"My dear Mister Trenton," the officer enunciated his guide's non military honorific primly to reinforce the point, "the 4th Kings own Infantry is just off of duty upon the English coasts, suppressing just this sort of activity."

"Ah, I see." The Loyalist nodded. For him this had been but a merry lark, he knew Trotter and is ilk for the traitorous villains they were and had sought both their comeuppance and his own social advancement as a side note.

"I dare say, we have spilled more white blood, English, Irish, Welsh and Scottish, than savage." He intoned it as if in passing, merely an afterthought. The lie was coming easier now to him. The 4th regiment had indeed just come from such sickening, bloody duty, but he had not. Lieutenant Wainright was in fact a supernumerary, an officer without a post, a man without a home, his commission purchased and set in this dreary frontier in hopes sickness or aboriginal arrows would quickly clear his way to a captaincy or colonelcy. In short, he needed to make a name for himself, and do so quickly to insure his advancement, less the mounting debts of his indenture here drown him.

The drably garbed Redcoat looked at his Tory guide and pasted on his best smile. This Loyalist had some meager influence among his peers and might prove useful to him. He was feeling the regrets of Mars, and Wainright did his best to offer some comforts. "But be of good cheer, Mr. Trenton, you have done the King good service this evening, and there will be rewards for it," throwing a comradely arm about his shoulder, Wainright turned him from the dead man toward the wagon, "rewards, both delayed, and very immediate."

With a deft lean, he got the man walking toward the fire flickering in the roadway. "Yonder, find a delicate young tart, the pride of dear departed Trotter's tavern."

"Young Meg?"

He did not know the little whore from Mary, Queen of Scots, but nodded just the same. "She had fully repented of her sins and agreed to work for us, for King and Country, as it were." The Redcoat officer confided. "But the wages of sin must be firmly embedded in her mind, and therefore I decree a lesson to be taught this evening. And I think I have found the proper. . . instrument to . . . thrust home . . . the lesson."

"Lesson, Lieutenant Wainright? I do not understand."

Damn these uptight colonials, even the dullest of his Lights would already have his trousers undone. "I have the little bitch lashed to a wagon wheel with her arse bared." Wainright's baser instinct snapped to the fore and he snapped crudely. "Does that draw the picture for you?" Saying this, arm around the Tory's shoulder, Wainright fairly dragged him toward the wagon and the smoldering fire.

Dimly, his rum soaked mind boggled at the fitful, smoky sparks of the fire, before such a flame as it facilitated his reading, and the heating of that chunk of iron he had used to...persuade young Meg. Then, in the mist of the rocky roadway, he saw his dented silver chalice glittering on the trail, the dark amber river of rum spraying like blood in the darkness to all but quench the kindled flame in the roadway.

"Lieutenant," spoke the merchant turned guide nervously.

"Not now." The besotted Wainright growled, turning the discarded tankard over in his hands. He remembered the precarious posting he had left the tankard in, chuckled quietly to himself. Saucy little tart, he thought, wasting good rum. He would get particular pleasure in taking that out on her.

"Lieutenant," said the Tory turned guide again.

"I said..." the Redcoat officer snapped, rounding on the civilian, but whatever he planned to repeat died in his throat as his companion stood beside the destruction of the tavern-keeper's wagon, alone. He boggled and staggered a bit, strained his eyes and his alcohol soaked mind in case he had somehow missed her. But while he could easily see the rawhide twine hanging from the wagon wheel, the girl was, inexplicably, unquestionably gone.

Braided rawhide, he mused, reaching out to touch the muddy, water saturated strand. The hand-woven strand had become wet, and doing so, stretched, not much perhaps, but the girl had done the rest.

"The girl, sir," said the purchaser weakly, "you said she was..."

"Be still, man." The lieutenant commanded. "Wherever she is now, it cannot be far." His eyes were scanning the woods line, searching for sign. Then, the shadow and moonlight of the trees resolved into a face peering back at him. The silver chalice slipped from his hand, rattling to the ground and drawing more attention than his next action. He snatched the flintlock pistol from his belt, pointed it into the air as his thumb drew back the hammer. The flint fell, spark flew, and....nothing.

Dimly, he recalled firing the pistol moments before, breaking open the chest, and his hand fell to the mechanical process of reloading as he raised his voice for attention. The distinctive snap of a flint on pan had drawn every eye like a whore in church, Wainright realized. "On her, lads, on her," he commanded quickly, "the little tart has slipped us. Get her! GO!" As he clipped the pistol back to his belt, he remembered the silver whistle hanging from his baldric and blew it loudly. "Get her!"

Soldiers in the drab wrappings of colonists leapt to the hunt, racing after the frightened girl, until all that was left in that scene of carnage was bodies, the Lieutenant and his Loyalist guide. "A fine night for a foxhunt, eh?", the lieutenant enthused with a wicked smile.

"Do you think it wise, sir?", the civilian asked. "Sending the whole band after one girl?"

"Let them have their fun," the officer boshed primly, "most of the bastards have been looking for a chance to desert since they got of the bloody ship."

* * * *

The tired horse seemed rooted to the spot, and Revere was content to leave it tied to the sapling before the young Scot's home. The menagerie of mongrel dogs circled it, sniffing and investigating this newcomer to their quiet, closed society, Revere watched their very canine perusal a few moments and asked. "Are you planning on opening a carnival?"

Daniel laughed, a happy sound that seemed out of place in the man. "Some were here when I arrived, 'tis as much their house as my own. They dinna' mind me, I always have a deer carcass hanging, so there are bones to eat and scraps abound." He shrugged. "We get along."

"Have you found work?" He asked as the two ambled toward the town green, and Buckman's Tavern.

Daniel smiled ruefully at that. "For a while, I did a fine trade in wolf and deer hides." As they drew closer to the tavern, Daniel realized his friend was serious in his invitation, drug a hand through his hair to untangle the worse of it.

That interested the silversmith. "How many hides have you, Daniel?"

The importance of the question eluded the young Scot as he drew a length of cloth from his sporran and bound up his long hair into something like a ponytail. "Some," he admitted, "but the pile is not soon apt to get larger."

"Trouble in the hunt?"

"Your Massachusetts wolves and deer have one advantage over the ones back home in Scotland, they have learned to mind the range of a musket." The Scot observed, running his fingers through his beard. "But that is the least of my troubles."

"What then?"

"The firelock I managed to acquire was not the best," Daniel admitted, "though a good enough looking Militia Fowler. I managed a few dozen shots before it broke its mainspring, and I lack the funds to replace it."

"That can be remedied." Revere returned brightly, reaching for the carved wooden door handle. "Do me the honor of delivering a post to Isaac Davis, he is the blacksmith of Acton. Tell him I sent you."

Daniel nodded at that. "I convalesced on charity," Daniel said it as if the very words tasted of bile to him, "at your behest I understand, and I do thank you for that."

"So you make rushes instead of buying candles?"

"Yes. The parson's wife traded me some beeswax for a day's labor pruning their orchards for smoking woods, and Ebenezer Munroe called upon me to help him kill and quarter an ox that broke his leg, he traded me some beef, fat and hide for my efforts."

"What need of you with an ox hide?" Revere could not contain his curiosity and guessed. "The shoes?"

"Aye, among other things," the Scot lifted a foot and looked at the homemade things upon his feet, then at the artisan works Revere walked upon. "I dyed them with Black Walnut husks, left them in the ochre a full week."

"And that did not do the trick?" Revere asked.

"If by "trick", you mean did they stain my feet brown for a month the first I wore them, then yes." He said in good jest, then his words sank to self pity and he said with a shrug. "None will ever mistake them for yours."

Revere threw a comradely arm about him. "No matter, no matter, my man. I applaud your creativity, and your industry." Revere smiled, and realized he meant the words he said, and realized how much he had missed the proud, quick witted Scot. The two walked in companionable silence, crossing the common and finally arriving at the distinctive red door of Buckman's Tavern. A man in a floppy hat stood outside the doorway staring at the horizon, a well-used pewter plate in his hand.

Daniel had seen the man about the town before, in his home-spuns of the approved Puritan style and unblocked grey hat, he was still of a singular, powerful build, with formerly brown hair now liberally sprinkled with a snowy white and intense eyes that seemed to be able to peer through the trees and the mountains. He was eating without looking, his eyes never leaving the roads as his hand mechanically shoveled food into is mouth.

"Good evening John Parker." Revere greeted formally.

Parker looked over Revere's walking companion with poorly concealed interest, but when he spoke to the silversmith, he was less concerned with the niceties of civilization's polite conversation. "Trotter's late," he said, pausing from lifting a sopping bread to glance at Revere, assuring himself that the gravity of his statement had been understood.

"I saw him, his man and a girl three hours ago. He got a late start."

"Always get a late start. Thrifty Scotsman wouldn't close his doors to a nickel." Parker scrubbed at the pewter plate with too much force, trying to hide his anxiety. "Always late, but he's never been this late before."

"Things could get confused out there. Lots of reasons he might be delayed," the silversmith soothed.

"I've sent expresses." Parker chewed at the bread again, then faded into staring silently at the horizon again. Dismissed, Revere and Daniel entered and found a quiet table in the rear.

The bewildered Scot asked. "What goes on here, Paul?"

"Liberty, the business of liberty."

"So you continue to say, but what does it mean?"

"It means the freedom to do as you will, deferring to no man. To succeed or fail on your own merits, without bowing to good King George, an ocean away..."

"None of this sounds new to my ears," Daniel interrupted, "the Scots have been trying to put Bonnie Charlie on the throne for years now. Too many years..."

"Not upon a throne, Daniel. We have no wish to exchange one tyrant for another."

No king? Daniel looked up at the silversmith in shock, like to ask a cow to crow in the morning, as for men to be governed without a king. "What then?"

"A republic."

"Republic," Daniel echoed, "like the Roman empire?"

Revere suppressed a grin and nodded at the Scot's acumen, there was a bright man beneath all the scruff and tangled, overgrown hair. "Even so...." He began, pausing as a serving girl brought them two crockery pints of beer.

"Paul, the Roman empire fell not long after our Lord was crucified." Daniel said quickly, curling his hand about the stout. He drank like a man who had lately missed meals, and Revere pretended not to notice.

"Yes, it fell, under the weight and stink of its own corruption." Revere smiled patiently; he was used to some intransigence. His words were safely enough spoken before the unknown serving girl, then the silversmith quickly ordered their meal and she left with a fetching switch of her skirts. "We will not be following in those footsteps, Daniel, with lifetime appointments, the curry of favors and the entitlements of Lords. We will build among us a ruling body of free citizens, by the people, for the people."

By the people? For the people? Daniel paused, his heart beat heavily in his chest at the thought of it. Imagine, no King, nor Lords, a nation of men, by the consent of the governed. It was a heady thought, strong enough for a man to be drunk upon it. No more peerage, no more tugging at the forelock. His hesitation seemed to melt away at the thought of it.

The silversmith looked about him, leaning forward as he spoke. "Things are a'acting in the Colonies." Revere confided. "The king is three thousand miles away, and he sleeps not soundly. King George has France and Spain to crowd his dreams, to say not less of the troubles that abound in Scotland and Ireland. If we trouble him enough, we are convinced he will forsake us for greater concerns."

"You know not what you speak, Paul. The Highlanders thought the same in the bold'45 to be rid of that dowdy, belligerent German, but Bloody

Billy Cumberland force marched his Lobsterbacks to Culloden, and then right down Scotland's throat."

Revere chuckled, King George was of the house of Hanover, where as the Scots saw James, and the house of Stuart as the rightful King of England and Scotland. "Three thousand miles, Daniel. How long does it take to cross the Atlantic?"

"Thirty days," Daniel answered with the assurance of a seaman, "with fair winds and a good hand at the sails." Then he thought a long moment. "Thirty days." He repeated, and realization dawned. The Scot found himself staring at Revere like a sinner to the parson on Sunday.

"Aye. Thirty days and a lot of good luck added to that, too. Thirty days to England, thirty days back, and how many days in the middle, do you think?" Revere paused for a moment, looking about conspiratorially and added. "We have friends in Britain, in Parliament and other places. Just as King George has friends here." Pointing with his nose, Revere indicated a nearby table. "That gentleman over there, in the blue vest and the Hanoveran cockade in his hat, you ken him? That is Collins, Master Artimus Collins, maker of both course and fine candles, and the Crown's eyes and ears in this shire."

"A fine looking fellow." Daniel opined cagily, though just to look upon the perfumed, well dressed man made him feel all the poorer. And he was, a gentleman to turn a lady's head upon the streets, and what's more he knew it.

"Word of advice," Revere whispered, as Daniel eyed the Crown's spy. The silversmith's strong brown eyes slid back to the table Collins had commanded and the men who shared it. "Tory's abound, even here in Lexington. Having seen you with me, you might begin wearing that sword of yours about."

Daniel nodded at that, observing the man who commanded so much of Paul Revere's animosity. Tall, of a lithe, almost wiry frame, he affected a powdered wig upon this evening. His eyebrows were a fine ruddy brown, his eyes of a particular, stunning blue. He wore a wool jacket over a silken vest, a tricorn hat with a red Hanovern cockade, all of a quality to rival Revere's.

But Daniel had these thoughts only fleetingly, the idea of fighting the British was like a fire in Daniel's Scottish blood. But fire only takes a man so far. Daniel shook his head like a dog, as if shaking off a dream. "When the Highlander charged the fields of Culloden," he hazarded, "the Redcoats stood in mass and fired so fast that it sounded like a single roar of thunder. The balls flew so thick that entire clans disappeared in it, clans, Paul, as in hundreds of men. How do you plan to stand against that?"

"Gage was at Culloden, you know." Revere mentioned it casually, but seemed to know the impact it would have on his friend. "General Thomas Gage, military governor of Massachusetts and the commander of the army here in the Colonies, he was there with the Duke of Cumberland."

Gage was one of Bloody Billy's killers? Daniel's jaw almost dropped, he felt his blood boil like not before.

"We do not endeavor for blood, my friend." The silversmith warned, "an army that does no killing is a lucky army indeed. We are convinced of the justness of our cause, but the regulars must be exposed before the world as those who have fired the first volley. Keep 'em wrong, and keep them there, says a friend of mine. There are no small stakes, the penalty for disloyalty to the Crown is hanging, from the nearest tree, without trial. We are but a small band, mechanics, farmers, men such as yourself. Our contestant is ..."

"The whole British army, and the Royal navy, and Loyalist fellows like this Collins." Daniel smiled. "But with a Highlander on your side, you reckon the odds about even?"

"But they are not," Revere said, quickly, "The colonies have many wondrous benefits. But we do not have powder, nor means to make it and scarce facility for the manufacture of arms." Revere's voice dropped to an even more guarded, harsh tone. "Do you ken the Provincial Powder House?"

"The one on Quarry hill in Cambridge? Aye, I know it."

"It was built to house all the powder for the providence, the town, the militia and extra powder for the Royal troops. For some time now, the towns have been quietly spiriting that powder away, in dribs and drabs. A bit here and a bit there, you understand, and we conceal it all about."

"The King's Reserve?" Daniel almost shrilled, he grasp the crock before him and fairly poured it down his throat, quickly gaining control of himself. The King's Reserve was a store of powder contained for the use of the Royal troops. "I want nothing to do with a noose, Paul! Poaching the King's property is bound to be a boatload of trouble."

"There's no trouble to it," the silversmith soothed, "nor is it poaching. Don't be a'feared just because they call something the property of the Sovereign. That ale you drink is the King's beer, the coins in your purse is the King's shilling, but it does not make it any less yours. That is our powder, our taxes bought it and go to maintaining its safety. It's ours, Daniel, and we have need of it."

"To load in muskets, and fire at the King's troops?" He said it dramatically, as if to shock the man he sat with out of his stupor.

"Maybe." Revere shrugged. "Not long ago, Redcoats opened fire on a shopkeeper trying to get payment and a crowd that had gathered. Five were killed, including a young boy...."

"That would be the bairn, I heard of in the *Green Dragon*."

Revere nodded, impressed the Scot remembered, then continued. "The Army said they had been fired on. The most those people had were snowballs, Daniel. Musket balls against snowballs. So, it may be we take the King's Reserve of powder just to keep the Lobsterbacks from using it against us."

The serving girl reappeared with two pieces of beefsteak, set them before the men and shifted off into the crowds again. Daniel barely noticed, in his mind's eye he allowed himself to see Redcoats lined upon the fields of Culloden Moor, hordes of screaming Highlanders racing toward them, and the Redcoats with nothing to do but stare at each other for want of powder. Revere felt his friends' change of mind. "Are we in accord?"

For a long moment, Daniel's mind calculated impossible odds, but his heart raced across the marshy fields of Culloden moor, into the face of redcoat guns, into the face of General Thomas Gage. He thought upon freedom, a dared upon, hoped for word. That was when a familiar face appeared at their table

Daniel looked up into the pale face of John Parker, eyes wild and mouth agape like a man pursued by the devil himself. "Paul," he gasp, "come outside, quickly."

* * * *

A half dozen men, clad in the rough cloth of day laborers moved with the careful, studious precision of trained skirmishers through the overgrown weeds and brush. They maneuvered by pairs, watching the other as they flitted from cover to cover with muskets at the ready. It seemed so much effort to find a single barefoot girl. They had rushed after the red haired girl with the wild abandon of fox hunters. However, of the half dozen men of the King's Own light company, they were enthusiastic but not experienced but for two. Those two had the woodcraft of experienced rangers, following her unerringly, forsaking her cagey blind trails and miss-trails.

"Come on, you laggards, we want to be in barr...er, home before nightfall!", barked the barrel-chested one the officer had called Kinkade. He had a tiny French moustache and the voice of a sergeant upon the parade grounds. At his command, the men immediately picked up their pace, searching more briskly along the overgrown grass and brush. All but the cagey ones, who squatted on their haunches and studied some bit of earth in the moonlight.

"What's that your malingering over, Private!" The officer demanded from somewhere behind. Wainright studied the man's face for a long moment to place him, then took the best guess he could. "You're Parsons, the poacher, aren't you?"

"Yes sir, judge said I could take the King's shilling, or the noose." The infantryman nodded, feigning flattery at his recognition. "Tracks in fresh mud, sir, going North, sir."

The Tory guide peered over the Light's shoulder. "So, she's circling on us?"

"So it would seem, sir, but it makes no sense. I think, me and Randal here, that is, that she's playing us cagey, a right tricksy rebel, trying to get us going the wrong way, begging your pardon, sir?" He added obsequiously, tugging his forelock to his officer.

"I see," Wainright nodded, then turned to his companion. "Mister Trenton, would you be so good as to tell me where the Hell we are?"

"I believe we are near the Sudsbury marshes, not the most hospitable of places, mostly brambles and thorns, that which is not flooded out right now with the thaws. When this area is settled, the old ministers used to say the Devil lived there."

"Did they now?" The British officer simpered, bemused. "Tell me more, are there any homes in it? Trails?"

"None, none at all. We do not go there and, if I may, sir, I believe there is a storm's blowin' in."

There was a storm in the offering, and rum disappeared from his system, which left the lieutenant painfully aware of his aching feet and throbbing head. "So Northward takes her deeper into these swamps."

"Yes sir, deeper into the brambles."

"We can do it, sir, me and Private Howe, we'll run her down," the former poacher offered.

Wainright fought a grimace at the soldier's offer. "Run her down all the way to Pennsylvania, I'll warrant."

"What, sir, desert?" Parsons protested weakly. "Me, sir?"

That was the pain of being a supernumerary, bloody rankers think you don't know their proclivities. As if one were any different from another, drunken, slovenly, disposed to thievery and rape, barely ahead of a noose, just out of reach of the lash. Wainright looked at the track in the mud, and the thick woods before him. "No, I do not think so. Sergeant, sound assembly, there are easier ways to go about this."

"So you plan to leave Meg here in the Sudsbury swamps?" Trenton asked as Sergeant Kinkade began blowing the whistle he wore in his baldric.

Wainright cast his eyes over the bramble and thorn, listened to the forbidding sounds of the woods. "Yes, yes I think so."

Chapter 4

A friendly rider out squiring some farmer's daughter had found

Trotter's burning wagon blazing on the roadside in the hilly, overgrown dirt

road paths between Sudbury and Lincoln. He had beaten a hasty retreat to

Lexington, riding overland through the trees and hills to report his discovery.

Fleet horses brought them there. It was far too easy for them to find the

wagon, a smudge of dark smoke still stained the grey evening sky from the

charred wreckage. Embers still crackled in the remains of a chest, broken open

and on its side in the blackened remains of the wagon, its fine linen lining and

contents an unrecognizable mound of char and ash.

Scattered, grisly piles of flesh that would roughly amount to two men

were scattered among the wreckage and spoiled goods. Scavenger animals had

already found their way among the offal, but the atrocities heaped upon the men

were readily apparent.

Daniel found himself unable to take his eyes from Trotter's disjointed,

scalped body. It was not these new indignities that caught his gaze, but an old

one. The tavern keeper's shirt was torn away, exposing his back, and the brutal

scars of the lash left there. These scars were an enduring gift from the strict

discipline of the British Army. Daniel found himself staring at them, and

brooding over his current path. "Who could have done this?" Daniel asked aloud, looking at the savaged form of the innkeeper who had harbored him as he rubbed at his furred cheek. "Pirates?

"Pirates? That sort of thing died with Blackbeard's head on a gibbet, back around 1620," snorted Parker, "not that I saw it myself, you understand."

The Scot peered into the trees again for danger, among his Clan in Scotland, there had been several veterans of the Seven Years War and Daniel had sat for many the campfire story of the aboriginal savages of this land, of their woodcraft and their savagery. "Indians?" Daniel offered a second thought, hefting his pistol. The pistol had produced more than a mild interest in his companions when the Scot had produced it, of Spanish manufacture, it mounted two barrels of .70 caliber side by side, each with its own flint and lock, and a sturdy metal clip mounted into the left side of the angular forearm, so it could be clipped beside a sword. The pistol and his green hunting shirt, a souvenir of his late adventure in Boston's harbor, were the only items he had fetched from his home before beginning this mission of mercy; indeed they were most of his true possessions.

"Mohawks? Ottawa's? This far East?" John Parker chided Daniel's apprehension, examining the wounds inflicted upon the bodies with a practiced eye. "But someone has taken pains that we might think so, or at least those who would know no better."

Parker, Daniel mused, was one who would know better. Daniel's eyes drifted from the tomahawk and knife thrust into Parker's belt to the well worn musket in his hands. The weapon was a hodge-podge assembly of parts British,

French and other things unknown, but it was oiled and ready for use. Parker himself moved like a wraith in the woods. Clad in his simple hunting shirt and stained breeches, he gave off a confidence now that Daniel had not noted before.

Revere had a heavy, brass butted pistol in one hand, the reins of his horse in the other. His eyes were scanning the foreboding woods. "So, Captain, who did this?"

Parker cast a baleful eye at the dirt path, coughed mightily and spat something tinged with pink upon the rocky, dirty trail. "Grounds been swept, absolutely swept like the deck of a ship. I see no tracks."

"There's some over here." Daniel intoned. Both men quickly picked their path through blood, body parts and wreckage to the Scot's side. There, in the mud of a neglected deer path, were four tracks. Three shod, and one small, partial bare footprint.

Parker flowed to one knee beside the evidence, studied it for some time. Revere also studied the marks in the earth, Daniel spoke first. "It makes no sense to my eye. I see three left feet, as if the same man stepped three times in the same area, dancing, and the heel of a bare foot, as if they were chasing the Indian."

"Not three left feet, son," Parker said, "three shoes cut on the same pattern. Note the toes strait and square like a box. Not like the fitted shoes Mister Revere wears, his shoes were made for him, and for each of his feet, left and right. These shoes were made to fit either foot.

"Brogans," Revere intoned, "army shoes."

Parker nodded, gravely. "When you look with eyes that see and know, you can see this is two left feet and a right, but of different men. This right foot, though not the shoe, is smaller than the other two, see the difference in the pressures of the track? And these men were running, chasing after . . ." He moved deeper into the woods, discovered another bare foot track in fresh mud.

"The Indian?"

"This was not one of your Indians, it is our Meg, I would stake my life to it. " Parker said definitively. "She has a light step, even when running like she is now. See the drag of her toes as she tries to dig them in the mud for purchase and for speed?" He pointed out the deeper tracks the toes had made, and scanned the foliage before him as if trying to peer through them, to find the missing girl. "She is out there somewhere, but where?"

"How can you know that?"

"Think, friend Daniel. Had our unknown friends in their army shoes caught our fine girl, she would be lying in pieces among dear Trotter and his man Pelenore, and our errand would be done, and not just begun."

"How do you know which is Pelenore?"

Interrupting a coughing fit, the man flinched his head at one stripped, scalped corpse. "The dim Norman had gone about without boots one winter, lost two toes for it." Parker said, disdainfully, and then stalked purposefully into the woods.

Revere slipped his pistol into his wide leather belt and gathering the reins of his horse. "Very well, you two range ahead, do what you can. I will return to Lexington, and gather yet more men for the search, and . . . other duties. If she still lives, she will be trying to find her way home." He swung into the saddle with easy grace, set spurs to the animal.

Parker re-emerged from the woods as Revere disappeared into the gloom, the salt and pepper haired Lexington man walked to the burned wagon where their two horses were tied. The animals were nervous, the scent of death was thick in the air all around them and they did not like it at all. The older man tried to quiet the fidgeting animals, led them off the roadside and re-tied their reins there. "Wind is freshening from the east," Parker said warily, "storm coming in from the sea."

"Nor'easter," Daniel crossed himself in a sailor's superstition. The wind was tinged with a salty smell, such as he had not noted since his brief time in Boston, "it'll be a cold rain, and a hard one."

"Meg's a cagey one." Parker spoke slowly, speaking to himself as if Daniel had not spoken. "She'll work to the river, not the road as they would expect her to. But the bustards chasing after her, they are what fear me."

Daniel crouched by the tracks in the mud, shook his head to clear it. "What's the army doing out here after them?", he mused to himself, trying to find the solution to the puzzle there in the dirt. "But why all this craft with the axes and daggers?"

"You do have eyes to see and know," Parker muttered appraisingly at the younger man, but said nothing else.

Daniel nudged a deerhide-clad foot against a part of what had once been Trotter, as if the corpse might answer him. "Maybe they don't want to hang a woman."

"Bloody Gage's admiralty court hangs women every day, boy. Just like the Crown courts of England." Parker barked darkly at that, his voice dissolving into a hacking cough that ended when he spat something veined with red upon the earth. "The sun tells me we have less than two hours to sunset, less with the storm sweeping in. I'm not of the best health, and too old to be out in a storm like what comes. You two are too young to die in it. We'll split up, I'll work my way to the river, heading toward Sudbury. You, Daniel, keep to their trail."

Daniel nodded, clipping his pistol to his belt before his left hip as he began walking toward the tracks again. Parker called after him, bringing him back. "A word, young Mr. Ferguson, Cap'n Rogers always said "look for the unusual things about you, then ask yourself why they stuck out."

Rogers? Daniel gaped. "You were one of Roger's Rangers?", he asked in awe, seeing the old farmer in a new light.

"That name did not come until later," Parker answered primly, offering the younger man one of the canteens from his horse. "But 'tis good advice, none the less."

Daniel shook the canteen, it was a wooden thing resembling a small keg. Parker nodded at it and said. "That's rum, good Jamaican, that will warm a body up enough to get through the night, if you can find her soon enough. God's speed, Daniel Ferguson, and I will see you again."

* * * *

Tracks in fresh earth, no heel marks, her bare toes dug in deeply. The world around him constricted to bare yards, sometimes to feet, or inches even. She indeed did have a light foot and long stride, almost like a dancer, which made finding her trail all the more difficult. She parted tall grasses almost like a ghost, leaving a path he needed good light to follow, and his light was fading.

He found a clearing where turkeys had scratched the earth, found a half dozen boots milling, part of a plug of tobacco carelessly dropped and spots where men had relieved themselves.

The frigid Atlantic winds were redoubling, bringing with them the unmistakable promise of rain to come. The wood around him was coming closer, thorns and branches reaching out like clawing fingers to drag him in. His instinct told him to run, to get to his home or find the warmth of an inn to pass a miserable evening. But if he did that, he knew, he would damn the girl to a death, a death to match that of Trotter's and Pelenore's, or death of exposure as sure as with a blade or gun.

Daniel could hear water ahead, a rushing river moving with abandon toward the sea. The promising green of spring did not hide the recently receding mark of high water from melting snow, dotted with uprooted trees and gashes in the bank where rushing waters had violently torn and eroded the earth.

Ahead, a fallen tree's roots clawed at the air like a hungry spider, he paused and looked at it, scoured the ground with his eyes and thought a long moment. The mud bore the prints of deer, the formless single print of British army brogans, of milling men stumbling about in the poor light of the overhang. An area stamped flat by their milling about, and then walking away.

The Sudsbury marshes were rousing from their winter's nap, vibrant, living greens covering over the grays and browns, new growth climbing over fallen trees and rocks. The melted snow charged the rivers, lifting their levels ever higher, though they now receded to leave behind fallen trees swept down its path, damming up areas with silt and limbs, a land of water, living and stagnant.

The colonials, of which Daniel had only begin to consider himself, never came to the marshes, but for a few intrepid hunters, this was an expanse ceded entirely to the other creatures, a land of fur and feathers.

A clawed, four toed track gave Daniel a thrill of fear, and he picked up his pace. Rushing after the sparse barefoot tracks rushing over a low rise, Daniel found where she had gone tripping over a root and rolled down a hill. Still she had scrambled to her feet, he found handprints in the mud, something like blood on a nearby branch. She had rushed across a rocky bubbling creek and he had followed, splashing quickly across the muddy, freezing-cold melted snow that swelled the water from ankle height to almost above his knee.

Rocks hid just beneath the rippling surface of the water, sneaking ambushers of his numbed toes and ankles. Daniel began pausing before each step to view its course before he would commit to it. He cursed them mightily, but seeing the rocks again reminded him of how few there were in this country. Scotland seemed to be all rocks and craggy hills, these colonies seemed to be all fertile flatlands.

Between two stones, he saw a strip of well used blue cloth, wedged there, Daniel pulled it up, felt the resistance as he drew the fabric free. To become wedged so, he realized, Meg would need to be going in one of two directions. One made little sense, the other even less, and Daniel charted his course deeper into the Marshes.

The water rose over his knees, now, gaining mid-thigh with numbing, painful splashes. But as the level began to slip below his knees again, he saw where someone had splashed ashore, scouring the rocky beach clean of greenish muck. The marks upon the earth reminded him of some of the marks painted upon some of his fellow Mohawks upon the Boston Docks, and that made him think of Revere and his words.

Upon the stony earth, he found a single bare footprint with a light step. Daniel crept around a thick, fallen bramble that had once been a tall oak uprooted and dragged by the melted snows of the past winter. He pondered Meg, chased by a bunch of men because of what she had seen. Peering over the tree, he reached for a secure grip of dead limbs, intent on sliding down the muddy hill. Blue gingham threads lashed at his fingers, and Daniel snapped back his hand as if struck.

He looked over that precipice again, then past it to a deer trail leading from the water. In the precipice, suddenly he saw a sharp slide down cold wet mud into the course of the rapid river, icy waters and currents to drag you down and foul your step. Shivering, he gathered himself and looked around the muddy path, found a partial bare foot track, heading away from the trap, and into the Sudbury swamps.

Liberty, Revere kept saying, but liberty from what? Daniel had been born a subject of the King, lived his whole life as one. Now, in this new land of Colonies and men who talked of Liberty, what was he expected to do?

Swiping a thorn bush aside as he kicked for purchase, he paused, looking at a steep rise that jutted up on his right side. There, he found a dent in the muddy earth, with blades of grass pushed into it.

Strange the turns of fate, Daniel mused, opening the tiny gap to detect the indentures of five perfect toes. Lo these long months, brief memories and remembered glimpses of Meg had kept his hopes warm as the summer breeze, and now he found himself scouting the marshes for the girl.

A bare arms length away, he found a heel print in the where she had stomped upon a root in the clay. A sticky grit of mud still clung to the root, she was not all that far ahead of him, less than an hour. "This way and close." He muttered to himself, scrambling up the draw as his neck registered the first touch of icy rain drops. Slow, fat drops came, not as the thunderous deluge that was to come, only a sample of the coming storm.

He was chilled to the bone from his icy dip, wading the marshes, and as the dark clouds gathered above, Daniel realized he would soon need to think to his own survival. To be trapped out in the marshes, in a seaborne spring storm would be a sure death sentence, less he find a fire and some shelter, soon. But, casting aside good sense for Samaritan concern of this girl, he trusted himself to chance and pushed onward.

The brambles and thorns grew thicker here, and he chopped with his dirk to make passage. Then, the jarring yellow of a broken branch hanging loose nearby caught his eye and caused him to pause, a length of it stripped of its branches and greenery where a hand had grasped it, where she had grabbed it. He looked down over the cliff and found where her knee had burrowed deep into the earth. If it had been he, Daniel nodded, chased, frightened, exhausted, he would have gone here also, go high and hide. He scrambled for a grip on the slick ground, pulled himself onto the path as the clouds gathered gray and heavy overhead.

Only, once he gained the height of the rise, Daniel found that he and the girl had gained but little. The ground sloped away, a gentle rise that would pass a walking man almost unnoticed. A raccoon, rising from its daylong nap to a night of foraging looked at him queerly before quietly setting off on its way. Daniel found Meg's path, a growth of berry bushes and beneath it the familiar tracks of bear, scraping at the earth for food.

The ground leveled quickly, a broken deer trail slashed through the cropped grass, but even at this elevation, slight though it was, he found a fine view of the horizon as the last rays of the April sun sank from view and a grey darkness spread over the land. The trees in better life at this modest elevation were all strong pines and tall oaks, casting a carpet of shadows about him. Hugging himself for warmth against the sudden chill, the Scot congratulated himself on seeing where a buck had pawed the earth for some morsel of food. He paused to look at the ground, mused the track of what must be a fine, big deer in the earth before he saw a bare foot jutting from beneath the spreading branches of a majestic pine nearby.

Find the unusual things around you, Daniel mused, almost missed the forest for the trees. He rushed to her side, drew up the thorny brambles of the pine to get to the prostrate girl. It looked as if Meg had tried to bury herself in the cast off branches and needles, he brushed the debris from her face. She had undoubtedly fallen in the icy creek several times, as her long hair was a sodden mass about her head and she was soaked to the bone. Her blouse was matted to her flesh like a second skin, the red bodice torn and some of the stays let out or bared, her skirt's hem was torn ragged. The girl's hands and elbows were worn bloody and her lips were distinctly blue, her arms cold as ice, but the gooseflesh came as he touched her. To make matters worse, it was at that moment the rains came, the cold wash of the Atlantic in each drip.

He gathered the girl into his arms, he had no hope of struggling back up the muddy trails to the roadways to Menotomy, and to the South lay only the snow-swelled river. Daniel held the girl close, and hazarded the tangling undergrowth and the icy raindrops. As rain soaked the back of his shirt, he whispered a silent prayer to Providence and stared hard through the haze for a miracle. The girl did not so much as turn her face from the droplets of water that exploded on her brow, and Daniel clucked his tongue at that. A fallen tree lay across his path, too thick to scale over with his current burden. The Scot turned from the river to go around it, and in doing so found a rocky overhang at the base of a low hill. It was not much, barely wide enough for one to crawl into, not high enough for a man to stand, barely enough to kneel inside, but it would do, it would have to do. He gently laid the girl on the dry, dusty earth and rushed back outside to yank dead branches from a nearby lightning-struck tree, threw them into the shelter of the overhang as the rain picked up in intensity.

Struggling back inside the overhang, he found he could sit with his legs crossed in a stoop and found himself strangely overjoyed at that. Smiling like a fool at that small victory, he began shifting through his sporran, setting aside items as he came to them, a spare flint for his musket, some dry tinder.

Meg lay in a heap exactly as he had left her, her breath so shallow he placed a hand near her nose until he felt the welcome breeze of her breath, then he drew a dead branch close to him, began breaking off branches and building a pyramid, filling the insides with the brittle woven twigs of an old cast off bird's nest and some dry leaves he found scattered in the deepest crevice of the overhang as he scoured the hole for bear sign.

A soft groan froze him in place, and he saw Meg's eyes, merely slits with which she observed him, but the drenched, frozen girl seemed to be aware of him.

"I know you," she whispered through blue lips, and Daniel winced, that was far too close to the grunted "Me know you" the Mohawks had exchanged that night in December, upon the wharves of Boston.

"Lay quiet, girl." He said, reassuringly, wishing he had found the time to shave and cut his hair before this rescue. He knew his neglect must be a frightful sight to this woman now. "Paul Revere sent me to fetch you back. You can trust me, you need not fear me."

She stared at him for a long time, her vision strangely perfect in the damp, shadowy recesses of a Sudbury marshes cave. She saw the tartan sash about his shoulder, a pistol clipped to his belt, the long bladed dirk thrust into his belt as he sat cross legged at the opening of the crevice. That familiar, overgrown face she had seen beside the stove in Trotter's Black Horse tavern, those eyes now calm and commanding as he looked earnestly at her. "I know you, Daniel Ferguson, and I am not afraid of you." She whispered around a strangely thick tongue. Meg tried to lift a hand in some gesture, but instead she shivered in the dirt, aching arms moving slowly to wrap her trunk and she clutched herself close and miserable before him.

Impetuously, he drew off the tartan scrap from his shoulder. "Here, girl," he said, draping it over her, "it's wet, but wool will keep you warm."

"N..n..no." She tried to form the word, her teeth chattered and her hands shook and seemed unable to grip the cloth. "What …what'll …."

"I'll live, girl," he said with false bravado and quipped, "I've got me beard to keep me warm." She muttered something that sounded like "scruffy looking" as he drew his dirk and sparked the flint off the long steel blade. "Take it." His voice was tinged with command, something she would have bristled at, but struggling to a sitting position, she wrapped it about her shoulders.

He knew the fire to be their lifeline, it would scare off the furred, toothed creatures of the marsh, and without its warmth they would not last that damp Spring night. Chilled as she was, the girl would not live two hours, he gave his own life only slightly better odds. But, he sighed, there was nothing else to warm them.

Shifting slightly, he felt the canteen about his middle slosh, and impetuously unslung it. "Here, girl, take some of this."

She took the canteen, jostled it suspiciously in her hand. "What is it?

"Jamaican rum, I am told it will..." Daniel answered guilelessly, looking up to see the girl take two full, deep swallows from the canteen, "....warm you."

Daniel collected his tinder starter again, scowled at the dampness and cast a jaundiced eye at the driving rain outside, "You seem troubled, Mister Ferguson," she said, the words came slurred and slowly. He did not know if it was the cold or the rum, but long experience as a barmaid, or just alert woman's intuition had picked up on his troubled mind. She forced out the words as she leaned heavily against the dirty rocky outcropping of the overhang, her head lolled to one side as though she lacked the strength to hold it up.

Troubled, you do not know the half of it, he mused, taking the canteen from her and hazarding a sip, lost in the woods with a weakened girl, a spring storm in the offering and bears and wolves in the tree-line. But to top it off, I cannot shake those damned words of Paul Revere, freedom, freedom. He pasted on a brave smile, one worthy of a Highlander. "No, girl, not at all," he said, pasting on his best smile as he set the canteen aside. The spray of sparks took to the dry bird's nest, the beginnings of the flame a fitful smoldering thing that fouled the close air with thick smoke. He fought the urge to hurriedly huff lungs full of air on the glowing sparks, instead methodically breaking twigs from one of his nearby branches, he began placing them carefully about the smoldering, smoky ember taking root upon the char cloth and leaves. As he did this, Daniel noted the girl was intently watching him and joked to lighten the mood. "Wish we had dry….something to encourage this fire."

Don't look to me, good sir." Meg said, her familiar serving girl front falling into place. "There is not a dry thing upon me."

Daniel raised his eyes, glancing at her through the teepee of sticks and bark he had constructed, smiled wanly and nodded. "Aye, so I see." Then he tried not to stare at the girl as the sparking embers sputtered, feeding it more sticks as with quick hands she chastely rearranged his frayed tartan to hide her shivering, taut bosom through the drenched muslin bodice.

Strange the twists of fate, Daniel mused again. To find this fine girl in the woods, drenched to the bone with her fabrics all clinging and sheer, and I too busy making fire to admire the benefits therein.

A flame! A tiny flickering thing not much bigger than a field mouse on its hind legs, but he thanked God for it, marveled at it for a long moment as it danced upon the char-cloth, stretched and reached for more fuel to add to itself. He fed it carefully into the pyramid of sticks and watched it with the fearful, protective eyes of a father to his first-born as it flared to life.

Kindled to a fickle flame, he watched the yellow flame climb from stick to stick, licking hot tongues against the meager tinder until it became a fickle, smoking fire. It cast a warm, sooty light about them, its heat a welcome ray of hope.

He looked at their meager supply of wood, rationed a miserly amount into the fire and watched the results of it with a jaundiced eye. Outside, the rain rattled down about them with the constant tattoo of a martial band.

"Are you hurt, girl? Wounded?"

She crawled close to the burgeoning fire, holding her hands to the smoky, scant heat. "No," she whispered through chattering teeth, "when the shooting began, I scampered into the greenery."

"Glad I am to hear that." The Scot smiled, and then turned serious, passed back the canteen. "They are dead, I am afraid."

"Yes... I presumed so." The red-haired girl whispered, tipping the rum to her lips.

"Who did this, girl? Who killed them?"

"I do not know," she lied, and then added a sorrowful shrug when the lie would not stand. "Indians?"

"Indians?" He parroted Captain Parker. "Indians, this far east?" But she said nothing, fussed at the hem of her skirts. He hazarded another start at the question. "At least three of the brigands wore Regular Army brogans."

The auburn haired girl flashed alight in anger like a candle dropped upon coal-oil. "Then likely as not they were white men dressed as Indians. White men can dress as Indians, you well know, Daniel Ferguson."

He did not recoil from her by force of will. It was certainly whispered about how he had come by his wounds, and the girl knew more than most, though this was the first time she openly voiced her suspicions. Instead, Daniel rummaged through his sporran again, found a small tin cup and set it out in the frigid deluge outside. In a surprisingly short time it had filled about halfway and he set it close to the fitful blaze until it bubbled. "Here, girl," he said, wrapping it in a scrap of cloth. "It's no Bohecia tea, but if you hold the cup, it will warm your outside a bit while the rum warms your insides."

"Were it King George's Chinese tea, I would not take it, Daniel Ferguson," she said stiffly, a production for someone so weak, "even from you."

"Take it girl," he said, shaking the cup again so the hot water almost splashed upon his hand.

"Megan," she said, finally taking the cup and clutching the hot metal vessel in her hands, and handing back the wooden canteen.

"Thank you, Meg…."

The sudden warmth of the wrapped cup in her hand was a tonic; bracing and most welcome. It emboldened her. "Not Meg, Megan." She said it with force. "People in taverns call me Meg."

"You don't like it?"

"Don't know," she admitted, surprising herself she so took the Scot into her confidence, "don't know if I hated it first, or learned to hate it. But I do now."

The canny Scot looked at her with appraising eyes. "Then Megan is not your real name," he said, adroitly, then rewarded himself with a sip of the rum

The girl looked at him with new respect. "No," she heard herself say, and was shocked by this strange man with his strange accent. "No it is not. You are the first to guess so, as you are the first I tell so much. I do not know why I did tell you so much, Daniel Ferguson, it has been a long time since I trusted another with so much." She said in a tone that ended the conversation.

"It is well you should, Megan, and it matters little. I can keep a confidence, assuming we survive the night." The Scot said it as a joke, but both knew the truth of the statement. A long time, and the canteen also, passed between them, staring at the fickle flames of their fire before Daniel asked with exaggerated, courtly politeness, "would you hand me that dry branch over by your foot?" As he asked it, he extended a hand like a courtier at a ball. Then his mouth fell open. Her feet were torn and bloodied, fresh mud staining her past the ankle. "Good Lord above, girl ..er.. Megan, look at your feet, 'tis barely Spring and you gad about barefoot? Where are your shoes?"

She yanked back her foot instinctively, covered it by rubbing at the dirty heel. "Shoes?" she parroted back, sharply. "May as well ask me where is my golden tiara, or my fine silks, Daniel Ferguson."

The Scotsman ran a hand through his long wet hair, looked at her and nodded, taking no offense at her tone. He fed more of their meager wood upon the flames and nodded contentedly as the fire grew higher and warmer, changing the subject when he spoke again. "Ah, yes, that will do fine," he said, rummaging in his sporran again, "a bit of a fire makes everything brighter." Daniel scratched at his beard self consciously, made of great, comic show of surveying the meager surroundings of the overhang, and the soaking chill outside. "May come back here and homestead."

Her easy smile returned, like the light of the fire it made everything brighter in the tight, cavernous overhang. The Scot continued to rummage in his belt pouch, finally drawing out a scrap of cloth that protected a spicy smelling piece of jerked venison. He looked at it with obvious relish, and then chivalrously handed it to the girl.

Her eyes were wide for a moment as she accepted it. Flexing aching muscles in her arm, she pulled free a thread of the meat and placed it on her tongue to soften. It was spicy with pepper and other, more provincial herbs. Tasting it was like eating a copy of a finer meal, made with poorer ingredients he had undoubtedly gathered the materials to make the meat himself. "I reckon you a man of finer breeding, Daniel Ferguson." Megan commented as the jerky's spices danced upon her tongue, then tipped the canteen to her mouth again before adding a compliment. "You have the manners of a lord under that horrid beard."

She had meant it as a compliment, obviously, but the Scot took it strangely. He cocked his head to one side and asked. "Must I be of the *daoine-uaisle* to know how to treat a lady?"

She did not know a *"daoine-uaisle"* from a Chinese fan dancer, but instead of asking, she shrugged and passed him the canteen, saying. "I remember Mr. Trotter sent me to the kitchen once, to fetch bread. You lay there in fever, I mopped your brow with a cool cloth, and your eyes snapped open, you looked at me and nodded, the sort of nod that is almost a bow."

Daniel did not remember that moment, he shrugged with a smile. "No, no kin of mine is part of the gentry." Daniel conceded, thinking of family left behind in Scotland as he busied his hands breaking the five foot length of dead tree branch into usable length for his tiny fire. He used both the strength of his limbs and the sharp edge of his great Dirk to do the deed. As he did, he realized his thought of Scotland, of his home, had turned to this new land, a land where clan did not matter, where the word *daoine-uaisle* did not even exist. "There are better set families, to be sure. We were no better than *buannachan*, fealty soldiers, called upon to raid for cattle, or vengeance, or defend against a raid."

"You were a soldier," Megan said without surprise, lifting a hand to brush wet hair from her face, "a soldier to your Clan's chieftain, and a good one, I wager."

"Aye, of a sort," he said self deprecatingly, looking down at the long steel blade thrust into the earth beside him and morosely sipped at their canteen.

"Why did you come here?", she asked in curiosity.

He paused, a long hesitation before he spoke, but when he did, she knew she heard the truth from a man uncomfortable with speaking of himself. "The harvest was poor, the Laird had need of gold, all the better if it left him with fewer mouths to feed. What he had was men, and the Crown had need of them. The Recruiting Sergeants came with a glad hand and an open purse, first among the farmers and tanners of the villages. Then, at my Laird's invitation, they began to walk among us of the…pugilistic class." He looked from Meg's face to the canteen, taking a long drink from it to kill the pain of the moment. "To us there was no offer of the King's shilling, no fine talk of adventure and plunder. Just a cold eye and "he'll do.""

"To take the King's shilling", she knew was a slang expression for joining the army. Recruiters would offer the prospective private their first month's wages up front, a shilling, and to accept it, even innocently, was enough to seal the contract. "Why?", Megan asked, gently taking the little wooden keg from his grip, tipping it to her mouth before she asked. "You would seem to be… in high demand."

"They knew us to be free for the asking, our duties about the Clan were specific. We fought, not a tanner or a cooper among us," the Scot said with an ironic pride as he accepted the canteen back. "To lose the town cooper meant no more wagon wheels, to lose one of us… did not mean as much, I suppose. So they walked among us like the butcher on meat day, not a smile nor drink or glad hand. Just "he'll do", and the Seneschal would tell us to kindly go with the man."

"I cannot imagine being so abused, yet thought trustworthy to hold a musket for the King."

"I'll say, the Laird even kept me bloody shilling!" He meant it as a joke, but it fell flat, even to him. His eyes drifted back to the fire, and he continued. "Trust has little to do with it, Megan, the Crown has realized they can't beat us upon the fields." Daniel shrugged. "Their new royal plan is to bleed the Highlands dry of men, between their Orangemen and their bloody sheep, they almost have. I decided not to be part of that." He took a long pull at the canteen and continued with a sigh. "I have stood for my Laird, the chief of the Clan for all my life. Had they raised Bonnie Charlie's banner once again, I would have fought and died for him. But this... this I could not bear. Were I to wear a red coat, I would have it be my wish, not another man's. So I stole off in the night, signed to the *Beaver*, and now, here I am."

"Bonnie Charlie." She smiled, "I have heard his name before. So you would fight for the Jacobite cause?"

Daniel waited a long moment before he answered her. "Back in Scotland, I prayed for it, for the King to come over the water and make all right. But here, in the America's, I... I have come to see things differently."

"Really?" She leaned forward intently, focused upon him in a strange way, and he, so starved for the company of another human being, answered.

"Aye. There is a different world here, a new world that free men and women can make in their own image. Without a King or Lairds over them, but being their own Lords, making their own way.

"There are those," she baited him, sipping at the canteen, "that see John Hancock as our next king."

"Aye, and he not the least among them. But that will not do him any harm for now. I cannot fault the man his riches, nor his efforts to extend them. That is the way of rich men. But maybe, just maybe this is the land where rich men will not do so on the backs of others."

"It would seem we both have known the injustices of men." She breathed, and the Scot fixed her with a strange look. Megan offered him a small smile, and the canteen, not knowing why she took this man into her confidence, but that his own honesty seemed to draw out hers. "You asked me about my shoes, I had a pair, once. Fine, glossy black, they were, with silver buckles." She smiled at the memory, a genuine smile that lit up her face, and faded just as fast as it appeared. "But, I was young. Young, proud and stupid, and I ran away with a boy, I thought him a man, but lacked the experience to know the difference." Time had not silenced this memory, and she paused a long moment.

"The thief," Daniel whispered too loudly, then tried to cover his words by courteously handing her the canteen.

"No." She smiled, sadly, shaking her head and sipping at the rum. "He did not steal them, I gave them willingly. I would have given him anything, everything - I did give him…everything. I…I trusted a boy to be a man, now I do not know if it is within me to trust again."

"The theft I accuse him of is plain. And it was not of shoes." Daniel said. "Nor do you need say anything more of it, though I do thank you for taking me into your confidence." He deftly added some more wood to the flames, then took the conversation in a different way. "There are many kinds of thefts, though. For instance, King George is a well-set lad, I suppose he could afford a loss here and there, don't you?"

"Theft of the King's property? At home, the … King's Judge would render verdict from the Royal courts on Sundays." She shuddered at a suppressed memory, drinking several long draughts to silence it before continuing. "Theft to the King's property is licentious treason, he would say."

"And licentious is bad, I take it?"

"Yes, and the punishment was death, by hanging." She whispered, not meeting his eyes and instead taking another drink, "and the trap would be sprung, and they would dangle and kick. They would kick and kick until they could kick no more. Then, the judge would give a speech, "none are above the law," he would say, "I would do the same to my own flesh and blood." And he would point at . . .his children."

"Bosh," Daniel said, "no man would do so, not to their own."

"So we thought, so I thought. Until he did, and his own son swung at the gibbet." She shuddered, a convulsive shake that became a sob, gathering the tartan shawl about her.

.   The gruff Scot gathered her close and held her reassuringly. "The winds still and the rain seems content to linger the night." Her rescuer soothed, "Think no more of it, as there is naught man can do. You dry out as best you can, we'll await the rainbow, and then, Miss Megan, I will see you home."

CHAPTER 5

"The rain stopped in the early hours." Captain Parker, red eyed and sore, intoned.

"T'was a frigid downpour," the Reverend Clarke growled in his deep bass voice, urging his horse onward with one hand as the other clutched a musket. He refused to equip the firelock with a sling, less the burden of it become too easy. "Is the Parson of Menotomy summoned? Or shall I be the one to serve over Mr. Trotter?"

"Revere headed for Menotomy before grey dawn." Parker said. "Be there help to come, they will be on the way, but in truth, I do not know if Trotter was in regular attendance for services there."

"T'was a cold rain last night," nodded Francis Brown, darkly and unbidden. "It came from the East, from the sea. Winds to chill a man to the bones." He was a round-faced, sturdy man with a fatalistic outlook. A fine man with a hammer or a saw, but a man with such a pessimistic attitude, he was not one to discuss the future.

Reverend Clarke looked up at the sky, but whether searching for rainclouds or offering a silent prayer, Parker did not know. "You have sent out a summons for men, more eyes to look for our foundling lambs?"

"I have." Parker confirmed.

"We will need all of them, the Sudsbury marshes are greening and thick, with many ways a man can meet his doom."

"It is well you are so close, Reverend, and that we bring shovels," muttered the stoic Brown as he curbed his horse sharply.

"Do yet keep a cheerful mind, Francis Brown." Clarke said, shaking his leonine head. There was undoubtedly more to his thought, but at a bend in the roadway, a man sat ahorse, as if awaiting them.

Parker set his musket across his lap with a purposeful, menacing eye and goaded his horse forward of the small pack of men, commanding. "State your name and your business!"

The man's horse remained perfectly still, a great demonstration of the skills of the horseman upon it. The rider looked at the half-dozen men and spoke. "I am Joshua Whittenmore, son of Samuel Whittenmore of Menotomy. He bids me to say to you, John Parker, that Paul Revere and the Whittenmores scour the marshes from the bend of the river and heading ever Northward. If they live, by the grace of God, we will find them."

"And what if they do not live," Brown snapped.

"We will find them none the less." The youth on horseback said with sharp finality. "My father swears it to Almighty God as his judge." Then, he whirled the horse and galloped off.

* * * * *

The Scot blearily reached for the canteen, found it light to the touch and it did not slosh when he shook it. He thought of throwing it from the cave, but his thundering head thought the better of it and he gently set it down.

The flames were burned down to mere coals and few of those. Daniel whispered a silent prayer of thanks for the life giving warmth the fire and Parker's rum had gifted them. Their meager supply of firewood was gone, not even a stick or leaf remained.

Since his birth, he had lived, served and toiled under the permission and pleasure of the King. His pains had been less his own, than granted to his temporary use by another, to be taken away at His Royal leisure, or upon His Royal whim. But upon these foreign lands, he had found in the words of another a strange idea, Liberty, freedom, a barely dreamed of hope before, now sprang to full flower. To go as he pleased, when he pleased and to do as he saw fit, never again to think of his children eating shanks and leeks for the taxman's demands. Beholding to none but himself, it almost seemed sacrilegious to dare think of it.

Propped comfortably upon his shoulder, the Scot lay cuddled up to Meg like two spoons in a drawer, she closest to the smoldering fire. His tartan was wrapped about her shoulders and she had pulled her bare feet beneath the fabric of her shredded skirts to keep warm. In her repose she looked like an angel, her tired, weary eyes closed to rest.

An errant strand of her long red hair graced her sleeping face and he gently eased it aside. At his touch, she gave a slow smile, and brushed her cheek against his hand. Then she shifted from her side, rolling upon her back to nuzzle at his shoulder, lifting her face toward his in a questing way, questing for a lover's first morning kiss.

Then, her eyes snapped open, and she stared up at him. Her eyes were not quite the same shade of red as her hair, and the grimace of pain she gave him, he hoped had little to do with his scraggly appearance and more to do with their drinking.

"Good morning," he enthused, as if he had noticed none of this, "the storm's passed."

Meg's eyes rolled, taking in everything in the close, rocky overhang, and gave a single, curt nod. Rubbing at her eyes and aching head, she asked. "Can we find our way back now?"

"Seems likely," he nodded.

"Good." The red-haired girl sat up, gathering the tartan about her to ward off the early morning chill. "Then we can leave this God-forbidden place behind." Without another word, she crawled free of the overhang.

Daniel watched her as she stood in the murky sunlight of the Sudbury marshes. I don't know, he thought, "I wouldn't mind staying on a bit longer." But he gathered his things and drew himself free of the cramped overhang. He clipped his pistol to his belt, careful fingers checking the hammers were set to half-cock for safety, though he wondered if he should bother, the priming and most likely the charge was undoubtedly wet.

She stood at the fallen tree that had guided them to their shelter, staring over it into the rushing river. "It is higher than yesterday," she said, nervously, "by a good deal."

"The rains," Daniel nodded, "higher and still quite cold, I will warrant."

"Yes," she confirmed, "cold enough to take your breath away." Now almost dry, she had no wish to be submerged in that icy stream again.

Daniel cast a sidelong look, but decided to drop the statement. Instead, he looked up at the Massachusetts sky. "You did not tell me who was chasing you, to force you into the marshes."

She looked at the rushing waters as if she did not hear him for a long time, then asked, lightly. "How did you sleep?"

"Naught at all." Daniel answered, giving up his previous question. "I had a great deal upon my mind."

"Such as?"

"Liberty." Daniel answered, truthfully, scratching at his beard in through. Then both looked at each other in shock as nearby a musket fired three rapid shots in quick succession. "That must be Parker," Daniel opined, "out looking for us."

"What do we do?" Meg asked, breathless at the thought of rescue.

"We answer." The Scot drew his pistol, pulled a small, flat horn from his sporran and freshened the priming in both pans. He cocked one of the hammers, pointed the barrels skyward and pulled the trigger.

* * * * *

"Answer!" Samuel Whittenmore declared, somewhat surprised as he lowered his smoking musket. "An answer and not that far off." He looked down from the rise, scanning about the greenery with his sharp eyes for some sign of his friend, but the world below remained a sea of emerald.

Curbing his mount beneath him, Joshua's young eyes were the sharper. "Down in the hollows," his son pointed from the back of his horse, "near the fork of the river, I reckon. That sow bear and cubs are down there, Father."

Whittenmore threw himself into his saddle with the zeal of a man half his age. His lively horse pranced in excitement as its rider gathered the reins in his hand, picking up its rider's own enthusiasm. "Very close, close indeed!" The grey haired man enthused, then muttered, "sow bear, you say?"

"Yes, the one that has been killing our cattle in the Eastern holdings."

The elder Whittenmore paused a long moment, then shrugged to his son. "Nothing to be done about it, but get it done." He said, then spurred the horse deeper into the marshes, toward the sound of the shot.

* * * * *

The echo of the pistol shot was barely gone when Daniel poured fresh powder and lead into the fired barrel, ramming quickly. Meg peered at the tree line, an endless line of green and shadows. "Where are they?"

"They will come," Daniel answered her.

"Where are they?"

"It may take them a few minutes, hours even," he soothed, thinking "You can't expect them to come boiling out of the greenery, just because you want to be home." As he said it, the bushes began to rattle and shake, and even Daniel fond himself expectedly staring at the rattling greenscape in disbelief, until with a lurch, two black fur balls tumbled free of the brush to roll and play in their makeshift campsite.

"Raccoons?", she whispered harshly as the two little lumps cavorted and played.

"No," Daniel said, grabbing her and dragging her to the other side of the fallen tree at the beach. "Bear cubs, duck down and pray Momma doesn't notice us."

"Momma? I didn't see…"

"Me neither, but she's there, and she's not far."

"Not far? But…" She began, and stifled a squeal as a deep, snuffling grunt thundered over the two.

Daniel cocked both hammers on the pistol in his hand, deftly glanced over the top of the tree. "It's snorting around the overhang." He hissed to Meg. "This isn't their cave, I checked it carefully for fur last night. There are some berries bushes nearby, Momma's checking a strange scent near her cubs."

"That scent…it's us."

"I know.

"She's coming this way." Meg hissed, voice shrill with fear.

"I know."

"Swim for it?"

"No, water's too cold, and bears can out swim a fish," the Scot answered, turned to look for the big carnivore and found himself staring into its big, angry eyes for a bare moment before it charged. The bear let up a roar that was all the worse for the rum he had drank the night before and lunged upon the log, slashing out with huge claws to rake the bark where Daniel's head had been a moment before.

The Scot lunged free of the tree trunk by instinct, cold water rushing into his Ghillie Brogues, numbing his feet as he whirled and presented his pistol. The bear stood on hind legs, like a furry wall before him, roaring with a mouth like a cavern teeming with white teeth. Daniel pointed his pistol into the furry mass, and fired both barrels. Recoil was horrendous as both .72-caliber balls belched out the muzzles with a flash like thunder. The bear staggered back, falling briefly to all fours before it rose again to brandish its black, sickle shaped claws. Blood poured from a massive wound on its torso and Daniel believed that its left fore-paw responded slower than the other to the bear's will.

Roaring his defiance in a red battle rage, he drew his Dirk from its scabbard as his left hand bore forth the pistol as a cudgel. But as he did it, his mouth went dry and his heart pounded in his chest. Daniel was about to fight a bear, hand to hand.

The bear took a swing at him, long hooking claws sliced the air, barely missing him. Daniel ducked beneath it, slashed with both dagger and clubbed pistol. Some loosened fur flew in the passage of the blade, but the bear didn't even notice the blow of the brass weighted pistol butt.

Even to a Scot who dreamed of the charge at Culloden, this was a losing fight, and he knew it. Two hundred pounds of bear was bleeding just enough to make it mad, but not enough to slow it down. It was strong as an ox, fighting for its young, and angry besides. Another swing of its massive paw clipped the pistol from his left hand with a glancing blow, and the Scot watched his improvised cudgel spin away. Daniel slashed at the offending limb, felt the blade connect but was more concerned with getting clear of the aggravated beast than what damage he had caused.

His graceful lunge free of the claws and teeth turned into a stumbling lurch that left him sprawling in the mud. He heard the bear's lumbering approach as he scrambled to gain his footing and then, two muskets boomed like a dual crash of thunder. So sudden and unexpected was the aid, Daniel glanced heavenward for the thunder cloud.

Sam Whittenmore's aim was better than Daniel's rushed shot, his son's ball also sailed true as two muskets boomed, one just a shade of time before the other. The bear lurched sideways and fell to the ground to rise no more. The grey haired man stood tall in the saddle and enthused. "Daniel Ferguson, we meet again!"

Daniel laughed like a child upon Christmas morn. "And well met indeed, Samuel Whittenmore!"

Whittenmore stood his horse in the cold, rushing waters, his long legs brushing at the mud colored waves. Though the icy rush of melted snow was past the brown stallion's knees, it did not move until coaxed by it rider, wading slowly to the beachside and into a dramatic leap to the sandy, muddy battleground before the overhang. Whittenmore allowed himself the slight arrogance of the leap, slowing the spirited mount in a slow pirouette to a stop, so as to offer Daniel his hand in greeting. The older man looked the shaggy Scot over a long moment, but smiled in recognition and said. "Glad to see you are both alive." He smiled a wide and uncharacteristically happy smile. "There are a great many looking for you two," He said as he slid from the saddle and decorously offered the horse to Meg, "shall we go and greet them?"

Daniel watched the girl slide demurely up onto the horse's saddle with a sad relish. Then he looked away with a will, sheathing his blade and reclaiming the Spanish pistol as he studied the fallen bear. It seemed so small now, the teeth more yellow and less glossy, its claws less massive.

"Daniel?" Whittenmore called again. "Daniel, do not concern yourself with your kill. My son, Joshua will see to it, won't you son?"

The younger Whittenmore, carefully picking his way out of the sandy, slippery watershed upon his horse, answered with a peculiar enthusiasm, "nothing I would like better!"

Whittenmore wound the reins for his horse about his left hand, saving his right for his long musket and with Daniel beside him, began walking into the wastes of the marshes. The old Dragoon knew the lands like the back of his hand, instinctively picking out the path back to the roads as he tried to keep a conversation going with the two, but both the Scot and Meg were too tired, and too relieved to hold up to a great deal of talking.

"You seem shaggier than when I last saw you, Daniel," Whittenmore said jovially, "but none the worse for wear. Come you round my home, and I'll have one of my daughters give you a haircut and a trim for that bird's nest you call a beard." As he spoke, he watched the Scot in the corner of his eye to see if his words struck a cord. They did not and finally, the former Dragoon soberly observed. "You seem troubled, Daniel Ferguson."

"Somewhat." The Scot admitted to his friend, scratching nervously at his cheek. "Samuel, may I ask you a question?

"Of course, on what topic?"

"If I may ask of you, Samuel," Daniel summoned a breath, "what are your thoughts on the topic of liberty?" He knew Whittenmore to have fought for the Crown, knew the man as a gallant, chivalrous adversary upon the dueling field, and as a steadfast friend. With the question, Daniel knew he had placed their relationship on the line.

"Liberty?" Samuel Whittenmore asked, seemingly shocked. "I would say liberty to be a fine thing, Daniel. A cherished thing even, but first I would ask liberty from what?"

In for a penny, in for a pound, the Scot thought. "Liberty from tyranny," Daniel answered too cagily, then looked at his friend and answered better and more completely. "Liberty from a royal German three thousand miles away."

"Ah, and what grievances can you list," the suddenly Socratic Whittenmore asked, "you, who has not yet spent a year here in the colonies."

"The blood of the clans at Culloden, the displacement of my people in the Clearances after," Daniel began, then paused a long moment and looked at his graying friend, locking eyes with the old Dragoon and saying, "the enforcement of illegal trading monopolies and taxation without representation."

"Ah, there are all good reasons, very good reasons indeed. But as to me," Sam Whittenmore said, "I would say that I wish my children, and their children, and theirs after to live free, and to rule themselves. Daily, I labor at my fields and cows, but freedom is my greatest legacy to them. To me, that is Liberty, and that is my answer to your question, too."

* * * * *

A small, sunlit clearing would be Trotter's and Pelenore's resting place until the final bugle call. Two of Parker's men hurriedly filled in their graves as Reverend Clark read from the Psalms. There was a nameless sense of urgency to their actions, consigning their souls to Heaven and their bodies to the Earth as each man worried about those still unaccounted for.

One by one, the search parties found them at that grave site with no new news of their searches. More and more hands found shovels and began the sad process of filing in the graves, or began dismantling Trotter's charred and savaged wagon. Reverend Clarke closed his Book and stood for an overlong moment in silent prayer. He looked over the group before him, their urgent looks and sad continence. Men took up pieces of sod or rocks and branches, concealing the graves as if they had never been there. Then each man looked at the tools he had used, picks, mattocks and shovels, none daring to ask the fated question, should they begin two more graves.

Clarke sighed compassionately, carefully pasting on his best, most sympathetic smile before summoning himself to giving that final, hated order. Then, over the rise came Daniel and grey haired Whittenmore walked down the trail, fiery-haired Meg astride the old Dragoon's horse, as hale and hearty as if the three had decided to take a stroll on a fine summer's day.

"The Lord of Hosts is with me and I will fear no evil." Revere whispered a not so silent prayer in gratitude that Reverend Clarke and a few others "amen'd" with reverent fervor. But then the Scot had walked through the crowd of grinning men to stand before him and say. "Alright, Paul, I'm in."

The duties of the gravesite, which before had seemed to be never-ending were quickly cleared up. With saws, axes and hammers, men with wagons took up the charred parts of Trotter's much repaired freight hauler and what was left of the contraband he had fetched, riding off quickly for Lexington, or the nearby hamlet of Concord. Reverend Clarke took Meg by the arm like a Queen and showed her to a seat on one of those wagons. "We will see you safe back to Lexington, the younger Harrington's have offered you a bed for as long as you have need."

"I cannot repay such…" Meg protested,

The reverend's shaggy head shook like a lion, or a rearing stallion, hearing none of it. "Nonsense, my girl, nonsense, 'tis our Christian duty. Besides, Ruth is just off her ninety days bed rest. No doubt, she would welcome the company."

"Ninety days?"

"Yes, God bless her, she delivered onto Young Jonathan a fine baby boy, strong, whole and well."

The last wagon left for Concord, Trotter's wagon was gone, as if it had never been. All that was left of the desperate, disastrous fight was spatters of blood upon the stones of the roadway.

Casually, Revere made his way to Daniel's side. "You have made a fine trophy there, Daniel Ferguson. Most here had given the girl up for dead."

"She has a spirit to her, a fire that would be hard to quench."

"That she is," Revere nodded in agreement. "But you have proven yourself a fine hunter again, a yeoman of the greenwood."

"I suppose." Daniel nodded cautiously, waiting for the silversmith to come to his point.

Revere smiled broadly at his friend. "We need folks of your skill. We will get you the powder, the powder we spoke of yesterday, you remember it?"

"Aye, all too well." He nodded

"With your knowledge of the lands and terrain, I bid you conceal it and keep charge of it, against the day."

"I am to be a night watchman?" Daniel asked.

The silversmith laughed a loud ringing sound that echoed through the woods. The grim humor in the face of his serious duties boded well. "There will be other duties, as they come up. Do you know of such a place?"

"Aye, I do," Daniel acknowledged, several secluded placed had already occurred to him. "It will have need of work, mind ye. Your cargo needs stay dry and well drained, but still accessible. I know of a place, close enough, but with green hides to shelter them and some digging to keep out the rain, your…cargo… will be well and dry… when you have the need."

"You have green hides."

Daniel paused, thinking of the salted deer skins tacked about on the walls of his residence. It would be a sacrifice, those hides, tanned and hung were to be his livelihood for some months to come. "Aye," he said simply, "I have."

Revere nodded. "Then we have an accord?"

"Aye." The Scot nodded, "You have my dirk upon it." Daniel said with great importance, drawing the blade partly from its sheathe. It was a knife with the character of a short sword, calling to Revere's mind descriptions of the Spartan Zaphos, or Roman Gladius, it also brought to stark relief the gulfs that lay between himself and the Scot before him.

Revere saw the intent of the drawn blade, an oath of fealty or death upon the very steel lain before him, but a simple glance at the Scotsman's eyes told the silversmith he would never grasp the weight of the act. Instead, Revere reached out and pushed the blade back into its sheath. "This is a new land, with new ideas. Here, you are a free man and owe fealty to none. No dirks, oaths or parchments signed in blood are needed between us, Daniel Ferguson," he said, stretching a hand across the table. "But I will take our hand on it, as one free man to another. Welcome to the Sons of Liberty."

Daniel's head spun, a lump rose in his throat as he in his home spun, buckskin breeches with their clumsy horn buttons and imperfectly dyed deer-hide brogues took the hand of a respected gentleman silversmith in his expensive riding cape and shoes custom made for each of his feet.

* * * * *

Reverend Clarke offered the shaggy Scot a horse. "It is a fine thing you accomplished, Mister Ferguson, a miracle unlike any I have heard of before." The Reverend said in a booming voice that somehow carried to Daniel and no further.

"I thank you, Reverend."

"Indeed, it reminds me I have been reticent in my own duties to the souls commended to my keeping upon this Earth. I had not ventured up to Cavanaugh's and invited you to Sunday services." Rarely had Daniel received such a loaded compliment, and the holy man left the statement there, hanging in the air between them like a cannon shell ready to burst.

"I had felt it in my best interest not to make myself a fixture in Lexington."

The Reverend Clarke nodded acceptingly at that statement, then added, conversationally. "Why, may I ask you, sir? In the strictest of confidences, I assure you. I sense the airs of a soldier about you, a warrior. Do you suffer under the Marks of Cain, son, do you fret over a life taken?"

"No, Reverend. I admit that sin, but my soul has already been shriven for those crimes." Daniel looked at the man, and realized as surely as if he had stepped into the darkness of a confessional, he was being offered absolution and what sanctuary the reverend could supply. "My Laird undoubtedly has pressed me as abandoning my clan in Scotland."

"So you were a soldier to a land owner." Reverend Clarke said without surprise, and hazarded. "and a deserter?" .

"Yes to the first, but not to King George. I never took an oath, I was commanded to go with the recruiters, and I did go, just not with the recruiters." Daniel said with the shrewd litigiousness of a Piccadilly Lawyer, but then drew in a deep breath, sighed and continued. "My Lord was considered loyal to the English, politically trustworthy, and he kept a cache of arms in his hall. I took my father's sword, this pistol and a Targe, though I broke it in order to bring it to the new world."

"Ah…your pardon, you "broke it"?" The reverend could not resist the question.

"Aye, I took the brass boss from it, pried free the brass pins and rim and packed them up with the lot of my dunnage when I signed aboard the *Beaver*."

"And you think this makes you a wanted man?"

"I am absent my Lairds will, and I took his property." The Scot nodded. "In Scotland, those would be deeds a man could stretch a rope for."

"But not ones a man would be chased to the ends of the Earth for, Daniel," The Reverend smiled paternally, "The Lord works in mysterious ways, my young friend. These are times which will test men's souls, and I think they will also see the day when we are right glad to have a warrior Scot among us, no matter his supposed crimes. Come 'round my house tomorrow, Daniel, and you and I will make a full accounting of your supposed crimes, to your satisfaction and the return of your sound sleep, I assure you." The massive Reverend leaned in his saddle and placed a fatherly hand upon the Scot's shoulder in reassurance, adding. "Also, my wife is a fine barber."

* * * * *

Mrs. Newman was a widow, her husband left her with a large, three story brick house famed for its scenic view of the harbor from the cupola on the North End, near the tall, majestic Old North church which you could see from anywhere in Boston, and even in Cambridge on the other bank of the Charles River. He also left her with mounting debts, mouths to feed and toward that end; she had converted that large house into a boarding establishment. Her accommodations, and cooking, while not overawing, had captured the attention of several of his Majesty's higher ranking officers. Colonel had followed Generals, then Majors, Captains and Lieutenants in their turns had followed. Toward that end, she was most likely one of the few who were glad of the

Ministerial army's occupation, or so Wainright thought. In truth, no one had ever thought to ask her.

Mrs. Newman made no offer of her own thoughts, she just charged the best coin she could for her accommodations, knowing that the young up and coming officers and supernumeraries would pay her prices in order to be close to their superiors.

None made much of Lieutenant Wainright's entrance into Widow Mrs. Newman's abode but for the two rankers at the door who raised their muskets in salute. Wainright was still in civilian laborer clothes beneath his riding cloak, but the men learned their faces. In the salon, card games were continuous, but Wainright was not interested right now, instead he sought his bed and sleep.

He mounted the stair to the third floor as quickly as his boots would allow. Throwing open his door to find, in his amazement, his roommate sorting through the bed linens.

"So, what new intelligences?", quipped Captain Henry Cochran as he quickly went on packing as if he had been doing nothing out of the ordinary.

Lieutenant Wainright paused in the doorway of the room he shared with this man, this pain in the ass, the son of General Cochran and currently assigned as Supernumerary to the Royal 23rd foot. The Captain had been going through Wainright's stockings, discarding some to the floor and packing the best of them into his grip.

Word had traveled fast, he realized. "Ah, no. I am afraid," Wainright said, wearily drawing himself to his bed. The civilian clothes he had worn were stiff with sweat and filthy, he was eager to get them off and get some sleep. Cochran was usually gone by now, sucking the ass of Colonel Maddison or Colonel Leslie.

"Oh?" Captain Cochran scoffed. He was possessor of the family's hawkish nose, which made his sneering continence all the more sharp, his chief promotions being his father's honored name, his father the general who had seen clear to purchase his son's way to Captain and this Colonial posting to make his fortune. The Captain had been in the America's for some two years now, and drown his boredom in the fleshpots of the Boston Wharfs one too many times. The diseases of Venus had not improved on his legendary bad temper. "Missed them entirely, then, did you?"

"Oh no, found them and killed the pair."

"Ah, quite right, quite right," His superior officer smiled sarcastically. "Filch enough from the wagons to buy your captaincy?"

Wainright bit his lower lip at that comment, not only was he being accused of common theft, but the Captain knew just the button to push. In order to purchase his way up to the next station in the British Officer class, he would need to find, by some means, the sum of 1500 pounds. Seeing that the Crown saw fit to pay him the pittance of four pounds a day, less his rent here at Mrs. Newman's, his mess fees, laundry fees, and other miscellaneous leeches applied daily to his pocketbook, Wainright felt he should see that sum sometimes after the dawn of the twentieth century.

"Wait a moment, "pair" you say?" The supernumerary Captain paused from sorting through the clump of shaving gear collecting on a nearby table and looked down his nose at the supernumerary Lieutenant, not missing a moment to belittle him. "But our little bird claims there were three of them."

"Yes, let the girl go. She's to work for the sovereign now."

Cochran dropped the best shaving brush into his bag. "Oh? Gave her solemn word did she? Pinky swear?"

"Oh, my no, you can't take the word of one of these Colonial girls, all whores and deceivers, they are. Most of them swear to anything. Some even say they don't have the pox." That stung the Captain, and he stayed moodily silent a moment, before abruptly beginning to whistle a happy tune and returning to folding shirts, dropping each into his bag. That alone brought Wainright's suspicion to a boil. "What are you doing?"

"What? Me?" Cochran simpered, taking another shirt from his drawer. Beneath it, he found a bottle of rum, cheerily added it to his bag before he closed it with victorious finality. "Packing my kit, seems I'm off to my new posting at Portsmith. Do have fun here with the regiment, bouncing about like an India rubber ball from unit to unit. I'm off to my command. Ta!"

The Captain even whistled a cheery tune as he sauntered down the hall to the stair, jauntily wishing the taciturn Widow Mrs. Newman the pleasure of the afternoon. Wainright sat on the bed for a long moment as the stiff, deathly silence resumed the room. Then, a string of profanity boiling from his lips, he lunged to his feet and almost made the door before he remembered he still wore the grimy clothes of a day laborer. Can't be seen upon the streets in them after sunrise, can't have a proper British officer gadding about in civilian clothes, people will ask questions they shouldn't. He drew on his best white leather small clothes and his scarlet jacket, affixing cross belt and garrison belt, and of course his gorget before stuffing his feet back into his boots and seeking the offices of the General, all thought of sleep forgotten.

Gage was absent, as Wainright expected the gentleman to be, but the man whom he desperately wanted to speak was in attendance. Samuel Kemble, Gage's personal and confidential secretary was posted at his desk, carefully recording the events of the day in a ledger.

Kemble held the esteemed position of personal secretary to the General by virtue of one salient fact, the General firmly believe that "blood keeps secrets best". The personal and confidential secretary's sister, Margaret Kimble Gage was wed most happily to the General, his deputy chief was a native of New Jersey, a Major in the regulars and his brother in law and another loyalist cousin had secured a position with the Horse Guards, and functioned as Gage's personal courier.

The personal secretary cut a singularly fine figure in his Scarlet tunic, especially since he was in fact, a loyal Provincial, born in the providence called New Jersey. "By the heavens, Lieutenant Wainright!", he enthused warmly as the Lieutenant entered, leaping to his feet in an enthusiastic greeting. "I had expected to see you later, what brings you to my offices so precipitously? Some good news, I don't doubt, as you have made so early an appearance from

your…exercises!"

"You can hang all that, Kemble! What the Hell is Captain bloody

Cochran doing dragging his diseased carcass off to a command while I'm

risking my ass on smuggler suppression duties." Wainright seethed, upsetting a

chair in his rage. He didn't care who Kemble's bloody cousin was, who his

sister was nor whom she slept with at night. "Why am I sodding about like

Galahad on bloody suicide missions when all I need do is go get the bloody Pox

off some bloody Belcher Lane whore to get a command."

"Calm yourself. Captain Cochran is off to Fort William and Mary in

Portsmith."

"I happen," The Lieutenant snapped angrily, "to be quite fond of New

Hampshire!"

"It's an invalid post! Not twenty men in the whole fort." Kemble

quickly whirled, shuffled some papers in a folder and nodded sharply to himself.

"Seven men, to be exact, and tubercular, malingering rankers all. The Corporal

has the gout, and the Sergeant only one eye and a wooden leg."

"And their commanding officer cannot piss without a tankard of rum!"

Wainright snapped back with rising rancor.

Samuel Kemble set the file aside, paused a moment and spoke again,

his tone conciliatory. "Lieutenant, though I will not repeat this, the General is

sick of Captain Cochran, of his malingering, incompetence, of his bloody father and his whining. He has found a useless post for a useless and poxed officer. Of

you, sir, the General has a much higher opinion."

Wainright paused a long moment, letting the enormity of the candid

statement sink in, then hazarded an interjection of his own. "Meaning?"

CHAPTER 6

"I'm in."

It seemed the words were no more than out of his mouth that he regretted them. Daniel had not, it seemed, known just how "in" he was to be, or how quickly. Less than a fortnight from his rescue of young Meg, and subsequent rescue of himself, there was a desperate tapping upon his door in the hours of darkest evening.

His heart had stopped at the sound, and as the dogs growled at the door, his first thought was to arm himself. Double barreled pistol in his hand, he opened the door to a man with his hat pulled low and mufflers about his face.

"We come at the behest of Paul Revere," the man said in a hushed voice. Daniel automatically assumed the man meant himself and the burdened horse he lead, until the tired Scot saw another man crouching near the path, watching in all directions.

"What, already?" Daniel boggled at the thought, rubbing a hand through his hair, which now only brushed his shoulders, unlike it had done less than a week ago.

"No time like the present." The muffled man quipped, and studied him with inquisitive eyes. "Are you prepared?"

"Like as not." Daniel sighed, clipping the pistol to his belt.

"Were you asleep?"

"No." Daniel said, truthfully. He would like to have answered differently, but sleep had eluded him since the marshes of Sudbury. He had lay in his bed, among the dogs, staring at a hole forming itself in the thatched ceiling above him and pondering the questions that crowded his mind.

The horse was burdened with two hogsheads of powder, both marked with the Royal broad arrow signifying them property of the king. Heavy wooden barrels about the size of a large dog, Daniel inspected them and mused he just might be able to get both beneath his bed and be back into it within a reasonably short time. "Alright, let's be about this."

"Right you are!" The muffled man enthused, and signaled his compatriot with a raised hand. The other man nodded and gave a sharp whistle. The shrill call summoned three other men with like-burdened horses.

They off-loaded the mounts and concealed the barrels in the greenery behind his house, carefully camouflaging them before the leader of the crew said. "We will be back in three days, maybe more. Be ready for our signal."

"Will I have as much again?"

"Doubtful. The others can…"

"Others?"

"Of course, you do not think you are the only man concealing powder for us in the district, do you?"

Daniel pondered that for the rest of the night, and slept no more. He found his thoughts turning to Meg. Days passed, and Daniel set to his new duties concealing the King's Reserve before it was to be brought to him once again. Daniel wished he could see the girl, but true to his word, the silversmith's friends made another trip to Lexington in four days. This time with pony kegs of powder and great half keg the size of an anvil.

His hunting duties served him well in this new employment, as in his wanderings he had found a cave set high in one of the hills in the greenwoods between Lexington and Lincoln. Daniel had spent several days improving that cave to its new task with borrowed picks, axes and saws. Shorn green timbers to lie across the stone and dirt floor to keep the casks, and their contents dry, and green hides lay over them as protection.

The task took days, in the evenings he busied himself into the dark hours with neglected chores, and a half hearted attempt at playing the slovenly, lay about Scot for the amusement of those who might be spying upon him for the King's shilling. When he found his tartan cloth, mended and laundered on his rude dining table, he wondered how long it had lay there, and he realized his new duties were causing him to neglect his own needs.

* * * *

Ruth Harrington had borne a fine, strong boy, who was the center of her world, absorbing most of her time and she was glad to see Meg, a woman of roughly her own age. Her husband, Jonathan, who everyone called Junior, was ever present and eager to attend the child, but, Ruth explained, there were things a woman needed another woman for. Try as they might, there were things a man need not try to do.

One of those things, Meg noted, was not to get up in the dark hours before dawn to feed the babe. "Ah, and what would he do but fetch a sucking bottle and ply the little dear to his slumber with warm beer and a hope?" Ruth gently chided the younger girl. "God hath equipped us better for these weary moments."

"I suppose," she considered Ruth's words, then, with a laugh, added. "Men, what do we need them for?"

"Well," Ruth rubbed the babe's head as he suckled at her breast. "They make it much easier to get one of these. Only happened once before, you know, and He was something of a special case." She smiled at the crucifix upon the wall, then crossed herself penitently at the possibly sacrilegious joke.

Meg did not cross herself; she smiled and laughed appreciatively. She found herself less a tavern servant and more an honored guest, wanted for her conversation instead of her menial skills. The first day of her arrival, she had slept late in a fine bed with blankets and a feather mattress, and when she had rose apologetically, was told her rest was all that was expected of her. The next day, she had attempted to clean the noon meal dishes, and was told, gratefully that it was not needed. Slowly, the grateful new mother accepted a set of spare hands, but the tavern girl still felt her value in the simple joy of standing about gossiping about women of whom she knew nothing about; who was pregnant, who was sweet upon whom and what they were doing about it and where.

It was a strange situation she found herself in, and in most any other time, it would be Heaven on Earth. But her dreams were haunted by the

Lieutenant's lusting eye and hot iron, and her ears rang with the officer's

demands she spy upon this Paul Revere and Daniel. Meg only wanted to escape,

to get free of Lexington, of Menotomy, of Boston, and to run.

"I appreciate you sitting up with me, at this chore. I could not ask

Jonathan to do it. He has a busy day tomorrow, the butchering time comes, long

days and late nights. A good time for a young lady to take store of the young

bucks about, with an eye to the future, though. Young Nathanial, Jonathan's

cousin is fifteen, old enough to think of a family. . ."

Meg watched Ruth with a hooded expression but Ruth eyes flashed

with hope. The tavern maid knew an invitation when she heard it, and

conspicuously did not take the bait. Ruth made a long pantomime of stroking the

babe's head as he fed, then ventured another try. "Of course that Wild Scot,

Daniel Ferguson, he would be a fine catch also, broad shoulder, rugged

Scotsman that he is..."

"A fine man to be sure." Meg heard herself agree, the words sounded

like they had been drug from her.

"But...?"

"I feel quite at sea in all this." Meg admitted. "The last time I chose, I

chose very, very wrongly. I am afraid I don't know what to do next."

"We can talk about that, I imagine." Ruth smiled softly.

But, Meg told herself, she liked the life she had carved for herself this

long year past, living without the permission of a man as a *femme solo*. "But as

we said, what could he get for me I cannot get myself."

"Words like that will end you a spinster." Ruth whispered like a friend might warn one dear to her, then Ruth offered a casual yawn to restart conversation. "Reverend Clarke gave a fine sermon tonight, don't you think?" When Meg gave no better response than a grunt, she added. "When he spoke of the evils of Allhallows eve, I was reminded of your Daniel's bravery."

The girl brushed a strand of auburn hair from her face and parroted back, "my Daniel?"

"He did risk all to tempt the marshes for you..."

"He was... quite brave."

"And industrious.

I am not quite so blinded by love as that, Meg demurred with a smile. "Of that I do not know, they say Scots have a lazy streak to them, or at least my father used to say such things. And there are those about town who say he lays in late into the morning."

"Not this day he did not, when I was feeding the boy, I saw him walking out of town, headed Concord way." She looked out the darkened window, as if the Scot had left a luminescent trail. "A man leaving so early in the morning must be about an important task, and want to be home in the early afternoon." Meg said nothing to that, also, and Ruth scowled at that. She fixed the girl in a knowing gaze. "You're leaving, aren't you?"

It took the red-haired girl a moment to answer. "Yes." She answered like a penitent child.

The knowing gaze turned misty, "when?" The mother begged as her child nursed upon her.

"Soon," Meg whispered, brushing an errant strand of hair from her face, "tonight, I think."

"Tonight?" Ruth parroted with misty fearful eyes. "Where will you go?"

"Away. . .far from Boston. West, I think."

"Lexington is west of Boston." Ruth teased, but the red haired girl did not answer. "Stay yet the night, Meg? All I say is that this is not the worst place to seek shelter."

* * * * *

The town of Acton was a good ten miles from Lexington, a long trudge through Concord and onward. It was a pleasant enough jaunt, and the making of a pleasant enough day for it, Daniel thought as he watched the sun rise from Punkatasett Hill. He had trudged across the North Bridge in the darkness, watched farmers and laborers walk to their daily duties in the grey of false dawn. But among the fading shadows of the military drilling field, he enjoyed the sunrise before once again marching onward toward the Acton smithy of Isaac Davis, a man he knew by name only.

Footfall after footfall brought him closer to their meeting, the Scot mused. Paul Revere had instructed Daniel to call upon the man, and said little else about it, but Daniel mused he had staked more than a day's walk on less from the silversmith.

Acton itself looked like every other Provincial settlement carved from the trees of the new world. A few inquiries had gotten him rough directions to the Blacksmith's, but none offered the stranger a friendly guide. He trudged along, enjoying the early summer breezes that traced at the air, the sound of the wind in the leaves

"To find a blacksmith, listen for the horses." It was one of those old Scottish witticisms his Da repeated endlessly, but once again it proved right. He heard the horses, and smelled them, before he found the smithy. Nervous horses pawed the muddy ground as a muscular man's hammer rang musically at his anvil, stopped abruptly to work a leather bellows to stoke the flames to a cherry red.

Footsore from the long walk, Daniel paused at the rails, observed the horses with a practiced eye. Then he looked into the confines of the smithy as all sound abruptly ended from it. The burly man, dirty from a days work, eyed him suspiciously but did not journey from the forge to challenge him.

He had been, he realized, unconsciously rude. "Isaac Davis?" He called, perhaps a bit too hurriedly.

"I am." The man answered, readily but warily. "And who might you be, friend?"

"Daniel Ferguson, sir." The Scot named himself. "I was sent by.."

"Paul Revere." The stocky blacksmith finished for him, nodding affirmatively. "Your reputation precedes you," Then he said nothing for a long time as his corded arms worked the bellows to stoke the coals to a red heat.

Daniel stepped close to the blazing coals of the hearth, took command of the

bellows and began stoking the coals with a practiced eye. The blacksmith eyed

him professionally for a long moment, then content that the newcomer knew his

employment, Davis took his long blacksmith's tongs and trusty hammer in hand.

He drew from the cherry red inferno a piece of blazing hot metal, examining the

shape of the piece and the color of the heat with a practiced eye. Then he thrust

it deep into the coals again, shifting it minutely in the red hot inferno as the

blazing coals roared around it.

At length, Davis drew the metal free again and beat it many stout blows

with a hammer before quenching it fully in a tub of water. Only then, he turned

back to the Scot with an abashed look. "Once begun I cannot stop, or lose hours

of work. I must appear to be a wretched host. You are no stranger to the forge, I

will give you that, Mr. Ferguson." He chuckled, toweled his face and arms of

sweat with a convenient cloth, leading Daniel from the smithy. "Paul sent me an

express some weeks ago, told me of your case."

Daniel followed the burly man, expected to go to the saltbox house, but

was lead to the barn instead. Behind the house and smithy, a long grassy field

lead to a berm of earth which could only be a shooting range. The tack room

was an arsenal, long muskets racked the walls and leaned in the corners,

cartridge boxes and bayonets hung from every available surface, from nails in

the wall to the backs of a few cast-off chairs on the dirt floor.

Impressed, Daniel surveyed the room, leaning his own musket in the

jamb of the door as he walked from each rack. Even in his Laird's great home, he had scarce seen such a collection of arms, he mused. Then the familiar, heart stopping sound of a musket hammer being cocked made the Scot whirl in a shock. The Acton blacksmith had walked around him on his inspection and took up the forgotten musket. In a casual way borne of habit, flicking open the pan and dusting it free of powder, "Wooley and Sons," Isaac Davis declared, inspecting the maker's marks upon the iron of the weapon, "Tory gun makers of Boston. You find yourself in possession of a fine Militia fowler, Daniel Ferguson. But how you came to hold it is the question."

Daniels' guts crawled up into his throat, a canny Scot, he knew a challenge when he heard it. The blacksmith thought him a spy, and worse, one bearing the markings of slovenly spy-craft, at that. Head spinning at the implications, Daniel tried to craft a reasonable explanation, and somewhere in the midst of his wool gathering heard himself saying. "It was a gift."

"A kingly gift indeed, sir," the blacksmith nodded and then demanded, "from who?"

"Samuel Whittenmore." Daniel supplied, there seemed no point in any subterfuge. "He is my acquaintance and particular friend in Menotomy."

Suspicion drained from the burly man. "Oh, alright then," he nodded and sat himself at the table loaded with leather cuttings being fashioned to cartridge boxes.

As if he had not heard the Smith's acknowledgement, Daniel further blurted out "He said he acquired it…"

"If Whittenmore gave it to you, I can well imagine how he acquired it." Davis nodded, gestured for the other man to sit himself at the table beside him. "You do well to call that man a friend, even in his seventies, he is a rare man, one to stand aside from." Davis fell upon the musket with screwdrivers and a twist of black steel called a musket tool.

"Seventies?" Daniel watched with interest as his musket fell to pieces on the scarred table,

"You are right to correct me. Mister Whittenmore had a birthday, last April. I believe he is eighty," the smith said, distracted by his labors.

Eighty, certainly, a rare age to gain in this time, as the Scot had guessed the man much closer to fifty. He pondered that until the piles of accoutrements scattered through the room drew his attention. From a discarded pile by the table he drew a simple black pouch with straps to carry it upon a belt. Beneath the flap, a wooden block nestled in it, drilled with a dozen or more holes for the carrying of paper-wrapped ball and black powder to reload a musket. "That an old cartridge box is a relic of the French and Indian war," Davis explained, never pausing in his work upon the firelock, "at first I thought to supply them to my men, but…"

"Your men?" Daniel queried.

"Yes, I am captain of the Acton Minute men. I sometimes forget that Acton is not the whole of the world. Everyone around here knows, but why would you." The man chided himself cheerily, like a man who enjoys his employment, then continued. "I thought to supply them to my…group, but the newer pouches slung from the shoulder which the Ministerial troops carry seem much more functional and popular. You may have it if you wish." The musket lock was spread before the Blacksmith in pieces smaller than Daniel had ever seen before, and the Scot fretted that it could ever be made whole again when Davis spoke again. "Your mainspring is indeed broken, no surprise there. Wooley has always been a poor hand at the crucible as spring steel goes, but we can remedy that." With precise movements, he sorted through the small parts of the mechanism. "You also have some cast off parts of ...Spanish or Portuguese manufacture, I believe. Well fit, but old. I think we'd best blunt tomorrow's tragedy and replace them also. I foretell a late evening to get all this completed."

Daniel's mouth dropped. "I...I cannot ask you to spend a day's labor for me, as my purse cannot possibly..."

"My labors have already been well compensated, Mister Ferguson." He assured the Scot, setting aside the disassembled musket parts and scrubbing his hands on a discarded scrap of cloth. "And, I think we might consider prying free this sun crest in the stock, unless you have grown fond of it, Mister Ferguson."

"No, no." Daniel said, trying to make it sound like a jest. "Pry away."

The gunsmith laughed. "And we shall begin." He said, and for a time unmeasured after, Daniel did not lack for activity. There were many other duties that commanded him aside from the furnace bellows. Under Davis's watchful eye, he cleaned and oiled every part of the musket, even the new ones the blacksmith created with files and other tools at his anvil and forge.

Daniel pried the sunburst crest from the wooden stock and Davis, without a word, gathered the brass plate and even the nails into a crucible and set it upon the coals. Turning back to Daniel, he handed the Scot a chisel and instructed him, "We'll turn that into a patch box to disguise the nail holes." Then the smith was at his bellows again, applying gusts of air into the coal until they were a flaring red orange like the face of the sun.

Daniel strayed from his duties at the chisel, watching the brass sun lose its form, folding in on itself until it seemed to collapse into a thick molten ocean. The blacksmith watched all this with a professional disinterest, gathering a mould from a shelf in the forge, grasping the crucible with tongs to pour the molten brass into its new form.

That done, Davis became talkative again, "You might benefit from a sling," he suggested, "there are a box of swivels I made during the winter over there in the corner, along with some stout leather straps."

Daniel fell to the pile in the corner, boxes of items and parts, some of military bearing, others as mundane as horse bits. At length, he victoriously found them, with a grain sack of leather straps suitable for slings.

When he turned, Daniel found Isaac Davis sitting upon the stone half-wall of his forge, the parts of Daniel's musket lock spread on a cast off piece of canvas before him. The Scot paced forward with a hesitant hope, could the work have been completed already? Would he now see the smith reassemble the musket with the same careless ease with which he had taken it apart? "Are we done?" He heard himself ask.

"Almost," Isaac Davis smiled, and presented Daniel with one of those twisted metal musket tools. Daniel hesitated, and the blacksmith laughed. 'Come now, my friend, there is no magic to it, as you will soon see."

Slowly, the lock, and then the entire musket went from pieces upon a scrap of grain sack to a whole and working firelock. Sling and lock, barrel and butt stock, Daniel hefted the weapon, screwed a flint into the jaws of the lock and tested it. The hammer fell, and sparks sprayed from the frizzen and pan. "So far, so good, now we shoot it." Davis nodded happily at that, handed the Scot a powder horn. "And best we hurry, as the sun does not seem well disposed to a long shooting session."

The British Army demanded a standard of three shots a minute, Daniel would not have done himself honors before them, but what shots he made were accurate enough for the smooth bore firelock. Davis watched him fire with a practiced eye, and when they were done, he asked in the fading light. "May I invite you for dinner, my Hannah is a fine cook, and we have a spare room for your use this evening. The roads back to Lexington are not so peaceful as I should allow you to wander them after dark."

The unsolved deaths of his benefactor, Mister Trotter, fresh in his mind, Daniel nodded gratefully and the two strode from the shooting range to the saltbox house in the middle of Davis's lot.

Hannah Davis was a tiny woman with a spirit that climbed to the mountaintops, with two children wrestling on the floor and a third a mere babe in her arms, she still looked at her husband like a virgin at a maypole festival. And Isaac Davis returned the favor to his lovely and lively bride.

The boys wrestling upon the floor stopped their contest as carved wooden horses upon the hearth seemed better sport. The Scot watched the two in their gallivanting and could not hide an admiring smile at the luck the smith had been granted in his domestic life.

Daniel instantly felt like an intruder between the two, but they assured him it was not so. Dinner was a meat pie and a warm new beer, all of a quality Daniel had not seen since the great halls of his Laird in Scotland. He restrained himself for pride and politeness, but his hunger was plain, and Hannah laughed and wordlessly shifted the last portion onto his pewter plate.

Daniel gratefully took up his spoon again. "Was my admiration so apparent?" He asked.

Hannah coquettishly dodged the question. "You have the look of a man who needs fattening up." She teased. "Surely with your manner, those blue eyes and fair hair, you are beating off the women of Lexington with a stick.'

Isaac, a fine young blonde haired girl in his lap, perhaps five and the spitting image of her mother, joined in the amusement at the Scot's expense. "You need a good woman in your life."

"Indeed." The Scot smiled, shoveling at the flakey morsels of the pie shell upon the plate before him. "Until these last few days, I had not noticed some of the great voids in my life."

Hannah laughed gaily, her husband and the children joining with

Daniel, until the tow haired girl in the blacksmith's lap clapped a hand to her

mouth and her laughter dissolved into a horse, wet cough. The room fell silent as

if smothered under a wet blanket. Davis watched the girl with a tinge of fear

upon his face, and Daniel looked from him to his wife, finding an identical look

on both parents.

The Blacksmith looked from his wife to his dinner guest, abashed.

"There is Canker rash about," he advised, warily, barely concealed a silent

prayer.

Daniel balked at the words, quickly caught himself and pasted on a

brave face. He looked at the husband and wife before him, to the baby in

Hannah's arms and the other three children. Of the four of them, Daniel knew,

the Davis's would be very fortunate to only bury two to the deadly disease.

The children were bundled off to their beds, and Daniel shown to his

room, where he sat silently staring out the window, worrying over the dear little

ones. Peering into the darkness, he watched Isaac Davis trudge back to his forge,

like as not seeking his familiar place where he could worry into the wee hours.

When the fear could do no more to him, Daniel sought the blankets and

found his slumber thinking about a red-headed tavern girl back in Lexington and

fretting about the gathering storms around them. There was, he knew, little he

could do, but see what the dawn would bring.

* * * * *

General Thomas Gage raised a silver thimble-sized chalice of Brandy by its thin stem and pronounced, in clipped, precise tones. "To your success, sir."

Lieutenant Colonel George Maddison inclined his head in a ceremonial bow of acknowledgement. "And to your very good health, sir," he replied unctuously, and both men effortlessly drained the tiny containers in a single throw.

It was an infinitesimal amount of a very good brandy from Gage's private cellar, the rarity of the vintage silent proof of the importance Gage placed upon this mission. Gage's latest entreaty for more troops for constable duties here in the Colonies had been pointedly, unquestionably dismissed by Parliament and dispatched to his attention by the first ship. He was allowed only a paltry number of Royal Marines and told to be on about it. With the Colonials becoming more bold by the day, the General had struck on a plan, brilliant in it simplicity, He could not defuse the mobs, but he could deprive them of the limbs of Mars. The Americas already had a paltry shortage of arms makers, little lead, and only a sad substitute for natural flint. Even their powder must be imported, and that was the meat of the present plan. It had been formed a short time earlier, when William Brattle, a strong Cambridge Loyalist whispered in Gage's ear of an ongoing rebel plot. It seemed the rabble rousers were spiriting away the stores in the provincial powder house.

The powder house was in Cambridge, atop a lonely hill, far away from the residential property of Boston, the powder stocks in it owned, variously by the towns and municipalities, excepting some casks and barrels marked with the broad arrow and called the King's powder, which these rebels and brigands sought to usurp. Gage was determined to move now, before one more horn of powder disappeared into the ether.

To do this, he had allowed Maddison, a promising, experienced officer, with a reputation for spit and polish discipline and unswerving loyalty, his pick of the garrison to complete it. Maddison deliberated and chose 260 men of the Grenadiers and light company skirmishers. Grenadiers were the strongmen of the army, big chested bully boys with the instincts of wolves. Light Infantry, or "lights" as they were called, were skirmishers who slipped ahead of the main troops to pot-shoot officers and artillerymen. Gage, having commanded light infantry in the earlier Seven Years war, found them to be quick witted, agile men with zeal and the initiative to fight independently.

Boarding thirteen navy longboats, two hundred and sixty men rowed across the harbor and up the Mystic River, landing near the Medford road. There, it was only a quick march to the outskirts of Cambridge, and the powder house. It rose from the gloom ahead of them, a looming tower-like stone cylinder mounted with a brass rod at its crown to discharge lighting bolts. Maddison recalled one of these Colonist chaps had come up with that last bit of ingenuity, seemed it dispelled the electrical current of the thunderbolts, rendering it harmless instead of devastatingly explosive.

Lieutenant Colonel Maddison caught sight of a small group of a dozen men hurriedly approaching him there on the green. All, save one, wore the tight fitting leather cap of the Lights, and that one wore his night cap and shirt. As distance closed and vision improved in the gloom, Maddison recognized Lieutenant Wainright briskly escorting the sheriff, Colonel David Phips, in his night shirt, to his presence. The Lieutenant, though technically supernumerary to the fourth, was fast becoming a favorite for his willingness to get things done, and Maddison had picked him for the duty of rousting the royally appointed Sheriff of Middlesex County, who had gained a reputation for sloth and inattention to his charges that bordered on the suspicious. Still, he perfunctorily announced. "Colonel Phips, I presume?"

"You may presume as you like, damn you sir!", the sheriff blustered. He was a portly man, his nightcap covering a balding, graying pate. "What is the meaning of this, dragging men from their home and hearth in the wee hours?"

"I am Colonel George Maddison, of his Majesty's army." The officer announced, imperiously. "The King has need of his powder, as his representative, I have come to collect it."

The Sheriff's jaw dropped, he made several attempts at speaking. When he finally did, his mood had changed considerably. "Your servant, sir," he announced, with a nod of his head that was almost a bow. One of the light infantrymen presented the suddenly docile sheriff with his keys, and clad in nightshirt and cap, the Sheriff of Middlesex County, opened the heavy wooden door to the stone fortification and warehouse.

"Good," enthused Maddison, handing Wainright a lantern with officious airs, "Lieutenant Wainright, do go and inventory the premises, please."

"Er....Yes, sir." The lieutenant of Lights said, hesitantly. Usually he leapt at such opportunities, to be the first in anything, All the better to garner that coveted "mention in dispatches", but in this case. "But, sir...the facility is stocked full, or at least we hope it to be stocked full of powder, sir. Explosive black powder and...." He held up the lantern. "This is an open flame, sir."

Good lord, Maddison chided himself, Too bloody early, silly bloody mistake. "He peered into the black cavity of the door. "Bloody dark, can't see a hand before your face," Maddison intoned stoically, clasping his hands behind him, "nothing to do but await the dawn."

"If I may, sir," The Lieutenant of Light Infantry offered, unctuously as he set aside the lantern, considering its light to be a fine mark to shoot at. "Intelligence mentioned a number of field pieces at the Cambridge meeting house, this pause seems an excellent time to.....:

"Yes, yes Lieutenant," Maddison said without looking back at him, "be on with it, fine lad."

Hiding a smile, Wainright snapped off a salute. "Yes, sir!"

Maddison was watching the grey of the horizon, as if he could command the sun to rise sooner. "Due caution and mind the time. We march at eight, sharp."

"Yes sir." Wainright simpered, called out for his company. Once safely out of the sight of the Colonel in the gloom, he quickly ordered his men to a fast jog, eager to get into Cambridge proper before the rising of the sun.

The cannon were hardly concealed, he found them easily before the Provisional house, two old iron six-pounders, their carriages half dry rotted but most likely serviceable enough to get them back to Boston, provided they go slowly enough.

"Private Howe," Wainright commanded, "requisition horses for the traces!" Howe was one of the King own Lights, a quick witted, shifty eyed bastard who showed a merciless efficiency as a forager. The soldier saluted and was gone at a trot, and within a few moments was back, not with horses, but the erstwhile Lord Trenton.

"Good evening, my dear friend." Wainright sketched a polite bow. Had he remembered that Trenton made Cambridge his home, he might not have so quickly volunteered for this mission.

"Good morning, Lieutenant." Trenton made a much deeper, even more formal bow. "I am amazed how the Lord works, sometimes, sir. I was in the midst of sending you a missive, your... sparrow, I had word not an hour ago she plans to fly west."

"West, you say?", Wainright asked, shocked. Trenton's men had been keeping an eye on the little tramp since her rescue, but the Lieutenant had presumed she had found comfortable quarters with the bumpkins there, and would proceed to burrow in like a tick to wait out the winter.

"Well, one of my…associates said Ruth Harrington was distraught this morning in his dry goods store, and said your…girl… planned to leave this day, indeed she was not found in her bed this morning."

The little tramp was giving him the slip? No, at least not immediately, for Trenton's men had been watching the dead smuggler's tavern, shuttered though it was. She had not gone there, but she would, she will go to Menotomy first, to that tavern, he would bet his life upon it. "What was the name of that place she worked? The dark mule?"

"The Black Horse, sir," Trenton answered unctuously.

"She will go there. When does the little trollop plan to fly the coop?"

"I believe this night."

"This night," Wainright nodded, forming a plan. "Private Randal, I will need three more horses. Sergeant, see the men home, quickly as the carriages will allow. What did you say that night, Mr. Trenton two hours by horse back to Menotomy?"

* * * * *

In the grey of dawn, Meg realized it was better to slip from the Harrington's door in the darkness, so not to concern dear Ruth. She had told herself that time and time again as she walked the six miles or so to Menotomy. The sun had risen as she walked and climbed to a cheery height over the trees, but it did not help her mood.

She slipped in the back door of the *Black Horse Tavern* like a thief, not in the front, beneath the carved, faded sign by which the tavern was known. The kitchen stove there was cold, as if it had not been used in months, instead of something like a week and a half, approaching two weeks. She padded slowly through the silent kitchen toward the barroom. Inwardly, her heart warred with itself, since abandoning her father's house, she had told herself to live by a single rule, "be ready to drop all and leave, at any time". There was no "thing" worth her life or her freedom.

Easy thing to think, easy to say when you lived well, until your entire life could be rolled up into a blanket. Then the idea of starting over somewhere without that tattered and patched blanket became a dreaded thought that could not be borne.

There was always a "but"; a single thought kept drawing her back here like a moth to a flame. The simile was a good one, there, as no moth ever survived his pursuit of a flame.

The things she came for now were neither gold, nor lofty treasure, they were so absolutely common as to embarrass her. Trotter had afforded her no room of her own, with the passing of the sun, she would sleep on sacks she stuffed herself with straw and fragrant herbs as her mattress and a simple blanket. In good weather, the sacks would hang on a line to air in the sun. In bad weather, they would fester in the barn with the horse flops and the pigs.

At the beginning of each day, she and Abigail would bundle their mattress sacks out, and roll their possessions into their blankets in a tight roll, putting these behind the bar.

So, she need only dash the few yards to the bar. Just a few bare yards, she told herself, a distance anyone could accomplish, she swung open the door. Just grab a single rolled up blanket and be gone, simple.

"Dearie!", the Lieutenant cried from the bar, where he lounged resplendent in his scarlet red coat, "come in, come in! Have a drink with me, a little nip to wear off the chill! We have so much to catch up on!" He was in his cups again, bottles scattered on the bar top before him, another in his hand.

Meg heard the heavy footfalls of army boots on the well trod floor behind her, she glanced back as one of the redcoats shut the door and then another familiar sound caused her to look back, the Lieutenant meaningfully cocked the pistol he had laid upon the bar top. "Do come in, Dearie. You're letting the heat out. After all, you left in the middle of our last discussion." At some unseen behest, a hand landed in the small of her back and with a shove, she found herself hurtling into the saloon, stumbling into the bar hard enough to take her breath away.

"Where's Abigail?" She demanded, fighting for air as she tried to turn and look at the officer of the Ministerial troops. The fire was out in the hearth, casting a cold gloom over the saloon.

"Oh, you mean the little black trollop? Gone, I imagine. We came here directly after you decided to go play wild Indian in the swamps, told her a patrol had discovered her master dead on the roads to the coast. She didn't waste a minute, gathered a few things, futtered a few of my men for tolls and fare and made for the trees." Wainright said with a droll shrug, and then added. "I'll note she never gave you a second thought. Now, are you having a drink or not, my sweet?" He teased, tinting his words with a dark, mocking tone. "Or does the house madam have a curfew for…gentleman callers?"

"I am not a whore," she protested, fighting for breath. The defense so constant it was almost tired. Near the main door, she could see the form of a man in the shadows. Another, bull-chested and mustachioed leaned casually in the kitchen door frame.

"No, no," he assuaged, his tone still mocking as he set down the heavy looking pistol beside him, "but, I think as I awaited your arrival, I have determined what you are." From his scarlet coat, he drew a newspaper and with great fanfare, read ". "From the Carolina Examiner. Absent this 17th instant, one Maureen Bulger, may use the name Higgins, or Ross, which was her Mother's maiden name." With glorious self confidence, he walked around the bar, struck a pose before her and continued reading with a dramatic flair. "Of red hair and singularly fine complexion, aged 17 years and has a peculiar birthmark upon her left shoulder in the shape of a gull wing." Taking great liberties, the Redcoat grabbed the girl, and drew down the shoulder of her loose blouse, nodding to himself in confirmation of the mark, and continued. "Had on or took with her sundry clothes of three distinct suits, and two fine new shoes of highly glossed leather, with silver buckles. Also has in her possession a quantity of silver, and may be in the company of a Nathan Higgins, a wastrel of ruddy continence who fashions himself an able seaman and may attempt to pass himself off as such, He is of strong build and is over proud of his looks and hair." The officer leaned forward. "Red hair, fine complexion, the birthmark is there, I believe I have found our long absent Maureen!"

Of all the violent, lustful abuses she had inoculated herself for, this simple familiar exposure took her breath and stole her wits and she said nothing.

"Is this you? Answer me, girl!", he demanded, drawing back a hand to strike.

Meg recoiled from the blow, gasping, "yes."

"This advertisement is almost a year old. How long has it been?", he asked, and when she did not answer, the lieutenant smiled. "Ever bit of a year and a half, I'll wager." With an almost casual wave of his hand, the burly sergeant and the other soldier drifted from the room, and the officer paused to listen for the click of the latch as they left the Black Horse, "but now, to supposition. Since our parting, what was it, a week, two ago? I have found myself often in the house of Trenton. He a gentleman and a most unquestionably loyal subject of the King, your father would undoubtedly love him. A most excellent host and has made his library available for me. Do you read, my dear? No, I suppose not, why would you. The ability to read is an asset beyond belief, post life can be quite dull, you know. The article does not start as others I have read, and I have found myself reading many. They say "serving girl, or servant, some say slave, this doesn't. I can only presume you are something other to the Judge. Not a milk maid, certainly not a whore. Dare I presume... his daughter?"

And as he said it, all of her resolve drained away, and she slumped to the floor, stifling a sob. She had prepared herself for debasement, for the chains of prison and even a rope, but not for that one word, exposing all her crimes and moral failings.

The Lieutenant made dramatic about face, said "I will alert your father to arrange your…joyful return to his fold."

"No." she squealed, more vehement than before. She was on her feet, real fear in her eyes. "No, please."

"I seem to have finally have seized your attention," the officer snapped. "I take it you do not want to go home?"

"No, please."

"And what, may I ask, are you willing to do for my . . . consideration?"

She presumed his meaning and shrank away.

"I have no interest in futtering you girl. I play for real stakes." Wainright snapped, then paused and asked, meaningfully. "Where is your love, the wastrel Higgins?

"Gone." She whispered through tears.

"And what of the silver? Gone too, I'll wager likely at the same time." The Redcoat officer paused and let out a dramatic sigh. "Love is like that."

She stifled her tears, commanding herself to stop this feminine display before one who cared not at all for her feelings. But the careless question brought to the fore of her mind a name she had forced herself not to consider for a time uncounted. His hair was the color of new flax, and hung past his shoulders, unfashionably long for the day, even in a queue. His eyes a unique grey, and she had been young, and swept from her feet by them. She did love

him, or had thought she did at the time, and thought he did so. "I did love him."

"And your King, girl? Do you love your King?" Wainright demanded.

"Your father is a Loyalist, his name has come to mean unwavering loyalty in

Military circles."

"What has my father's name to do with anything?", she demanded,

shivering in tearful fright.

Giving voice to such a statement brought bile to Wainright's throat and

thoughts of Captain Cochran's mocking face. "You will find, girl, a fine name

means a great deal. But I judge you too young to note that now." He paced back

toward the bar, spun on his heels and commanded her. "Get you back to

Lexington, there is a tavern there called Buckman's. Find employment there."

She hesitated, but saw a glimmer of hope in his words. "I do not know

what employment may be found there, sir."

"I could care what sort of work you find; bus tables, lay upon your

back. Women hear things in a tavern, take note and report to me. Go at once."

"I would be little good in the middle of the wilderness, sir. You mistake

me, sir, for one of Roger's Rangers."

"I mistake you for nothing, girl." Wainright spat. "Get you to

Lexington, there is a pit of vipers to work your ways upon."

"But you know this Revere, your actions were plain enough in that,

why am I not to watch him?"

"Ah, had I only found you earlier, my dear. Revere lost his last doxy to childbirth, just a few months ago. He's found a new one now, so your idea just

won't do. Aside, with a thousand or more redcoats in Boston and you searching

me up for every bit of trivial, you would be exposed in days. Lexington's not far

away, not twenty miles, I'll ride out to visit you." He smiled maliciously at her,

reaching behind the bar for another bottle. He pulled the cork with his teeth,

looked at it for a moment before continuing to speak. "Take this with you,

though, my chickadee, my sparrow, and whisper it in the right, treasonous ears.

In New Hampshire, there is a fort called William and Mary. It is guarded by a

pitiful force of less than ten men. Tell them there it is ripe for the picking, but

they must act fast. Can you remember all that?"

The though of Captain Cochran reminded the British officer of another

of his superiors, and he hastily checked his pocket watch, it read 8:15, the sun

was finally and fully up, certainly Colonel Maddison had begun his victorious

march back to the protection of Boston, even his own Light company must be

close to the eerie gallows erected near the checkpoint at the water-bound stretch

of land called Boston Neck. It was time for himself and his little party to seek

the familiar ports of Boston also. "I must depart you now, my sparrow. But I

will call upon you soon, do not disappoint me."

Meg sank to the floor, lying prostrate among the smooth rubbed

floorboards and wept immodestly and uncontrollably in something like

exhaustion as the British officer walked out the doorway. Still racked by sobs,

she remembered her own mission there and crawled behind the bar, to the cubby

where she and Abigail would stow their blankets for the day's duties.

Her hand reached into the shadowy crevice expectantly, questing for the familiar woolen softness of her blanket, rolled with her meager possessions and found only the unyielding gruffness of hard, wooden oak. Her blanket, and all that was in it, everything she could call hers in the world, was gone.

For a long moment, time seemed to escape her and she sat, not moving, not comprehending, barely breathing with her eyes locked upon the vacant cubby where her property had absconded, as if it might grow back and be restored to her.

The enormity of it; the long walk to Menotomy, to find herself once more in the power of the sadistic lieutenant, and her meager possessions, the whole of her reason for coming, gone. Tears came freely again, much though she tried to stop them.

The lieutenant had helped himself to several bottles from the bar awaiting her, scattering the drained glass on the floor about him. She reached to pick up the closest of them and the bottle slid from her reach across the scuffed floorboards. Meg let the tears come free, rolling onto her back like a martyr.

Trotter had made a habit of standing at the same spot behind the bar, to the point he had worn scuffmarks into the planks. Meg felt the roughness of that spot upon her elbows. Mounted high above the bar, invisible at all angles but this one, Trotter had mounted a pair of rods, whittled to the dimensions of the pistol barrel he had slid upon it. She reached up and drew down the handgun, one of those all metal ones the Scottish regiments always carried, the single barrel of a caliber to rival the Army's muskets.

She had never touched a gun before in her life, had shied from them like the plague, like sin. Now, having fallen into the clutches of sin, she measured the weight of the pistol in her hands, and did not shy from it.

Her meager things were gone, this lethal bequeath from Trotter her only means to make a way in this wicked world, that and a command from the sadist who, through his gift of literacy, controlled her. She rose from the dirty ground, Go to Lexington, he commanded. "He can go to Hell," she snarled to the vacant, echoing room. The world was wide, the continents no less so. She would find her way, and with her meager goods gone, she mused wryly, that meant that much less to carry.

Meg slipped out the kitchen door again, closed it securely though she doubted any would ever open it again. The sun was fully up, it was nearing nine o'clock. She looked up at the sun, the world was wide to her, all roads lead somewhere, but she paused at the one that lead to Lexington. She thought of Ruth, of her dear boy and her husband. She thought of Reverend Clarke, and she dared to think of one other man, "Daniel", she whispered, dared to dream a moment, to remember, and then she turned away.

Nearby, the Lieutenant stood back from the windows and nodded as the girl began walking in the correct direction. He looked at Lord Trenton beside him and smiled. "I am afraid you will have a long walk today, my Lord, follow her, if you would and see she returns to Lexington as I directed. Send word to me in Boston."

"Yes, of course, but of what…"

"I am afraid any more information is of…classified significance." Wainright said importantly, adding, "I am sorry."

There was a ruckus in the midst of town, men were milling, some shouting. Powder, something about powder, Meg tried to stop someone and ask, but they shoved her aside. Silly girl, events are unfolding, happenings too important for a girl.

Finally, a grey-beareded man soothed her curiosity. "The powder, the Ministerial troops seized all the powder in the provincial store! The army is out and raising the countryside."

"What?" Meg's jaw dropped, her heart leapt to her throat.

"'Tis the God's truth, my girl, I swear it. Troops landed in the darkness. Red coats march on Woburn and Acton, seven dead in Cambridge alone so far, with more to be found, for sure."

She thought of Ruth and Jonathan, of the babe in Lexington. She thought of Lexington aflame, of tubercular Captain Parker and his men trying to hold back the best army in the world. She thought of another who would stand also, stand until the last drop of blood fell from him, crying to his Gallic forefathers to grant him one more Lobsterback before he fell. "Oh, God, no." She whispered, found herself rushing into a stable and seizing a horse by the bridle. Before she knew it, she had left Menotomy behind and was riding for Lexington upon thundering hooves.

* * * * *

The morning found Daniel rising to eggs and fresh bread. Then the Acton blacksmith had made him a present of a small packet of fishing hooks, and some lead and powder, before handing Daniel his musket.

Daniel swore the blacksmith must be a Scot, as he acted like a Laird upon Christmas day. Their shooting yesterday had been done without the new patch box concealing the absent brass sun's nail holes. Now, it was in place. The hinged brass plate carefully embellished with a Scottish thistle, where once the anonymous BR's initials had been.

In truth, he had hated to leave the Davis's, partly for fear of the little ones, and for their generosity and hospitality. The fishhooks netted him a fine brace of spotted trout from one of the rough-hewn bridges between Concord and Lexington, easily enough for several days gorge and the Scot set out on his walk again, finding his life suddenly carefree for perhaps the first time since arriving in this new world.

The brace of fish upon his back, Daniel fell into a familiar, mile eating pace and relished the feeling of the wind upon his face as he walked onward toward his home. The twists and turns of the roadway were familiar old friends to him, now, and he sank into a thoughtful contemplation of his case, and the promise of Liberty.

He was a Highlander by the grace of God, Daniel reasoned, The King commanded by no less spiritual authority. From time immemorial, men had been ruled over by a Regent, a Royal who drew his powers directly from God above. Or, more directly, from the fact he had been born to the right combination of man and woman, an authority by birthright. How many members of the officer class of the British army owed their commission to the same arrangement? The Scottish Church had purposefully omitted "God save the King" from its prayers, every Sunday, and every mass besides, but even they had not gone so far as to consider replacing the monarchy with this fanciful Roman republic blather.

The right of Kings argument had almost swayed him, until he turned the corner near the bridge over Tanner's brook. A wagon sat to the side of the road, and Daniel's Gallic instincts bid him to take to the weeds. In the anonymity of camouflage, he crept closer, though stayed well removed from musket range.

The wagon was loaded with fresh cut straw, some farmer's hope to feed his livestock for the coming winter, and the product of a hard day's work. Like as not, the family had reaped the feed through the day and slept under the stars to get a jump on this new day. A beaten, stained chunk of canvas lashed across the feed held it fast, or did, until several eager Lobsterbacks slashed the ropes holding it and leapt into the wagon bed, laying about them with bayoneted muskets like pitch-forks.

The farmer was beside himself, having been drawn across the roadway before the private soldiers began their work undoing his labors. A Redcoat officer, his scarlet coat and fine breeches distinct among the dusty rose color of the enlisted who served him, maintained the man's attention, demanding to know his name and his place, his business and what he was doing so far from hearth and home in Bedford this early in the morning.

Upon the other side of the wagon, a proud woman of some fading beauty, protected the two frightened children at her skirts as she fended off the groping hands of a Welsh sergeant well practiced in his subterfuge. The breeze picked up his words with the scattered straw, "keep a still tongue, dearie," he hissed, "hate to have your man hear. Fine goods such as yours are wasted upon a dirt grubbing provincial."

Daniel clutched at the musket in his hands, but the range for shooting was too far, the odds too dear. He stayed in the shadows of the trees, and watched helplessly. Here is the final end of divine right of Kings, Daniel hissed as he bit his tongue, the power of the sovereign delegated to bullies, to keep the peasants in the field and afraid.

After some time the Lobsterbacks departed and he walked out to the bridge, hailing the farmer as he approached. Setting his musket aside, Daniel helped the family gather their scattered cargo, though in the end it did not fill the wagon as much as it once had. He waved as they rode off, never giving hint of what he had witnessed, and was on his way again.

Homes were rising from the earth closer to the settlements as more new settlers came to try their hand in the fertile milk country of Lexington. Hired men scampered over the rising structures, applying their trade. One caught Daniel's eye like none of the others.

Though dressed in the manner of other laborers, in breeches, good shoes and shirt, his head shaded from the sun with a wide brimmed hat, he was as black as midnight. Daniel stopped and stared at the man as he balanced upon a ladder and swung a hammer with the skill of a tradesman.

His hair was curly and speckled with grey, his eyes, when he glanced over at the Scot standing there like a gibbering fool in the roadway, were of a marked brown that matched his skin tone. Daniel had never seen anyone like him in Scotland, nor on the *Beaver*. He stared unabashedly at the tradesman, until the carpenter had enough of the rude man in the roadway. The black man set aside his tools. "Is there something I can help you with, friend?" He called from his ladder, then slid down its sides and walked closer to the man who had given him offense.

Daniel blushed sheepishly, he bowed penitently and said. "Your pardon sir, I have never been so close to . . . one of your color. My curiosity got the better of my manners, but that is inexcusable."

"That accent," the black man said in surprise, "and you are not one I know about town. You are the wild Scot? The one who lives up at Old Man Cavanaugh's place, yes? You go about making your way trapping wolves and such?" He shook Daniel's hand as the Highlander nodded. "In truth, had you not stopped to stare at me, I might have done so to you. I am David Lambson, carpenter and free man."

Free man? Daniel knew that this meant he had purchased, or been granted his freedom, and a carpenter to boot. "Strange to meet a tradesman such as yourself," Daniel mused, "as I have need of such as you to mend a hole in my roof. "

"And I have need of a few of the spotty's you bear." The black man laughed, gesturing at the trout hanging from Daniel's line. "Where do you go now, Daniel Ferguson?"

"I journey home with my fish, whom I have invited to my supper.'

"Then I will delay you no longer, continue on, and I will attend you there before the sunset." The black man smiled widely. "Then your spotties can attend me, and I shall therefore attend your roof. Agreed?"

His grip was firm, the hand of a tradesman used to making his way with his hands and his tools. Daniel waved as he began his trudge onward toward Lexington, convinced he had made a new friend. As he walked, he pondered the associations he had made in this new world, from Bodkin to Paul Revere, Sam Adams and even this carpenter, David Lambson. To a man, they judged him by the content of his character, not the lofty assumptions of a title or baronage. It was a foreign feeling to the Scot, and he liked it.

Ahead, his eye caught movement in a field ahead. Daniel's heart leapt to his throat and he scanned his environment for cover. Moving from tree to tree in his best imitation of a Red Indian, he looked for best advantage to see the object in that field. Finally, he beheld a wizen old woman standing in the ruts of a harvested field, she held a cast-off tree limb pressed into her service. Daniel recognized her errand, few Scot that would not. She was grubbing, digging at the furrows for some scrap to fill her belly, the work was strenuous, and her

weak arms shook from the effort.

Daniel stood, leaning against the tree and felt his heart go out to the old

woman. Then, he self-consciously adjusted the string of trout upon his back, and

he piously pondered for a long moment.

* * * * *

Mother Batherick had been upon the earth so long she had long ago

discarded the habit of keeping birthdays. Instead, she did her best to make her

way in the world, finding the best path for an old woman and doing no harm to

others. Most went out of their way to avoid her, and there were those who would

do far worse, as someone had done to poor trader Trotter, weeks back. Pausing a

long moment from her labors, the old woman crossed herself, hoping the

Taverner's last moments on earth had atoned for whatever sins he might have

committed, and he found rest.

Mother Batherick had long ago given up on the idea of others

brimming with the milk of human kindness. Best for an old woman to keep to

herself and ….

"Halooo!" A voice called from the roadway, and the little old lady

cursed her wool gathering, letting some ruffian close upon her while she talked

to herself like an old fool.

Her aged eyes were still sharp, and at the roadway, she saw a tall, broad

man of sandy hair waving a hand over his head. Timidly, she raised her own hand and waved back, staring at the man like a lamb stared at a wolf, knowing her aged body would not be able to outrun one such as he.

The broad shouldered man dropped his hand, turning to fetch something from his back, Mother Batherick's heart skipped a beat, as she saw a musket across has back.

But the long, lethal looking musket stayed on his back. Instead, he raised up a fine brace of fish, hanging them off a convenient branch of a tree, and walked on with a wave.

* * * * *

The dogs massed in an accusatory pack at the half open door, as if he might have shot a deer and kept it all for himself. Daniel laughed at them, pushed his way through the inquisitive, furry mass and set musket back into the pegs over the fireplace.

It was ten o'clock, or so, close enough to noon upon September 1st of 1774, that Daniel was thinking of his lunch. His act of charity had shorted his meal from a gorge to a more miserly graze. But Daniel looked forward to nothing more than a long rest before his own hearth with his feet up, possibly followed by an early night and a late mornings rising tomorrow.

Then the clattering of horse's hooves made him hang his shoulders in dismay, picturing the arrival of another mule loaded with kegs of the King's powder he had sparse place to store. "No rest for the wicked," he muttered, but then his ears perked. Whoever came was riding a fleet footed horse, not a saddle worn pack animal, and he was putting spurs to its flanks to urge it to speed, instead of nervously allowing the beast its footing, less a sudden shock blow them to kingdom come.

"Town borne, turn out! Town borne, turn out!" It was an ancient call of distress that had crossed the Atlantic, a call summoning the citizens of the militia, boys of 16 to men of 60, to assemble and prepare to fight. Daniel's heart leapt into his throat at the sound and he rushed out his door. A young man on a wild eyed dun colored stallion raced up the dirt road toward Reverend Clarke's parsonage, shouting his summons at the top of his lungs.

Daniel stumbled out onto the grass. "Town borne, turn out!" The youth called again, sending a thrill up his spine and fire racing through his veins. In Scotland, the Chieftain's levy was summoned by a man wielding a burning cross, somehow that urgent cry seemed the better of the two. Daniel put his hands to his mouth "Nathanial Harrington! What is the ruckus?"

The youth wheeled his mount, raced overland up the hill to Daniel's door. The horse was wild eyed, already lathered and panting, sides bloody from the rider's spurs. Young Nathanial sawed back on the reins, the horse dropped his withers, gaining the incline and racing up to stand before the Scot. "The Army is out! They've stolen all the powder from the Provincial Stores!" the fifteen year old youth was shouting, unaware he was doing it in his zeal. "The Militia is called, we march to relieve Boston!" The dun horse leapt at his traces, lunging into a gallop that would take them to Bedford towne, and was gone.

For a month he had played the part of the lay about Scotsman, slipping out in the night to meet men on mountain horses with half-kegs of powder stretched about them, to conceal them about the woods and the glens against that frightening, fateful day. Daniel stood staring into the distance, almost unaware that young Nathaniel had gone. It was begun! Could it be, was this the beginning of the awaited, dreaded revolt against King George?

* * * * *

Buckman's Tavern was a bustle. Women readied food, or poured molten lead into molds to make bullets with a dread note of preparation. Children rushed about, getting underfoot, men packing haversacks, or pouches, sharing what little news they had, or had heard, or sometimes made up from the various bits others had told them.

She had worn out a horse to get back, to find the town still standing. She was in fact, the second rider with the news, and once again found herself welcome with open arms. William Munroe, the owner of Buckman's and Sergeant of the Town Militia had welcomed her help in the kitchen, baking for the gathering men.

"Meg, when you get a moment, run some more biscuits."

The red haired girl ran a hand through her hair, felt bits of flour there. "Already have, and I baked them hard, to travel."

"Fine." The Tavern-keeper nodded appreciatively. "You have a fine grasp of a tavern, girl."

She made a small curtsey at the compliment, "thank you."

"Would you want for a job?", Munroe asked appraisingly, "I could make good use of one such as you."

For once, she heard those words and did not think they would end with her flat on her back. In the back of her mind, she heard Lieutenant Wainright's demand she make her way to this very tavern to find employ. There was a note of the divine in it all, Meg mused, enough to start believing God is an Englishman. The tavern keeper was looking at her for some answer to his offer, but Meg feigned that someone was motioning her to bring her tray of biscuits, and slipped around Monroe, rushing off.

"The Royal army is out," confirmed Francis Brown with an assured, fatalistic voice, "King George has finally let slip the Dogs of War."

"Means to teach us a lesson," Joe Vile added, "my man said a peddler told him Boston was burning. What news do you have, John Parker?"

Jonathan Parker sat by the fire, smoking his long clay pipe and watching the door. He was the duly elected Captain of the Lexington's ready company, holding the position for some years mainly on the strength of his long experiences serving King George in the Seven Years War. "What news?", he parroted, snatching the fired clay stem from his lips. "I know that an express rider informed me the bloody Lobster backs had pillaged the blessed powder stores on Quarry Hill. I know that the Militia marches on Boston, for whatever end. That is all I know, and I am too old a campaigner to be unnerved by what a slave says a peddler was told by a deaf serving wench, who heard it from a blind-mute, who saw it with his own eyes."

Rebuffed, Joe Vile shrank back. Looking about, he took a quick headcount, then hazarded a second question. "We are assembled, my Captain, why do we tarry?"

"I await someone." Parker answered cryptically, nursed his pipe a few long moments. His eyes were glued to the door as he blew smoke rings at the roof, feigning carelessness for a goodly long time, until the expectant eyes of the gathered became too much and Parker finally gave up the act as hopeless. "Guess he is not coming." The captain of militia sighed.

The door creaked, then swung open wide, and the crowded room gaped. Megan, standing with a tray of biscuits stared also. Before them stood Ferguson like a statue to some Scottish Mars, musket in one hand, a small leather faced shield draped the other. He wore those familiar buckskin breeches, now patched and stained from a hard life, his hair was clipped and drawn up into an acceptable ponytail, his beard neatly clipped close. His familiar tartan, which had sheltered her through that long frigid night, hung from his broad right shoulder to drift beneath his left arm, and a leather baldric from left to right supporting his great curved, basket hilted sword. Girding his middle was a thick belt, supporting pistol, his sporran, an old fashioned cartridge box and dirk.

A stattico tapping broke the crowd's stare, Jonathan Parker tapping his pipe against the bricks of the fireplace. "Now we are assembled," he announced, "make ready to march."

The Scot chuckled, entering and leaned his long flintlock against the wall among others. Parker watched him, surveying the arsenal slung about the man. "A double barreled pistol." He whispered again in hushed admiration of the weapon, clipped to his belt on his left side.

"And that spike mounted on that shield. Lord, protect us from the fury of the Northmen," jovially quipped the characteristically morose Brown.

"I think you mean, "Glad he's on our side," don't you?" Meg snapped, protectively, stabbing with the tray of hard biscuits to make her point. "Or maybe "Glad he's one of us.""

"One of us, Meg?" Another of the militiamen mocked the girl. "You forget yourself. He's a wild Scot, runs about in the woods, making his living killing wolves and deer. He has more in common with a painted Ottawa than us." The Scot, at that moment, did not seem such a Wild man. He had found a child crying in fright of his father going off to fight, had sat down beside the boy and was singing to him softly in Gaelic.

"He is come to us, to fight with us in the Militia," she rejoined, "you are just not seen a warrior Highlander in action."

"But you have?" Nathaniel Farmer smiled luridly, twisting her words to a totally new, more base and sexual meaning.

Meg blushed a deep crimson and drew back, affronted. "I would slap your face for that, Daniel was a perfect gentleman. I owe him my life, Nathaniel Farmer," she snapped, pulling the tray of biscuits out of the man's reach in passing for good measure.

Parker laughed, a dry, frail sound that was not lately heard. He reached up from the comfort of his warm seat and took one of Meg's biscuits, broke it in half and chewed thoughtfully, offering her the other half.

She took it, surprising herself. Setting the tray aside on a nearby table, she scooped out the soft inside of the biscuit, holding it, warm and pliable in her hand as she chewed the hard outer shell. "A wild Scot, indeed."

"Farmer's point is well taken. Daniel has not made himself a fixture of the community. Oh, he comes to services, and makes himself available to the old and those who need help. But he keeps to himself, gadding about with his gun and his skins."

"He is a good hunter, and a Christian. The Militia needs men like him and unbidden, he comes." Meg added. "And you knew his character, for you tarried here an hour waiting for him."

Parker nodded without rancor. "He is undoubtedly a good man to have about in a fight."

"And you love him." Meg goaded the older man.

"True, but not as much as you."

Meg started, began to stammer a mild rejection of the statement and the older man chuckled. "These grey hairs have garnered me more than just this warm spot beside the fire, give a man his due. I noted the new spring in your step when you came home from that cold, rainy night, how you brighten when he walks into a room." Parker smiled at her warmly, scooped his long clay pipe from his lap, sticking it and the remains of the biscuit into his home-spun hunting shirt's pocket.

She stood in silence for a long time as Parker disappear out the door, quietly watching the Scotsman with a thoughtful eye as he circulated through the assembly of Militia crowding the tavern. He moved like a cat, an island unto himself, this bold Highlander who had saved her life. She pondered another thought, this might be the last time she saw him alive, and felt a tear well in her eye at that thought.

Was it true? Could it possibly be true? Her long ago oath to herself rang in her ears, Never again, never again to be a cog, a tool to some man's needs and forsaking her own, but....

But...

"Meg! The biscuits over here if you please?" Sergeant Monroe's voice drew her from her reverie, snapped her back to reality and she attended these men who might not be coming back.

"Who are all these people?" Daniel asked Parker as the older man sidled up beside him.

"Every able bodied and willing man between 16 and 60, less clergy, contentious objectors and the mentally infirmed of course, though some might argue that Simonds here is mentally infirmed," a laugh went up at the joke, Simonds laughing as hard as the others. "Reverend Clarke is outside, he insists upon coming along. Yonder is Jonathan Harrington, those two men there, both of them, the younger has allowed your Meg to stay with his wife. I'll introduce you around as we march."

"You know them all?"

"I'm related, by blood or marriage to most of them."

* * * * *

The crackling fire was the only noise in the room, the men were gone, women and children gone. The corner which a bare moment ago was stacked with muskets and swords was bare. The Militia must be moving out, she realized and rushed outside.

On the cool green, the quiet sobbing of women and children was punctuated by the occasional order by a sergeant, or the clatter of equipment. Nineteen year old William Diamond and his rattling drum set the pace of the march, but he was nowhere to be seen with the men straggling off in the direction of Boston. She scanned the forms around her and found Daniel's familiar frame. He stood still, alone and apart from the others, but resolute to his task and duties, and she hurried toward him, heedless of the indiscretion of it all.

Daniel spun on his heel as she rushed to his side, and when she looked into his eyes, she was struck dumb. All that had filled her heart and mind the moment before deserted her like leaves swept away by the winds. She stared into those deep blue eyes and felt herself falling into them. Daniel smiled at her, a timid, careful smile that seemed to be daring to hope. "Yes, Megan?"

She brushed a strand of red hair from her face, searching for something to say. When she did speak, even she was disappointed. "You... you go with the

Militia," she stammered, and felt foolish for it. It was the sort of thing people said when they could think of nothing else.

"Yes," Daniel nodded, "We march for Boston, to whatever end." He tried to make it sound solemn, or noble. But even to his own ears it only sounded dead-panned.

"You look well." She whispered.

"Thank you," he said, scratching at his cheek, "I have been attending to my grooming more than when last we met."

She reached out impulsively and drew a hand through the sandy brown hairs covering his cheeks. "I still do not know if I could abide a man with a beard." She thought aloud.

Daniel said nothing, looking into her eyes like a mythic beast dazzling its victim. His eyes drew her in, pulling her in like drowning pools.

"Do you… do you have needs?" She stammered, the question seemed brazen to her mind, but the preoccupied Scot only shook his head. Other Lexington men were filing past the two of them, standing and staring mutely at each other in the dusty road to Boston. But to Megan, there was no one else in the world but the Scot. "Do you need food? Bullets?"

He hefted the long militia musket in the crook of his arm, reached out and stirred the pile of lead balls in her outstretched hands, though it was just an excuse to touch her. The freshly cast, pea sized balls of buckshot would turn his musket into a shotgun, something he had never thought of doing. He had always loaded the militia fowler with a single ball of .72 caliber, as the Redcoats did, instead of loading shot and using it like a long shotgun. "No, thank you." He

smiled, rather than point out what to her mind must seem a trifling discrepancy.

"I am well supplied."

"Oh." She said, taken aback. The mere brush of his fingertips was

electric to her, a luxurious burst of sensation that sent her heart into her throat

and left her breathless, the call up of the militia, the frightful knowledge that this

might be their last moments together, the realization of her feelings for him

giving the moment special poignancy. She felt the caress of her flesh and lost all

reason, wanted him so badly to touch her again, to touch her forever. But then

icy fear chilled her heart and she bristled at his refusal of her offer. Her soul

rebelled at the thought of falling once again into the control of a man. "Go, then,

Daniel Ferguson! Take your big gun and go to Boston."

Daniel's face fell, and his arm, which had stayed poised over her out

stretched palm, fell to his side with the finality of a hangman's trap. The Scot

spun on his heel and he strode off, the long legged, mile eating stride of an

experienced warrior. Megan watched those long legs heading for Boston, for

British guns and Redcoat bayonets. "My prayers go with you," she whispered to

the wind, and felt tears stain her eyes.

CHAPTER 7

The trail to Boston, all seventeen miles of it, stretched out before them, reduced to the mile eating strides of the armed Minutemen. The mind, unburdened in the endless repetition of pacing out the distance, wandered, some to duties unfulfilled or words unsaid, others to more personal thoughts.

"My prayers go with you," she whispered to the wind, and tears stain her eyes.

The Scot stopped, not the pause of a tarrying man, but the immediate halt of a hunter who had scented prey. He whirled and in the space of a breath her wild Scot looming over her like a mirage. Megan gasped at the suddenness of it, opened her mouth to say some words that never came out. For Ferguson had other plans, his strong left hand swept her in, pressing her body to his, musket trapped between them, and he kissed her.

It was not a chaste kiss of greeting, nor the petite peck that austere Puritan Massachusetts looked down upon, but permitted. It was the kiss a man gave his lover before he bedded her, the kiss to hold and keep, and she should slap his face, but she didn't. She melted into it, cast her arms about him and held him close.

I should have done that. Daniel Ferguson mused at the daydream, that dreamed-of kiss as he trod the long road to Boston, and the dream floated away like a mirage.

They marched, some fifty men against the most powerful army in the world and Daniel both despaired and chided himself as a coward. As they journeyed a strange thing happened, at each trail crossing, each farm or collection of buildings, their numbers grew. Men from Lincoln town ran over hill and stream to join them.

I should have kissed her, the Scotsman thought again, oblivious to all in his musings.

They marched, now eighty strong to the crossroads of the Lexington and Cambridge road and the road to Woburn, where a single man in black stood, cradling a battered musket in the crook of his arm. He lit a pipe and commented. "A fine day for a stroll, eh, Jonathan Parker?"

Parker, no spry chicken at 46 years of age, was brought up short by this new arrival. "Deacon Haynes, you saw the fair side of seventy years ago. You have no need of this march."

The old man took in Parker's comments with no notice but to shift the weight of his musket, then brought his hand to his mouth and whistled shrilly. A dozen or more men stood on both sides of the road, two drew Daniel's eye. Both were the spitting image of this acerbic deacon, one in the prime of life, the other barely out of teen years. "Perhaps my best years are behind me," Haynes admitted, eyes never leaving the teen who wore his face, "but I will not leave to grandchildren a fight I should have made."

"What news have you heard?"

"We heard our powder was stolen, Boston shelled as we speak, a dozen or more dead, women and children among them."

Parker nodded, thoughtfully. "The powder we had heard about."

"And we go to war?", the old deacon asked.

"We go to war."

* * * * *

They marched onward, in a strange commingling of deadly purpose and festival. Men greeted each other with firm handshakes and gossiped about long separated friends and kinfolks. Daniel marched among them in silence for a long time, nodding at some polite joke he did not comprehend, and morosely reflecting on Meg's parting words to him.

Jonathan Parker seemed to sense the dark clouds troubling him, and endeavored to shake him from it with a continuous stream of introductions. Daniel met neighbors of Lexington, Lincoln and a half dozen other hamlets. Captain Parker, like as not would introduce him as "The Wild Scot who has been chasing down wolves in the trees, we are right glad to have him with us."

Parker, for all his infirmities, had the stride of a man half his age, and seemed to have no need of rest, and the growing string of men straggled as they closed the distance to Cambridge. Setting the pace was Moses Harrington of Lexington, 63 years old and so was considered a member of the Alarm List, old men who were not required to fall out with the Militia, but rather to guard the town in the younger men's absence. But he set a marching pace that left many younger men gasping and struggling to keep up.

Younger men, winded and struggling under the unfamiliar weight of lead, powder, gun and blade were falling back, straggling out of line but unwilling to drop out and return to their homes unbloodied. Daniel carried twice the weight of many of the minutemen, dripping, in the Highland fashion, with dirk, long gun, sword, pistol and targe. But hard living and familiarity with the load kept him safely in the vanguard of the marching war party. Inwardly, he was divided. In his heart, he could see Meg standing there, her hair undone and fluttering like the wings of a bird, and he remembered every line of her, the tilt of her head, the way the light danced and played on her face.

I should have kissed her, Daniel muttered again, in his mind he saw the fields of Culloden, kilted Highlanders charging close packed Redcoats firing so rapidly it sounded like a continuous roll of thunder. He saw the clansmen falling in heaps in their desperation to bring the charge home against the hated British. The flower of Scotland, the whole of the warrior clans of the Highlands could not stand against the British Army, and now he marched against them with farmers and tradesman?

The Militia did not march so much as all the men purposefully strolled together. Some smoked a pipe, almost no one had his musket upon their shoulders, though some did approximate the marching order of the red-coated ministerial troops. Others held their guns parallel to the ground, or slung over their shoulders. If they had a thought or word for this man or that, they would simply jog up and pass some of the time with that man, drifting off or not as they would. Daniel watched this for a time before joining Parker in the leading van of the march. "What plan have we, my Captain?", Daniel asked, in his closest approximation of military speech.

"I must admit I do not know, friend Daniel," the older man said, glancing over his powerful shoulders to meet the Scot's eyes as he did, "and I find myself pondering that very thing as we march. General Gage can choose to meet us with anything up to five thousand men, and in truth, could meet us anywhere he likes, but were it me, I would stay where I am strongest."

"You mean the Neck?"

"Yes, yes I do. I would command the ferries upon the Charles River be moored, and wait at the works upon Boston Neck, supported by the great guns of the Royal Navy."

Daniel thought upon those military works, stuffed with cannons and muskets sitting in the shadows of the Governor's Gallows and the pauper's graveyard. "There are a great many Lobsterback there." Daniel muttered.

"And cannon, friend Daniel, do not forget the Ministerial cannon," Parker nodded, "or rather ponder our lack of field guns."

"Suicide," Daniel whispered, "this can only be suicide."

The Captain licked dry lips and nodded. "I do not argue this."

"Then why?"

"Why? Deacon Haynes said it best, so as not to leave to grandchildren a fight we should have made. There are things bigger than us, we fight here for progeny unborn, who will either reap the rewards of our toil now, or struggle under the yoke of our inactivity." Parker paused to look past Daniel, seemed amazed at the size his levy had grown to. "But ponder that not for now, things may yet be salvaged. Have you met Jonathan Harrington?" Among the marching mass was a younger man whom Daniel remembered as a Lexington man he had seen about the town. He was breathless in his efforts to keep the pace, and pale as a ghost. Concerned, the Scot called out in friendly greeting. "What troubles you, Jimmy? Yer white as a sheet," the Scot observed, cryptically, "and look like a stallion about to bolt."

"Jimmy?"

"Ach, we all call ourselves that, back home." The Scot waved off dismissively, with an infectious laugh. A quick round of introductions followed.

Young Junior Harrington was not in a laughing mood. "I have found myself recalling the displays of arms the Magisterial troops will put on." The young man said airily, as if a man trying not to betray his fears. "All those muskets sweeping down, and the bayonets gleaming in the sun. I suddenly find it rather…off-putting."

In point of fact, Daniel did know, and had been trying very hard not to think about any of that.

"I have a fine wife at home, and my son is a strapping lad, I could not be prouder of either of them." He swallowed several times, and his voice took on a maudlin, sad air. "Now the though of leaving them alone in the world is… should I fall, would you be so good, sir, to…"

"You'll not fall, laddie." Daniel said with forced bravado.

"That is in God's hands, my friend," Harrington said morosely, "and I must admit it crowds my thoughts."

"Don't let it." Daniel advised, and then his advice went bloody and practical. "When the time comes, load your musket with double ball. Stand proud in your line and listen. Before the Lobsterbacks shoot, their officer will command them to "prepare", then he will call for them to "present" and the last command will be "fire." The last two come quick on each other so listen sharp, but when the officer calls out "fire", the flints will fall. At that moment, you hit the dirt, aim your musket into the smoke at their bellies and let fly."

Harrington stared at him a long moment. "You sound like a man who has seen the King's troops in action before."

Daniel paused, fixed his eyes upon his comrade in arms and wondered how much he should say. Should he admit to the hours dedicated to observing British troops in their evolutions, working out his own plans to preserve his life should Bonnie Charlie, the rightful King of Scotland, ever return. He decided on a simpler course. "That I have. You just stick near me if there's a dust up, Mr. Harrington. You'll see that fine boy grow yet."

"Yes." The Lexington man nodded, gratefully. "I am wondering why one would consider carrying a shield in matters such as this. It would seem a bit… outmoded."

True enough, Daniel considered the brass decorated, leather covered Targe upon his left arm a long moment before he answered. "A man fights the way he trains to fight, as he lives the way he is taught to live." Daniel spoke

through gritted teeth. "Such as you, I take you to have been born here."

"Well guessed, but not a great hazard. Most of the county is named

Harrington, and has been for two generations." He glanced in several directions

and whispered, conspiratorially. "The Parkers had a string of girls that took them

out of the running."

Daniel snorted appreciatively at the humor, "Aye, and a broad, proud

land you have here. I came from Scotland, would you have guessed."

"No, never would have guessed you for a Highlander," the other man

guffawed. "And a beautiful country it is, I have heard."

"It is, Johnny, it is. But I think you might have the better of me there."

Daniel said, wistfully. "There is something about this land, something in the air

that won't tolerate a king, or a potentate, that tells every man to go forth for his

own sake and..."

A voice called from the very head of the column. "Rider approaching!"

All eyes flashed to the front.

Harrington's eyes went wide, he made a false start at speaking before

cracking a strangely calm smile and he said, "I'm afraid we must continue this

discussion later, my dear friend Daniel. But continue we shall, as it sounds to be

a topic to rival Reverend Clarke on a Sunday."

Bedlam ensued, Captain Parker ordered lines of battle, the bellowed

call answered by a confusing crush of men who had never drilled together

tripping over each other in their haste to obey. "Oh, bloody Hell and perdition."

Parker croaked, trying to hold in a wet, hacking cough. "Junior Harrington, you, Daniel and Mister Simonds, line up here, now kneel down. You, you and you, Francis Brown, do the same." Brave colonials shuffled to the line in a rough approximation of the British duel- tiered line to repel cavalry, one kneeling and the rear line standing. Daniel quietly checked the powder beneath the frizzen on his flintlock pan. "You, Joe Vile, and Reverend Clarke begin the second rank behind them. Have ye' not loaded, this might be the time to do so!"

Those last words, powerfully bellowed, set off a spasm of frantic activity. Those who had bayonets, and they were a desperately small few, fixed them to their muzzles. Others busied themselves with ramrods, or whisking at their flash pans before freshening the charge, giving the screw that held their all important flint a final, good luck twist.

"Who comes?", demanded one of the Woburn men in the rear ranks.

Daniel peered sharply at the horseman, at the familiar way he sat his mount and the easy grace he displayed in the saddle. "Revere," he muttered in recognition, nodded in assurance and repeated at a shout, "it's Revere! Paul Revere!"

The name, which short months ago meant nothing to Daniel, had an electric effect on the citizen militia. Muskets, before so belligerently brandished were raised almost as one, hammers lowered carefully and bayonets returned to their scabbards.

Revere rode like the very demons of Hell were upon him, pulled the reins much later than Daniel would have to curb the lathered, spirited horse and caused her to rear dramatically, iron-shod hooves pawing at the sky. "Hold!"

Revere roared, "Hold, hold!" On the third demand, Daniel realized the

silversmith was speaking to the assembly of men, and not his horse.

The gray mare reared again, majestically tossing its broad head as

Revere waved both hands before him. "Hold, my countrymen! Stop!"

"We are at bay, friend Revere." Parker said, deferentially, as the hastily

formed firing line dissolved into a rush of men crowding around Revere's horse

to hear the silversmith speak.

"My countrymen," Revere spoke almost rhetorically to the crowd.

"Why come you with sword and bayonet?"

"We come for hair!" Parker snapped, brandishing that worn, lethal

looking tomahawk above his head. It was a poetic, even heroic sight, and it

ended far too soon, and heart-wrenchingly as the Militia Captain clapped a hand

to his mouth and the defiant martial ardor dissolved into a wet coughing fit.

"Word reached Lexington, Paul!" Another voice toward the front

added. "T'is spreading like wildfire."

"Word of what?", Paul queried, but his voice, to one who knew him

such as Daniel, suggested he already knew.

Dozens of voices spoke up at once, shouts of blood letting and rioting

Lobsterbacks, of shelling and thefts in the name of the British crown. Revere

listened for a long moment, then held up his hands for silence. "Raiding there

was. Skirmishers of the Ministerial troops confiscated the stores from the

Powder House in Cambridge, and likewise stole cannon from the Provincial

Courthouse. But by the grace of God, there was no killing." He allowed those words to sink in a long moment. "No killing, none."

That seemed to silence some of the blood ardor in the crowd's heart, until a voice cried out. "And what of Boston, silversmith, we were told the King's Navy reduces it as we speak!"

"Aye, and that Cambridge burns!" Another voice added.

"Common sense tells these as lies!" Revere snapped like a man on the edge of losing patience. "Hear you the thundering guns? We are a bare five miles from the Harbor, surely we could hear them. Nor do we see the smoke or flames from your blazing Cambridge, which I just rode through in my haste to arrive here."

More muttering rippled through the assembly, some 250 armed, belligerent men now disjointed from their course. The Deacon puffed at his pipe thoughtfully. "Powder and cannon taken, you say Paul?"

"Aye," Revere spat from atop the horse, "but naught else!"

"Yet these are crimes alone demanding redress." The old man bared his teeth in a wolfish leer, and the crowd picked up their sanguine lust again.

Parker and Revere struggled for order, Daniel slipped to the older man's side. "We cannot regain the stolen powder, nor the guns. Not with every man in New England." He heard Parker say.

"We have marched all the way on a pretext, liberty." The deacon, no stranger to debate and speech, parried the argument. "A pretext you yourself

have spoken on many times, John Parker. Better now, when we are prepared,
than later...I say on and be done with it."

"I would expect cooler thought and more deliberate words from a man
of your years, Josiah Haynes." Paul Revere scolded from atop the borrowed
horse. "This small theft be not provocation enough to plead our case, we must be
unmistakably in the right."

'They quarter troops in our homes, and we do nothing. They shoot
down a seventeen year old boy in our streets, and we wait. Now they come as
thieves in the night and steal our powder from beneath our very noses." The
belligerent old man paused and shook his head. "I go on, I swear I continue, and
God above is my witness and my judge."

"I judge this a fool's errand, Deacon Haynes," Parker spat, "and a
waste of fathers and sons."

"Now, John." Paul revere said, suddenly all soothing and reasonable.
"We cannot fault the man for martial ardor and patriotism. We shall ride on to
Cambridge, so Deacon Haynes can see it still stands. And I will ride beside
him."

Such was Revere's prestige and indomitable spirit, that the party began
to move onward to the East, some men, satisfied with Revere's words slip away
and begin the journey home, still others continued on, Revere and the Deacon
riding side by side on the trail, speaking back and forth in hushed, rapid tones.

Miles disappeared beneath their paces, and the horizon coalesced into
the steeples and buildings of Cambridge. Revere, with the instincts of a

showman waited until the clergyman could see the milling forms of men upon the cobblestones. "There!" He announced theatrically. "You see for yourself, Deacon, Cambridge and Boston beyond, standing and whole."

The Deacon said nothing, standing there chewing his upper lip with his well oiled musket cradled in his arms. Daniel, standing at the pair's left, looked at the fine towers and steeples of the town with some satisfaction. Then, his sharp eyes noted other things, the millings of the people on the streets, and yet another horseman riding express out of the town. "Another rider, Paul," the Scot intoned thoughtfully.

The rider put spurs to his animal, dashing free of the town, then, noticing the party in the distance, wheeled his horse and rode straight at them. As he closed, Daniel could see he was a fine, ruddy looking boy with dark hair under a curiously floppy hat.

"We've got trouble, Mr. Revere!" He announced, adding, "Brattle, do you know of the man?

Revere had to think a minute. "William Brattle? He who lead troops in the Seven Years War? The doctor?"

"Aye, Doctor, Colonel, clergy and lawyer, too, that William Brattle."

Daniel was impressed, doctor, clergy, lawyer and an accomplished military officer, this was a learned man. And if he was in the circle of Revere, a high minded Son of Liberty, to boot, Daniel felt better in their chances in this mad scheme.

"He's not regularly in my correspondence," Revere said it lightly, in the manner of a joke, "but I know of the man."

"Be glad he is not in your correspondence, Paul." With that ominous comment, the rider handed the Silversmith a much folded copy of the Cambridge newspaper. "He had always kept strict neutrality between the Loyalists and Sons of Liberty here in Cambridge, or so we thought."

This Brattle was a loyalist after all. From the ground, the confused Daniel could see little more than the offered page was a reprint of a letter, Revere provided the rest, picking out choice phrases like "plunder their effects and put all to the sword", and naming Sam Adams and John Hancock, among others, as he read quickly to himself, and Daniel's spirit plunged. The express rider was nervous, glancing over his shoulder often and could finally bear no more of Revere's thoughtful contemplation. "There's a mob forming down there, Paul, it's going to get very ugly, soon."

"Have you need of us, Paul?" John Parker asked, deferentially to the Silversmith. The implication was here, a trained body of armed men stood ready to march into Cambridge, at Revere's word.

"Send you against neighbor and cousin, to rescue a bunch of Loyalists?" Revere scoffed at the thought, trying to maintain calm by the force of his spirit. Daniel could see in his eyes that the silversmith fretted. Finally, he said. "No, John, send them home."

Somewhat taken aback, the Ranger turned Captain of Militia ordered his young drummer to beat out the tune for assembly and the rag tag group of men in homespun gathered close, listening intently as Parker calls the various town militias together and ordered them to disband. Some reacted with disappointment, most with relief, and Harrington was one of the latter. The strain of the long day seemed to slough away like an old skin, and hefting his heavy musket, he felt as if he could run all the way home. His heart was light and his mind filled with thoughts of Ruth and his young son. Then, looking about one last time, he saw Daniel standing alone, unmoved from the place he had stood, near Revere's horse, quietly, contemplatively staring at the town of Cambridge, as a thick black smoke begins to rise from her Northern warrens. "Are you not going home now, Daniel," he asked his newfound friend.

Home, Daniel rolled the word around on his tongue and thought wistfully of dear red haired Meg back in Lexington. He wanted to go, to return to her, more than anything else in the world. But, "Ah...yes, I shall, in a bit there, Johnny. It's been a while since I...stretched my legs, thought I might see the sights with Paul here before I go back."

Paul looked down at him in surprise, then his shocked continence turned to gratitude, "and I shall guarantee you the rental of a fine stallion to ease your passage home if you do, Daniel."

"Well, then." Harrington enthused. "If you will do the same for me, I shall come along too! Seems sort of like fair day in Lexington down there, anyway."

* * * *

Revere, now afoot, narrowly dodged out of the path of a mounted man, lashing greater speed from his horse as he heedlessly hurtled through the streets of Cambridge. Dusting off his coat, Revere mused, "I believe that was Hallowell, the King's Commissioner of Customs."

"What was he doing riding bareback on a horse harnessed to pull a carriage?" Harrington wondered aloud, looking at the retreating rear of the horse as it made best speed for the Boston Neck. Unencumbered by his musket and other tools of war, he gadded about like a sightseer. The whole day had taken on an aspect that was equal parts fever dream and carnival, and he had determined to enjoy every bit of it.

"I know that not, Johnny," Daniel said, quickly, "but I think that party coming on may know his reasoning." A full dozen armed horseman were charging down the road in pursuit of the Royal customs man, and Daniel and his friends quickly stepped aside for them and their heedless, trampling horse's hooves.

Ahead, a mob had formed around one of Cambridge's homes, some bore torches, and others waved muskets or swords, or pried bricks from the cobblestone streets. Even as they approached, Revere could easily see that bare few of the windows of the house still contained their expensive glass panes.

"This can not go well for our cause," the silversmith muttered to himself. The image of a riotous mob abusing the citizens of placid, bucolic Cambridge would not advance their cause before the world as anything but the ruffians the Crown had attempted to paint them. Revere looked at his stalwart friends and smiled, embarrassed at his wool-gathering. "Come, my friends, we may yet be able to talk these folks out of their current course." He said, with an enthusiasm he did not feel. Cambridge, Boston, all of Massachusetts even was a powder keg of emotions ready for any spark to set it off. Revere feared this might be the day.

"Come out, Trenton, ye' bastard!", demanded someone within the mass of milling Colonials, his powerful voice carried above the general voice of the crowd. Like a command of "fire" might loose a volley upon a battlefield, so did this man's words release a shower of rocks and bricks upon the home much abused siding. One of those rocks shattered another fine glass window and rattled across the polished wood floor inside, and was answered with an affronted, and very terrified, feminine scream from inside. The Scot looked up in shock at the gut-wrenching sound, to see the face of a frightened child staring out of a different, ragged-edged window in abject terror at the crowd below.

Daniel's heart leapt to his throat, looking about wildly, he saw two mechanics of the sort Revere and Adams drew his men, wearing the simple clothes of the working class and prying bricks from the cobblestone street. "Stop!" Daniel called, rushing toward the two. "Stop! There are women and children in there!"

In response, the first man threw his worn cobblestone, and the second turned upon Daniel as if he were a simpleton. "There's no bloody women or children in there, friend, only Tories."

I marched to make war for this man, Daniel growled incredulously as a red rage seized him, yet if I had my musket now, I would shoot him down like a dog. But he did not have his musket, it sat in the barn beside Harrington's, with the Scot's spiked Targe. But he drew back a fist and struck the mechanic so powerfully he flew into his friend and both tumbled to the ground.

With a bellow, Daniel drew his basket hilted blade. The sudden, sheer violence of it caused the crowd to recoil from the wild Scot. "Alright, come on, heroes!", the warrior Scot roared, "Come On! I know ye' can frighten children, now who wants to dance with a Highlander?"

The crowd parted before him like waves upon the rocks, and he stalked them, driving them away from the abused house. "Come now, you'll throw rocks at women and children, there's not a story to tell your grandchildren there. Not a battle to make men weep nor a virgin's thighs quiver." He pounded the brass basket hilt of his sword manfully upon his breast, declaring. "This is Daniel Ferguson, *buchannan* of the Clan Ferguson, chief of his lordship's reavers. Many's the *ghillie* who rues the day we upon moor or dale, and there were many, but not one still wore diapers."

"Never thought I'd see the day a free Scotsman would succor a damned arse-licking Tory!" A female voice shrilled, and another gravely male voice took up the cause. "I only hope Trenton pays you well to spit upon your freedom!'

"I'd not ever set eyes upon him, or if I have it is not in my ken, But there is a fat German bastard in London who wants to say we riot. Make him a gift of that, and he'll have his damned Dragoons here upon us before

Michaelmas!" Daniel brought up his sword, sighted down the upturned arch of

the blade at a man in the crowd like the finger of Damnation. "Have ye ever

seen Dragoons in their games, Jimmy?", he demanded of a blonde haired man

standing at the front of the mob. Unaware of the act, the surprised man shook his

head. "Well, I have. They ride you down like hounds upon a fox with a great

bloody sword that's only half sharp, so you're all the more sure to linger with a

busted skull, instead of a quick killing stroke, and not man, woman nor child is

spared the touch of their sport."

Daniel stopped and stared pointedly at a child of about ten in the

crowd. A woman nearby immediately dragged the boy from the wild man's

basilisk glare. "That's a fine looking bairn you have there, lassie," the Scot told

the woman, "but he'll not be so fine after that day, after the Dragoons come

riding through here, hacking away and his brains are leaking out his ears."

He stalked the small stretch before the house that his stalking and

ranting had earned him, looking in all directions. This barely determined plan of

his did not seem to be working, the crowd he was trying to break up seemed to

be growing with men and women eager to see what all his shouting was about.

"Go home!" He demanded, bellowing at the mob, "go home now, you crazy

bastards, go home and stop putting your necks onto King George's block! Go!"

Slowly, by ones and tens, the mob of angry Colonists drifted away,

until all that was left was Daniel, and his two wildly grinning companions.

* * * * *

Upon the floor of Buckman's Tavern, exhausted men slept the dreamless sleep of those who had diced with death and won. A warm fire cleansed the early September chill and Revere and Daniel sat close to the hearth. Daniel stared at the flame with red veined eyes, too exhausted to sleep and too tightly wound by the events of the day to try.

Buckman's door was open, but the tavern was all but closed, Sergeant Monroe, the old campaigner that he was, plodded back into his tavern exhausted, mounted the stairs to his bed without a word. Meg, the redheaded beauty that had inspired him to march to battle like a Spartan queen, was still there at the bar, thought she was all but the last one there now.

Daniel stole glances at her from the corner of his eye. The girl he had gone to war for, the thought of whom had kept him going, was within his reach. The crucible of war and of a hopeless fight had failed to extinguish his temper, but had left him focused upon things that had before seemed important yet now became trivial, and things trivial were now in sharp relief. Daniel had marched to Boston and back, he had found there no Lobsterback offering battle, but instead common men in riot, and had quelled them. He had done all this and come home atop, as Revere had promised, a fine horse. Redeemed by his triumphant return, he focused on the thing that had brought him home. He thought of pretty red-haired Meg, and a kiss.

Revere smoked a long stem pipe, brooding some question with waking intensity, he thought of Redcoats and their muskets, and the theft of their powder, of the British Government's element of surprise, and how best to blunt it. At length, he spoke. "There are lessons to be learned here." He intoned.

"Aye," Daniel agreed in a tired voice. "That the King stole our bloody powder."

"Bosh, we've been stealing it for over a year now." Revere smirked good naturedly, as if he had today lost nothing more important that a chess match over a pipe and a beer at Buckman's hearth. "He just did it faster, all at once. We need to gather faster too, the old way is not working now."

Daniel was confused; the horsemen calling the gathering had worked through history. "If we don't use expresses, how do you propose to . . ."

"No, the expresses are not what I spoke upon, we need to follow that with something new, more massive... perhaps bonfires, like in the old Indian raiding days."

"It does bear thought, Paul," the Scot nodded, watching as Meg wiped down the bar top a final time before turning to leave the tavern and he quickly rose to follow, "but in the morning. I bid you a good night, and I will seek your company for breakfast."

Revere took the pipe from his mouth to bid the Scot a peaceful sleep, but his companion was already gone.

* * * * *

"Megan, may I have a word? With you, I mean." He called gently after her as she wearily walked to the kitchen door.

She turned to see her brave Scot standing at before her, sword at his side and his belt bristling with arms, but she marveled at her confidence in the presence of his lethal kit. "Of course Daniel, can I get you something? The stove is out, but..."

"I...I did not need food, Megan, nor drink." Daniel stammered, head whirling to find the words he'd presumed would come so readily. "I...."

"You? . . . ." She mimicked him, coquettishly.

His mouth was dry, his heartbeat curiously strong in his ears, but Daniel also felt the confidence of a man who had charged into the haze of battle, and come out the other side. "The...the face of war, confronting a man as it does, give him pause to new considerations. I would see you, Megan. I mean that. . . I mean to court you."

Megan, before so poised, so in command and confident in her own right, stared at him, her mouth fell open in a surprised little O. She looked at the broad, bearded face before her, and in her mind saw Nathan Higgins proposing his mad, impetuous idea to run off, escape from her father's judgmental claws and start a new life somewhere, anywhere else, then his leering taunting face as he boarded ship and sailed from her. It was a memory that rarely left her, that tortured her in the night. But this night, she could not shake off the eyes of this Highland Scot who had braved the marshes to bring her home. Though Nathan Higgins' roguish smile was burned into her memory, it could not overcome those piercing eyes with that blue like the sea after a storm.

Daniel hazarded. "I have ….today, made the acquaintance of Jonathan Harrington, I am proud to call him my friend. I imagine that I will be calling on the Harringtons often, and I have heard that you had taken residence there…"

"Oh, Daniel." She simpered, strangely enjoying drawing out the clumsy Scot at his purpose. "Though I am very glad you have found a friend, I must tell you I have gained work here at Buckman's Tavern, and your Sergeant Monroe has granted me lodging here as part of my pay."

"Oh?" The Scot lifted an eyebrow. "I suppose that is only just that Sergeant Monroe seized you for your talents, as you were always a fine ornament to the Black Horse, back in Menotomy." He meant it as a complement, but she could not conceal a grimace of pain flittering across her face at the thought of her last, and perhaps final visit to old Mister Trotter's tavern, and Daniel saw it, with an acuity that surprised her, as most men had a more difficult time cracking her armor. "I have…caused you pain, my lady. I apologize if my Highland manners are too brisk for your ways."

"Daniel." She whispered, drawing him back. Her throat felt thick and she felt tears wet her cheeks, "oh, my brave, one of a kind Daniel. You know my case better, I think, than any living thing in this new world of ours, but at the same time, you do not know me. I have resided in Massachusetts for soon approaching two years, I have had some fine offers in that time, more than you would care to think of, I am sure. Some from men of wealth and prominence, but I have not had an offer that made me tremble until now. But I would never place myself to be used like that again."

The Scot looked at the attitude of her face, the hardness of her eyes and paused a long moment. He made an attempt to speak, but thought the better of it. She looked back at him from the second step, eye to eye, a strange thing for the Highlander, somewhere above six foot as he was. He daydreamed upon the kiss that had carried him through this day like a Lady's favor for her chosen Knight, and he wanted it badly, needed it. But those eyes spoke volumes about the thinking the girl needed do before she could give it. Wordlessly, he took her left hand in his own with the gentleness of a man picking up a fallen bird, pressed his lips to it, and walked back into the main room.

Francis Brown, one of the exhausted Lexington men, worn from their hazardous trail but too tired to sleep, had returned to the fire and he sat in discussion with Revere.

"Women," Daniel muttered to himself, reclaiming his seat.

Revere chuckled. "I believe, friend Francis, that when a man sets his mind to something, there is naught else he can do but attempt the prize. God will decide the matter, as He always does." He pretended to address his comrade at the hearth, but hoped the advice might offer Daniel some comfort.

"I respect the point, Paul." Francis Brown rebutted, also tempering his words to Daniel's plight. "But I believe the Lord has placed us upon this dust speck for a certain number of days, and a man needs to husband his time, weighing the time expended against the prize of a battle won. What think you, Scotsman?"

Dimly, Daniel rose and walked to the bar, pulling himself a pint of beer from the keg there. "I believe I shall get blind drunk, now." He declared, to both men's amusement.

Brown cast him a sardonic salute. "That's the spirit, lad!"

* * * * *

September gave way to October, and the hurried times of harvest, as the feared snows of December and the New Year were in the offering in the cold Atlantic breezes. Daniel set aside his musket for the scythe and butchering knife, and did not lack for employment. Late nights lead to early mornings as everyone rushed to put up the foods to see them through the winter and into the spring.

But when the last beef was hung, the last pig blanched, scraped and rendered to sausage and hanging hams, a different fervor embraced the hamlet of Lexington. That last beef became a banquet for the whole town, with chickens and other meats roasting beside it, cooking slowly over a wood fire as a tired looking Reverend Clarke gave a shorter than usual Sunday sermon as distracting breezes drifted through the meeting house, perfumed with the smell of cooking meats.

Walking unobtrusively from the meeting house, Daniel wanted nothing more than to slip home to a well deserved rest, but dour Francis Brown slid an uncharacteristic arm about his shoulders and said. "Daniel Ferguson, I would invite you come sup at our house this Saturday, the pork is one you helped to slaughter, after all."

Captain Parker and other men, tending the spitted beef waved the Scot to their side to test the doneness of the cooking meat. Across the roadway, Sergeant Munroe and Meg were rolling kegs of the season's new beer from the bowels of Buckman's Tavern to quench the feast, as tables and all manner of benches were filling the drilling green for the convenience of all, a makeshift bar-top before the tavern filling with familiar crockery tankards. The fire-tenders waited with ill conceived enthusiasm for the kegs to be tapped before they rushed for the first sample of the beer, Daniel swept along with them.

To his chagrin, it was Munroe who served Daniel his wooden tankard of ale. "Thank you, Sergeant Munroe, and good day to you, and you also, Meg." His heart jumped as Meg smiled warmly back at him.

Munroe smiled also. "Meg," he said, cagily, "I have need of something to sit these kegs upon in their chases so as not to bruise the wood. Something like a wolf pelt, do we have one?"

"Uh, no." Meg answered, confused. The heavy kegs of new beer had sat on the floor in the basement, or the outbuildings for so long without concern. This was the first the master of Buckman's tavern had seemed to give any thought to their bruising.

"Oh." Munroe said, turning unctuously to the Scotman. "Good friend Ferguson, would you know where I could acquire two wolf pelts?"

"I have some, at my cabin." Daniel answered, guilelessly.

"Splendid, could I entreat you to borrow them?" The sergeant of Militia asked genuinely, but without waiting for an answer, turned to Meg. "Go with him, girl, and get me two fine, winter pelts. Take as long as you want."

Somewhat stunned at her sudden leave, the red haired girl nodded dully, wiping her hands on a loose rag and slipping from behind the ad-hoc bar to follow her Scottish warrior. This was the first time the master of Buckman's Tavern had so commanded her to take her leisure, also.

The military green was a bustle of non military activity, filling with the citizens of Lexington, each with nothing more pressing upon their minds than a fine meal and perhaps a tankard or two of ale. "You are not leaving, are you, Daniel Ferguson? My son will not hear of going home unless you sing that song again," called Esther Parker as Daniel began threading his path through the milling population of Lexington. She was one of the many Lexington Parkers, her husband a sire of Jonas Parker, and kin to the Militia Captain.

"Ach, no, Mrs. Parker, I promise, just on a bit of a lark," He began, glanced at Meg and, fretting her reputation for the flippant remark, he quickly added, "for Sergeant Munroe."

"Ah, well, I am saving you a piece of this cherry pie," she called at his back as enticement.

"You sing?" Meg asked the Scotsman.

"Ah, no, at least not well," Daniel answered modestly, but with honesty. "But the bairn was beyond tired and fussy, and, to be honest, t'was the end of a long day of butchering and we had been passing about some ale. I was a bit in me cups and sang him "Rally for Charlie", an old Jacobite tune. He seems to have taken a liking to it."

Meg laughed her real, bell like laugh and beamed at the Scot. He was a different man now than the one she had helped to nurse in the kitchen of the Black Horse Inn, different still than the sulking hermit that had rescued her in the Sudbury swamps. "You're changed," She mused, quickly covering when the Scot cast an eye toward her. "You've changed your clothes, I mean."

Daniel spread out his arms with a self conscious grin, modeling his clothing. He wore new buckskin pants, and a deer-hide coat of a decidedly Scottish cut. The sleeves were laced onto the vest with home made hide laces, as were the buttons, bound in an elaborate knot that formed a globe. The whole was dyed a patchy nut brown and beneath it, he wore his familiar tartan and a white shirt, obviously new. His hair was cut, done up in a queue, the militant ponytail that was so the fashion of the men of Boston, and his face was cleanly shaven.

"Your jacket and pantaloons cut a fine figure." Meg commented appreciatively, and quickly flushed at the forwardness of her words.

Daniel took them without rancor. "Aye, I am becoming quite the hand with buckskin." He smiled.

"And that is a fine shirt, have you become your own seamstress also?"

"No, as I was busy butchering hog and beef, I asked Ebenezer's wife to do so for me."

"How much?", she inquired cannily. "Ebenezer does nothing for free, nor would he abide any of his own to do so."

Guilelessly, Daniel answered, "two deer skins."

"I would have done it for much less," Meg said, smiling coyly at him. She had meant it to display her desire he come to her with such need of this sort he might have.

"You think I do not deal shrewdly?" Daniel asked, like a lad expecting a scolding.

"No, no. Not at all, Daniel," Meg rushed to assure him, floundering for a complement, "it is very Christian of you to ask your elders to…"

Sensing her discomfort, Daniel pressed his advantage flirtatiously. "Then those are the words of a woman who would impress a man with her sewing skills."

Meg laughed. "I doubt you would be so impressed."

"I doubt it not." The Scot rose to her defense, then he glanced over his shoulder and a strange smile spread over his face. After a long moment, asked. "Have you considered the words we spoke last month, in September?"

Meg's head swam at the memory of his words, and she inwardly wondered at the rush of words that came to her mind. Thankfully, that was the moment they arrived at Daniel's door. His home was of a much better order now, though his legendary pack of dogs still seemed to wander the grounds at their leisure. Inside, the house a masculine sense of order prevailed, musket and horn over the fireplace. Upon a crude table was his leather-faced shield, with its long steel spike jutting from the bowl-like brass central boss. Daniel drifted to a corner where a stack of furs were placed above dog height, sorted through them for two fine wolf pelts.

The stack of skins was high and carefully tanned. They would bring a high price and the red haired girl said. "I had wondered what you had been doing to stay busy."

'Ah." The Scot smiled. "The Gods of the hunt have favored me, but that has not been my only task." He set aside the two wolf skins and sought out another corner of the room, returning with a package wrapped in cast off newspapers. Without comment, he set the package in her lap, and withdrew to the furs once again.

Meg undid the simple string, delving into the wrapping to find a pair of Scottish ghillie brogues, more expertly tanned than his first attempt. The leather was soft deer hide, tanned to a pleasing, even light brown, and sized to her feet.

"Try them on." The Scot urged from the confines of the cabin, evidently watching but afraid to approach too soon.

"My… my feet are dirty." The girl demurred, unable to take her eyes from the gift. She remembered Nathan Higgins taking up her last pair, bundling the shoes under his arm to trade for his sailing kit, her tears and his indifference to them. A flood of emotions rushed over her, and a rush of words to say, too, but before she could bring any of them to full form, the Scot was before her, kneeling gracefully. Her heart leapt in her throat as he did so, but he took one of the shoes and gently laced it upon her foot, smiling as he did. "A fine fit." He commented to himself in congratulations. "I was concerned about that, though perhaps the stretch of the leather is more to credit than my poor skills." He took the other shoe and claimed the privilege to put it on her, then quietly withdrew and left her to her thoughts.

Perplexed, Meg watched him at his duties for a few moments before drifting to the spiked targe upon the table. She lifted it up tentatively, it was heavier than it looked. There were two straps on the rear, and she slid her arm through them, feeling the weight of the device as Daniel approached her. "I know," he mused self-effacingly, "that it is an old-fashioned piece, but it is how I learned my trade."

"It is heavier than it appears," she observed, hefting it.

"Well, it is two layers of wood," smiled Daniel felicitously, "heavy leather upon the face and more upon the back, to say nothing of the spike, and the boss itself."

She observed it again, looking at the heavy ox-hide front. "The face if it seems plain somehow."

"You must have been a Scot in a past life." Daniel marveled. "You are right, most of them are decorated, with tacks or paint. I have lacked the time to give it a proper decoration – perhaps over the long winter, time allowing." Then gently, he took the straps from her arm and set the Targe to one side. "You have not answered me, Meg, so I will be bold before you and ask again. Have you considered the words I asked you last September?"

Her heart was throbbing in her throat, "My days are quite busy at Buckman's, you know, Daniel. Mister Munroe – you probably think of him as Sergeant Munroe, says I have a fine instinct for the work..."

"Have you," Daniel insisted, "thought of what we spoke?"

"Yes," she whispered. "Yes, I have. Every night."

"Thank you, Lord." The Scot whispered, too loudly and moved to take the girl in his arms, but she stepped back out of his range.

"But..." She began.

"But?"

"It is complicated, Daniel. I am complicated. You in truth know little about me, little but that which I want you to know. . . "

"You disapprove of my work with the Sons of Liberty?"

"Liberty." She breathed the words like a prayer. "Daniel, only you, as a free Scot ought understand my heart's reaction to that word. I am so very proud of you. . . in your work. I pray for you every night." She took a long moment to think before speaking again. "You are a fine man, any woman would be glad to have you, and rightly so, I know that, but I am not any woman, I have made my way in life as a *Femme Solo* for some two years now, and.."

"You had little choice, after that bastard abandoned you..."

"The reasons for my path are unimportant, or rather it may be because of them I find myself here. Regardless, I will not be so sorely used again, though I do not think you that hard sort." Tears in her eyes, she gathered the wolf pelts and rushed out the door.

The October winds swept around her and chilled her bones, Meg looked down into the crowded, joyous streets of Lexington, and then, impetuously looked back over her shoulder, at the beaten upon cabin, and her bonny Scot, standing in his doorway, and watched a confident smile spread upon his face.

"Complicated, ye are, yes." He smiled. "But that is not a no."

* * * * *

The beer kegs sat perched upon their wolf-pelts, and Meg found it hard to look at them. Ruth Harrington stood chatting with her, holding the fine looking boy that seemed to have sprung overnight from the babe they had tended, and Meg found it hard to look at the child, too.

Up the hill, Daniel had yet to return to the harvest celebration, she found it hard not to look up the path. Ruth was eyeing her strangely and Meg realized in her wool gathering, she had missed a question in their conversation. "I'm sorry," she demurred, "it is very noisy here, what did you say?"

"I asked if your new employment was to your liking?"

"Oh," Meg nodded. "Aye, I suppose it is."

"Aye?" Ruth parroted back to her. "Aye? Next thing I know you'll be babbling in Gaelic." She smiled at the girl's discomfort, adding. "And you're not running around barefoot anymore, glad to see it, I was worried about what the winter might bring this year."

Meg looked down at her feet, at the nut-brown Scottish brogues she wore, muttered. "They are a fine fit."

"Yes, a very fine fit," Ruth smiled widely, "the two of you, I mean. It is well received." She looked around. "Where is your Scottish warrior, anyway?"

"Wandered off, I think," she said, looking once again up the trail to Cavanaugh's, "to do what, I really do not know."

Adjusting the wriggling boy in her arms, Ruth nodded. "I saw Paul Revere some time ago, most likely they are together." The youngest Harrington wiggled yet more, and Ruth smiled for indulgence sake. "Seems I should be on, think about what we talked on, a girl could do far worse than a Highlander."

Meg smiled, fearing she would think of nothing else for some time to come. She took up a tankard and drew a beer for herself. The sun was low in the sky, bringing the close to another day. The revelers of Lexington were disappearing by ones and twos, soon there would be little left but the clean up, she thought as she approached one of the remaining patrons. "Done for the evening, Mister Whittenmore?"

"I suppose so, Meg." The old Dragoon smiled widely at the young girl, he had drunk enough to be sociable this day, and then some more. "Where is your Highlander this fine evening? It is not a night to tend strangers."

"He is off with Revere," The girl groused, slurping again from a wooden tankard, "helping someone or other."

So much Whittenmore had presumed, indeed Ferguson's absence had made him tarry longer than the beefsteak and company might have made him normally stay. He looked at the fiery haired lass with her sad, world weary eyes again and wondered what might give a girl so young such a flinty edge. "An evening such as this is a time for tales, such as my father might tell late into the night," he ventured, "tell me a tale, love. Tell a tale to your dear Uncle Samuel, a story to ease a tired soul to his slumber on a miserable late October evening."

"Alright." She smiled patiently, drawing a long draught from the wooden tankard before her, a nutty warm ale that would, most likely be her dinner that late night. Beer on an empty stomach was making her light headed and slightly dizzy, but she felt the warmth of it in the pit of her stomach, and it made the tale easier. "I'll tell you of a young girl, who fell in love with a man."

"A swashbuckling former Dragoon, no longer in his prime?", He half-teased.

"No," She giggled coquettishly with her clear, bell like laugh. "A stable boy, an outlander even, and she of good Scotch-Irish stock and of a fine house, the tongues that would have wagged had their love been known, he a mysterious, handsome swain who told tales of the sea and far away places, and she the daughter of a royally appointed judge. It was forbidden for them to be together, so one night, they boarded ship to start a new life together in the Pennsylvania Colonies."

"But they did not get that far?" Whittenmore finished, astutely.

She shook her head sadly. "No, they barely made it past the first saloon. And when their money was gone, she found out his worldly knowledge, so glamorous before, had a hard edge." Her face was frozen in a look of sad fear and pain, staring at a point far away and some lifetimes behind.

"A hard edge, you say? What could that be?"

"He came for her in the early hours, one morning." She whispered, coughed and drank from her tankard before continuing. "Before they stole away into the night, he asked her to get food for their journey. She did, returning quickly, but not before he had helped himself to her father's silver tableware, something she did not discover until much later."

"The brigand."

"He did much worse before…" She began, but stopped herself.

"Before he left? And what happened to this young swain?" The grey haired man asked. Finally, he reached for her and gripped her arm. "Dear Meg? What happened to your young man?"

She snapped from her reverie, wiped at her face and then snapped up a rag, began scrubbing the bar top. "He left."

Whittenmore felt the moment of honesty slipping from between them, and quickly threw the charade of the tale back between them, threw his arms wide and exclaimed grandly in a fake French accent. "No, no, no, this will not do! A great tale of life like this must have an equally exquisite ending. Try again, s'il vous plaît?"

She toyed with a twist of her hair for a long moment in silence, then spoke again. "He spent all that remained of their money on kit for a sea voyage. She begged him, who was the whole world to her now, not to leave her, but he signed onto a whaler out of Boston. She saw him to the dock that morning, and her last words to him were his last hope to get him to stay. "I won't wait for you,

Nathan Higgins!" She said, and he turned and looked at her with a sarcastic smile and said. "Then, don't."

"So what does happen to these star-crossed lovers?"

"There is no need to give them such lofty titles as that," She scoffed darkly, "there was only a silly girl and a man who knew how to . . . pluck her heart strings like a harp."

"But certainly life does not end there, what happens next?" The old Dragoon prodded. "What happens to our dear heroine? Does she find love again?"

"I don't know." She whispered again, the long suppressed pain of a broken heart boiling over her again like a drowning wave of ice. She forced it down by habit, crushing all that she had allowed herself to feel. Silly girl, how could she even consider the idea of love again, of casting hard-learned lessons aside for impractical mewling and dove songs.

"But there is no hope for her?" Whittenmore dared again.

Meg stared at the dwindling fire in the hearth for a long time and whispered in a voice like the wind. "I don't know."

* * * *

The last of the plates and tankards were soaking if not washed. Meg consoled herself that it would be best done tomorrow, when there was some help for her to complete the job.

It was late in the night, the crowds of Lexington festival goers had drifted to their homes, or found their beds for the evening, as she would do now.

Upon the third level of Buckman's Tavern, in a little called for corner room, the ever industrious Monroe had strung blankets as walls, making them fast with nails in floor below and beams above, as small living cubicles for his staff's repose. Lit by a single window of smoky glass, they were dark and spartanly furnished with bed and cast-off table, and simple oil lanterns they dared not leave burning unattended, but Meg was right glad now. Her days were long and this night's rest would be short but welcome. In her mind, she thirsted for the thin blanket, and the scent of the lavender she had scattered through the mattress straw to perfume her dreams.

The door was ajar, a glimmer of light from beneath the woolen, draping doorway of her cubicle caught her breath in her throat, and brought her newly shod feet up short on the creaky floor. Her instincts screamed to run, and she would have, but for that laughing, dark voice calling. "Dearie! Do come in!"

With the long blade of his sword, he reached out and shifted the blanket aside, he lounged on her bed, muddy boots propped on the wood blanket, a scarlet covered arm stretched out behind his head, and a heavy looking pistol in his lap. "You're letting the light out," He purred like a cat toying with its next meal, raised a rum bottle to his lips and took a long pull at it.

Eyes darting this way and that, in her mind's eye Meg saw the stairwell behind her. Then, she looked back at the Redcoat officer lounging on her simple bed, and the heavy pistol lying on his belly. "Do lower your voice, m'lord" She begged, heart beating so fast in her chest she feared she might swoon.

"I had grown worried, my dove," the lobsterback officer simpered dramatically, "I had not heard from you in some time, nor has Portsmith fallen to your Sons of Liberty. I was afraid you had fallen sick, or something, so I rushed to your bedside."

Portsmith? It was his Fort William and Mary again, she mused, wondered why the man placed so much stock there. But, she stepped into the threadbare blanket sanctuary, and with a beaming smile, he withdrew the sword and the curtain-like doorway fluttered closed. Her eyes were glued to the pistol propped on his red coat. It was long of barrel and heavy looking, as if the King, in his thriftiness had refused to buy two sizes of flint-locks and simply ordered the pistols built large to accommodate the same ones the muskets used. Both barrel and lock were set in a wooden grip with a heavy brass butt that seemed made for cudgeling. It was not at all like her steel-framed Scottish pistol.

Her pistol! She was suddenly reminded of her own gun, hidden beneath some sewing in the cast off biscuit box by her bed.

"I was summoned to the office of the Governor of the Massachusetts Colonies recently. You, of course, know General Thomas Gage?" He name dropped remorselessly. "Of course, I don't mean personally, my dear, but you know of him? He has a great interest in the deportment of the outlying villages, their feelings on the King's most benevolent rule, and more specifically if they are hoarding arms and powder for insurrection. I, of course, set myself above the crowd when I told him I had confidential friends in the villages eager to display their loyalty to the Crown by divulging whatever information he might desire."

"Why do we need a king or anyone over us?" Meg heard herself ask. "We get on fine here in Lexington without one."

"Ah, I see you have been infected with this sad disease also," he tisked morosely at her political condition. "Do you ride, my lady?"

She pressed her back to the woolen wall, keeping the best distance from the redcoat officer. "Somewhat, yes m'lord." She nodded, stepping quietly into the dimly lit room.

"What say you we have a race, you wager a ha'penny, and I a thousand pounds, Hmmm? But only I may use my reins, you shall relinquish yours and disdain your stirrup and spur. What say you?" He did not give the girl a chance to answer. "Of course you will see the folly, the beast would wander to the nearest hummock and you aboard like a bump on a frog's arse. So it is with most men, left to their own devices they will drink themselves blind, futter with the first milkmaid they come across and scurry off to do so again, but for the hand at the reins."

"A hand at the reins," Meg echoed, "a hand like King George, or you?"

"King George and his poxy Queen can go hang," Wainright growled, tipped the bottle to his lips again. "I am an officer in his Majesty's army, granted a minor one, but I have ambition. Ambition, but sadly no money."

"I do not understand." She stepped to within a bare foot of the simple wooden crate that housed her worldly possessions.

"The British Royal officer corps is fueled by two things, death and commissions." The Lieutenant said morosely, tipping the rum bottle back again, so that the amber fluid poured from his mouth and down both his cheeks. "You must buy your way in, and after it is deemed that you have suitably debased yourself, you may buy your way up. A Captaincy can cost as much as fifteen hundred pounds, and my dear father has managed to drink away what he has not gambled off before he died, that well is dry. So, if I wish to go anywhere, I must distinguish myself. To do that, I must have war, or at least a good insurrection and in order to play chess, my dear,' He preened, "I need pieces in play."

"Meaning me," she said with a quavering voice, hazarding another step. Her foot bushed the rough box in a sort of victory.

"Well," he purred like a cat toying with a mouse. "Yes."

"No," She snapped, snatching her pistol from beneath the mound of pins and fabrics in the cast off wooden crate. "Get out!"

But he was every bit as fast as she, up like a shot, his heavy looking pistol in hand. "Dearie! You surprise me! It seems my kitten has claws!"

"Claws and the will to use them, Lieutenant, I warn you."

'That is a fine firelock you have there, dear Meg." He made a show of perusing the steel pistol. "Now, this gets me thinking, where might you have come by a Scottish handgun, and a scarce one at that. Even after all your proclamations of innocence and chastity, I find you've been spreading your honey about the town. I do wonder, though, if the Boston docks exchange rates apply out here in the Indian backwoods?"

"I am not a whore!"

"And how else might you have convinced your Scotsman to part with such a fine pistol from his belt, unless you were playing sheath to his dagger."

"It is nothing like that." She heard herself bark back at him, wondered if she was defending her own honor, or Daniel's.

"Not a dagger then," Wainright smirked, intentionally misunderstanding her. "but…what do they call it… a Claymore?" He pantomimed a two handed sword of immense proportions with a mocking tone.

"You are a bastard and a brute!"

Wainright smiled slowly at that slander and said, in a simpering voice. "I don't know what to make of this, dear Meg. You seemed so much more tractable leaned over that wagon wheel with your delicates exposed." Even now, facing down a pistol every bit as lethal looking as his own, he seemed to be enjoying himself.

Meg flushed crimson with embarrassment and then a rush of anger, almost bloody minded rage. She could still feel the rough, damp wood of the spokes of the wagon wheel against her cheek, the red-hot metal scrap's heat upon her thighs and the fear in her throat like vomit as the sadistic Wainright raised it unerringly higher and higher. In her mind, she saw the Lieutenant saunter through his lupine soldiers in colonial garb as they killed and mutilated two men and looted the wagon. With a will, she fought down panic, commanding herself to not give in to fear of this man and what he had done. "I do know," she said, her voice trembling, "I know where you were the night Mister Trotter and Pelenore died. I do know, I saw and I can swear to it."

Wainright's left eyebrow rose the barest fraction, but otherwise he retained his perfect poker face. "Dearest Meg, this is no time to banter confessions of your larceny…"

"But a fine time to wake the King's Magistrate, and tell him who killed them." She hissed over the broad steel barrel.

"You've been hanging around your Sons of Liberty too long, something in the water here in the colonies."

"They tried the men who fired at the Massacre upon King Street, the only thing that saved them was John Adams is a fine lawyer. You will not get such treatment."

"A fine lawyer and a treasonous rabble rouser," The British officer snapped, he did not know John Adams, but knew Sam Adams all too well. "I do declare you are mad. You've listened to your Sam Adams too much, and thinking too little. The British Army is the finest in the world, undefeated. Your batch of bandits is nothing we have not faced a dozen times, and will vanquish again, best to think of being on the winning side, my girl."

"I am not your girl." She growled in a low voice.

Wainright boggled, trying to think of some clever turn of phrase to get this little tart back under his thumb. "You over-speak yourself, whore."

"I am not your whore," Meg growled over the pistol barrel, "I am not your girl. I never was, and never will be. Get out of my sight."

"You are a whore, a liar and a thief, and you will not take that tone with your betters, girl," Wainright snapped with clipped, barbed jabs, "or you will suffer for it."

Megan raised the steel pistol unerringly to the Lieutenant's face. "Go now, or I will not need a King's Magistrate."

"You have been careless of the company you keep, they've given you foolish thoughts." Wainright simpered. "I doubt your father would…"

"Get out!" She fairly screamed, but for fear of waking her neighbors.

"Or what, exactly," he smirked, "a pistol shot will be loud, my lovely, and draw a crowd. How will you explain to your treasonous friends that a British officer was in your bed."

That thought did give her pause, but she rushed to cover it up. "But you will still be dead."

"Perhaps." He smiled that Cheshire smile again, heedless of the pistol aimed at his back, he slowly clipped the heavy pistol to his belt and sheathed his sword. "Very well, my dear, I will take my leave of you, for now. I do hope on our next meeting you will be more agreeable." He paused to pick up his rum bottle, taking a long, final draught before wiping his mouth daintily on the woolen blanket walls. "Remember; arms, powder, guns, where they are and who has them, the leader's names and their whereabouts." He snapped at the girl, as if she had agreed to his commands instead of pulled a pistol upon him to elicit his exit. "And do not forget Fort William and Mary, Portsmith, New Hampshire." He turned abruptly, dropping the crockery jug to shatter on her floor, and departed as if she had never dared to point the pistol at him at all.

Now her hands shook, they shook so hard she feared the pistol might fire, and set it carefully on her mattress. Sharp shards of crockery were scattered about the floor, perfuming the room with the scent of cheap rum. On shaking hands and knees she piled them together, trying to gather the fragments before she split open her heel on one.

The floor creaked outside her blanket shell, and she froze, not daring to move, not daring to breathe until she realized it was simply the wind. Her heart was in her throat, the world swam for a moment and she realized she was alone in this dark place, and that the Lieutenant could return at his will and do what he would with her. What nebulous security she had purchased with his assumption that she was his agent was gone now.

She snatched up her shawl and raced out into the darkness, the streets of Lexington, before so familiar and safe, were a mass of evilly moving shadows and wraiths made of darkness, each a potential hiding spot for Lieutenant Wainright and his lethal intent.

Still, she ran onward, until she collapsed against the door of what the locals still called Cavanaugh's place, and banged frantically upon it.

Daniel, his strange double barreled pistol in his hands, swung open the door and Meg had a sudden thought of her own gun, lying forgotten upon her bed in Buckman's tavern. "Megan," He declared as she collapsed against him.

He seized her in his arms and fairly dragged her into the house, kicked the door closed behind them. Clutching her close to his breast with wild eyes, he asked. "Are you pursued, girl, who chases you?"

Meg stared into those wide blue eyes and in her mind, she heard her hated blackmailer's voice. "How will you explain to your treasonous friends?" How could she say, what could she possibly say. Meg looked Daniel deep in the eyes, and she lied. "I was. . . I was frightened."

Daniel held her close. "Frightened? Of what?" He asked, burying his head in her hair, stroking the length of it down her back.

"Someone banging upon the door. . ."

"At Buckman's?" Daniel completed for her, "upon the door at Buckman's?"

"Yes." She too readily agreed. "And I was afraid, and I ran. . .to you." She looked deep into his eyes and felt herself melting there until a third voice spoke.

"Do not be afraid, Meg." Paul Revere said soothingly from the hearth. The silversmith placed his clay pipe upon the mantle and walked toward them. "You could do no better than to come to Daniel in your fright." Standing beside them now, he placed a comradely hand upon Daniel's shoulder and smiled.

The Scot held her close a moment more, and then set her in a chair before the fire. "Rest, Megan," he said, wrapping a blanket about her legs. "It will take but a moment for me to prepare, then I will take you home."

Meg leaned her weary head back against the chair back, felt the chair rock slightly. She studied the legs and realized that two were repaired, one whittled from a branch and guessed Daniel had done the work himself.

At the hearth, Daniel thrust his long dirk beside the pistol in his belt, whispered to Revere. "Look at her, she's terrified."

"She stinks of rum," the silversmith cautioned, "and ale."

"I know, I smelled it too," Daniel conceded, taking rolled charges from his cartridge box and stuffing them in his sporran. "But, she is not one to be chased by ghosts in the dark, Paul."

"I understand, my friend. We can continue our conversation when you return. We need to disperse that powder."

"Your powder is safe and well cared for." Daniel said, too quickly. "It is stored in several caves, high and dry."

"I do not doubt you." Revere nodded, soothingly as he took up his pipe again. "But it may do us little good in the middle of the greenwood, if we have need of it in Woburn. And the day may come when we need every grain we have, and more."

"There is powder to be had, Mr. Revere," Meg caused them to jump as she suddenly spoke up, "in Fort William and Mary."

"William and Mary? Portsmith? There is powder there, to be sure, Meg, but also stout walls and men with cannon."

"Not now it is not, sir. It is guarded by ten men."

"Ten men, are you serious? Are you sure?"

"How do you know this, Meg?" Daniel asked.

"There was a man, in Buckman's today, a traveling dealer, in breads and meats, I think." Meg lied. "He talked of it. Said but ten men guarded the whole of the fort."

"When did this man come?"

"Today, as the festival was in swing," she said, adding, "he said he was just come from there."

The two men glanced at each other. "Can it be true, Paul."

The silversmith was already tapping out his pipe. "I do not know, but it bears investigation. I ride tonight."

CHAPTER 8

"Greetings to you, Mr. Townsley." William Tidd nodded cordially

from the wagon-driver's seat. "We have fetched up the load of fresh straw you

wanted, sir."

Mr. Townsley, was a nondescript man in the golden time of middle age,

sandy hair going grey with gentle dignity and alert brown eyes. He nodded with

ill-concealed fear painting his face. "Ah, very good and welcome, Mr. Smith.

My son will show you where to put it."

Neither Tidd, nor Daniel used the moniker "Smith", but all was done as

Townsley, if that was his name, requested. The three of them took the wagon to

the rear of the house and Daniel turned out the horse in the corral. The dark

brown mare walked slowly into the corral before realizing she was free of the

wagon's traces, then began to move with a sprightly gait. Daniel watched with

some humor, but past the corrals split rail and stone fence, he could see the

Black Horse Tavern,

William Tidd, second in command of the Lexington Militia, was on the

happy side of forty, a well thought of man about town in Lexington, and, as

Revere had termed it, "a high-minded Son of Liberty". He was Daniel's

conspirator in this latest crime against the Crown. At Revere's direction the two

had, at odd times in the past months, transported powder stolen from the

Cambridge Powder Stores, to Patriot vigilance committees of Woburn and

Acton. It had allowed him to once again see the Davis family. The blacksmith's

home was as welcoming as ever, though Canker Rash still stalked the environs,

and cast a pall over their reunion. This latest direction was, to Daniel, much

more personal. Revere had taken to sending a man with directions "take two and

go to Woburn, see this man or that", this time he came in person. He stood at

Daniel's plain hearth and asked. "Tell me, friend Daniel, how is your memory of

the Black Horse?"

"My memories?" Daniel repeated, "mostly favorable."

Smiling mirthlessly, Revere corrected him. "Not your ruminations of it,

do you remember the floor plan?"

Still not quite seizing the meaning, Daniel nodded. "Yes, well enough."

"Do you remember the stairwell up to the second floor?" Revere asked,

and with rising dread, the Scot nodded. "Well enough to stash a few kegs of

powder there in the dark, quickly?"

Daniel, loathe to say it, nodded instead. Satisfied, Revere nodded back,

put his pipe to his mouth and breathed out a long stream of smoke.

Young Mr. Townsley was a 20-ish image of his father, with the arms of

a man used to the scythe, the wary eyes of a hunter, and a pistol concealed

beneath his jacket. With their mare turned out upon the pasture, Daniel watched

Tidd haul down his bags from beneath the wagon's seat as Young Townsley

tossed a hay-fork into the rear of the wagon. It gave a hollow thud that made the

young man look back in consternation and he quickly scaled into the wagon,

shifting the straw to reveal one of the powder kegs before Tidd could stop him.

Wordlessly, the younger Menotomy man shifted the straw back over the barrel, and jumped down.

The young man made a bee-line for the house, with Daniel and Tidd hurrying after in close pursuit. Daniel cleared the door frame to see the younger Townsley talking animatedly to his father at a rough table. The house was spartanly furnished, though not to the degree of Whittenmore's, it made Daniel wonder if it was a Menotomy trait. There were some apples arranged in a bowl upon the table, providing the barest of a splash of color to a flat, drab room. A blanket covered a doorway he assumed led to the kitchen, and fire burned in the fireplace, a bubbling pot of something aromatic cooking there. Three sets of pegs over the hearth, two filled with muskets, the middle pegs were empty.

"I am concerned as to your purpose here in Menotomy, Cousin," intoned the older Townsley.

"No hospitality?" Chided Tidd. "No greeting for kin?"

"Cousin, your politics are no new news to me. Speaking in a pub is one thing, concealing powder marked with the King's broad arrow is quite another. You endanger this home and all who dwell here, if you have not been caught and set us up intentionally for arrest, I must ask your intentions."

"My intentions, my intentions. What about, how is your family, what news from Lexington?"

"Or, perhaps, who is your new friend?", offered Townsley, as his son began to quietly move around to Daniel's side.

"My name is no concern of yours, thank you," Daniel growled, not taking his eyes from the younger man, "nor my purpose in Menotomy."

"That was to be my next question."

"And I have already answered it."

"Smug bastard." The younger man growled, and went for his pistol.

It was a move Daniel expected, and he cleared the sparse two paces between them before the young man could fully extend the single shot French made gun, the Scot's sixteen-inch Dirk free from it scabbard in a blade-downward left hand grip as his right clamped down upon the hammer and pan of the flintlock pistol the other man had pulled. The blade was between them, its sharp point bare inches from the younger Townley's throat. In his peripheral vision, Daniel saw the blanket curtain flutter and a blonde haired angel with a musket stepped out, bringing the gun expertly to her shoulder and locking back the hammer.

"Stalemate." Townsley the older smiled serenely, but his son had other thoughts.

The younger man had a strange look on his face, staring not at the blade inches from his throat, but at the face of the man who bore it. "That is a big knife you have there, sir," he said, eyes locked to Daniel's, "I must ask again, please, for your name."

The hairs on the back of Daniel's neck stood at full stand, as if he had been too close to an electrical strike, he knew the girl's musket was pointed surely upon his back. But he looked back at the younger Townsley and something in the way the man spoke drove thoughts of lying from the Scot's

mind. "Daniel Ferguson."

The name did not seem to be a surprise. "I hunt with Joshua

Whittenmore, he speaks of your talent hunting bears."

Daniel smirked at the flood of memories. "I was right glad to see him

that day, or I would not be here now."

The young man let out a breath he had not realized he'd held, loosened

his grip on the pistol and motioned for the girl to lower her musket. "He tells it a

bit differently. As you are in Menotomy, you might stop at their home, Samuel

had the bear's skin tanned, I think he intends to give it to you as a gift."

Daniel was amazed at that generosity, but did not know why it

surprised him so. It was typical of the man. "I thank you."

"But for now, I must, for my father's sake, ask your intentions for this

powder."

"I intend to conceal it." Daniel answered truthfully, but cryptically.

"Where?"

"That is not your concern," snapped Daniel, then softened the statement

with, "rather, what you don't know, you cannot say."

The younger Townsley nodded at that. "I imagine it would be best to

wait for nightfall?"

"Yes, I suppose it would be." Daniel nodded, hesitantly.

"Then I would grant the use of my home until the sunset."

"I will go and check my cargo, then," Daniel said plainly, "so as not to further your troubles." Without another word, he turned and walked out the door, in his mind, he saw that rearing sow bear, heard the roar of her, and marveled that Whittenmore had saved him twice that day.

He wandered the town, Menotomy had not changed a great deal, the Black Horse Tavern down the path was boarded up in a disinterested manner, as the afternoon stretched on, he toured the drilling fields, the shops and homes, little seemed to have changed. Then, a voice broke him from his reverie. "I take you, sir, as one of those Sons of Liberty." The man said studiously. There was a formal tone to his voice as he hobbled toward Daniel on a stiff, maimed leg.

Daniel looked the man over slowly, and seeing no reason to lie, nodded. "I am, sir."

"Well done, lad, well done. So many today will skulk about, Royalist or no, and try to conceal their allegiances. Good to meet a plain spoken gentleman." The lame man enthused, offering a hand. "I am Jason Russell, and I would greet you, should you offer me the confidence of your name, sir."

Daniel returned the man's infectious grin and took his hand. "I am Daniel Ferguson, Mister Russell."

"Jason, please, just Jason. And may I say, sir, that is a fine, full brogue you have in your speech. I take you to be only recently arrived here?" The Scot nodded and his lame companion smiled sympathetically. "I suppose it is no surprise to find your people among the Sons, as sorely used as you were."

"You speak warmly of the Sons, Mr. Russell. Are you also a member?"

"Me?" The lame man recoiled as if stunned. "No, sir, no, I doubt if they would have me as a member, I am not the dancer I once was. I am content to live my life without the entanglements of politics, as free as a man may be upon his own lands."

"And should the King come to your lands and declare you not as free as you thought?" Daniel prodded.

"Let him," the hobbling Russell said dismissively, "I have no less the rights of an Englishman here than in London or Avon. "Though the wind blow through the shutters and the roof may leak, the King himself must knock and beg leave of entry.", that is strait from the Magna Charta. Disobedience to the Regent is a young man's game, a game of speeches to stir the blood and absolutes, which is no longer my realm."

"So you are content to live and let live?"

"Yes."

"And be the servant of a German three thousand miles away, who does not allow us the basic right of Englishmen?

I am content to live, and give unto Caesar's that which is Caesar's, so long as he allows me what is mine. So far as I may see, that limited contract is inviolate. However, I see in your face that you see my stance as invalid."

"Not so." Daniel responded automatically, then in a moment's consideration added. "That I wish to be free, I must defend your right to your own anonymity."

"Well said." The crippled man nodded. "Besides, I can see both sides of this debate."

"Both sides, sir," Daniel sputtered, "what of the King's refusal to allow us say in our own governance?"

"True, that is an affront to civic privilege," the studious man allowed, giving off the subtleties of an attorney as he warmed to this debate, "but it is not new for a ruler to insist on ruling. How do you answer for the Divine Rights of Kings, sir?"

"I do not, I made no contract with King George, nor any other, and do not consent to be governed by them."

"I sense in those words the epitaph of Wallace."

"Even so," Daniel allowed, "but what do you say of the Divine rights of man, good my friend Jason. God did place us upon this Earth to take dominion over the creatures of the sea and land, to better it for ourselves and our prosperity, not waste our lives in toil for the enrichment of a sovereign six thousand miles away."

"Well stated, and a point I had not considered before. To which I say to you, "the people cried out for a King, and God gave them David". The Divine right of kings is our lot of life, as it was our forefathers and theirs before. Indeed, why would anyone think to compel a sovereign to pick up his toys and go home, He is the King, he does as he likes, 'tis how it always was."

"But not how it will always be." Daniel swore with a wolfish growl.

"Indeed? And how, once you compel the regent to leave, how will you command his obedience, by the tyrant's *Linguae François*, force? King commands more muskets than a farmer, so for your dream to see the light of day, and not dissolve like the fog in the sun, force can only mean the force of law. But, I say to you, if you believe so strongly in your Roman Democracy, put this question to a vote "of the people" you are so fond of. Should "the people" wish to remain with the King, would you be content?"

"Yes, yes I would." Daniel nodded truthfully. "But should the vote go the other way, do you think good King George would pick up his Lobsterbacks, or choose to compel our subservience?"

Russell blinked as if struck and smiled broadly. "Well said, Mister Ferguson, well said indeed, a fine debate!" He shook Daniel hand warmly. "A fine debate indeed!" A weary smile slowly spread across Jason Russell's face. "Best of luck to you, friend Daniel of the Sons of Liberty, I will think of you in my prayers."

* * * * *

Sam Whittenmore was glad to see the Scot, and had indeed gifted him the tanned bearskin. A pleasant hour was passed as the two talked over a bottle of Whittenmore's wine, as Daniel watched the setting sun with dread of his coming mission.

When conversation dried up, Daniel returned to Townsley's barn, removing a portion of the hay as he thought on the topics discussed with the enigmatic, legalistic Russell, when approaching footfalls brought him back to reality and he turned to see the lady of the house hesitantly watching him from the corral gate.

"Thank you for the straw, what price did my Father-in-law contract you for it?"

"Keep it as a gift." Daniel tried to smile disarmingly, but it only displayed his nervousness at the coming of the sunset.

"Take this as payment, then." She smiled warmly back, handed him an apple. "Is this your first trip to Menotomy, Mister Ferguson?"

Daniel took the fruit and bit into it, it was softer than he usually liked, but for so early in the spring, not bad. "Thank you, and I am Daniel. It is not my first visit here, I spent time here…a while ago. It is much more pleasing now."

"I am Rachel, then." The girl said, but Daniel stood watched the setting sun for a long time, before the lady spoke again, pointing with a finger. "That will be my garden, right where your wagon sits."

"And what will your garden grow, Rachel?"

She shrugged disarmingly. "Everything. I am the mistress of the house."

"You are quite industrious," laughed the Scot, "your husband is a very lucky man. How long have you been married?"

"Last fall." She said, proudly. "Mother Townsley passed beyond last Spring. I find myself the woman of the house, now."

"How do you…how do you feel about," Daniel paused, thought briefly before concluding with, "what we do here."

"It frightens me," she answered with more honesty than she perhaps intended, "as I imagine it does you, also. But I think of young Chris Seider shot down upon King Street, and Crispus Attacus beside him and I weep. Should God grant me a child, I would that he, or she, would see old age after me. Each night I pray for peace, but a wolf at the door will not respect prayer, only a gun, it seems it is so with some people too, even Royals."

Daniel watched the sun's last rays lick at the sky and disappear. "My work summons me, Madame, and I shall go."

"Will we see you again, Mister Ferguson?"

"I hope so, madam, I think I would like that."

* * * * *

"Come, my stalwarts," sighed Lieutenant Wainright, straightening the front of his fine scarlet tunic, flicking distractedly at some dust that had settled upon his royal blue facings, "let us go and overawe the bumpkins." Sergeant McNeal, a gruff, lean Scotsman who had been in His Majesty's army seemingly forever, called the men to stiff attention before barking "Forward… march", and twenty or so men of the King's Own lights marched smoothly down the cobblestones, into the military green off Hanover Street and Cold Lane.

A crowd had already gathered, but more milled in behind the marching Redcoats, as these military maneuvers were high drama in their dreary days, it also provided a handy reminder of the strong punitive arm of the King of England. Toward that end, it had become a standard practice among junior and supernumerary officers to lead a company through the streets, and into the military park to the delight of the crowd.

You could quickly pick out the Tories, who showed a preference to applause, but the lieutenant's mind was not on the alliances of his audience, right and left facings, or evolutions. Instead, he pondered his recanting informant in Lexington, and what to do about her. That the mewling little tart lived was an annoyance, rather like the buzzing of a fly. More, he pondered the words he had said in her presence while she was in his power and seemed of no more consequence than a potted plant. That, those words, were what he *feared*.

With a rattling crash of boot soles, they halted before a copse of trees, the crowd edging closer to watch as Wainright paced before his men. "Company," he bellowed, "Form ranks!" To the rattle of a drum, they melted to two lines with crisp precision. Then, the drum ceased like a slamming door.

"Do be quick." He urged the men, quietly the drum rattled and he walked before them. "You are only shooting powder, you know." The men grinned at that, though the lead balls the Brown Bess muskets shot were slightly undersized, firing caused fouling in the barrel which quickly render the passage of the ball impossible.

The lieutenant took a most military pace back, commanding "Company, load!" and twenty men poured blank charges of powder down the gaping maws of ol' Brown Bess. "Five rounds, rapid fire! Prepare!"

"Oh, good lieutenant, do give Sam Adams his comeuppance!" cried a voice from the assembly of onlookers.

The voice was in earnest, and female. For the second reason more than the first, Lieutenant Wainright scanned the crowd for whoever spoke, then dramatically replied. "I would, good citizen, but I do not have a rope." Tories laughed appreciatively at the jest, rebels stood disapprovingly stone faced. The Lieutenant leered wolfishly at all and returned to his duties.

The soldiers held their pieces before their faces, the heavy Brown Bess musket locks at the level of their eyes. "Present!" He commanded, and as one the muskets leveled, each man staring down the long barrel at some imagined point in the distance.

"Fire!" He bellowed, the word drown out by the blast of twenty muskets sounding like a single cannon blast. It was a lovely sound, echoed through the military park with the rattling of ramrods and then another blast like an echo of the first, and more still like the echoing roll of thunder.

Speed was the thing, rapidity of firing making up for the lack of accuracy the sightless smoothbore musket boasted, speed even making up for the pitiful range. It all came down to speed, the lieutenant told himself and far too soon, a shocking silence descended like a blanket of the green, swept away by applause. Beaming, Sergeant McNeal asked from the side of his mouth "How long, sir? What was our time?"

"Who cares, Sergeant," Wainright soothed, casually slipping his neglected watch into the inside pocket of his Scarlet jacket, "our point was made." Then he gave a very courtly bow as William Brattle approached, offering his hand in friendship. Brattle was something of a local hero of the

Seven Years War, and lately had become well-known as an unrepentant loyalist who had been run out of his home in Cambridge. Gage had allowed him to maintain arms in his new housing against the hooligans, as they referred to the Sons of Liberty.

"An excellent display, lieutenant, quite martial," Brattle said, and Wainright opened his mouth to speak his thanks, but the local legend continued. "I cannot tell you how welcome a red coat is to me and mine in these times of troubles. If there is anything a clergyman can do for you, please do not hesitate."

Hmmm, thought Wainright,the man had lead troops, carried license as a doctor and a lawyer, but he calls himself clergy. The Lieutenant wondered if these late events had stolen his pluck. "The time may come when the King will need much from his subjects."

The words had the proper flattery for Brattle. "By God's will, lieutenant, I keep my musket oiled and by the door, waiting for your call, sir."

* * * * *

"Friend Ferguson!", enthused a nearby voice, one that drew Daniel back to that blustery, eventful night upon the docks of Griffin's Wharf, Daniel craned his neck in all directions to find its owner. Then, the familiar visage of Doctor Warren materialized in the crush of men and women, the Scot inclined his head in a friendly half bow. "Good to see you again, sir. What brings you back to Boston?' The Doctor asked as he shook Daniel's hand.

Daniel smiled warmly at the man who had once stitched him back whole. "I am invited to South Church this evening, on the anniversary of the

Boston Massacre." Daniel spoke truthfully, "you are familiar with it."

"The massacre? I should say all of Boston knows of it."

"I meant the church, Doctor." Daniel corrected himself

"Yes, you could say. I will be delivering the address," he said humbly. "I did so last year, and apparently was though of well enough that I was asked to repeat my performance."

A passing corpulent business man with red cockade in his tricorn looked at his attendant manservant and said, loudly. "That reminds me, Perkins, I am in need of new feather pillows." The Doctor smiled widely at the comment and turned, giving an extravagant bow.

Daniel's confusion must have been evident, though, for Warren tossed an arm around him and said, "do not concern yourself with his lordship, he lacks the courage to do his own misdeeds. True, we Sons of Liberty and the Tories trade tarring and feathering parties like favors at a May-day dance, but with that short sword stuck in your belt, you have none to fear."

"Have the Tar and Feather parties come for you?"

"No." The doctor said with finality, allowed his coat to fall open. The good doctor smiled in a way that confirmed Daniel to be in his confidence and swept aside the skits of his coat, displaying a pair of pistols thrust into his stylish green-grey sash. Daniel admired the diminutive pair of flintlocks, as they were a work of the gun-maker's art, jutting muzzles swelled from palm sized grips, fittings of polished brass ornamentally accented a pair of weapons to stand aside from on a dark night.

"In truth, I did not take his meaning." Daniel admitted, shyly adjusting the long dirk thrust into his belt.

"Good!" The doctor enthused. "Indeed, I daily receive notice of some violence to be done unto me. I am afraid I have become somewhat immune to it. But in any case."

"These must be interesting times, that a doctor of your skill and renown must gird himself like a Highwayman before journeying from his door." Daniel remarked.

"As that a Highlander such as yourself has laid aside his Lochaber axe for a simple dirk." He reached out and jovially touched the carved hilt of Daniel's sixteen inch blade, thrust into his belt so the carved brass guard touched his belt buckle, as the Scot always carried it. The act was done in token of friendship, and out of respect for the doctor who had saved his life, the Scot allowed it, though in the Highlands, it would have been a deadly insult. "Would that mean that trouble is expected of us?"

"It all depends on what the damned Lobsterbacks have planned."

* * * * *

"A most audacious plan, sir!" Ensign Henry DeBerniere enthused.

"Do you think so?" Captain Chapman preened his moustaches at the praise, taking a pinch of snuff from a box carved from a clamshell and set with a silver hinge.

No, in point of fact, Lieutenant Wainright did not think so. The blithering, inbred bastard had all but damned them to an inglorious death, being torn apart by an enraged mob. His so-called plan commanded a few dozen or so of the King's officers to march into the lion's den, the Old South Meeting House, where the ruffians had held their meeting before sinking some eighteen thousand pounds worth of his Majesty's tea. The Captain had come around the barracks almost as Wainright had returned from the days evolutions, informed them that, having the ear of General Gage, he knew that the General had finally had enough of these ridiculous upstart colonists, and the deed had fallen to them."

It was a suicide mission tailored to the desperation of supernumeraries, nonexistent planning, ridiculous risk and with that, the possibilities of incredible rewards should they succeed. Careers had been made on lesser assaults.

Dear Ensign Henry DeBerniere, Wainright's new roommate at the Widow Newman's boarding house, held no such powers of examination. Instead, taking as granted that this drunken Captain did indeed have Gage's ear, he had fallen into a particularly unctuous form of flattery. "And what a fine snuffbox that is, sir, quite unique."

"Paul Revere did it for me, and at a fine price, I should mention." Chapman held it out for the inferior officer to examine. "A fine tradesman he is, though a poor judge of politics."

"Revere?" The Ensign fairly squealed, oozing hero-worship from every pore. He was a shorter man, of French extraction on his Father's side and merchant money on his mother's. His Daddy had given him his dark hair and sharp features, his mother's money had given him his commission. "You

ventured into the lion's den to stare face to face with the propagandist, sir?"
Everyone knew the name, but damned few had bothered to walk down to Fish
Street and look the devil in the face. Wainright thought to himself, and made a
note to himself to make the journey to Revere's silver shop and do just that.

Ensign DeBerniere had all but dragged Wainright on this fool's errand,
insisting that the chances for promotion were so obvious and fairly dripping
from the Captain's finger that he would be a fool not to go. Wainright was more
inclined to sullenly drink himself to sleep, but succumbed to the Ensign's
enthusiasm. Besides, it was better than staring at the ceiling of his overpriced
room, hoping a solution to his problems with the difficult, disobedient Meg
would materialize from thin air. So, Wainright found himself standing in the
gathering darkness of Boston's side streets, mulling over the barest sketch of a
plan Captain Chapman had detailed for them. They were to walk into the
imposing, ornate meeting house, surreptitiously making their way to the front;
such an easy thing for a half dozen men in scarlet coats and white leather small
clothes amongst a sea of colonist drabs. Then, at the podium, they were to await
the signal, and upon it, arrest…well, everybody; the vociferous Dr Warren, the
Machiavellian manipulator Sam Adams, idle rich pretender to the American
throne John Hancock and any others who dared sedition. The signal, ad-hoc
though it appeared, was strangely appropriate, upon the Captain's signal, young,
pimply Ensign Murray, all fifteen years of him, too young to shave and too
stupid to see this for the suicide mission it was, was to throw a raw egg at
Warren as he spoke his treasonous bile.

Huddled in the shadows of the alleyways, the Captain tipped a silver flask of brandy to his lips, watched hordes of people pour into the meeting hall, the other men watched too, with a growing sense of dread. Lieutenant Cooper, a stocky, self prepossessed officer of a regular company checked the priming powder in the pan of his pistol for perhaps the eighth time, The Captain had seen fit to muster the group of them and issue or confiscate arms from the officers as he saw fit, though he wore his fine sword and a pistol, as did his two favorites, Lieutenant Cooper and the already pleasantly drunk Ensign DePage. The rest of them apparently were to make due with swords only, something Wainright saw as an insult to his proficiency, but he kept his own secrets that none need know.

"Captain, if I may presume to say," Wainright said unctuously, "this isn't going to get any better looking at it."

"Yes, quite." The officer nodded, in a muttering tone that made Wainright sure he had injured the drunken bastard's fragile pride. But the man got moving, slowly toward the Old South.

* * * * *

"Today is the sixth of March, the year of our Lord 1774," Captain Parker, wearing his best Sunday suit, said formally at the kitchen door, "five years ago was the bloody Boston Massacre. I go to Boston to honor those fallen, and I am asked to invite you and a select group of others to this attendance."

"Yes, my Captain," Meg demurred shyly. "But is not today the sixth? Yesterday was the date of the King Street massacre."

"Yes Meg, it was, and also a Sunday," The Captain smiled paternally at the young girl. "It was decided to delay the memorial so as not to disturb the Sabbath with warlike speeches."

Meg's stomach flipped inside her. "Will there be warlike speeches, sir?

"No doubt, Meg, no doubt," Parker smiled flippantly. "Doctor Joseph Warren will once again be the speaker. T'is his third year and he has always brought the walls down like Joshua."

The wagon ride to Boston was uneventful; though Menotomy left a pang in her heart for those lost in the shadows. Not valued so much as accepted in life, Meg found than she missed their presence in their deaths. More soldiers seemed to be patrolling the Boston Neck, that narrow strip of land that led into the town. The pauper's graveyard for the poor and suicides seemed fuller, nor did the gallows at the fortification gates lack business.

Dour Sam Adams was master of this night's ceremony, standing beside his constant shadow, the dapperly dressed John Hancock, one of the richest men in the America's, and who's name was often mentioned as the monarch of this new world, should it break from English rule. Crowds were already filling the meeting house when they arrived.

Megan unconsciously smoothed her skirt as John Parker guided her into the presence of Paul Revere. He looked excited, but tired, like a man who had just won a horse race, clad in his best brocade vest and brushed green coat for the evening. She had worn her best for this evening, her just finished white blouse and red bodice with her newest green skirt over her Scottish brogues.

"Good evening, Miss Megan," the silversmith said, with real warmth, "you are most welcome this night. If you had not heard, the…information you provided me on our last meeting was very fruitful." She smiled demurely at the tubercular Parker beside her and the beaming Revere. "The young lady is indeed the hero of the hour."

More and more people were crowding into the old meeting house, chairs filling rapidly, and the small group quickly seized a row of seats in the third row. Meg looked about the room, marveling at the mass of humanity that had come to hear the speeches, long residence in small towns had left her unused to crowds. The crowd was so vast it blocked the doors and the featured speaker had to shimmy up a ladder and crawl in a window behind the altar. Striking in his robes, Doctor Warren solemnly approached the black crepe-draped dais and the Bostonian audience respectfully hushed and a scattering of Lobsterbacks hissed under their breath. He wore a fine representation of a roman toga to add solemnity to the event, clutching a handkerchief in his left hand, his right at the belt line of his breeches.

A scattering of some forty Redcoat officers were in attendance among the throng of Bostonians, easily outnumbering the soldiers a hundred or more to one. Sam Adams, ever the chess player, had noted their entrance and invited these "honored guests" to the front rows, the best seats in the house. Several refused these offers as still too trifling, planting themselves upon the edge of the stage itself as their seats. The Captain was one of these, placing himself near the dais with an intent look upon his face and Wainright seized the opportunity to ingratiate and stood to the officer's right, placing his back to the wall.

* * * * *

The good doctor began to speak, and the milling crowd stopped muttering and turned to him like flowers to the rising sun. All but the Lobsterbacks in the audience, who hissed or boo'd in blatant attempt to drown the Doctor out, others laughed outlandishly or coughed like tubercular monkeys. That they gave offensive utterance was a testament to their bravado, Daniel thought; that they did it surreptitiously was a demonstration of their good sense.

The crowd did not so much part for the six foot Scot with a dagger thrust through his belt as he managed to dance through the citizens of Boston and red-coated British officers like the river swaying around the rocks in its path. All were almost ridiculously polite, a sightseeing Lobsterback Lieutenant trod upon Daniel's foot and apologized so profusely that Daniel was embarrassed. It was a strange feeling to be so close and so polite to these men in their scarlet coats when seven months ago he had marched to war against them. Now we stand about complementing each other and pretending nothing had happened.

Finally seeing his intended person in the crowd, Daniel approached Revere, who greeted him warmly. The act seemed to embarrass Daniel, who stammered for something to say. "I… have delivered the items entrusted me, safe and secure."

"Of which I had no doubt." Revere smiled broadly, "though good to hear, just the same. Was there any difficulty?"

"None." Daniel lied, the Black Horse Tavern had been darker than he remembered it, and he dared not strike a light to guide his way. In complete darkness, he snuck two barrels of powder into the abandoned building, creeping through the shadows, as he dared not make a sound to conceal them behind the old stairs to the second floor. Abandoned bottles and things unidentified contrived to trip his steps and beams and doorjambs seemed eager to seek out his head. But with long effort and silent persistence, he had completed the goal.

"I only wish it had been more." The silversmith lamented, voicing the opposite sentiment that Daniel had been musing. "Had the British not stolen their powder, I believe we could have made off with all of it!"

Daniel's jangled nerves were still on edge, and the crowd making him paranoid. He looked at the faces about him and said, with forced casualness. "What is this matter, Paul?"

"It is a memorial to the Boston Massacre." Revere said simply, fixing him with a queer look.

"So much I know, but I am afraid I do not know the event which is memorialized, past that it was a Massacre, and presumably somewhere in Boston."

Revere nodded in sudden understanding. "Do you see that fellow over there, with the hat that needs blocking?" Revere nodded over Daniel's shoulder and Daniel looked quickly, seeing a thin, dark haired man with his back to the

260

wall and a set look to his mouth. "That is George Hewes, a cobbler and a fine, high minded citizen," Daniel had known Revere long enough to know that meant the man was a Son of Liberty, "a British soldier contracted him to repair a pair of brogans, which he did, but upon his return the Soldier refused to pay, just threatened George with his bayonet and left with his shoes. Come that fated day, George sees that same soldier standing guard on the King Street customs house. George demands payment once again, and the soldier threatens to run George through. Being a sensible man, George high-tails it across the street, well out of bayonet range and begins railing against the soldier.

"A crowd gathers, someone starts throwing snowballs, the custom house calls out the guard, a dozen redcoats with musket and bayonet getting pelted with snowballs, one of them commands present arms most likely to scare the crowd, but an officer in the building hears that and rushes out, screaming "no, soldiers, don't fire." Course, in the confusion the only word the bastards heard was "Fire", and they did." Revere drew in a breath and let it out in a sad sigh. "Crispis Attacus, Samuel Grey, James Caldwell and Samuel Maverick died in the snow, more were wounded. Muskets against snowballs, Daniel."

* * * * *

Warren was blathering on about innocent colonists, as if these litigious rebels could be credited, Wainright thought, standing against the dais, he could see every angry eye in the meeting house. "Where was bloody Murray and his damned egg. Get on with it," he inwardly raged.

"If we sought rebels, we seem to have come to the right place," noted Captain Chapman at a whisper, beckoning with his chin, "yonder sits Revere."

Wainright followed the gesture to find the man. He had never set eyes upon the hated rebel agent but indeed, there was the silversmith, in rapt attention of the ridiculously dressed, preening Dr Warren at the podium.

As befitted a coward, Revere stood in a tight group, a blonde-haired man with a dagger thrust into his belt, an old man with the eyes of an Indian fighter and... beside those two was that bane of his existence, the little red haired tart from the forest. She looked different her Sunday best, instead of dirty with soot and scared to death, but it was her, without question. Lt Wainright was so shocked, he almost dropped his flask.

Feeling his gazes upon her, the fire haired little wench turned and started. Her eyes boggling from her head in fright at him, that plump little set of red lips dropped open in shock, then quivered in fear, which only strengthened Wainright's resolve. But he felt the strong hand of his erstwhile leader, Captain Chapman, leader of the group, and heard his slurring fatherly voice suggesting "Stare at the vixen later, the fox is afoot. As you were moon gathering, I have sent your fellow DeBerniere on an excursion," the Captain advised with rum soaked breath, "I have a fine prank in mind."

"Yes sir." Wainright muttered, but was unable to tear his eyes from the shocked, beautiful continence. Meg's eyes were wide as a shying colt, breaths coming quick, straining the stays of her bodice so rapidly she might hyperventilate. As was his way, the Lieutenant opted to press his attack, and see what developed. Casually he glanced for witnesses, but found every eye but hers

locked upon Warren in his crowing, then he locked eyes with the frightened girl

and deliberately drew a finger across his throat.

* * * * *

Her corset was too tight, her throat constricting and cutting her air,

Megan's head swam and the world took on a sable edge, shrinking around her.

She fought a swoon, battling back from the edge of the abyss, and losing.

"We stare wildly about, and with amazement ask, "Who has spread this

ruin around us?" Is it the French? Perhaps the Spanish or the Red Indians?"

Warren, upon his podium, paused dramatically and then continued. "No, none of

these, it is the hand of Britain that inflicts this wound."

In drunken, sarcastic response, Captain Chapman held up a handful of

bullets, the round lead balls clinked ominously in his hand. "This hand of Britain

can inflict many a worse wound, Doctor." He slurred with ill concealed malice.

Without losing a step, or any composure, the Patriot doctor dropped his white

handkerchief over the captain's hand, and continued his speech. Meg watched

all this dimly as the world constricted to a pinpoint around the evil eyes of her

red-coated tormentor.

Revere was lost in Warren's oration. Warren was oblivious to her state,

an entire congregation of friends and neighbors about her, and she might as well

be alone in a pasture, just she and the man who had butchered her friends in the

Sudbury woods.

Then, a familiar Scottish burr purred. "Megan? What's the matter, girl." Trust her "Wild Scot" to note her distress. But she peered into the deep blue pools of the Scotsman's eyes, eyes like the sea after a storm, dark and vibrantly blue, and that drew her back from the brink. Her hands found his and seized it, felt the warmth of him, the iron of his strength. "Are you alright, girl? Do you need some air perhaps?"

With a rising panic and horror, she remembered the officer and his affection for shadows, the ruthless efficiency of his men, hatchetting dear Mr. Trotter and the officious, presumptuous Pelenore at their leisure in the privacy of the dark woods. Her throat clenched at the thought of relinquishing the comfort and safety of Old South's crowd and giving the Lieutenant his chance to do so again. "Mr. Warren is…a fine speaker." She hazarded.

"A fine speaker?", the Scot repeated, "a fine speaker you say? 'Tis just as well he closes, then, less you faint dead away." He gestured toward the podium as Dr Warren stepped free of its draped dais. The Bostonians hesitated and looked from their own to the Red coated officers in their midst like rats in a corner, afraid to give themselves away. Then, Sam Adams rose majestically and declared in his grand manner. "Shall the committee agree to commend Doctor Warren's fine oratory with a return engagement on the next commemoration of this most bloody anniversary?" The room broke into thunderous applause.

Ensign DePage looked at his fellows, once again tipped the flask to his lips and blew a contemptuous raspberry. Captain Chapman laughed as the crash of a military drum and fife drifted through the window. An eager junior lieutenant swung up to one of the windows. "It's the band from the 43rd foot!" He declared proudly as the tattoo of rolling drums crackled like rain upon the assembly, and the shrill of fifes made Lt Wainright's blood boil hotly in his ears.

The crescendo of applause seemed to rise, an attempt to drown out he music of the King's Army. "Cheeky bastards," growled the young lieutenant, as the handsome Doctor Warren tarried a bit longer on the dais, acknowledging the applause. Emboldened by rum, DePage rose and raged at the Doctor on his podium. "Fie!" He called in menacing derision. "Fie! Fie!"

Military music filled the room with an electric current, women paled and clutched at their suitors, men rose in mute, fearful notice, and the commanding boom of "Fie! Fie!" sounding like "Fire! Fire!" sending the room into panic.

There was a panicked rush for the doors, women swooned or screamed, men brandished walking sticks like cudgels, plainly willing to go down fighting. No few swords were produced, as were daggers and privately owned pistols. What seating there was had been abandoned, much as whatever orderly, polite attention was forgotten. The Colonials were milling against each other like cows to pasture, all hope of civilization or community gone. Wainright saw Revere in a huddle at the stage with Adams and Warren, Captain Chapman attempting to amass his fellows into something like a defensive position. Then he picked out the flaming auburn hair of the girl, alone, not far from the spot he had observed her before.

Secreted in Lieutenant Wainright's boot was a small pistol, a parting gift from the uncle who had all but raised him. He palmed the little firearm as he slid away his pocket flask, then he abandoned his messmates to a delicate game of maneuver through the crowd, a mass of angry, confused faces and lethal arms of every make and size.

"Hello dearie." He muttered, just loud enough to be heard. She spun, eyes wide like a shying horse, or more appropriately, a hen-bird before the axe came down. He grinned a death's leer smile, directed her gaze with his eyes to the wide pistol bore jutting from his fingers. "I've been thinking a lot about you lately."

"Oh God, you!" She whispered, eyes glued to the bore the size of an acorn protruding from between his gloved fingers.

"Yes, 'tis I. Our last meeting was so…terse. I was hoping we might patch things up." He smirked the same leer again, gesturing with the pistol toward the door. "It is a fine night, and good King George, God bless him, and General Gage have seen fit to give me the entire evening to myself." His voice was smooth, with a hissing lisp that reminder her of a serpent. "Why don't we take a nice long walk, in the woods, just you and I?"

"In the woods. . ." She repeated, and the color drained from her face. She knew it was a walk she would never return.

* * * * *

Two men in the crowd had the same thought "It cannot begin here, not in a church" One was Sam Adams, white as a sheet upon the podium and fearing the loss of their moral case as much as a hangman's rope. The other was the Scot, remembering tales of Robert the Bruce and his excommunication. It was a tale every young Scot knew, in 1306, Robert the Bruce met with John Comyn in a church to discuss a secret agreement, but daggers were drawn and in an instant, Comyn lay dead before the altar, and the Bruce under the condemnation of the church.

It could not happen here, not again. "Good sir, put up your blade!" He begged.

"The Lobsterbacks come for us!", declared the man. He wore the powdered wig, fine vest and jacket of a lawyer, but the hunting sword of an accomplished fox-hunter and seemed intent to use it this night, so much so Daniel had imposed himself between the man and the red-coated soldiers. "It's war, son, war!"

"Yonder Redcoats offer no fight, sir!", observed Daniel, pointing at the clutch of officers in scarlet huddled upon the walls. "They fear us more than we fear them."

The barrister paused at that, observing the mass of red coats and white leather pants with a new humor to his face, and slid the much loved old hunting hanger back into its sheathe.

There was no time to savor the victory, as a time-worn voice reached his ears. "Lobsterback bastard, I'd like to twit your nose!" A withered old lady had cornered a broad shouldered officer of the crown, his hair every bit as red as his jacket and was berating the bewildered man for everything she was worth.

"Mother," Daniel offered the chiding word as an honorific, "can't you see that this officer has no…" His words trailed off as, over the Irish Guard's shoulder, Daniel spotted a new vision which made his heart jump. Daniel forced himself not to run, walking deliberately at the pair, Scarlet coat and fiery red hair, they were easy to find in the riotous mob. Her eyes seemed glued to his middle, fear plain on her face. Daniel scanned the Lobsterback for the reasoning of this terror. His sword was still sheathed, hanging at his waist, but there was no doubting that look in Meg's eyes. The Redcoat shifted constantly, watching in all directions, and as he did, Daniel saw the tiny pistol in his hand.

Yet another of the tiny things, much the same as Doctor Warren had carried thrust in his belt this very day. Daniel's mind whirled and twisted, plotting some way to extract Meg from this unwelcome attention without one of the two of them gaining the contents of that little pistol. "You English have the manner of pigs," he growled as he neared them, both started at his sudden interruption, "in Scotland, a Ghillie escorting a lady to a shindy has reason to expect he might escort her home as well."

"And you must be dear Meg's Scotsman!" Wainright smiled his brightest smile, glancing between the newcomer and the red haired girl. "Meg spoke so highly of you upon our last meeting! I do hope you've gotten your pistol back."

"Pistol?" Daniel fixed the man with a look of confusion.

Another provincial dullard, Wainright sneered with a resigned sigh. "Stand aside, peasant, this is King's business." Wainright snapped as he seized

Meg by the arm, fully expecting this insolent provincial to mutely obey. But the man stood resolute, like a six foot statue, a strange smile fixed upon his face. "I said move aside, you rascal, by the command of his Majesty, King George."

"His Majesty, King George." The Scot repeated, slowly chewing each word as if he had never heard them before, mulling over their meaning a long moment as the crowd of the meeting hall mulled around him, unnoticed. Meg stared at the two men, these two warring embodiments of her soul, one meaning freedom, the other her chains, one the embodiment of Royal law and order, the other the chaos of this strange new ideal, "the rights of man".

His brawny arms were folded across his broad chest, like a blind man upon a cliff's edge, Daniel tried to feel his way along the precipice. From the moment he had set foot upon this new world, he had played at being a revolutionary, destroying the King's tea, concealing stolen powder, merely twitting His Royal nose. But now, standing before his home-made shoes – both pairs, in fact – was a royal officer giving him an order in the name of the King, and giving it with insolent, commanding eyes. Those eyes were like reflecting pools shining back the Highland clans falling at Culloden and their widows and bairns being swept from their homes in the Clearances after, to be replaced by grazing sheep. He saw the icy, calculating eyes of recruiting sergeants, Royal Navy press gangs seizing free men upon ships at sea and a German King in Buckingham Castle, dictating who and what the colonists would be permitted to trade with, and the army placed there to insure it.

"Command of the king," Daniel said again, expounding, "and what command can a Royal German usurper give me? What command can a King's lieutenant, by right, give a free citizen?"

"Those words smack of treason," Wainright growled, tightening his grip upon the girl, "more so than the words of that fop of a doctor caparisoned like a drapery upon the stage."

"Aye, they do. And strange they taste upon my tongue." The Scot said, his voice strangely conversational, the smile upon his face elated, like a man finishing a journey, "strange like the dawn of a new day, and all the more welcome for it."

Wainright stared at the man a long moment and mused the tone of his words, but he had no time for conversation this night and snapped a final time. "Get out of my way, villain."

"Villain am I, now?" Daniel cast back to the British officer, "by what right do you take to address a man so common?"

"Fie upon you, madman," Wainright spat, "go and find yourself an asylum, as if this entire continent were not madhouse enough." He began to twist away, dragging Meg toward the doorway, but felt a poke in his ribs and glanced down.

A blade jutted from beneath the Scot's broad arms, steel the length of a short sword closing the bare six inches between them and touched his red-coated breast. "She's sixteen inches, Jimmy, every blessed bit of it." The Scot whispered to him in a voice pitched like a lover's. "Enough to go through both your lungs, one after the other, your heart and come out the other side too, I'll wager. She's tickling your eighth rib, that's a straight shot through. Trust me."

He did believe the man, and at the same time accepted that the Scot was just the sort of man who could commit the deed. But instead of voicing those thoughts, the Lieutenant turned back to the quivering girl at his side. "Dearest Meg, I had more hope for you than to find you in the company of a filthy Scot."

"When dealing with the English," Daniel quipped, "a Scot be the best friend to have."

"What do you mean by that impudence?"

"T'is we filthy Scots who pushed back your Edward the Long shanks at Falkirk, when the rest of the world was pissing in their boots at the name of him, and stood off you English at pike point upon Flodden fields…"

"…And lost," the Lieutenant said sharply. "You lost, at end of things, over and over."

"We won at Sterling Bridge."

"Even a broken clock is right twice a day, my Scottish vagabond. Those who lack the wit to distinguish brilliance from belligerence will be disappointed in the end. Now out of my way."

Still the Scot did not move, the short sword he called a side knife protruding from beneath his arm, ready to burrow through Wainright's body and rob him of his life in a single effort. The officer smirked evilly. "I can pull this trigger and this treasonous bitch will never see the morning."

"Aye, that you can," Daniel agreed. "If the powder be not damp and the load a well done thing. If the flint has not jostled loose, or the priming be in the pan and not sitting in the heel of your boot." The Scot, trusted warrior of his Clan, was in his element. Megan held her lower lip tightly so as the hated Lieutenant would not see it tremble, but Daniel's voice was hypnotic, she found herself wondering how the man could sound so calm when she was about to lose her water right here on the floor of Old South. "The difference here Jimmy, is I know I hold your soul in 'me hand, as to you and her, 'tis a less known thing."

"There is a regiment of King's men outside, and better than three dozen of his Majesty's officer in this room." Wainright snapped, and jabbed the little pistol hard into Meg's side to punctuate the threat. "One word from me will have you both arrested, and hung, and that does not require my pistol to work."

"Ever tried to sing with a blade the length of a belaying pin through your innards?" The Scot said, conversationally. "I have not, but I have spoken to those who have. They marveled at the difficulty."

"I grow impatient." The Lieutenant snarled. "I have better thing to do than talk to an ignorant Scot about a whore. I may just pull this trigger and do us both a service."

"Aye, you might, an' that be the thing I cannot abide." Daniel smiled slowly. "You can still walk from here, Lieutenant, and live another day. But not with the girl."

Someone bumped into Daniel, hard enough to unsettled his balance, but the nimble Scot kept his feet, glanced back to see the angered face of the Lord

Trenton, dimly remembered from that day in December after he had fallen from the *Beaver* and into the Sons of Liberty. The man's face was twisted into a scowl. "Tis a crime to molest a Crown officer!", the Tory said, incensed at the Scot's lack of manners.

"No more so than to accost a lady, aye, and possibly for the same reason." Daniel quipped, glancing down at the man's hands and the short barreled pistol there, another of those blessed muff pistols! The grip, which was barely held by one and a half fingers was almost as long as the barrel. This man, the third he had encountered carrying one of the things, was enough to make the Scot wonder if they were the fashion about town. So tiny, they were, it was hard to believe such a little thing could hurt a man, but for the broad, wide bore staring at him like a Cyclops. He wrenched his eyes from it and looked at the Redcoat officer whom he had at dagger point. "You are a fine trainer, Lieutenant. I dinna hear you whistle, yet still your dog comes at a gallop."

"I warn you, villain, I am prepared to do what I must." Trenton snapped in his best military tone, and a quavering voice.

Eyes still locked on Wainright, Daniel smirked. "Your puppy needs to bark more and lick less, lieutenant."

Trenton started at the insult, began to menacingly raise the small pistol to Daniel's face, but Wainright hissed. "Put that down, Mister Trenton." His eyes never left the Scot's face. "We must be civil among the bumpkins."

"Villains, ruffians, bumpkins." Daniel locked eyes with Trenton. "Wonder what he calls you when you're not around.'

"He calls me a loyal subject to King George, God love him!" The tradesman shrilled defensively.

"Please be quiet, Mister Trenton." Wainright snapped, his mind spun as he tried to divine a way from this mess with his skin unpunctured and intact, and this troublesome little tart. Wainright scanned the crowd about him, upon the dais, Adams and Warren were watching with interest, apparently aware of what transpired, but unwilling to yet raise the alarm. More than a few other sets of eyes were upon them on the Meeting Hall floor also."

The girl knew too much, should she realize the value of what she knew, what she could say, Wainright would be sunk. She could not be made to work for him, she had made that clear over the barrel of a pistol. With startling clarity, Wainright realized what must be done, but it could not be done here, in so public a place, not now.

Wainright opened his hand and let the girl's arm drop.

Daniel smiled. "Thank you, sir." He said, genuinely

"I will be seeing you, ruffian."

"No doubt, no doubt and this is not over between us, Tory." The Scot grabbed the red haired girl and was gone into the riotous crowd before Wainright could phrase a reply. The crowd seemed to part before them, and before either realized it, they were out of Old South and dashing through the back streets of Boston, turning down alleys and back paths to lose pursuers.

After a time unmeasured, Meg gasped, "Where are we?"

"Unless we took a greater turn than I foresee," The Scot answered wittily, "Boston, Massachusetts."

"Are we lost?

"Though 'tis been a great while since I wandered the streets of Boston, I dinna think we are so turned about as that." Daniel smiled disarmingly. "Asides, I can think of worse fates to be wandering the streets of Boston on a fine night with a pretty girl."

"With a bunch of redcoats after her, uh . . . them." Meg added.

"True, but that is not so unusual of an occurrence for me." Daniel looked in all directions at a crossroad, then a strange sight filled his eyes, and he asked Meg, "What is that?"

It was a majestic, spreading elm, messages were tacked to its trunk, and lanterns swung gently in its many branches. Daniel felt drawn to it, stretched out a hand to touch its abused, nail studded bark. "This is the Liberty Tree." Meg said behind him, almost feeling as if she intruded.

"It is well named." He nodded, looked back to see her shiver in the darkness surrounding them. Chivalrously, he draped his jacket about her shoulders. "Do you want to tell me about that red coated Johnny with the wee-little pistol?" He probed gently.

"No." She whispered, shuffling closer to the Scot, standing in the warmth of him.

"As you said, Meg, you're a complicated girl."

You'd best be rid of me." Meg heard herself blurt out.

"Well, I dinna say that…"

"You should," the red haired girl said, seizing the dreadful theme, "I should say it, I should run away, never return to Lexington."

"I will come find you and drag you back." Daniel deflected the barbs of her words. Meg swung her face toward him like a cougar, and the Scot put a gentle finger to her lips. "What I say, girl, is when times get tight, there is no place to be but among friends and family."

"I have none of those."

"But you do." Daniel said, and smiled a wide grin.

"You?" She boggled at the thought, heart in her throat at the thought of dragging the Scot into her problems, terrified of what he might find, and what he might think of her. "Daniel, you don't even know me."

"I know enough."

"You know enough?" She mimicked with eyes wide. "Daniel, how can you think that, how can you say that? Do you know my father, my family? What of my circumstance, Do you?"

Compulsively, with a suddenness that took her breath, Daniel swept the girl up in his arms, their previous closeness forgotten as he crushed her close to him beneath the sheltering branches of the Liberty Tree. Her eyes went wide like a shying colt, flashing in all direction for a path of flight as he tangled a hand in her hair and pulled her head back, finding her soft lips with his own.

She should run, she should slap him, she should fight her way free and dash away into the Boston night, never looking back. But she did none of that, her hazel eyes went wide, then fluttered closed and she melted to him. Their bodies seemed to merge together as she clutched him close, their lips hungrily greeting each other as Daniel finally claimed his victory kiss.

CHAPTER 9

"Captain Chapman was very pleased with your conduct that night," The

Ensign said reassuringly, "he has told me so himself on several occasions."

"Yes, but it has been over a month since, my promotion seems long in

coming." Wainright dryly groused as he looked up from his quill pen to stare out

the window as the warming April breezes banish the last vestiges of the winter

months.

"Captain Cochran's commission is still for sale." Captain Brown

offered, inking his quill-pen. "He seemed a fine fellow."

"Yes, after giving the ruffians a hundred barrels of powder, some

hundred plus muskets and sixteen cannon, he was one of the best officers these

Sons of Liberty had." December the 13th had presented Lieutenant Wainright a

fine early Christmas gift. In the early morning hours some hundreds of armed

men handily overwhelmed the garrison of Fort William and Mary, in snowy

Portsmith, New Hampshire. Poxy Captain Cochran surprisingly refused their

offer to surrender and fired a single, unimpressive volley of three artillery pieces

before being smothered under Provincials with pitchforks.

The garrison of seven was not so much paroled as forgotten about. The

once proud fort was stripped to the walls of arms and powder, one of the saucy

bastards made to haul down the Union Jack, for which Captain Cochran stirred

up enough patriotism through his inebriation to attempt to draw his sword, and was shot in the arm for his troubles, or so he claimed before he was shipped back to London. Wainright made a point of waving from the dock as his ship pulled away with the tide, a doxy on each arm to sweeten the soup. Cochran's fall from grace had swept through the garrison, between his drunkenness, unfortunate exposure to the diseases of Venus, and the inglorious end of his career at Fort William and Mary, there was some belief that his commission was cursed, and none wished to risk the Captain's foul luck.

"He will need money in London," DeBerniere mused, sympathetically, "that wound he received will require tending."

"Yes," Wainright agreed with ill-concealed contempt, "pistol wounds are the easiest to self-inflict."

With that bit of dry regard, everyone settled back into their task until the ever effervescent DeBerniere again needed noise in the quiet room and asked "General Brown, has my dear roommate told you of his involvement in the Salem caper?"

Wainright laughed at that, the doldrums of early 1774 had faded into February, and, because of General Gage's high opinion of him, Wainright found himself under the temporary command of Lieutenant Colonel Alexander Leslie, an amiable, professional Scottish officer of distinction and importance, who, duly impressed, would assure Wainright's meteoric rise.

"You were with Leslie?" Brown enthused. "How was it, do tell, sir!"

"It was …eventful." Wainright said cryptically.

"I heard there was some trouble in some villages." Brown nodded, knowingly.

"Trouble does not carry it, sir." Wainright agreed sharply. They had sailed through the night, 240 soldiers stuffed into the leaky hold of a Royal Navy sloop like so many savage Africans to gain complete surprise, even offloading as the bumpkins sat in their meeting house at services. So what does that bloody Scot bastard do next but order the fifers and drums to strike up "Yankee Doodle". "The upstart colonists pulled up the drawbridge over the damned North River and sat swinging their toes in the tide."

"Yes, but it was handled, was it not?" Said his roommate in a voice full of the self assurance of one who was not there.

Wainright smiled slowly at that. Colonel Leslie, with great élan and little common sense dramatically drew his sword and demand the Salem villains to lower the drawbridge "or I shall clear it with musketry!" But the bastards were mighty brave with their damned Salem militia trundling in at the Redcoat's backs. "Fire and be damned" came the reply, "You've no call to fire without orders." He smirked at the memory. Then the Colonel commanded the troops to seize fishing boats, but the damned Sons of Liberty were already going at their wooden bellies with axes. Still, we rushed over, and one of the soldiers, frustrated and worn down from long day, and long months of legalistic colonist cat-and-mouse games lunged at one of the bastards, pricking his chest with his bayonet, and almost getting them all torn apart by the mob in the process.

The town priest probably saved them all, a recanter, one of those bastards trying to have it both ways by signing the King's loyalty oath, then recanting the act and begging the town's forgiveness, the holy man was good to his holy oaths and he and Leslie worked up a devil's bargain. The redcoats would be allowed across the bridge, after which they would walk a precise hundred yards to a falling in blacksmith's shed. If no cannon were found there, and of course they weren't, they were to about face and march back.

The march back to the ships was the longest of his life. He distinctly remembered a blonde doxy hanging from her window, daring them to shoot amidst the insolent cries of "Lobsterbacks! Bloodybacks! Damnation upon you." They had lost all respect for the army, all respect for their King! But then, why should they have? Colonel Leslie ceding to their demands was not disease but symptom, His agreement with the damned recanter priest to "go 100 yards but no further, and then come back" was not the surrender of a coward, but a good subordinate Colonel following the lead of his commanding General. Tommy Gage had capitulated again and again to the haughty demands of these overreaching colonists, could poor, damned Colonel Leslie do any less?

Wainright remembered the return to Boston, looking at the faces around him, exhausted, dejected, and even ashamed. They had been bested by rabble with pitchforks, hooted down the street and run out of town by the shrilling pipes and cast-off drums of a cod-fishery militia, as good as being run out of town on a rail. "Yes." He smiled at his roommate. "It was quite a time."

"I read some of the Colonel's reports," confided Brown, "seemed a near run thing. You and your men acted most gallantly."

Read the report? So had Wainright, and were it not for that creative bit of fiction the Scottish officer had written, the whole travesty would have been more of a farce than it was. Now it only seemed like a dirty little assignation in the dark, that the officers who had served knew, but only whispered of in private company. "Yes, thank you." Wainright hazarded. "Something must be done about these upstart colonists."

"Must be what ol' Tommy Gage is thinking, eh General Brown?" The young ensign smiled at Captain Brown, then demurred to his roommate with a smile. "Oh, we can't very well talk about secret missions and all that,"

"Secret mission my arse, the whole of Boston knew what you were about before you hit Cambridge." Wainright said like a scold. "You were out mapping the country for an expedition."

The Ensign did not rise to the bait. "How is our report coming, Colonel Brown?"

The more taciturn Captain Brown had been elected to write their report, probably for no better reason that dear Henry didn't feel like it. He was about Wainright's age, of a more affluent family that did not mind parting with fifteen hundred pounds for a Captain's commission. He seemed more world-wise than dear Ensign DeBerniere, which was most likely why Gage had sent the two men out together on a fool's mission to scout the Massachusetts outskirts for nests of rebellion and stores of powder.

Brown took up his pages, clearing his throat and began, "as it pleases your lordship, myself and Ensign DeBerniere departed in brown cloaks with red handkerchief at our throats." He read aloud to the room. "Your lordship will recall the excellence of our masquerade, as when we presented ourselves to you, you did not recognize us."

"Oh, that sounds fine, Major Brown." DeBerniere enthused. The two got on so obscenely well that Wainright had for a while assumed they were pederasts. They teased each other mercilessly, calling each other "general, major or captain without rhyme or reason, reminders of the promotions they were sure they would get for this spy mission the two had undertaken.

"Are you sure, Colonel DeBerniere?" Brown asked as the Ensign nodded enthusiastically.

As the two congratulated each other, Wainright read over the Ensign's shoulder. "Dearest Mother," Henry's letter began, "I hope this letter reaches you in good health, as I am whole and hale here in the new world, with many interesting tales to relate." DeBerniere took up his pen again and scratched momentarily at the paper, Wainright continued reading around his arm. "As we walked off the Charleston Docks, dear Mother, we pass the pilloried, bleaching bones of an assassinating slave named Mark, and the damned ranker on guard duty brings his musket to salute, exposing us to all and sundry! We walked through the day, the three of us, your truly, my companion Captain Brown and my faithful batman," Wainright suppressed a smirk, trust DeBerniere to take along a body servant on a reconnaissance mission, "until we arrived at a provincial inn and determined to seek food and shelter there for the evening."

"Our table servant was a black girl not quite into her teens. Being seated we commanded food be brought us, and attempted to allay fears by engaging her in conversation. "It is a fine country" seemed an innocuous enough way to begin, but she answered "It is, and we have brave men to defend it. If you go up any higher, you will find that out." This disconcerted us greatly, but no less than when the owner of the inn approached and told us the little wench was newly from the city where she had worked at Ft. William. It was apparent that the slave had recognized us and we resolved not to say the night."

The letter continued, speaking of his trip to another tavern, of meeting with some Loyalists who hurried them home less the Sons get them. Their mission, of course, had fallen flat, as worthless as his trip to visit the little harlot in Lexington had proven. Wainright had almost been content to put the whole trip out of his mind as a foolish indiscretion brought on by too much drink, until the raid on Fort William and Mary, and he had realized that the girl had indeed been playing both sides of the gate.

A dramatic clearing of the throat drew their attentions to the door, Samuel Kemble, Gage's personal servant stood at a respectful distance away. "The General requests that you gentleman attend him at your earliest convenience," he announced

"Did the general confer his purpose?", asked DeBerniere, edging insolence. When you were the son of a peer, you could occasionally twit at the noses of social inferiors who happened to outrank you.

"I believe General Gage wishes you to personally attend him, with your servant." Samuel Kemble said officiously, then looked about and added, conspiratorially, "I believe he intends that you renew your previous assignment, but this time to Concord."

The two men exchanged hurried, consenting glances, leaping at the opportunity to escape dreary garrison life for a few more days. Wainright was instantly jealous. "Tell him we shall attend him forthwith!" DeBerniere enthused as he heard a clattering upon the table beside him. He turned to see Brown had bared his dagger and his two queen Ann pistols, and was beginning to clean them. "Oh, do come, Colonel Brown." The Ensign chided his comrade, insinuating yet more great reward, and advancement.

Wainright could take no more, biting his tongue as the two began their childish games again. "I believe I am for luncheon."

"Well," Brown called unctuously over his shoulder, "don't wait up, ta."

He tossed open his trunk, drew on his fine scarlet coat and his best Light Infantry cap, a leather thing with a small brim that fit tightly to his head. As he dressed, his thoughts turned once again to the girl who had twitted him in Lexington.

Foremost in Wainright's mind was a red haired problem with indiscreet lips and too much knowledge, and how best to resolve that problem with minimum exposure to himself, but maximum speed and effect. As a scout, the British army's kind euphemism for a spy, the girl was of use, potentially much use. But as another doxy loose in the brambles with the ruffians, she was a liability. Wainright left the warmth of the Widow Newman's rooming house for the chilling breeze of the streets of Boston, cursing his rum soaked tongue as he walked the cobbled streets. Talk it in circles all you wish, he mused. Your fault, her fault, it came to the same conclusion. The girl knew too much, she had refused his kindness and now, she had to die.

Wainright tried the knob on a certain door on Purchase Street, near the wharfs, entered without introduction, fairly bursting into the private office. "Lieutenant Wainright!" shrilled Lord Trenton, rising respectfully from his chair. "What service may a simple merchant offer you today?"

Yes, thought Wainright, what service indeed.

* * * * *

"I ask you to put no blood on your hands, dear sir. Simply acquire the little slut and meet me at Spy Pond. My men and I will accomplish the deed."

Spy Pond, thought Trenton, how aptly named. He knew it of course, it was a little slip of water nestled against the Waltham road and woods near Menotomy. "And how, sir, will you accomplish that?"

"We will be there within a fortnight, until then you may enjoy her as you please." Wainright yawned. "General Gage set my roommate and a Captain Brown to reconnaissance Concord-town and the Lexington road. The light companies are set off the duty roster and we are ordered to repair our kit and mend out kettles? We will be in the field before the twentieth of this month." He finished with assurance.

"My lord, may I ask your ... association with this wench?"

The rebel's ways were contagious, Wainright thought darkly, even Loyalists see fit to question their betters. "She is a runaway. My men and I tried to counsel her on giving up her rebellious way, but…" he picked up a piece of the hard bread and buttered it thoroughly to buy a moment to think. His first thoughts were of Captain Cochran and barely hid a smile. "She…uh…gifted one of my men with a social disease," he lied.

Inwardly Trenton chided, yet moments ago you encourage me to enjoy her as I would. But, he nodded his understanding and paused a moment before continuing. "And, if I may inquire. You understand, in this world, a man must look to his own…."

Smiling, Wainright looked over his shoulder before continuing. "The 4th Kings Own is to be assigned to the Colonies for extended duty, Mr. Trenton. Units with experience in…pacification are highly sought and my men and I are well thought of in this area. To that end, I am sure that we can be of…assistance… to each other." He drew up his crock and drained the beer from it. "Further, General Gage has been commanded by his Majesty to assemble a corps of loyal Colonists from which to draw Friends of the Royal Government, as you are termed. Should you and yours become part of this unit, I will endeavor to assure your rapid and…safe ascension through the ranks."

"I am still unsure how you can be so certain that you can meet me, sir."

"I have made it a point to be in the good graces of General Gage's personal secretary, this gives me insights that others do not have. I also ride with several other officers, and regularly sup with them, but the last few days, they have been busy with their saddles and swords. Rest assured, the Royal Army will march, and we will be in Concord within a fortnight. I will send you word when to move, and I will see you at Spy pond before the 21st." Without another word, Wainright rose and, spilling some coins onto the tabletop, left the tavern.

For a long moment, Trenton sat deep in thought. Then a wiry, hawk faced man slid into the seat emptied by Wainright's absence. "What thinks you, my Lord?" He asked deferentially.

"I think we are in a fine predicament, Lenstock." Trenton grudgingly groused to his faithful servant. To think he had once called the Lieutenant a friend, even come to his rescue at Old South. "We cannot say no to this officer; nor can we be absent our homes and our businesses a fortnight without questions being asked when the girl turns up dead."

"You do not believe that he will meet us?" the servant queried, the use of the plural pronoun sounded strange, but there was no doubt that the Lord would expect his company. Accepting every Sunday, Lenstock had his own holy trinity, George, King of England, and his right Lord and Lady Trenton.

"Meet us, oh yes, I believe that he will, but with a squad of Lights to complete the business. Witnesses are a complication he does not need." He paused to drain his crock of beer, sloshing the contents of the pitcher upon the table as he refilled the mug before he spoke again. "Does your sister still do the laundry for the garrison at Ft. William?"

"Yes, among other tasks." Lenstock said snidely. "One of the few women I know that wears out the arse of her dress before her stockings."

"Could she be convinced to loan us ten or so uniforms?"

"Yes...."

Trenton set a crock before his faithful servant and filled it with beer. "Do you know Colonel William Brattle?"

"What right thinking Englishmen does not? A fine Loyalist gentleman he is."

"Yes, I am currently in his good graces. I believe I could impose upon him for the loan of proper arms and ammunition for a small company of men. General Gage noted his prestigious service in the Seven Years War and warranted him permission to possess proper arms and powder upon his estates, less the ruffians rise up again as they did in September. I think we make quick work of this diseased wench, and the good Lieutenant may find a body and a note saying we are gone north for the grouse season."

* * * * *

The April rains had washed out part of a pathway to his powder cave. A quick hike had confirmed the contraband contents reasonably dry, the green hides weathering their stay nicely. But a long week of work lay ahead of him to clear the path.

His walk back through the Lexington woods had been fruitful; a fine stag fell before his musket, the carcass hung from a tree in the front of Cavanaugh's old hovel. There was meat to put up, a hide to cure and his musket needed cleaning and looking after. But there were other things afoot that night. Daniel had strayed down into town that late night, found a welcome meal and company at Buckman's, and Meg's manic hot and cold temperament decidedly warmer. He had asked the red-haired lass if she might like to take a stroll down the lane that evening, and Meg had not shut the door in his face.

He had rushed back to the cabin for his newest shirt, sharpened his razor and shaved with greater care than his racing heart warranted. His heart raced with anticipation, excitement, and hope. He saw the world stretch out before him in a string of endless possibilities, each more wondrous than the last.

Then, the dogs begin barking, growling at the door, memories of the troubles in Scotland filled his mind as shaking fingers curled around the familiar grip of the Spanish double barreled pistol. But even as the icy memories gripped at his heart, chilling his veins and setting his flesh on edge, he realized he was no longer in Scotland, but in the New World and though not out of the reaches of King George, certainly further from the Royal grip than he had ever been before, and at that, a familiar voice called out. "Hallo the house!"

His hand found the horn handle of his home made rush light lantern and, pistol sheltered behind his back, he peered out the door. Then, with a smile, Daniel took his thumb from the flint. "Evening, Paul Revere. What's acting, to bring you out so late on a chill April night?"

"Oh, nothing," the silversmith said with a forced casual air, "just out for a ride."

Daniel clipped the pistol onto his wide belt, striding out to where his friend sat patiently in the saddle, "That horse is half rode to death. Says I, there is more to this." Revere smiled slowly, saying nothing and the Scot relented.

"Well, I have hides aplenty to sleep upon, if you need, and venison enough for two. Come in."

Revere shook that off. "Do you have any plans for this day?", he asked, swinging himself easily from the saddle and walking stiffly into the home.

"This day, Paul? It is long past seven in the evening, the sun has little life left in it." Daniel protested, eyeing his friend as if he were mad. "Is it the fourteenth, or fifteenth?"

"The seventeenth, were you not at services this Lord's day?" Revere asked, and received a dull look from the Scot as his reward. "Well, it is Sunday, the seventeenth of April, though as you say, there are few hours left in it. You might as well call it the eighteenth of April and we need hurry." Revere had found a bucket of water upon the table and a cup of acceptable cleanliness and was drinking eagerly from it. "I was wondering if you might help a friend of mine move?"

Suspiciously, the Scot asked. "What friend?" As thoughts of an evenings walk with Meg slipped away with the fog.

"The less you know the better, for now." Revere intoned, setting down the cup, but the Scot seemed more recalcitrant than would usually benefit a man and the silversmith sighed. "Daniel, we have…friends… all through Boston, some might surprise you,"

"Go on."

"…and I shall, friend Daniel." Revere paused a long moment, seemed to consider the Scot before he continued. "Daniel," he repeated, "on the fifteenth, the Provincial Congress in Concord received a message from one of these friends. A simple message, but one of momentous importance, it said "It will be soon." Do you know what that might mean, Daniel Ferguson?"

"It apparently means you will ride a horse to death seventeen miles to fetch me so I can help a man move. Do you trust this Ghillie with the note?"

"Enough that the entire Congress adjourned, and the delegates scattered to the winds."

"And this friend of yours, he is one of those winds I take it, but what man might that be?"

"A good friend," Revere paused dramatically, "to me and to Liberty."

A friend of liberty? That enigmatic reference from Revere was enough for Daniel, and the Scot bid the thoughts of an evening whiled away with carefree acts goodbye. The cause of liberty called, and he could, of course, do nothing but answer. "I have nothing pressing, I suppose." Daniel admitted.

"Good," Revere smiled widely, and scooped up Daniel's sword and baldric from a peg mounted by his bed. "You'll have need of this."

* * * * *

They trudged to the stables near Malt Lane Road, passing Nathan Munroe's darkened home on the Concord road. The tired brown stud horse walked behind Revere like it was being lead to the gallows, and the silversmith seemed long resigned to the fact he would require another, and Revere also rented a horse for him, and begged the loan of a riding cloak.

It was a dull eyed Suffolk Punch, brown coat dappled with grays and blacks, short in the legs and thick of body. She looked mistrustfully at Daniel as the Scot checked the girth on the saddle, loosening it to give the animal more wind. From the looks of her, she would need it if he had a hope to keep the pace Revere wanted.

Peering past the meeting house, Daniel could see the fading lights of Buckman's tavern. It was late into the evening that Sunday, the seventeenth of April, 1774, very late. The mid-week crowd had departed and Meg was closing earlier than she might. Closing to entertain the idea of a short walk, Daniel grimaced, looked at his friend who was quickly exchanging his saddle to this new mount. "Paul," the Scot began hesitantly. "Before I go, there is one thing I must do, a small duty, but an important one."

The silversmith grunted unintelligibly, looked from his duty to where the Scot stared into the blackness and nodded knowingly to himself. "Be quick Daniel, I beg you."

With utmost speed, he trotted before the meeting house, but found himself hesitating at the door. He stood silently at the weathered, abused red door of Buckman's Tavern for a time unmeasured before he took the handle in hand and entered. She stood at the kitchen door with a batch of crockery tankards in her hands, at one of the million mundane tasks that filled her day and wearing an older white blouse and her bodice with a familiar blue gingham skirt, now patched at the hems, the skirt she had worn in the swamps. She looked tired, her hair flowing past her shoulders but limply as if the long day had taken some of the life from it. But her eyes twinkled with a welcome smile that light a poor man's world like diamonds.

"I am summoned to assist Paul Revere." Daniel blurted out, with all the elegance of a rampaging bull.

The spreading smile turned to a frown of confusion. "In what cause?", Meg asked, with a worried edge to her voice.

"Uh…liberty," he answered. It sounded so much better when Revere said it.

"Where do you go?"

"I do not know."

"Do not know?" She returned. "Do not know?"

"He did not say," was all Daniel could add.

"When will you return?"

He sighed and said with a smile, "in truth, I do not know that either."

"Do not know, or will not tell a mere woman?" She snapped back, and her vehemence almost melted before his wounded glance. In her mind, she heard Ruth's advice to her lovelorn soul. Allow him his life, support the things he favors, her friend had said. "Never mind, Daniel Ferguson, if you are summoned by Mr. Revere, it is without a doubt you are justly summoned to the cause of liberty." She paused dramatically before adding "My prayers go with you."

The last stung him. "I do not know what it is you expect of me, girl.'

Arms crossed, she spun in a flurry of red hair and strode to the fireplace mantle. "I want you to serve the cause." She snapped.

"Yet when I do, as I do now, this is my due?"

"The travails of the world are sometimes too big for two small people such as we.", she said with her back to him, not daring to look back for fear he would see the tears welling in her eyes, tears that belied her words.

He flowed to her, was upon her before she could react and wrapper his arms around her from behind. "Then come away with me, Megan," he hissed in her ear and her heart pounded for it. He spun her around, holding her in the spell of his blue eyes and said. "Come now to Boston, we can be rid of these shores and Revere, if that is your wish, aboard a clipper ship by the dawn, and from there the world is wide."

She heard his words and her jaw almost dropped, wondrous words, word to make a woman's heart swell to bursting in her chest, had she not heard them before. In her mind the burly Scot disappeared and was replaced by blonde haired, grey eyed Nathan Higgins, with his embroidered shirts and his silken tongue.

Daniel looked at her faraway, sightless eyes and sighed in disappointment, and wordlessly he turned and walked toward the rented horse, and Boston. Without speaking another word to Revere or anyone else, he mounted the horse and was gone into the darkness. Meg watched him disappear into the darkness, and long before that, the tears came, washing down her face like the rains that had soaked them both in the swamps of Sudbury.

She rushed back into Buckman's, locked the door behind her, and in the darkened confines of the tavern, her tears come for a time unmeasured. The burning hearth as her pillow, she cried for a life left behind, she cried for a life offered beside the Wild Scot and she cried because for so long she had refused herself the right to do so. She cried for a time she did not know how long, and somewhere in the midst of it, she slipped unknowingly into sleep.

* * * * *

Gabriel Collins stood in the shadows of the meeting house as he had done for hours now and whispered silent prayers for those he awaited. They were late, and by hours, not minutes. Each creak of saddle leather or whiney of horse from the stables made him jump, every sound in the darkness set his hair on end until he wanted to run home. Wanted to, but he did not for this was his duty to King George, as his father had impressed upon him.

Finally, they came, not a single man but a dozen or more, and in the red uniforms of the Crown. Lord Trenton, the author of the night's exercise, rode a brown Punch short enough to be a mule and not at all up to the fine horses Trenton was know for insisting upon. Gabriel hurried to their side. "Good morning, my lord." He said formally. "That is a fine mount you have there."

"Quiet, you young fool," the red-eyed Trenton snapped, 'do you want to wake the town?"

"Got us lost," someone muttered behind the Lord.

"Stole the bloody horse," added another voice.

"Confiscated." The Lord growled. They had set out from Cambridge to Lexington on foot to a man, but after an hour or so of plodding on sore feet. Trenton had taken advantage of his uniform's captain's bars and seized the first horse they had come upon. The hour was late for marching soldiers, but the townsfolk were used to seeing troops on the march now, General Gage was making fine use of the Spring to toughed his rankers up after a long winter. The tired Trenton fixed the eighteen year old Gabriel Collins in an irritable glare and demanded. "Have you kept the watch, as I asked? Is the little tart still there?"

Since Lenstock had come to his father's candle shop and gained their assistance in this matter, Gabriel had lived in dread of the command to begin his watch. "Yes," he nodded "I have watched, as you commanded, sir. The last patrons left hours ago, one of them was Revere. The lantern in the second floor windows never came on. I think her still on the main floor."

"Good, good." Trenton nodded. "Our first bit of luck." He looked over the men who had accepted his command this night. The selection of the men he had left to his faithful batman, tenant farmers and laborers, a blacksmith and cooper, all loyal to their sovereign, King George, each of them was a tenant to Trenton, the tough times had left them all behind in their rents and each realized he could be on the streets by the morrow, they had agreed to the errand for their Sovereign and their landlord most willingly.

Each of them understood his duty to his King this evening, though Trenton had couched it in careful terms, the enforcement of a King's warrant falling to them because of its delicate nature. They had been loaned the uniform and arms of a soldier of the king, from the musket and bayonet right down to their cross-belts and breeches.

"Dale," Trenton commanded one of the Loyalists, "you slip around to the back of the tavern. Be sure the little trollop doesn't slip out the back. Hellard, you take the front with young Collins here." Trenton slid from the worn saddle of the little Punch, absently handing the reins to the candle-maker's son.

Under his ill-fitting red coat, Hellard had the bandy shoulders of a blacksmith, and a musket in his hands. Collins found he could not take his eyes from the weapon, and the blacksmith caught his stare. "Like it?", He asked, "She's the pick of the litter." The muscular man explained, holding up the lead sphere in his fingers. "The ball is cast at .68 caliber, but the barrels are anywhere from .72 to .78, depending on who cast them."

"Ah, I see!" The younger man nodded. "So you searched for the narrowest bore, one of the 72 caliber ones?"

"Quite the opposite, I sought the widest I could find." The Boston Blacksmith answered. "The wider the bore, the faster the reloading, and the more rounds fired before the powder fouling begins to plug the bore and slows your ramming of the ball."

"Yes, I see…" the boy pondered, "but … there are many who feel that such a sloppy bore leads to the poor accuracy, as the ball bounces all about in the barrel in its firing."

That's…. interesting," the blacksmith said, with the air of a man amusing a child or simpleton.

Trenton marched with assurance toward the door of Buckman's Tavern, but inwardly he found himself remembering that terrible February, two years back, trooping out to the Sudbury road to sit in ambush for Trotter and his man, they had left in disguise, he the lone civilian in the group. Now, his position was reversed, he mused, chuckling gaily to himself.

Then he turned to Lenstock, "Sergeant, if you please, affect the warrant."

* * * * *

The whinny of a horse broke her from her slumber, eyes red and sore from tears, the fire long gone to coals in the hearth, but she did not ponder the time lost. She did not wonder at the visitors, only decided, "If it is him, if it is my Daniel, I will go with him. I will go with him and I will tell him all."

Outside, a nervous horse pawed the stones. The latch rattled in its casement and Meg stood to unlock it, but before she could, a heavy booth thudded against the door, and then another as Meg's heart clawed up into her throat.

Since finding the unwelcome Lieutenant in her bedchamber, Meg had kept Mister Trotter's pistol close, in the Tavern room, she had taken to keeping it rolled in her drab grey shawl at the bar. This night, she had placed it upon the bar to take upstairs when Daniel arrived, and with a glance she saw that it still waited there. She hurried toward it as the weathered old red door groaned under the assault of boots and musket butts, and gave way.

Men in red coats rushed into the dim confines of Buckman's. She looked over her shoulder at them, saw an officer in his Scarlet cloth in the midst of all that dusty rose red wool, pointing a pistol at her and demanding in a voice that must be obeyed. "Halt in the name of King George, or I will fire!"

She froze so quickly her slight weight threatened to carry her over her legs into a heap of ginghams. Her hands flew up of their own volition and she heard the officer speak again. "Seize that traitor, Sergeant, in the name of King George!"

* * * * *

A dozen men of the mechanic's class were hurriedly bundling John Hancock's life and possessions into a ridiculously small number of wagons. It was not the first time they had done so, from the hurried evacuation of the fifteenth to now, the wagons had been packed and re-packed, acquiring items from the trunks and bundles or discerning the amount of damage the pieces had received in their movement.

Doctor Warren, Paul Revere and a small band of men stood in the darkness, watching the shadows with fearful dread. It was these others which caught Dolly Quincy's eye. They bore the haunted looks of dangerous men, peering into the night, peeling away from the safety of the group to search out the meanings of sounds in the night or a fleeting shade.

Daniel sat the borrowed mount's reins like a man born ahorse, worn leather reins in a single hand, and the other resting on his beltline beneath the riding cloak. Their cordon about the house containing John Hancock and his guests was a loose one, but would have to do. The house was situated in Cambridge, far from the citizenry and within earshot of the shores. It was far from ideal, even he could see that, ripe for a raid such as the Redcoats had done in September, which sparked the Powder Alarms.

Footfalls upon gravel behind him rang in his ears like church bells, the sound made Daniel grip his pistol tighter, turning in the saddle.

Pretty Miss Dorothy Quincy approached him with a pitcher in hand, and the measuring eye of a woman used to appraising men and taking the ones she desired.

"Would you like a drink, Mr. Ferguson?" She asked, gestured to the amber liquid in the golden carafe. She was a small woman with a fine, pinched face. Thin as a yearling branch with an elfish way about her, this Queen-presumptive of a new world, all laughter and gaiety, as if the subterfuge of the night held no real importance to her.

"What is it?" Daniel asked, less politely than the pretty lady was used to, his voice clipped and his eyes not leaving the streets.

"Ale, heated upon the fire." She chirped with a voice like a bell, ever the lady of the house and hostess. "Something to warm you this cool night."

Daniel made a regretful face. "No doubt, ma'am, but thank you, no."

Taken aback by the briskness of his address, Hancock's fiancé bristled. "I assure you, I make a fine Alewife."

She was obviously not used to being refused, the Scot hastened to sooth ruffled feelings. "No doubt of that either, ma'am, but I am loathe to busy my hands right now."

Dorothy Quincy stood for a moment, then spoke again. "I take it you do not approve of my fiancé, Mr. Ferguson."

"'Tis not my lot to neither approve, nor disapprove, Ma'am."

"He will be the king of this land," The sprightly lady prophesized with pride, "your king, King Hancock."

"I have heard it said so, sure enough," he admitted without rancor, "and by none less than he himself, this very night. But I ken a different way of doing things in this land, a path to freedom, where all men are created equal…"

She forced an unladylike snort from her nose that was supposed to display both her amusement and his folly. "I sense you have been talking to Mister Revere," She mocked him, "And how do you like the thought of life without a head of state to guide the lesser instinct of your fellow man."

"I like it fine, ma'am." He smiled wistfully. "The thought of being allowed to make my own way, me and my woman, and, should the Lord smile, my family, stirs my blood."

"Ah, I see, you are in love." Lady Dorothy smiled knowingly. Daniel started as if stung by a bee, he opened his mouth to protest, but she would have none of it. "Tut tut, Mister Ferguson, none of your Gallic denials, a woman knows that look."

"And what should be my look, ma'am, that it so betrays my soul. Or do you claim the Second Sight?"

"That look, that look on a man's face that he will move mountains for the one he loves, that he will tame dozens or storm castles if only to see a smile upon her face. Every woman knows that look, every woman…' Dorothy Quincy paused and glanced back over her shoulder, at her Intended, the man who had proposed yet refused to set the date of their wedding. It was not the first time Hancock had asked for the hand of a woman, he had vigorously, persistently, scandalously pursued Sally Jackson, who had spurned him, wed another and promptly died. In truth, the gentleman's intransigence had shaken the pretty woman's confidence, as the only person who's affection she was sure of was Hancock's Aunt Lydia, who had played matchmaker for the two. "and some lucky few will see it once in their lives."

An errant breeze blew back the skirts of his borrowed riding cloak, and the lady glimpsed a twinkling pistol butt, dagger and massive sword hilt besides. She drew back at the arsenal spread about the Scotsman's middle, and abashed, he settled the woolen cloak around him once again.

"You seem…well girded for this nights work." She simpered to cover her shock.

"I pray not." The mounted Scot answered reverently.

"Will you not reconsider and accept some of the hospitality of our house?"

Daniel stared morosely into the night sky for a long moment. "In Scotland, when the lord would call on his levy of troops to go a'raiding, he would pass about the brandy before the killing. It made the thing easier –easier upon the mind, if not the soul. I ken a different way here, a different world in this land." The Scot smiled quietly in realization. "But I disturb you, ma'am,"

"No, you do not, good sir."

"Then the cold evening does not agree with you, for you are white as a sheet, and from your breathing, I fear you may swoon. May I assist you back to the fire?"

"No, no thank you."

"Then I will be about my duties." He said, familiarly using his knees to urge the rented horse into motion.

Midnight was long past when the wagons were ready to begin their journey. Daniel and the other men suspiciously wearing riding cloaks formed a cordon about the wagons. Revere had long since disappeared, but Hancock, riding a tall white charger every bit the match of his carriage horses rode silently beside the Scot. This man who would be his King wore a blue wool riding cloak, though of better manufacture than Daniel's, and beneath it carried a sword at his hip, a fine thing with a gilded grip and a long stabbing blade, something more for the court than the battlefield. The charger was of high spirits, chewing at his bit, and stood as easy five hands over Daniel's poorer, stubby Suffolk Punch. Daniel would not be a bit surprised to find out Hancock's mount had Arab blood.

"Thought I might ride tonight," this man who would be King said airily, "stretch my legs, as it were."

"As you like." Daniel said noncommittally. The Scot, with his broad basket hilted blade at his side, a blade bearing more in common with a butcher's cleaver than the fine thing at Hancock's side, noted that the man on the fine

Arab charger waited over long before speaking again, and Daniel supposed the man awaited some sort of honorific, "your honor", or "your grace", some rot like that. Daniel scanned the road instead, his hand found its way to his pistol, concealed beneath the heavy cloak as he watched the shadows in the darkened alleyways and deserted streets of Boston.

"You have the manner of a man upon a fox hunt." Hancock mused humorously, then morosely sulked as Daniel said nothing.

Daniel curbed his horse, allowing the animal to take a place near the ornate carriage and more plain wagon passing them. Hancock stayed by his side. Watching morosely as the carriage rumbled and cranked on iron shod wheels through the potholes and puddles toward the Boston neck. "I did not want this, to slip away like a thief in the early hours. You cannot imagine the turmoil that raced through our household yesterday when the message arrived."

"Message?" Daniel asked, only half listening.

"It was not a message in the traditional sense. Just a few words, delivered by a mechanic who had our trust, "it will begin tonight," that is all that was said, but then that was all that need be said, isn't it. General Gage plans to move, and those of us who… risk greatly, of our fortunes if not our blood, we will absent ourselves." He sighed, muttered to no one in particular. "I simply wanted a land where we could be free."

"Free has a fine sound to it." Daniel said, a bit too sharply. "But the word rings hollow from a man who pretends to the throne of this new nation." In his sudden anger, Daniel, in his borrowed riding cloak, rounded his rented horse on the richest man in Boston. "I have come here from a land under the thumb of a King, and I have scant need of another."

"A sentiment many share." Hancock nodded, in desperately flattering condescension, "if I could but offer this new nation a single bit of advice, it would be despise the glare of wealth. People who pay greater respect to a wealthy villain than to an honest, upright man in poverty deserve this royal enslavement. They plainly show wealth; however it may be acquired is esteemed to be preferred to virtue."

Daniel looked on the rich man as if he had struck the Scot a blow. "That is well said." He said in genuine admiration.

"Yes it was," Hancock said as if he too were surprised by his eloquence. "I shall do my best to remember it for another day."

"You have a fine voice, it puts me to mind of Reverend Clarke in Lexington."

"He is my cousin, you know. My father was a preacher, some of my earliest memories are of Lexington, but I was taken away by my Uncle Thomas, to Boston. He was a merchant, taught me his trade." Hancock mused for a long moment, watching the carriage and the poorer wagon trundle upon the rutted dirt road. "Forgive me, this has been a strenuous time for me, for us. Sneaking from our home to huddle here in Cambridge, under the guns of your hated regent, it has worn upon me. Can you get us to Lexington?" He asked in earnest.

"I would think so," Daniel nodded, he had been advised to take his charges to the Clarke's parsonage in Lexington. He could not help but stare at the gallows looming from the foggy shadows. A long legged corpse hung there, creaking in the slow sea breezes that evening. His borrowed horse's ears went back at the smell, carried on that salty air. "But then where, if you can tell me?"

"I can tell you, a Continental Congress, in Philadelphia, a place where representatives of the colonies can meet for a short time and discuss our issues in respectful, honest debate."

Dr Warren interrupted them. "Mister Ferguson, Mister Hancock, I go forward to arrange our safe passage with the night watch." He smiled warmly, but in a forced way. His hand was in his jacket, and he drew it out gripping a leather bag that jingled like gold as he did it.

"I was afraid you bore your pistols." The Scot half quipped, letting out a breath.

"I have them too." He nodded dutifully. "Remain here at the wagon. Should you hear a shot or two, please hurry up."

Scandalized by the intense doctor's sanguine words, Daniel reined in his mount and sat quietly, unobtrusively watching the dirty, muddy trail back to Boston. Doctor Warren rode casually ahead of the carriage and wagon bearing all of Mr. Hancock – pardon, King Hancock's possessions, including the young Miss Quincy and the good doctor approached the pickets standing their posts that miserable night with a smile painted upon his face and gold in his pockets. Then the wagons journeyed on with Warren returned to his home with only his smile.

* * * * *

"We call this "the rocks", sir." Young Gabriel said, tugging his forelock. "Everyone for twenty miles knows it, should you say "the rock" and they will know exactly where you are."

That was precisely what Trenton feared, that everyone did know where he was. His foot weary levy of Loyalists sat in lumps at the side of the dusty road, grumbling at their hard use and groaning at sore feet and backs. Some, betraying all hint of their disguise, sprawled in the grass in their misery. They sat on their tired rumps by the stone formation, draining their canteens and rubbing cramping muscles. Some had begged to remove the white pipe-clayed cross belts which were wearing bloody calluses on their shoulders and cutting their wind.

Only two stood, Lenstock, wearing the stripes of a Sergeant stood nervously scanning the roadway, a medieval looking spontoon in his hands, and the all too familiar red haired girl. She stood resolutely, hands bound before her, the rope trailing from her wrists to the tired Punch's saddle.

Trenton continued to sit his horse, looking in all directions in the dim light, gauging how long his party had been at rest, perhaps twenty minutes, he decided. He also thought of their position, "the Rocks", not a half hour outside Lexington. They needed to be moving, enough time wasted. "Sergeant Lenstock, get the men up and moving."

The grumbling began almost immediately. "Come on, lads," his faithful batman tried valiantly to stir spirit in the exhausted men, "Cambridge in three hours, home by the morning and a pint o' cheer at Piper's Tavern this evening to toast the good King's health." Even as he said these things, Lenstock considered them to be very generous estimates, after a long night of marching, then the brief terror of their duties, these men, city bred and unused to the ways of a soldier, would never keep that pace, but he reasoned men needed these slight truths in such situations as they found themselves now.

"That is not our target, Sergeant." Lord Trenton announced, becoming far too used to those officers togs he wore, in Lenstock's estimation. "From here, we cut for the woods, like a deer." He turned in his saddle and told the young candle maker's son. "You boy, we need a way to Spy pond, the path need not be the shortest, so long as we remain unseen."

"To what end?" Snapped one of the tired Tories as he struggle with screaming muscles to his feet, his voice more sore than respectful.

High atop the horse, feeling this first exhilarating breath of military command Lord Trenton was willing to be magnanimous, even loose lipped. "Straight to the Pond, Mister Dale, and cool our aching feet in the waters as we await our benefactor, Lieutenant Wainright of the Lights," He saw the pretty red haired girl pale, then swallow in fear at the mere mention of the officer's name and felt compelled to add, "to whatever end."

The Lord was tempted to string together a speech, but Hellard, the road guard rushed back, hissing "armed man upon the roadway", and Trenton was obliged to get his small party into the greenery.

* * * * *

"Armed man upon the roadway," hissed one of Hancock's guardians, others picked up the call, summoning Daniel from beside the carriage's team of Arabian horses. The sun was full up in the sky this new day, and Daniel, wet from the dew, tired of eye and muscle was hard pressed to coax a trot from his recalcitrant mount, but he eventually did.

A man in a beaten-upon hat did indeed sit a plodding horse in the roadway before them, and he did indeed balance a musket across his knees. But there was something familiar in the way the man sat a horse, something in his carriage that jogged a man's mind as Daniel rode closer, so that when he neared the rider, he held up a hand and called "greetings Sam Whittenmore, and good morning to you."

"Good morning, my bold Scottish steel bonnet. Out marauding, I see." Whittenmore smiled, his voice cracking repeatedly until he warmed to the exercise of speaking. "I am on the way to my South holdings, I fear a wolf among my cows."

Daniel nodded at that, then offered, "come to Lexington with me, we'll share a pint and then we'll both go hunt your wolf."

"A fine bargain and a fine idea." The old Dragoon smiled widely at the invitation, guided his mount into a graceful turn and fell in beside the Scot upon his borrowed horse. "Right glad I am to see you Daniel, hale and hearty."

"Hale I may be, should a night in the saddle and the soaking dew not spell my grave." Daniel groused to his friend. "But hearty... the bloody wagons slow our progress, we left in the early hours, now the sun is high and I am still not in my bed."

Whittenmore nodded companionably at that. 'How is your lady friend, Meg?"

"I swear I do not know, the lady runs hot and cold. One minute I would swear the next face I see to be Reverend Clarke, and he with the marryin' book in hand, the next she rears like a lightning spooked colt and rails of "never being at the mercy of callous men's hearts again." Daniel sighed and marked their passing of the Rocks, only a half mile to go to Lexington. "I tell you true, Sam, I would not be surprised to find her gone."

"Or with a marrying book and Reverend Clarke?" The Dragoon teased, and both men laughed.

The familiar shapes of Lexington began to take shape in the darkness, and Daniel peered hard, to see if his prognostication had proved true or false. The hour was right for Meg to be seeing to breakfasts in Buckman's, and he prayed to see her standing at the roadside, awaiting his return. Instead, as the Tavern appeared in the long shadows cast by the meeting house, he saw men and women crowding about the shattered tavern door and Daniel gave a start, instinctively grasping the threat, and looked at Whittenmore beside him, as if the old dragoon might reassure him of some other reasoning, or that it was a dream.

"Go, Daniel," the old man barked it like an order through a strangely stiff lip. "I will tend to these charges. Where were they to be delivered?"

Even now, the Scot hesitated, he looked at the older man and imagined his head in a noose. "I cannot ask you to become involved in this, my friend."

"You did not ask, I offered. Now, where do I take these charges, Daniel?"

"Do you know the parsonage of Reverend Clarke?"" Daniel answered, his head, and his heart already bursting through those shattered doors.

"I know it well," the grey haired man said reassuringly to his young friend, "I will see to this, and then return. Go."

Without further encouragement, Daniel spurred his horse forward, his heart in his throat. He did not remember leaping from the saddle and neglected to tie his horse to the hitching rail before rushing in. He scanned the interior of a room he had been in more times than he could count, as if he saw it now for the first time. At the bar, Daniel recognized Megan's shawl left abandoned upon the wooden top in the shadows of that great stone fireplace, the hearth now gone cold. He walked over to the bar, gathered an end of the shawl in his dirty fingertips began to rise, but stopped, feeling an unexpected weight inside and began to unfold it carefully.

Sergeant Munroe rose from a hunched stoop, where he was gathering the shredded parts of his destroyed red door. "She is gone, Daniel." He intoned, taking the chunks of destroyed timbers outside to dispose of.

"What? How?" The Scot boggled, chasing the tavern master. "Speak to me, Sergeant."

Before the distraught Munroe could answer, another voice spoke up in the crowd. "She was taken by ministerial troops, a dozen men." Jonathan Harrington parted the crowd. He was breathless as a man who had run a race with the devil. "Bloody Redcoats with a King's warrant, I saw it with my own eyes."

"When?"

"Not three hours ago, in the early dawn they came, and marched her back toward Boston."

"I am come from Cambridge," Daniel blurted out, "we did not... our paths did not cross." Remembering his charges, Daniel peered over the crowd as the wagons of King Hancock's possessions rattled loudly past. "We did not see these soldiers, not before the dawn, nor after." He intoned as the wagons rolled out of sight, then rushed back into the tavern.

Captain Parker, floppy hat clapped to his head, walked soundlessly through the bustling crowd in the dim street about of Buckman's. He wore his hunting shirt and powder horn. "Greetings, friend Ferguson," he said with a cold, military aspect, "was your delivery a success?

Daniel did not answer for a moment, looking down into the wool at a steel frame Scottish pistol. He turned it to see the military markings for the King's Royal Highlanders, one of the Scottish units that had fought in the Seven Years War, checking the pan and finding it loaded. "My captain, Meg is..." Daniel began, and the militia commander held up a hand.

"I have heard, Daniel," he said with real emotion, "but sadly, other matters come first. Is your package delivered?"

From the fading darkness, the Scot's sharp eyes scanned over the military drilling green and picked out Sam Whittenmore's brown mare rounding the curve of the Bedford road, riding back from the reverend's parsonage. Hancock was safe. "Yes."

Parker nodded at that. "That is news both good and bad. Had they not arrived, it would free the whole of the town's muster…" The tubercular man trailed off, his meaning clear. Daniel's errand was a success and the man he had delivered, he who would be King of this new land, would have to be guarded.

Daniel bit off a sarcastic comment, glancing down at Parker's feet out of respect for the man. Beside the Militia Captain's shoe, Daniel saw tracks. One was Meg's soft soled Scottish brogues, without a doubt. The Scot whirled on his soft soled heels and bellowed "Jonathan Harrington!"

The young man dashed from the building to find Daniel kneeling upon the earth, pointed at the ground beside Parker's feet. "These are the tracks of the soldiers who arrested Meg, are they not?", he begged his friend.

"Yes, I would stake my life upon it." The young man answered without hesitation. "Why?"

"They do not wear Brogans, they wear city shoes!"

The gathered men of Lexington crowded in, studying the marks in the earth in the gaining light. "Left and right," Parker nodded, "not just the officers, but in the ranks, too. One of them rests the butt of his musket heavily on the ground here, and – look here - he chews tobacco – which no Sergeant would allow in the ranks. Here, also, is a butt of a Spontoon, ground in so it would almost stand by itself, something no British sergeant would do."

"Something is rotten here." David Lambson growled from the crowd.

"You say they headed east, toward Boston?" Daniel demanded of Harrington, and when the other man nodded, the Scot turned to the black man. "Take my horse, David, if you please, scout the Cambridge road for them."

The black man acted without hesitation, rolling into the saddle and urging the tired horse to a trot. Daniel noticed none of this, his eyes never left Harington. "Tell me swiftly, now Jonathan, what did you see?"

"I saw them force the door, and I followed them into the establishment. I demanded their purpose, and a warrant from their officer. They threatened me with firelocks, but I said I would not be moved, until one cocked his piece."

"What of the others? Think, any trivial item could be of importance."

"I saw the Lobsterback Sergeant steal a handful of flour, "just enough for a spotty or two" said he. Another at the tables filched some dice and cards.

"Spotty's? That means trout?" Parker observed.

The sharp report of a musket snapped their eyes to the East of town, and Daniel found himself running with Parker and Jonathan Harrington toward the sound, he dropped the heavy riding cloak into the dirt as he moved, casting off Meg's shawl and clipping the pistol to his belt absently as he raced onward.

David Lambson held a musket in one hand, the reins of Daniel's tired punch in the other. He pointed with the long musket like it was an instructor's stylus. "They went off the roadway here." He said, breathlessly.

Parker disappeared into the greenery. A bare second passed before the man coughed, retching blood. Then a tired voice called out in warning. "An extra pair of feet here"

"Meg?" Daniel asked with a dread sense of apprehension.

"Her also," The familiar, weathered face appeared with a confirming nod, "but a youth with a spring in his step, too."

"And here I find foam from a tired horse." Samuel Whittenmore was by the roadway, brushed a hand on a scrap of bush growing there, and held up wet fingertips.

"Tracks for a horse I found also." Parker confirmed with a nod. "The officer took it with him."

"Into the scrub?" Lambson shrilled, the newly greening wood was thick and close through this forest, to take the horse into it made no sense.

"His horse I remember." Jonathan Harrington nodded sagely, "a mare, no English horse like the Redcoats favor, but a good, sprightly Suffolk Punch, or I'm no judge of horseflesh."

"Foot sore men in city shoes," Whittenmore wondered, "cutting a path a blind man can follow, and moving fast to the east by road. They certainly aren't afraid they'll be followed."

"No, they almost blaze a trail." Parker concurred. "They seemed to make overland for the neck, not the Cambridge road, which t'is the quickest way to the ferry, and back to Boston." The former Ranger stared at the marks in the earth a long time before coming to the obvious conclusion.

"They will not go to Boston." Daniel hissed, in the voice of a general commanding his men. "They cannot go to the ferry, too many witnesses. The ferrymen know every Lobsterback in Boston, a dozen new ones with a pretty little prisoner would draw too many questions. Dice, flour for a spotty or two, playing cards, and now they break from the Cambridge road for the greenwood."

"Not near a village, somewhere quiet, where a man can have a few spotties for a meal without notice, but near a road." Parker muttered, almost speaking to himself as he reasoned these men's course. "Their Captain has retained his horse, so he will be expecting to use a road to return, as befitting an officer."

"They have three hours or better on us." Harrington mused aloud, looking at the greenery as if it might spit out the answer.

"Bah!" Whittenmore snapped. "Three hours stumbling in the dark on unfamiliar goat paths and brush, that horse is no gift to them. We can get ahead of them, if we can discern their course." Sam said, then he breathed like a man in a trance. "Somewhere like Spy Lake, my God, Daniel, I feel it in my bones, I would bet my life upon it."

"It is not your life in the wager, but hers." David Lambson observed gloomily.

"It makes sense, 'tis an easy to find landmark, and close to the Tory abodes of Cambridge." Parker nodded in defense of the guess. "Spy Lake is on the way to Cambridge, on the way to Boston, it occurs to me that we will lose no time to it."

"It occurs to me," Whittenmore snapped, "we lose time talking about it now." His old body had taken on a lean, wolfish aspect. He had his course, he had his purpose, and he would not be turned from it.

All eyes turned to Daniel, somehow elected the leader of this mad expedition by virtue of having the most to lose. His was the anguish, so his was the decision. "Alright," the Scot pronounced. "We go. Run the ridge lines and arrive at Spy Lake with best speed." Saying it, he whirled and stalked back toward Lexington, his musket was there, and in his soul, he knew he would have need of it today.

"I do not run fast these days," Whittenmore spoke hesitantly, damning his aged body as he raced to keep up with the determined Scot.

'Nor do I," Parker muttered, fingering the tomahawk in his belt as he moved. He turned his eyes up to the Lexington meeting house steeple, adding as an oath, "but I will today."

"Get there when you can." Daniel whirled upon the former Dragoon he called a friend, his blue eyes had taken on a determined, steely cast. "Take horses if you must. I will run the ridge, meet us this Spy pond, at least one is sure to catch them."

"I go with you." Jonathan Harrington intoned, his eyes locked upon his wife nearby. She started at his words, then with a quivering lower lip resolutely walked into their simple saltbox house, returning with her husband's musket and shooting kit.

"I am mounted," volunteered the mullato man as he swung back into the saddle, "so I will range the roadways between here and Cambridge, should I happen upon them, I will fire another signal shot."

* * * * *

Lord Trenton did not open his shop that fine April morning and Wainright took that as a fine beginning. He had returned to Widow Newman's for a game or two of cards, and waited. He waited impatiently into the afternoon until doubt crept into his mind, and then he began to drink.

How much he had imbibed, he did not know. That it was rum was a foregone conclusion, nothing else was so cheap and easily available as rum, and nothing else gave him such a pounding headache. He had, apparently managed to return to his room and even take off his boots, or at least they were off when Ensign Henry DeBerniere shook him awake and told him to dress.

He was, he decided in drunken terror, being arrested. The bitch had finally found a magistrate and told all. His dear roommate was fully dressed in his finest uniform and bearing sword and pistol, he was also gathering things from their writing table as Wainright found his boots and began to pull them on.

They had sent DeBerniere to do the work of a squad, he seethed, and it would be their undoing. The hung over Lieutenant felt the little palm pistol secreted in his boot, his thumb finding the hammer as DeBerniere turned from his attentions and dropped a pistol, and ammunition pouch into Wainright's lap. "Gather your sword, too, Edward," He urged, "time is a'wasting."

Edward? Wainright thought, blearily. Who is Edward? Then, his rum soaked mind clicked. Bless me, I am. I'm Edward, been called Lieutenant for so long, I'd bloody well forgotten. What had DeBerniere said before that? Grab his sword? Wainright took his thumb off the lock on his little pistol, maybe he wasn't being arrested after all.

But if it was not an arrest, what was this? Wainright took up his sword, and the offered pistol and ammunition pouch, as the earnest Ensign thrust his own finest uniform onto him, and quickly polished the shiny gorget.

The sun was almost down, it had to be after seven, and the two left the Widow Newman's, rushed past the Old North Church. The streets were patrolled by armed Redcoats, they always were, but this evening there seemed to a special urgency in the searching eyes, the way they held their muskets.

The two hurried through the darkness, the Lieutenant padding quickly after Ensign DeBerniere, but the two did not speak, not even when they left the cobblestone streets for the wharfs. And the first voice to speak that evening was neither of theirs, but Colonel Smith.

Wainright froze at the unmistakable sight of him. Lieutenant-Colonel Francis Smith was a career officer, a man of substance and gravitas, or perhaps more accurately, a portly, self important man of good circumstance who needed help getting upon his horse, so fond of fine eating was he. But this was a man who could make, or break his career. "Ah, Wainright, of the Lights," the corpulent Smith said imperiously, saying all and nothing at the same time, "you are well spoken of. Do well for me today, and there cannot help but be rewards."

"Indeed," Wainright mused as Royal Navy lifeboats rowed out of the gloom and reefed upon the shores of Boston, "sir."

* * * * *

Atop a small rise, they lay close, so close that Daniel could not only reach to his right and touch Whittenmore, but to his left, over Captain Parker and touch Jonathan Harrington. Below, some bare ten yards away was a depressed deer trail worn into the earth, muddy with run-off from recent rains and scattered with leaves. Daniel knew it well; he had stalked it until the deer had abandoned it for safer grounds before the snows.

"Are you sure they come, Daniel?" Harrington whispered.

"T'is the best trail to Spy Pond," Whittenmore whispered back, "and I know them all."

"I am just...worried."

"At worst, should they be beyond us, we are close enough we should hear..." Parker stopped as the brush shook. Daniel willed himself to be still and peered intently at the movement. A moment measured as an eternity passed until the branches parted and a young man stepped through. Certainly not beyond his nineteenth year, like Lexington's drummer boy, William Diamond, he wore the clothes of a prosperous young man, coat and vest, breeches and stocking with good shoes. Had he a tri-corner hat, Daniel would have presumed his cutting the path as a shortcut to church, but for his manner. He slid through the path, squatting and looking about for a long moment. Daniel froze as he imagined the youngster's eyes upon him, but the youth uncoiled himself and spritefully crept up the trail.

"Well, well," Parker rasp, "Gabriel Collins. His father is…"

"Artimus Collins, the candle maker."

"And Tory," added the former Ranger, then he looked at Daniel and admitted penitently. "I doubted before, but I believe we are upon the right path." Parker voice was of a timber that made Daniel wonder if he were speaking from underwater. Then, the Scot realized the tubercular Captain was restraining his coughing fits to stay silent in the wood. Allowing himself to drown in his own juices to allow Meg's best chance for survival. In his heart, Daniel wanted to bless the man for his silent suffering, to seize him in a great hug and thank him, but there were no words for the things he felt, and just as suddenly, Daniel realized that Parker would rather be no place else in the world, and the Scot wanted to weep, and thank him all the more.

Another's coughing snapped him back as the sound rattled through the leaves. Daniel strained to hear, and caught the "clip-clip-clip-clop of horse's hooves upon the path. The scouting youth dashed back into the greenery and Daniel's strained ears heard him say "The path is clear, captain, all the way to the Pond. I saw it with my own eyes, sir." At that, a cheer went up.

The raucous huzzah went up, it had an electric effect on the four concealed men. Parker, all though of his misery gone, placed his thumb precipitously upon his musket's hammer. As the clip-clop of the hooves grew,

Daniel watched his companions do the same. Snatches of red and white began to

flit between the drabber colors of the greenwood, and the soldiers came on with

a racket.

This time, the young scout had an officer's sword, and was chopping

about himself with abandon, hacking a path through the greenery. Behind him,

on a tired Suffolk Punch was a gaudy officer in a broad brimmed cap and

officer's scarlet. Daniel remembered the lithe form of the hated lieutenant at Old

South, and wondered at how this man before him compared. "The winter has not

been kind to you, lieutenant," he thought, "too much carousing and wassailing,

not enough drilling and riding. . ."

The next in the line brought him up short, a length of rope trailed from

the officer's saddle, and it bound Meg's hands before her, pulling her along to

her fate at Spy Pond. Daniel licked dry lips and cautioned himself not to cry out.

Two dressed as Sergeants, battle-axe like spontoons in hand, followed behind

the red-haired girl, then a bustling riot of red coated soldiers straggling to keep

up, and Daniel's suspicions were confirmed. They were not in formation, they

were not marching, they were definitely not Redcoats despite their costume, but

they were definitely armed. Each bore a firelock, bayonet and cartridge box.

"Steady." Parker hissed to Daniel. "Let us get a count of them."

The group struggled through the shrubs and tangle-foot lining the

overgrown deer trail, and the little party above watched. "Steady." Parker whispered. "Steady."

"I count thirteen," Whittenmore growled, "less our foundling lamb."

"A full baker's dozen." Harrington confirmed, checking the priming in his old French musket's pan.

"I concur." Parker whispered, then he nestled himself behind his musket of cast off parts, and said. "Let us open the ball, on three."

"One…" Whittenmore snarled like a leopard as he familiarly brought the hammer on his musket back to full cock.

Daniel hurriedly drew the wooden stock of his gun to his shoulder, settling the crude sights of his musket upon the mounted man in the bright Scarlet coat. The guide had treated him as a leader and Daniel could only think of one officer who might want to kidnap Meg, and Daniel meant to kill him. "Two…" He said, and he said it in a resolute voice.

"Three." Breathed Parker, and four provincial long guns fired as one smoky racket.

* * * * *

Trenton tried to kick some life into the sullen, exhausted mare to get her to jump a fallen branch that stretched across the mucky path like a rotting black snake, at the same time shoving at some tangling overgrowth that snatched at his hat with woodsy fingers and tried to scratch at his eyes. The tired Punch, sore to galling from the unfamiliar weight in her saddle and gouged by spurs gave a single, spastic effort and lunged forward, with shocking results. The young sapling branches lashed out like a live thing, snapping back to pick

Trenton clean out of the saddle to plummet to the ground as overhead, muskets crashed like a clap of thunder.

The errant April breeze played with the stinking white-grey cloud that swirled about them. Peering into the acrid, reeking cloud, Daniel rejoiced to see the hated lieutenant fallen from his horse and prostrate upon the muddy earth and one of the false Redcoat soldiers lay in the mud, clutching at his belly and drumming his heels. Four doubled shotted, heavy charged muskets, eight.72 caliber balls, at less than sixty yards, had failed to cause three casualties. Overall, it was probably better than he had a right to expect.

The men in dull-rose red jackets whirled, three brought their muskets to their shoulder and made to fire back, only one of the ponderous weapons fired. Their sergeant, a bull shouldered man with one of those medieval looking pole-arms shoved and threatened the mass of them into something like two lines, ordered them to "present", and then, "Fire!"

With a crash, the canopy above them was scythed with flying lead, leaves drifted down from above. Harrington leapt to his feet. "Twelve to four, let's get 'em." He seethed, "Run down there and serve them some of their own pudding!"

Whittenmore stared down at the mass of Lobster backs with a jaundiced eye, "Long odds…"

"I will go," Daniel slowly rose to his feet, "alone if I must." His eyes were glued to the red clothed men below.

"Has your blood turned to water?" Parker snarled at Whittenmore almost at the same moment. The former Ranger's blood was up, teeth bared in a killing rage. He had his worn tomahawk in his hand, and he thirsted to use it.

"Hold." The King's Dragoon held up a placating hand. "I did not say no, just that there are gentilities to be heeded." The grey haired man was rising stiffly to his feet, a strange smile upon his face, and eyes upon Daniel. "Go ahead, Chieftain, I have always wanted to be in a Highland charge."

The Scot drew a breath, stared long down the hill at the mass of Red coated men below him. His heart thumped in his chest, and all thought and fear drained from him. The long barreled musket slipped from him, clattering to the stony ground as his right hand wrapped the worn grip of his Falchion at his hip and his left found the straps of his Targe.

His arm drew through the heavy leather strapping as his left hand slid his long dirk from the scabbard. The motions of his arming dissolved into a muscle loosening twist as Daniel drew in a long, deep breath. "Claymore!" He bellowed, in a voice to wake the Gods.

He was running before he knew it, thick hide soles of his home made shoes eating the yards between he and they, roaring his defiance and blood lust as the miniscule line of men in red loomed closer and closer. They had measured a baker's dozen of armed men, a party that had so outnumbered his tiny band before, and now he took all on alone.

Breath hot in throat, he angled the Targe from his face, the simple barrier of wood, hide and some small scraps of brass the only protection for his face and heart. He did not think on that either. With a crashing "Sprang!" a musket ball bounced off the brass boss of his targe, still he came on. The very shape of the hill added to the velocity of his coming, rushing from the sun with steel in his hands and retribution in his heart.

The Tory's double line, a pitiful crush of men trying to masquerade as troops of the Crown was collapsing in on themselves as men huddling close against the coming onslaught like dogs hiding from the rain. In the van of the charge was a six-footer wearing leather pants, waving over his head a blade with the curved, deadly aspects of a sickle, and bearing a shield. The shield's middle was a large brass disk, but as its decoration, its coat of arms, was the greenery and spreading limbs of an elm tree, and a single bannered word. "LIBERTY".

Then came the dreaded moment of impact. . .

Roaring like a bezerker, Daniel leapt into the air, throwing himself bodily into the mass of Loyalists. One of the men had the forethought to mount his bayonet, and now made to use it, thrusting the 17-inches of steel at Daniel's breast with the length of his musket and his body weight behind it. Daniel caught the blade upon his targe's leather face, deflecting it to the side as he lashed out into the second row of men with his slashing sword, halving a man's head at his eyebrows with a single hacking blow.

Like a thing with a mind of its own, the blade continued on, parting steel and wood, the bladed musket's butt stock spun away into the weeds and its wielder lurched for dear life into his mate's side, spoiling his aim and landing the two in a muddle of arms and legs in the mist of the muddy path.

His voice a keening thing that ripped from his throat, Daniel swung the targe over his head like a hatchet blow, the heavy shield's rim, decorated with brass tacks crashed down upon a red-coated arm, cracking bone asunder like a cleaver. Then, the thick spike, a full eight inches long and sharp as a needle met a man with a sick, wet resistance contesting the full force of his weight behind it. As he had been taught, Daniel muscled the false Redcoat aside with a toss of his shoulder, throwing the man like a farmer with a manure fork, all the while hacking on still with the sword in his right hand at the rear row of standing men. He wrenched the targe's spike free with a wet sucking sound, slashing with the dirk in his left hand at the wounded man and plunged it sideways into the third Tory.

His sword was stuck, or seemed to be. It was buried deep in the chest of the man from the second row, cleaving him from shoulder to mid-chest. Daniel wrenched at his sword to free it, twisted and tugged, then put a foot to the screaming man's chest and yanked with all his might.

The Tory's shied from the blood spattered man yanking at his wickedly curved blade embedded in one of their friends. Their pitiful line was broken, a blood covered monster standing in the midst of it, foot upon the breast of their fellow and wrenching to free it and continue his terrible slaughter. Their minds boggled at this sudden turn, their day had gone from the simplicity of arresting one girl to battling for their lives with a blood soaked creature of nightmares in an instant. Then, as one they seemed to realize, they possessed arms also.

Meg stared in open shock, Daniel stood awash with blood, ichor and gore dripping down to his shoes, covered his sword and awash upon the leather cover of his shield. Beneath that gore on his targe was a device, and one she recognized, the Liberty tree, which they had stood together under in Boston, that night he had saved her in Old South. Like a stalking wolf, the Scot abandoned his sword and turned toward her, his blue eyes resolute upon the remnants of the Tory skirmish line.

Lenscott's head spun in all directions at once, to the empty saddle of his employer, to his blood soaked man who had hacked a hole into his meager force, and was now turning toward him, and the suddenly so pathetic looking spontoon in his grip. Without hesitation, he threw it aside, snatching the red-haired girl's rope from Trenton's saddle as he commanded. "Get him!"

A snaggled toothed man at the far end of the line responded as if he woke from a dream, drew up his heavy musket at Daniel's back an instant before Parker was upon him, tomahawk streaking through the air like a bird of prey. Another man, this one closer, made to defend his leaders and their red haired prize, drew up the brass banded butt stock of his musket to brain the Scot.

Abandoning the quivering sword, Daniel lashed out with the targe, punching that Tory in the face with the brass tacked edge in a spray of teeth and blood and the Royalist staggered back, dropping his musket to clap both hands to his shattered face.

Jonathan Harrington appeared at his friend's side, pressed his back to the Scots as he dropped his musket's wooden ramrod and swung the broad .75

caliber maw to bear on the far end of the false Red-coat's poor battle line. Without hesitation, the flint fell, and his heavy charge of powder went off with a roar. A dozen or more balls of shot fanned out in a lethal hail, slicing down two Royalist as Daniel, standing in the gaping hole in the firing line, locked into combat with a charging man who bore the white stripes of a sergeant upon his arms, and a spontoon in his hands.

The medieval looking blade was an axe head mounted beneath a spear point, a wicked raven's beak jutting from the back of it, all mounted to a five foot long pole. It was a wicked weapon now relegated to ceremonial duties as a Sergeant's badge of rank. It was like plowing with a war horse.

Daniel palmed his dirk from left hand to right, replacing the abandoned sword as the spontoon loomed closer to him. He brought his targe up, so he peered over the tack-decorated edge at the charging Redcoat. His red-coated nemesis, a man with little fat to him nor wasted movement, had the arms of a tradesman and the scarred knuckles of a man who labored for his bread.

Meg stifled a gasp, watching the man with the Sergeant's pole arm rush at her Daniel. Furthermore, behind him came one of his Red coated mates, bearing a musket affixed with seventeen inches of gleaming, edged steel glowing bright in the greenwoods. Two men rushed almost in a line to take on her blood-dripping Scot, the musketeer trying to hide behind the massive shoulder of his friend. The doubled odds favored her captors, she knew, as did the hawk-faced man who held her bonds, a pistol in his hands and a spreading smile upon his face.

Then the Scotsman flashed into action with the suddenness of a released spring. He caught the steely point of the Spontoon with his targe, tossing it high into the sky and was beyond the deadly pole arm before the redcoat could recover from the block. Weaving between the two soldiers like a steeple chaser, he was upon the second man before the muscular first could turn, his long bladed dirk flashing.

The Scottish blade traced a bloody line across the man's forearm, who let up a cry as his blood flowed, stumbled and flopped to the far side of the trail, desperate hands working to stem the flow of his life's fluid with panicked speed. Spinning in a red fury, Daniel grasp the leather, tacked edge of his targe, rushing like a charger and slammed bodily into the disarmed man with the Sergeant's coat, throwing him over his shoulder like a bag of purloined tea as his feet worked for speed. The Royalist screamed as Daniel crashed into a greening oak, the soles of his city shoes barely brushed the ground with the targe nailing him in his dusty rose-red coat to the tree by its needle-like spine. Daniel whirled, a soft soled shoe kicking the center of the shield with all his strength to see it well seated as the pinioned man keened in pain.

Meg's stomach flopped inside her, and she felt her last meal rising to be seen again, but before that unwelcome event could come, she saw a bloody armed man lunging to his feet, his wounded, bloody palm splayed against a tree for support. His other hand steadied a musket against his hip, the broad muzzle at Daniel's back. "Daniel!" She screamed.

The Scot whirled, dirk slipping from his fingers as his hands went to the pistols at his belt. He stared down the muzzle of a cocked musket as he did, even he knowing it was a lost cause.

The report of the shot was like thunder, the flash and smoke ripping through the overcast grove like the crack of doom, and the bleeding Redcoat spun, his musket flying useless into the ferns, to collapse into the mud.

Daniel spun, catching sight of Samuel Whittenmore a bare yard from him, tossing aside his smoking musket. The Scot had his double barreled pistol in his right hand, the newly found Scottish one in his left, without thinking, he called "Sam!" and threw the Scottish steel pistol as the Spanish double barrel came to the full extension of his arm.

Lenstock tried to hide behind the red haired girl, tried to cock the pistol, he tried to track onto the old white haired man and the blood covered Scotsman at the same time, his mind whirled and he tried to discern which was the greater threat, who to use his single shot upon, or should he shoot the girl, or threaten the deed in exchange for his escape.

Daniel's first shot hit the Loyalist in the right hand, the .70 caliber ball tore his thumb from his body, burrowed a funnel through the wood on the Queen Anne pistol continued on to bury itself in his shoulder. Lenstock flinched, his entire body turning away from the bound girl with the impact, and the second ball struck him midpoint on the breastbone.

The old Dragoon plucked Daniel's gift from the air, thumb finding the hammer and locking it back as his eye picked up the crude front sight.

Whittenmore's shot hit just to the left of Daniel's last, cut the legs from beneath the Tory and dropped him in a heap at Meg's feet.

Whittenmore was like a man half his age, racing on, he paused before the red haired girl only a moment, dropping the empty Scottish pistol for a discarded musket, racing ahead toward Spy Pond at all hazard, and a strange, sulfur scented silence gripped the deer trail, Daniel let out a shuttering sigh, looking in all around him. Parker stood negligently gripping his bloody hatchet, Jonathan Harrington was near him, holding a Brown Bess musket by the barrel, the stock broken off and bloodied.

Meg stood amidst bleeding red-coated bodies like a supplicated pagan goddess, her hands still bound before her. Errant breezes danced in her long red hair, playing the tresses about her pale face and breathless lips, her eyes were locked upon Daniel. She stooped and picked up the steel framed pistol which Whittenmore had dropped, offered it to the Scot with both her bound hands. He, gore dripping from his dirk and blood spattering his face, seemed lost in the blood lust, scanning for more men to quench his blade in, and did not seem to notice her.

He turned toward her in a way more animal than human, she gasp and almost retreated from him. But he snatched the pistol from her offering hands without a word of thanks. Almost as an afterthought, that long bladed dirk flashed and the rope that had bound her wrist for these long hours parted. Blood rushed into her clumsy fingers in a sudden, almost painful sensation of tingling heat.

She looked again at Ferguson, heart pounding in her ears and made to whisper her thanks. But he had no ears for her, his hands flying over the metal pistol, drawing a load for it from the pouch at his belt. Within moments, he reversed it and handed it back to her. "Your pistol, Meg, found in Buckman's, where you left it. If you no trust me now, girl, use it and be done."

"Not trust you?" Meg boggled, "once again you rode to my rescue…"

"Aye, I have. The night you were lost in the woods, I found you. When the Lobsterbacks marched on Cambridge and stole the powder, I answered the *Clannarch*, and marched with your Militia, for you. When that painted Lobsterback peacock tried to filch you from Old South in Boston, last March, I brought you home with the point o' me dirk. Now, I stand before you, with blood on my blade and the Mark of Cain upon my soul once more, and I must ask you, do you now trust me? Do you trust me now to have and keep you?"

Her eyes went dark at the edges; her heart pounded in her chest, the world swam around him. The world went black, all but him, all but that craggy face like the shores of Scotland, and those blue eyes like the sea.

Daniel stared at her, watched here eyes as she stood there looking at her, and let out a slow breath. "Then I shall see you home, Megan Bulger." And without another word, he turned to walk away from her.

Captain Parker turned in slow circle, observing the still bodies scattered in the clearing. Even a casual counting revealed the lion share of them had fallen to the Scot's blades. "The sun sinks in the sky, Mister Harrington," He barked, wiping his hatchet in the grass, "retrieve our arms from the crest above, your legs are the youngest."

"Aye, and my face the prettiest. . ." Harrington rebutted, but then he dashed up the embankment like a deer. Halfway up, he paused and turned back, bowing gallantly, ". . . second prettiest."

Meg's eyes were locked upon the Scot's broad, bloodied shoulders, her mouth was dry, her face pale. Harrington's familiar voice snatched at her attention, but could not hold it, she wanted to laugh at his humor, but could not. She could not tear her eyes from her savior, could not rest her mind from anything but his words.

Whittenmore reappeared into the shelter of the leaves, holding the reins of the little Punch, which had made a half-hearted bolt when the shooting began. The animal was foot sore and tired, its head lolling toward the ground, cropping at newly greening grass. Whittenmore reached down to seize its bridle, as the animal bent its head toward Meg's feet, and the former Dragoon gave a start and muttered a soft prayer.

Lenstock was still alive, staring at the three of them with ill-concealed hatred. Whittenmore and Meg crouched beside him instinctively to lend aid, Daniel came without thought, looking at his adversary in his final moments with a strange sympathy. Blood pooled at the edges of his mouth, dribbling down to puddle in a muddy, trampled horseshoe print there. "I may die now," He gasped, drawing in a ragged breath, "but you and your rebels will join me within the fortnight! The Regulars march, and good King George, God bless him, will pluck your Adams and Hancock like ripe…grapes."

The rattling of leaves behind them announced someone approaching. "Bring him, then, and your Tommy Gage, too," Parker growled at the dying man as he walked up, "and all he will find is his Royal grave."

The dying man could say no more, nor lift his head. His eyes dimmed, then closed and did not open again. Daniel stood staring, then crossed himself and whispered a silent prayer of protection as his mind spun with superstitious tales from Scotland of dying prognostications and the Second Sight.

"Time is against us," Parker clapped Daniel upon his shoulder, "and we need to be elsewhere."

"Can we not bury them?", charitably asked young Harrington, walking toward them from the heights with a collection of muskets slung about his body or in his arms.

"Possibly tomorrow, or soon, but not now. Gather what you can."

"Yes, my Captain." Nodded Jonathan Harrington, handing Daniel his musket.

Daniel nodded his thanks, saw his friend's hands bloodied. "Are you hurt, Jonathan?"

"No, I am unmarked. But that man over there obliged me to finish him." The Lexington man smiled, inclining his head toward the mounds of fallen men.

"How?"

"By pointing a musket at your back," Harrington said innocently. "You were none the wiser of the event, Daniel. I tell you truly, after seeing you here I do not see how your people lost at Culloden. Of the thirteen red coats, you account for …."

Thirteen? Daniel looked in all directions at the carnage he had visited upon this quiet wood. "My captain, Captain Parker!" He called out, scrambling to feed a fresh load into his musket."

"Yes, Daniel, I am here."

"We are missing men, here. We counted thirteen, but only have eleven bodies."

Parker's sharp eyes swept the battlefield, "all the more reason to be elsewhere!"

Musket upon his back, Daniel fell upon the corpse hanging pinned to the tree with his targe. The man was long past to the next world, throat cut with the handy swing of a razor sharp tomahawk. Daniel wrenched his targe free of the oak tree, let the dead weight carry itself free of the spike with a nauseating sucking sound. Then the Scot coolly saw to the corpse's pouches and pockets.

Nearby, Whittenmore was pulling the cartridge box from a body, picked up the dead man's musket and inspected it carefully. "Look at that," he marveled to no one in particular, "muzzle wide as a blessed blunderbuss, and fine broad touch hole! Going to have to keep this one!" The old Dragoon set the musket beside his own, went back to his duties.

Daniel glanced over his shoulder, not so much at Whittenmore's newest acquisition, but at Meg, standing quietly, looking at him.

"You noted?" Whittenmore voice in his ear shook him from his reverie.

"Noted what?"

The old Dragoon campaigner smiled wryly. "These muskets, almost new and each and every man has paper-wrapped cartridges in pre-packed five round bundles. "

"They are not soldiers." Daniel said with finality.

"The uniforms are perfect, though not the men in them." Whittenmore nodded, waiting for Daniel to speak his thoughts.

"Who are they, and what is their interest in Meg? T'is a lot of trouble to go to for a girl not fully into her twenties." He asked aloud, finally.

"That is the question for which we have no answer."

"And one that will have to wait." Parker barked. "The sun says it be not quite afternoon, the wind freshen from the sea, that means a storm, and we have a long ride home, one that necessitates few witnesses."

* * * * *

The kidnappers in red coats had left a broad trail, and when the skies opened upon them, it was still easy to find. Rain spattered the horses, and soaked the riders, as they picked their paths through the greenery to find their way home.

Whittenmore had loaned Daniel his horse, that fine dun mare that had brought Meg out of the Sudbury swamps, and had left their party with a strange melancholy. He was closer to home than not, a distance fit for walking, he had said, and wishing them well, departed.

Parker coughed that deep, hacking retch that tugged at Daniel's heart, but the Militia Captain insisted they not ride directly into Lexington, but swing wide, coming up the mill road to the stables, billeting their horses, and walked briskly around the meeting house, and though the militia fields, up the hill to Cavanaugh's old place.

The dogs let up a racket, protesting their eviction from the bed as first Daniel, then everyone divested themselves of whatever booty they had gathered upon the straw mattress.

Meg lay two dripping cartridge boxes upon the deer hide blankets, looked again at Daniel. The Scot, soaked to the bone, dropping his targe and baldric upon the bed but the drenching rain had washed away a good deal of the blood that had coated him after the battle, washed it from his clothes if not his soul. He looked at her, she at him and neither could look away.

Meg broke the silence between them. "I'm leaving Lexington." She said with finality, and just as forcefully, Daniel said. "No."

"I am troubles you do not need, Daniel Ferguson."

"I will not allow it."

Harrington looked at Parker, and the old Ranger signaled him to be silent.

"You will not allow it? Who the Hell do you…I will not allow any man to…"

"Not allow any man, bosh!" Daniel shouted back. "You've allowed this Nathan *ghillie* to rule you from beyond for how many years now. He's gone, Megan, gone, but I am not, nor will I."

Meg opened her mouth, but then stopped. She stopped and looked at the Scot, really looked at his wet face and matted hair, and before she knew it, she had closed the space between them, wrapping her arms about him as she felt his own encompass her. The Scot seized her like a drowning man will seize a lifeline, holding her so tightly she could scarcely breathe. Her lips melted to him as he kissed her with a passion that boiled through her like an inferno.

Meg pulled at Daniel with an urgency born of love suppressed; her body so long unused to the touch of a man sprang to the recollection. She ran a hand beneath his shirt, touching the taunt skin of his belly, and the meeting was electric. Then remembered herself, that they were not alone in the cabin. "Send them away." She whispered breathlessly into his ear. Sheepishly, the Scot nodded, but when Daniel looked for his companions, they had already slipped out the door.

"I asked ye' a question once." He said, hazarding all one last time. "I have asked it more than a man should have to ask. But this last time, Megan Bulger, I will ask it again, and I would have an answer."

"Call me Megan Ferguson."

CHAPTER 10

"We are rested enough for this night." Revere smiled from his borrowed brown horse. Beside him, William Dawes, the second of Boston's dispatch riders. "William and I will ride on to Concord, and alert the committee of safety there."

Captain Parker nodded, his eyes scanned the men of the Lexington Ready Company as they slowly appeared in the misty post-midnight black. He yawned, and his yawn turned into a hacking cough.

"Are you alright?" Revere asked with real concern in his voice. "You look as if you have not slept in a week."

"There were matters, Paul," Parker drawled as if he spoke of thing of no concern, "matters that needed my attention."

Revere did not press further, scanned the faces of the assembly. "I do not see our young Daniel." He offered when the silence had become unbearable.

"Nor do I," Parker rasp hoarsely, "nor do I expect to. He and Meg have finally…come to an agreement."

Revere started at the matter-of-fact statement, then a rare grin of pure joy spread across his face at the Scot's good fortune. "That is fine news." He pronounced happily, and then the look on his face melted away as he scanned the pitiful number of townsfolk with muskets before him. Fifty men, he though, perhaps on the outside seventy, "certainly not a hundred," he muttered.

"No, and not on our best day." Parker agreed, pointing at two men standing off by themselves. "See yonder? That is Sylvanus Wood hailing from Woburn, not even of Lexington, simply passing through, yet he agreed to stand with us this day."

"Smith has almost a thousand men." Revere whispered to himself, his face losing it color and grim. The silversmith fought down his fear, glancing at Dawes beside him and said, firmly. "We will need every man and every musket. I will rouse Ferguson as we ride."

* * * *

"The regulars are out! Turn out! Turn out your militia!" The feared words thundered on speeding hooves in the darkness. The time had come, before the dawn of April 19, 1773.

Signal guns and tolling bells shattered the momentary silence that replaced Paul Revere's approach. Megan clutched at him spastically at the sound of the shots, but sat bolt upright as a heavy stick clattered at the wooden corner of his home. "Up! Up! Up, Daniel Ferguson, up! Events are unfolding and good men needed!" The horse whinnied as Revere wheeled his mount and applied his spurs. Then silence settled upon them again like a dark blanket. She turned up the lantern sitting on the fireplace stoop. The bed was still the repository of arms and other prizes, and a few dogs that had reclaimed their places.

He had taken her to the bearskin draped before the fireplace, the same bear he had fought for her in the Sudbury swamps. He had laid her upon it and taken her there, taken her as wife, taken her as lover, taken her forever. Then they had lain there together for time unmeasured. She propped herself on an elbow and looked at him, looked at him a long moment then rose and padded, naked across the dirt floor. He allowed himself just a moment to watch her, and then struggled for his breeches.

Signal guns echoed into the darkness Daniel stumbled to the sheepskin and glass covered windows, signal fires painted the skyline with pinpoints of orange. Signal fires that had once forecasted Indian raids or French actions, now with a different purpose. He pulled his muslin shirt over his head, found his fringed green hunting shirt and draped it over his neck, settling them onto his chest, a chest that moments ago had been the repose of his Megan and her flaming auburn hair.

He was scanning the ground for his thick soled *ghillie brogues* when the padding of feet behind him caused him to whirl. His red haired Meg stood there like a beautiful statue to Mars, the steel of his musket and the dim gloss of polished wood created a maple hued stain against the luminescence of her bare skin. In the stern military manner of a Spartan wife, she offered him his gun. "Get ready." She offered. "I'll fix you food to take."

He took the musket in his left hand, staggering toward the forgotten bed, decorated with dogs and all manner of bandoleers and bags. He saw canteens and Musset bags, his baldric, sword and dirk, two or three horns of powder.

His belt was mixed in with the crush, he buckled it around his middle, looped the baldric over his shoulder. His left hand found his sporran, scrabbled inside it for coins. "Rent a horse." He commanded her, with a force that surprised even him. "Head for …Concord, or Menotomy. Hide, I will seek you there."

"No, I remain here, it is my place now." She said, meaning not Lexington, but his meager home. But she said it with a timber to her voice he had not heard before.

"Yes, it is." He agreed, and seized her bare body, dragging her to him and kissed her, hard. Megan started at the suddenness of it, opened her mouth to say some words that never came out, for Ferguson had other plans. His strong left hand swept her to him, pressing her to his body, his musket trapped between them, and he kissed her.

It was not a chaste kiss of greeting, nor the petite peck that austere Puritan Massachusetts looked down upon, but permitted. It was the kiss a man gave his lover when he bedded her, the kiss a man gave to hold and keep, and she melted into it, cast her arms about him and held him close. "My prayers go with you, Daniel Ferguson."

"Aye, and a fine thing they are, and no doubt I will have great need of them." The Scot said with a queer smile upon his face, looking deeply into her eyes. "Now tell me your heart goes with me, too.

Megan Ferguson looked at the Wild Scot of Lexington and all thought of a callous youth gone to sea washed away with the tears that welled in her eyes. "I swear it, Daniel Ferguson."

* * * * *

Musket slung from his shoulder, he trudged into Lexington Square, Parker's eyes seemed to light up as the Scotsman appeared from the gloom and the Captain offered his hand, cool to the touch, but firm and sure. "You are welcome, Daniel Ferguson, take your place in this line." Daniel's heart swelled as his neighbors clapped his back in greeting. For a moment, he was afraid he might lose his composure to unmanly tears. He found Jonathan Harrington making him a place beside him in the line of armed free men.

Jonathan shook his hand firmly. "Glad to see you, Daniel. Glad," he said as Daniel slipped into the line. "Good to have a warrior Scot beside me today."

"No." Daniel whispered with a tear welling in his eye. Croaking the single word was all he could do, his throat tight with emotion. His eyes were peering sharply into the gloom, seeking glittering points of bayonets in the pre-dawn grey. He cleared his throat and summoned his voice, saying again. "No, not a Scot, I am an American."

FIN

<u>Author's Analog</u>

Consequential, transformative men tread the Earth in 1774. Brave men blocked the path of tyranny with the only thing they truly had, and the thing they held dearest, their "lives, fortunes and sacred honor". But most importantly, real people, who worked and lived, failed only to rise and try again, men who loved fiercely and created a system of government so insanely radical that it espoused the King himself no better than the lowliest commoner, and from it sprung a spark that would set the world afire. The words you have read in these pages are my poor attempt at re-introducing them to you, or for some of you, introducing you to your history for the first time.

I, the author, freely admit to adapting some of the historical time line to my literary purposes. If the readers would like to explore the historical account, I would strongly recommend David Hackett Fischer's *Paul Revere's Ride*. Other books consulted in the writing of this book include *Tories*, by Thomas B Allen and *Paul Revere and the world he lived in*, by Esther Forbes, the author of another great work of fiction, *Johnny Tremain.*.

Though Daniel, Meg and Lieutenant Wainright are fictional creations, most of the characters you have met in this work, Paul Revere, Captain Parker, Samuel Whittenmore and Jonathan Harrington, among others, are real, men and women who found themselves in the thresholds of history, and were forced to ask themselves that age old question of Hamlet, "…Whether 'tis Nobler in the mind to suffer the slings and arrows of outrageous fortune, or to take arms against a sea of troubles, and by opposing end them…" The monumental weight of this decision cannot be understated; to take up arms against the King was suicidal treason in a day when any British officer could hang you from the nearest tree, without preamble or anything like a trial.

In the prism of history, which is far too often the only way we look at these figures in our past, it is easy to say that the colonists need only "get through eight years" before the logistical stress of this costly war would cause King George to forget his plans for the America's. The men who stood on Lexington Green could not know this, they were staring at the red coats of an undefeated army, the greatest army in the world, and a Navy that ruled the sea, and all lead by a King that was the only ruler they had ever known. They stared into a dark room that they didn't know if they would ever see the other side of.

Why? Why did they do it? John Adams answered that, "Posterity"- us. After riding the bloody trail from Boston to Concord, he wrote. "Posterity, you will never know how much it cost the present generation to preserve your freedom! I hope you will make a good use of it. If you do not, I shall repent in Heaven that I ever took half the pains to preserve it." His words speak through the years, to you and me, as Tom Hanks said at the sanguine conclusion of "Saving Private Ryan.", he tell us to "Earn this."

The Appleseed Project is an all volunteer organization, a 501C3 formed by Fred Dailey. Every weekend, somewhere in America and likely several somewheres, a group of your friends and neighbors band together to remind their fellow citizens of their heritage, and teach a little marksmanship in the process. With some of the finest instructors, volunteer or otherwise, on the planet, Appleseed has instructed Police Officers, and several units of our military prior to overseas deployment.

Daniel has answered the call of liberty on the fields of Lexington and his fate is intertwined with our nation's in its difficult birth. As for me, I'll see you at the rifle range. I'll be the guy in the red hat that says "RWVA". Ask me what it means.

Aim small, miss small

Nelson Abbac.

A brief selection from *Freedom's Forge*, book two

Lord Trenton sipped gratefully at the hot tea, the warmth of it spread through his chilled, aching bones. The welcome relief revived him to the point he risked to speak a few words. "I will need clothes to return to Cambridge." He said slowly, his tongue still thick in his mouth, a dark bruise forming under his nose from the tree branch that had whipped over the horse's head, bloodying his nose and loosening his fore-teeth as it swept him from the saddle.

"Of course," said Artimus Collins, though Trenton could not determine if it was agreement, or sarcasm in his voice. The man, a dedicated loyalist in the hive of vipers called Lexington stood at the window, peering out the curtains.

"You have not yet asked me why I wear the Scarlet of an officer." The trader of goods lisped at the candle-maker, his teeth ached from the blow of the branch, his back ached from the hard landing when he was unhorsed.

"I imagine it has to do with Revere coming through town."

Trenton jumped at the mention of the name, almost upsetting his tea. "Revere? What?" He forced the words through his aching mouth.

"Aye, M'Lord, calm yourself. Revere came through just after midnight. He spoke to a few, all of the treasonous sort, and departed. Young William Diamond is sweet upon my Becky and came to see her just hours ago, with the grey of dawn. He said the ministerial troops were on the march, I ken you to be one of them, as I had heard that General Gage was authorized to raise a regiment of those friendly to the King."

Trenton's mouth went dry, the King's troops were on the way here? Well past Spy lake, where he was to have met Lieutenant Wainright with his charge. Trenton sipped at the hot tea again, but now it seemed to have lost all curative powers. It scalded his tongue and tasted like ashes, but he downed it anyway.

"Yonder comes young Meg for Buckman's."

Young Meg? He had deluded himself to think her dead. "What?"

"Yes, a fine enough lass to look upon, but she spends too much time among the ruffian class, those Sons of Liberty. She spent the night at that Scot's home, I believe."

"Where does she go?"

"Why, to Buckman's, by the back door."

There was yet time before the dawn and he found that he had much to do. "I will need those clothes now." He pronounced in his pained lisp.

"Of course, and anything else?"

"Yes." He said in his best commanding voice as he drew the Queen Anne pistol from his belt "Powder and ball, and a good knife or hatchet, I have unfinished business."

* * * * *

"They're coming." Someone shouted.

"They're running." Corrected balding, acerbic Francis Brown, eyes wide and his flesh pale in shock at the sight of them.

"Lights run everywhere." Parker snapped, and he was correct. But to know it and to see it were two different things. "Stay in formation."

Daniel had no intention of moving, but as he watched those bayonets like a steel hedgerow rushing down the Cambridge road toward them, and saw a barrel-chested Marine lieutenant detail off the forward companies at the fork and charge in their direction, his stomach went cold. It seemed the whole redcoat Army was at a dead run straight at the meager line of perhaps eighty Militiamen. Red coats, white pipe-clay belts, and a gleaming row of bayonets, throwing up a cloud of dust as they raced toward them, then, with a sudden bark from the Marine Lieutenant, the line shifted, at a dead run, into two long lines facing them over the green, and the tromping of feet ceased, to be suddenly replaced by the bellowing roar of "Huzzah! Huzzah! Huzzah!", each explosive exultation like a scything blast of canister slashing into the little group of Lexington men's souls.

Then silence, a silence so sudden, and so complete it made your ears ache. A bare seventy yards separated them. Men in Red coats glared belligerently at farmers in home-spuns.

Wainright picks out Daniel in the mass of Militia. "Yonder see that tall blonde with the tartan about his shoulder. I bounty that scrap of tartan at a Guinea, provided there's blood upon it." The Lieutenant shouted to his Lights, but at Daniel particularly and smiled to himself as the stoic Scot reacted to his prod. It struck the Officer to announce the bounty more fully, and he drew in a breath, rolling his head to better broadcast his voice to the line, and as he did, he caught sight of a familiar mane of red hair disappearing around the back of Buckman's Tavern. It truly is my lucky day, he thought, and signaled to Ensign DeBerniere. "Henry, old chum," He called out unctuously to his roommate, "take over for me, I need to pop off, only take a minute."

Ensign Henry, dear sweet, dull Henry DeBerniere gave a confused, frightened but eager-to-please nod, and Wainright dashed off. Another unit of redcoats stood at parade attention between the meeting house and the Tavern on the road to the green, so it was easy for Wainright to dash into them, as if he needed to confer with some other officer, then cut through and into the Tavern.

The door was brand new, and creaked slightly on its unfamiliar hinges as he burst in. The girl stood in the center of the room, and Wainright smiled, God was an Englishmen, he mused silently and pointed his heavy pistol at her. "Your Hancock and Adams, we know they are in town, where are they?" He demanded.

In answer, the girl produced her own pistol again, that damned steel Scottish thing with the barrel like a cannon. Strangely, Wainright had noted earlier that the Royal Marine officer who accompanied them, Major John Pitcarn, carried a brace of the things on his saddle, but then the Major was a Scot also. His were, befitting an officer, more ornamental and embossed, but the girl's was no less lethal. "I swear, if you do not tell me, forthrightly, I will end you!" Wainright roared, drawing back the flint. "You try my patience."

Meg was undaunted, sighting down the grey steel barrel with a surprising determination underlining her words. "I will live no longer in fear," She swore, her voice an even, cold growl, "no more in chains."

There was something different in the girl, some new focus, or fortitude. Wainright put it out of his mind. "No, no more in chains, girl," Wainright gave an oily smile, "just a rope, beside your Adams and Hancock." He set the sights of his pistol upon the girl's lovely chest and pronounced, "You know where they are, I will give you one last chance."

"You will go to Hell!" She snapped back and her flint fell with a "Foosh" and a roar, the British officer fired also.

* * * * *

"Must be a thousand of them," breathed William Diamond, the Militia's drummer, his face white as a sheet as he fingered his drumsticks, his only weapon.

A thousand, Daniel wondered, looking coolly at their bladed muskets and deadly stares. Not a thousand, perhaps two hundred or so, but when your own force numbered not quite eighty, and those all beardless boys and men past their prime, two hundred Redcoats was bad enough. Daniel scanned the ranks of hateful faces, trying to find that familiar one again, Meg's Lieutenant and his bemused look were nowhere to be seen, and that was perhaps more worrisome than having a bounty placed upon him.

Parker paced the line, speaking in a low voice. "Do not fire unless fired upon, but if they will have a war, let it begin here." Do not fire unless fired upon? Daniel wondered. The militia, outnumbered at two to one or better, was going to stand and receive fire, take the first punch?

Jonathan Harrington caught his eye beside him, eyes wide enough with fear Daniel could see the whites all around his blue-grey eyeball. Daniel tried to give him a smile of confidence he did not feel. "Remember that advice I gave you on the road to Cambridge that day?"

"That bit about "when they say fire, hit the ground", it's never left my mind."

"Well, keep sharp, look to your front and be ready, this could go badly in the blink of....." Daniel's voice went silent in awe of a magnificent sight. Before him, an officer in scarlet, a Major of Marines by his facings and decorations, on a beautiful white charger, a horse to rival Hancock's matched Arabians, leapt his animal over one of the crude Lexington piled stone fences and raced to the field. The man sat a horse as if he were born there, curbing the spirited animal effortlessly in the no-man's land between armed Lexington farmers and the elite forces of the most deadly army in the world.

He seemed genuinely shocked by the presence of this belligerent body before him, leaned in his saddle as if to be sure it was not a mirage. "Disperse, damn you!" He demanded, disapproval fairly dripping from his eyes like an angry father at some drunken, lay-about son. "You villains, you rascals, lay down your arms and disperse! I said lay down your arms, why don't you disperse, damn you!"

The Militia, if anything, seem to take resolve from the Major's words, Daniel watched backs stiffen, eyes grow hard and set, except for Captain Parker, he looked from the Major on his white horse to his men, friends and families all. Daniel had a flash of Parker's words last September, as they marched for Cambridge, "related to most of them by blood or marriage", he had said. He watched Parker look from the lines of Redcoats, to his Militia, and back, and then watched the captain nod to himself.

The former Ranger turned toward his men. "We've made our point," he said with not a hint of defeat in his voice, and commanded his friends and neighbors, "disperse, but don't lay down your arms. Turn around and walk away, but don't lay down your arms."

Harrington let out a long breath he did not know he had held. "Sounds like sense to me." He whispered to Daniel in a voice so low only the Scot could hear it.

Daniel said nothing, his eyes were locked upon the Redcoat line, seeking for the officer who had tried to make off with Meg with one eye, and the other locked on the Major who apparently commanded here.

The Major was affronted that his command to these ruffian farmers had been rebuffed, turning in his saddle and commanded. "Soldiers, encircle them and disarm…."

I will not be disarmed, Daniel seethed at the insult, one the Scots had know far too often. But now, to have come so far, endured so much, found so much, only to…

A pistol shot rang out, so loud it had to be close, but a pistol shot none the less. Daniel's heart turned to ice and leapt into his throat, and he dove for the ground.

Dumped from leaky lifeboats into the swampy marshes of Cambridge, the Redcoat soldiers had marched through the night in a waking, hostile land, to this point barely after the dawn. Frightened, exhausted soldiers heard the barking report of a shot, and did the thing they had trained for, with a snap, flints fell to ignite heavy charges, and the rising sun was obliterated by the grey-black powder smoke of a Shot Heard 'Round the World.

LOOK FOR <u>FREEDOM'S FORGE, book 2, Gathering the Tinder</u>

Nelson Abbac is the pen-name of a former SWAT police officer, lifetime shooter, history buff and current Appleseed Instructor. He holds a Bachelor's degree and is currently an elected official in his home town. While he has published several magazine articles, this novel is his first work of fiction. He is a proud husband and father of two in Northwest Ohio, where he is ardently admired by his two dogs and occasionally noticed by the family cat.